BLACK CHAMBER

S. M. STIRLING

ACE
New York

ACE
Published by Berkley
An imprint of Penguin Random House LLC
375 Hudson Street, New York, New York 10014

Copyright © 2018 by S. M. Stirling
Penguin Random House supports copyright. Copyright fuels creativity, encourages diverse voices,
promotes free speech, and creates a vibrant culture. Thank you for buying an authorized edition
of this book and for complying with copyright laws by not reproducing, scanning, or distributing
any part of it in any form without permission. You are supporting writers and allowing
Penguin Random House to continue to publish books for every reader.

ACE is a registered trademark and the A colophon is a trademark of Penguin Random House LLC.

Library of Congress Cataloging-in-Publication Data
Names: Stirling, S. M., author.
Title: Black chamber / S. M. Stirling.
Description: First edition. | New York : ACE, 2018.
Identifiers: LCCN 2017047810| ISBN 9780399586231 (trade paperback) |
ISBN 9780399586248 (ebook)
Subjects: | GSAFD: Alternative histories (Fiction)
Classification: LCC PS3569.T543 B58 2018 | DDC 813/.54—dc23
LC record available at https://lccn.loc.gov/2017047810

First Edition: July 2018

Printed in the United States of America
1 3 5 7 9 10 8 6 4 2

Cover design by Adam Auerbach
Book design by Laura K. Corless

To Jan, in all possible worlds!

ACKNOWLEDGMENTS

To Kier Salmon, longtime close friend and valued advisor, whose help with things in Spanish and about Mexico—she lived there into adulthood—has been very, very helpful with this one, as well as her general advice to which I always listen carefully. My mother grew up speaking Spanish too (in Lima, Peru), but alas she and my aunt used it as a secret code the children couldn't understand, and Kier has been invaluable in filling in those lacunae, as well as being a fine editor (and promising writer) in her own right.

To Markus Baur, for help with the German language. Though he did chuckle at "pigdog."

To Dave Drake, for help with the Latin bits and a deep knowledge of firearms acquired in several different ways.

To Alyx Dellamonica, for some really good advice on how to handle a crucial relationship. Bless the aunties!

To my first readers; Steve Brady, Pete Sartucci, Brenda Sutton, Lucienne Brown, and Scott Palter.

To Patricia Finney, for friendship and her own wonderful books, starting with *A Shadow of Gulls* and going on from there.

To Roland and Sheila Richter at Joe's Diner of Santa Fe—for putting up with me using their place as an unofficial office, not charging me rent, and for Roland helping me with some German subtleties. Besides, Joe's is a *really good* diner.

And to: Walter Jon Williams, Emily Mah, John Miller, Vic Milan, Jan Stirling, Matt Reiten, Lauren Teffeau, and Sareena of Critical Mass, our writer's group, for constant help and advice.

Only those are fit to live who do not fear to die; and none are fit to die who have shrunk from the joy of life and the duty of life. Both life and death are parts of the same Great Adventure.

—THEODORE ROOSEVELT

PROLOGUE

Sagamore Hill, Long Island, New York
MAY 25TH, 1912–1912(B)
Point of Departure plus 4 Hours

There was a rising murmur of voices in the entranceway of Sagamore Hill's great North Room. Theodore Roosevelt and his advisors ignored it.

"Your tour's really fired up the Party's supporters, Colonel Roosevelt," Lucius Swift said. "As far as the ordinary members are concerned, the Party's ours. We took Ohio by nearly fifty thousand votes . . . Taft's home state! It's the *Progressive* Republican Party now in all but name."

"Bully!" Roosevelt said, sincerely.

He'd broken with tradition and whistle-stopped the country as a candidate for the nomination, and he intended to do much more along those lines. Tradition was good, but you couldn't let it become a set of shackles, turning a young vigorous country into a bunch of prissy lawyers . . . like his ex-friend and the current president, William Howard Taft. The North Room of his country estate, lined with books and maps and hunting trophies—he was very proud of the elephant tusks framing the entrance, and the rhino horn—showed what *he* was and how he led. From the front, as he'd led the Rough Riders up San Juan Hill with the 7mm bullets of the Spanish Mausers making that ripping-silk sound as they punched past his ears.

Senator Dixon nodded. "They can't win it now unless they steal it, so they're panicking and punching below the belt. They stole New York outright with fake ballots, and they'll rely on stuffing the selection committees to disqualify our delegates and put in theirs."

Roosevelt tapped his knuckles on the table thoughtfully. "The Old Guard controls the state machines and Taft has his hand on the federal patronage spigots. Right now we need to—"

The voices rose to near-shouts, and the men around the table looked at each other. Some, like the newspaperman Frank Knox, had fought with him in Cuba; others like Croly had furthered the reform cause with their books . . . and Roosevelt was an author himself many times over. Only one was older than his own fifty-three years and a few were new to serious politics; earnest young men who reminded him of his earlier, unbattered self. He'd left strict orders that nobody should interrupt this late-night meeting with his closest advisors, and there were a couple of ex–Rough Riders at the entrance to enforce it, men whose real duties involved six-shooters and brass knuckles rather than the chores of stables and farm. Assassination wasn't unknown— McKinley's had put him in the White House a decade ago—and Roosevelt had been outspoken enough about the need to do something about Mexico's gathering chaos that some wild-eyed fanatic might have traveled north to slay the gringo devil.

"What is it?" Roosevelt said.

He felt a welcome quickening of the blood. Whatever the news was, it would be a challenge.

A flash of memory: that time in the Badlands of the Dakota Territory, walking into Nolan's saloon and the taunting voice of the killing-drunk gunman demanding the four-eyed eastern dude buy the drinks all 'round, and the two Colts pointing at his gut. He'd laughed then . . . just before a quick right-left-right to the jaw had left the man unconscious on the sawdust-covered boards with the smoking pistols in his hands. The bullets had come close, but he'd never felt more alive.

A fight gave life its savor . . . and so did an opportunity.

"Telegraph, Colonel," the pale-eyed man in the bowler hat said as he came to the balustrade at the entrance and waved a Western Union flimsy; there was a bulge under the left armpit of his cheap blue suit, a scar kinked his beaky nose, and his voice had a strong western twang. "You're going to want to see this one *right now* and no mistake."

Whitlock's a reliable man. This has to be something big . . .

Herbert Croly went to the entranceway landing and reached up to take the paper. It took a moment for him to cross the big dim room, and the others had an instant to look at each other again with growing speculation. His usually stolid moon-shaped face went slack in surprise as he read.

"Hell and damnation!" he said, even more uncharacteristically, being rather prim and reserved by nature. "President Taft's dead!"

"Good God!" a young Harvard man murmured under the chorus of gasps and oaths, which was a Boston Brahmin's way of running around the room waving his arms and shrieking.

"*What!*" Roosevelt said, almost a shout.

After surprise came a stab of grief. He'd meant what he said when he called Taft a fat-headed Old Guard flubdub, but they'd been friends and allies once.

"How?" he said sharply.

"Just didn't wake up from his nap after dinner. They think it was his heart. A gentle way to go, at least."

Roosevelt shook his head as the brief message was dropped on the table, looking at it as if it were a carrion bird cawing *nevermore*. Croly slumped back into his chair and gulped at a hitherto-untasted glass, choking a little on the brandy.

"He never did exercise enough," Roosevelt said sadly.

Taft had looked like a walrus on legs for decades, and it had gotten worse since he moved into the White House and ate more to cope with the nervous strain. They'd had to install a custom-built bathtub seven feet by four after he got stuck in the regular one and was left roaring for help when he couldn't pull himself out. The terrible grinding labor of campaigning in the new fashion must have been the last straw that broke him . . .

"God rest his soul; he always meant well. As a judge, he'd have been magnificent. A patriot and a scholar, but he just wasn't made to be a leader."

Theodore Roosevelt was a bit stocky himself these days, but it was nearly all muscle. He rode and wrestled and swam, hunted and hiked and split wood and pitched in on the farm here at Sagamore Hill with gusto, enjoying the strenuous, outdoor life he'd pursued since he was a sickly little boy dreaming of adventure. That was why he'd gone west to be a rancher, that and sorrow after his first wife died bearing her namesake daughter, Alice: for the challenge and the adventure of the rough frontier life. The same spirit had taken him through the East African wilderness and down the Nile, and it would take him back to the White House whatever the conservative faction thought.

Everyone was silent for a long moment, in respect and speculation. Then Knox cleared his throat.

"There's Sherman," he said, naming Taft's vice president. "He's able, and popular with the Old Guard. They could rally around him; he's the president now, after all."

"No," Roosevelt said incisively. "Sherman is very ill."

He'd known, but hadn't mentioned it before because it hadn't been directly relevant and a gentleman didn't refer to another's personal matters unless he must. Now it was something that had to be said.

"How sick, Colonel?" Knox asked.

Only men who'd fought with the Rough Riders called him that without the name attached; as a nickname he liked it a good deal more than *Teddy*, to which he was most unwillingly resigned when it came from other adults.

"He's dying, Frank," Roosevelt said. "His kidneys, Bright's disease. His doctors don't think he can survive the year. He may not live to November."

Roosevelt wouldn't wish that long painful passing on any man; he'd always carried a vial of morphine in dangerous situations, so that if death was coming he could choose its manner and time and not die like a beaten beast. But in practical terms . . . Possibly you could be nominated as a vice presidential candidate with a fatal disease. Not as a contender for president.

And I'm as healthy as a bull moose!

"We've got them, if we move quickly," he said. "Their candidate is . . . gone, and now Sherman's a sitting president but too sick to run. The Three Witches from Macbeth couldn't have cursed them more comprehensively."

"Good God Almighty," Knox said . . . but in a very different tone, and looked at Roosevelt with a tinge of awe. "Colonel, didn't Bismarck say something once about Providence and America—"

Roosevelt knew the German statesman's saying, but let Croly supply the quote:

"'A special Providence of God protects drunkards, small children, and the United States of America.'"

Roosevelt waited for laughter, but nobody was treating it as a joke . . . or even smiling. He didn't believe in divine intervention of that type himself, but he did believe in destiny, for men and nations. He could feel his stirring now, and with it America's, like boulders shifting at the tipping point of an all-conquering avalanche. And all because of one blocked artery in a fat man's heart, a tiny thing moving mountains. He went on thoughtfully, but with a growing feeling of exhilarating certainty:

"The Old Guard probably can't even *agree* on a candidate without an incumbent to run, not in the time they've got before the convention . . . and they don't have the guts to bolt the Party when we carry the nomination."

Which I would have done, if they'd stolen it!

Dixon broke a brown study of concentration: "Taft's ordinary delegates will come over to us in the next week, or enough of them. But the big boys, and the corporations and trusts behind them . . . they'll sit on their hands all the way to November."

The campaign manager's warning meant he was already looking ahead to the general election. It was just dawning on the rest that the struggle they'd met here to plan was effectively over. The senator from Montana continued:

"They'll close their checkbooks too, and hope we're discredited if the Democrats win."

"I don't care if they pout. All the better! We can put reliable Progressives in every position while the malefactors of great wealth are sulking in their tents," Roosevelt said.

"We can build a Progressive Republican Party that's a disciplined political *army*, not a divided rabble!" Croly said.

"And we'll have the people with us," Roosevelt said; he liked Croly's ideas, even if he wasn't overfond of the man himself.

His fist thudded on the table.

"By God, we've got them! And if the Democrats are stupid enough to nominate that prissy sissy of a Princeton professor, that fake Progressive and sad excuse for a man Woodrow Woodenhead Wilson, we've got them too!"

"And then . . ." Dixon almost crooned; he'd earned his Progressive spurs fighting the well-named Anaconda Copper Mining Company's crushing hold on his home state. "There are some scores to pay, by God—the railroads and the trusts will learn to walk small."

That brought a rumble of agreement, and Roosevelt nodded. It was time to show that the people's voice . . . spoken through him . . . was master. Half measures hadn't worked.

Croly nodded too. "And we can finally get the nineteenth century over with, make this a planned efficient *nation* instead of a mess with a few efficient spots in it."

Roosevelt grinned, his fighting grin. "We can set this great country of ours to rights, and give it a government worthy of it!"

A wolfish growl ran around the table, hungry and determined. The Rough Riders had followed him up San Juan Hill, and now the Republican Party . . .

No, the Progressive *Republican Party—we'll change the name to let people know a new broom is sweeping clean!*

. . . would follow him to Washington.

And might God have pity on those who got in the way, for he didn't intend to do much along those lines himself.

ONE

I've never flown before, Senior Field Operative Luz O'Malley Aróste-gui thought.

She looked up at the docked airship, a study in light and shadow beneath the glare of the hangar's banks of lights, silver-bright above and reflected off the rippling water of the berth below.

And my first trip . . . three thousand miles over an ocean, to a continent at war!

At seven hundred fifty feet from nose to tail and a hundred forty across at its broadest point, the great silvery whale-shape of the *San Juan Hill* was the pride of American National Airways—four months out of the yard at Lakehurst and with its three sisters the only dirigibles in the world capable of routine transatlantic trips. The *Battle* class were a leap even for the brilliant, daring young engineering wizards of the National Aeronautical Administration, with a more advanced teardrop shape than any zeppelin and bigger too, larger even than the one that had spent a hundred hours in the air recently to reach German East Africa from Bulgaria despite the Entente air patrols.

And fortunately not one of their occasional brilliant daring failures, like that

*six-engine flying boat that kept crashing and sinking, or bursting into flames . . .
and then crashing and sinking.*

The airship above her was so large that its floating over the water
seemed utterly unnatural, as if the giant silvery-gray thing were in an
eternal mid-fall ready to topple down on you . . . though it was also a
fragile lacework of aluminum covered in fabric, when you thought of
Atlantic storms. The interior was vast, millions of square feet, but most
of that was bags full of hydrogen and gas fuel for the ten engine pods.

She couldn't tell if the stirring she felt and the shiver on the back of
her neck was excitement or apprehension. Not fear, certainly not that.
Luz inhaled deeply; that smell of brackish harbor water, fuel oil, lubricants, and the doped cotton covering the giant flying machine was a
new thing in the world. A coughing roar sounded as the engines began
to turn over; the four-bladed aluminum propellers started to spin and
the breeze of them went washing over her and tugging at her hat and
skirt and fluttering cool fingers into her hair.

Excitement, verdad. *Fear I leave for others . . . I left it behind with my
childhood.*

Luz wasn't afraid of much; she had never been timid, and what
remained had been scoured out the night Pancho Villa's men burned
the hacienda where her family had been staying, back before the Intervention.

Her face changed as she remembered, and for a moment her
midnight-blue eyes might have been black, as the lighter streaks around
the irises vanished. Remembered waiting in the back of the wardrobe
in the dark, with the muzzle of the pistol pressed under her chin. Listening to the Villistas kill her parents while she swallowed her sobs,
then crawling out on her belly like a snake below the worst of the
smoke, past their machete-hacked bodies and through the sticky pools
of their blood. Five years ago now . . .

"Miss?" the ticketing officer behind the counter of his kiosk said,
alarm in his voice and a startled look in his eyes at what he'd seen
in hers.

"Sorry," she said, blinking back to reality.

The stabs of uncontrollable memory were rare now. Now that every man involved was dead, including Villa. She'd watched most of them die, the ones she hadn't killed herself.

The agent was still puzzled by what he'd seen, frightened without knowing why. She gave him a charming smile as she handed over her passport along with the ticket.

The passport was forged in the name of one Elisa Carmody de Soto-Dominguez; there were more formalities to travel these days, what with the war, but the Black Chamber's documents section was on the job. Mexicans who wanted to travel abroad also had to get U.S. passports to do it, but that and the requisite dual citizenship were fairly easy to acquire for wealthy ones in good odor with the American authorities who ran the Mexican Protectorate now. Elisa had been one such, until the Chamber found out she was also a secret member of the Partido Nacional Revolucionario and conspiring with the German Empire against the United States.

While Luz traveled under her name, the luckless actual Elisa was either dead of what the file would say was heart failure—a .45 slug in the back of the head did make your heart fail very badly indeed—or still undergoing a series of exquisitely unpleasant experiences in El Palacio Negro de Lecumberri. The Black Palace of Lecumberri was a hulking ill-omened pile northeast of Mexico City that had been built as a prison by President Porfirio Díaz back around the turn of the century, and one that made her skin crawl every time she came near.

It had been the sort of place where you went for offending one of the Indispensible One's *jefes políticos* and slept tied upright to the walls because there were five thousand inmates in cells theoretically designed for seven hundred fifty. And there you stayed until you died or some guard made fifty pesos under the table by selling you to a labor agent from the tobacco estates of the Valle Nacional, which was about the same thing with fresh air.

It was still a prison for the Protectorate today, though much more select in its client list. It also housed the Black Chamber's southern headquarters, a Federal Bureau of Security station, and representatives from what she thought of as the Heinz 57 Varieties of military intelligence.

The ticket agent visibly relaxed under the beacon of her smile, dismissing the unguarded emotion he'd just seen in her eyes. Charming smiles were something Luz did well, along with other, hidden talents. She was in her mid-twenties, with straight fine hair the color of raven feathers, so black that it had metallic-blue highlights in the sun. It was done in the bobbed style the French actress Polaire had recently made fashionable among the daring, and framed a comely straight-nosed, full-lipped, olive-skinned oval face with high cheekbones under a round turban-style hat with a single peacock plume and a scarflike silk fall that was looped under the chin and fastened on the other side with a silver clasp.

Her clothes were modish but a little more conservative than the bobbed hair, a dark maroon *tailleur* outfit of jacket and lower-calf-length skirt of light worsted suited to the humid heat of New York's summer, with a cream silk shirtwaist and a few small pieces of day jewelry in the popular southwestern style. She'd picked those up in Santa Fe while debriefing from her last mission in a Black Chamber safe house.

Being obviously a bit of a dashing New Woman of the era of the New Nationalism was one thing, but she didn't want to stand out as a full-scale flapper with a cigarette in an ivory holder and a whiskey flask tucked into her garter. That would be bad tradecraft, both because it would attract attention and because it would be another layer of pretense she'd have to keep track of. It was much easier to disguise *who* you were than *what* you were. Like most of her generation and class Luz regarded the old Victorian conventions of Mrs. Grundy and her ilk with a degree of amused contempt and enjoyed herself without qualms, but she wasn't basically a frivolous person.

Thank God the corset is dead, though, she thought. *My luck!*

She'd just barely missed the period when you were a hopeless eccentric or a free-love advocate in odd-looking William Morris–style aesthetic gowns if you didn't start corseting by your late teens. The change had been very swift. Nobody her age wore one now, except dowdy lower-middle-class provincials who hadn't gotten the news or a few pinch-mouthed conservatives in enclaves like Beacon Hill in Boston where they tried to pretend the twentieth century hadn't started yet.

And thank God that looking active is fashionable now, too, everyone living Uncle Teddy's "Strenuous Life" or pretending to.

Her honorary uncle approved of strenuous *women*, too. Luz knew he meant it because she'd visited the Roosevelts often since girlhood; her father had been a Rough Rider and, as an MIT man who made his living as a consulting engineer in wild and woolly places, was just the type of scientific modern buccaneer the president admired.

I'd have been out of luck in the era of the tight-laced swoon and interesting pallor.

The middle-aged man in the blue uniform behind the booking booth's counter concealed any annoyance at her carefully calculated last-minute arrival and looked at the baggage the sweating porter had piled up behind her with his dolly. There were two expensive Vuitton steamer trunks in yellow leather with brass corners to go into the hold, and a large ostrich-hide suitcase and a hatbox by the same maker for the eighty-odd hours of the journey. They were plainly visible, since an airship boarding process wasn't the mob scene you'd get at Grand Central or Penn Station, especially when you were the last passenger to arrive. In fact there were several hundred people in the hangar, but they were mostly ground crew lost in the hugeness of it, disconnecting the lift gas and fuel gas and ballast water pipes and electric power cables and standing by the mooring lines.

None of them were paying her any special attention, except the corporal in charge of the very bored but reasonably alert Federal Bureau of Security squad in their new turtlelike steel helmets, baggy olive-dust-brown-green uniforms, and buckled gaiter boots.

He'd been giving her a few uneasy glances, his knobby narrow-chinned hillbilly face puzzled. He had a long scar over his sandy eyebrows, a very deep tan, an Arkansas toothpick tucked into his boot, and a drum-fed Thompson gun with a use-pitted muzzle in an assault sling across his belly. The rest carried the light self-loading rifles Browning had developed and Colt manufactured, or battle shotguns. The Bureau got their pick of the new toys, of which there were many these days since Uncle Teddy loved gadgets and inventions, particularly those that shot bullets. Or flew, or better still flew through the air shooting bullets.

His hand worked on the grip of the machine pistol as he frowned at her in puzzlement, and he was obviously listening to instincts that had kept him alive. She disarmed him with a brilliant smile and he flushed and looked away scowling, unable to match the inner prompting with what his eyes told him.

"You're traveling alone, then, Miss, ah, Carmody?" the ticketing officer said, grizzled brows rising on a face like the map of Ireland.

She nodded casually. Even in these enlightened modern days—and when years of war and Roosevelt's Equal Rights Amendment had changed many things—it was still just a little risqué for an obviously well-born young woman not to have even a maid with her, or an older traveling companion. Her mother's family, those stiff-necked birth-proud Cuban hacendado sugar barons, would have fainted in shock. But then they'd cut off her mother as if she were dead for eloping with the dashing young engineer Patrick O'Malley a quarter century ago, and she'd been raised very differently from the gloom and almost Oriental seclusion her mother had endured. Mima had enjoyed that adventurous tomboyish girl's life vicariously, even when she felt her daughter and only child was going too far and insisted on spells in finishing schools.

And besides, the Black Chamber doesn't have enough female agents to waste one playing my maid.

"If you'll stand here on the scale with your things, miss, we need to have the exact weight . . . ah, your cabin baggage is a bit over the maximum . . ."

She paid the stiff extra charge without a qualm; it fit her persona as an arrogant headstrong rich girl, which Elisa Carmody had been . . . though being a secret revolutionary had been arrogantly headstrong and very, very foolish. This was on Uncle Sam's nickel anyway, through the clandestine budget the Treasury funneled to the Secret Service and they to the Chamber, though she could have afforded it herself. Her father had left her the house and real estate in Santa Barbara and the ranchland near Los Olivos and enough income from conservative investments to finish her education at Bryn Mawr College and live very comfortably for the rest of her life, if not enough for the Upper Ten Thousand's social whirl. She'd chosen the Black Chamber instead because she wanted it. First for revenge, and then because . . .

Well, it would have been very dull to have nothing important to do. Even in Santa Barbara, where you can spend a month ambling around without noticing whether it's Friday yet. And I had to show Uncle Teddy he was right to trust me, and not let the other women in the Chamber down either. Peace someday . . . but not today.

A stamp on her passport ended the process. "That'll be cabin A-12, Miss Carmody . . . Miss de Soto . . . Miss . . . Dominguez . . ." he said, gradually running down as he ran through the names, mangling the Hispanic parts with a nasal big-city, East Coast, *dese-and-dem* accent probably acquired growing up in the Bronx.

"All three, technically, but Carmody will do," she said patiently.

Her own natural accent in English was pellucid General American of a Californian variety with a very faint western tinge, though she could have donned one that would make her sound like the man's younger sister. She *was* letting a very slight hint of both Mexico and Ireland into her speech, to match the report of Elisa Carmody's patterns.

He continued, with obvious relief at not having offended someone who could afford to spend better than his yearly salary on a ticket.

"Dinner will be served from seven, Miss Carmody. Welcome to the friendly skies of American National Airways, and have a swift and pleasant flight. Please follow the steward who will carry your cabin baggage."

She turned and strode with a gracefully springy step up the ramp that led to the gondola entrance, ignoring the passengers looking down at her disgracefully late arrival through the inward-curving windows of the lounge above; the three-level inhabited part of the airship was built into the bottommost curve of the hull save for where the semicircle of the flight deck jutted out like a chin near the underside of the prow.

There was work to be done before they left . . . and possibly a man to kill in the skies over the gray northern seas.

The attendant who carried her gear answered her smile as she paused and looked up at the great machine, taking it for admiration. The real cause was the thought of another historic first, like her vote in the 1914 midterm election.

Only better. Uncle Teddy, qué Dios te bendiga, *isn't the only one who can make history.*

Millions of other women had voted, and helped put in the first and so far only woman senator. But Luz doubted *anyone* had assassinated a German spy on a dirigible yet. According to the grapevine and the implications of their new orders, Teddy had said the gloves were well and truly off. He was . . . peeved. There were good reasons, too.

Sinking the Mauretania *and killing two hundred Americans on board her, for one. It would have been interesting to be a fly on the wall in the White House when Uncle Teddy got the news about* that *back in the spring.*

She'd been mildly surprised that he hadn't declared war then and there. Reportedly, his old Cuba comrade and current Chief of the General Staff, General Leonard Wood, had talked him out of it, on the grounds that the United States wasn't quite ready.

Readiness had gone into high gear since.

I can smell war coming, smell it down the wind from the future. And not far away, either.

TWO

L uz stepped through and looked around the pale elegance of the little cabin as the stewardess opened the door and followed with her
bags. The walls were taut fabric over an aluminum frame like the outer
covering, though in this case linen printed with a willow-leaf pattern,
with cellular paper shaped like the newfangled egg cartons filling in behind it to soundproof the compartment. There was a well-upholstered
sofa that would turn into a bed, a chair and a table discreetly bolted to
the floor through the carpeting in case of storms, and a sink covered by a
folding top that turned it into another table. From what she'd heard, the
idea was that you'd spend the time you weren't actually sleeping in the
airship's well-appointed public spaces.

Another bunk hinged on the wall struts folded into the space above
the sofa, but the Chamber had secured the whole compartment for her
by the simple expedient of buying two tickets and having the fictional
other woman cancel at the last instant, forfeiting the price.

Transatlantic travel had nosedived because of the war in Europe,
especially after the *Mauretania* met its torpedo and its sister the *Lusita-
nia* got its close shave, but for the same reason many who *did* have to
cross the ocean anyway wanted an airship passage if they could possibly get it. The risks of a means of travel only six months old looked

good by comparison to running the iron gauntlet of the U-boat packs, and every commercial trip had seen the airships fully booked both ways three times a week. Fortunately for the company and for American prestige they'd all made it across even in the worst weather with nothing more than airsickness and the occasional stretch of hull fabric torn off.

"Thank you," she said to the stewardess—there were three to attend the twelve female passengers—and slipped her an Indian Head quarter eagle, which was a very generous but not outlandish tip. "Please turn down the bed while I'm in the dining compartment."

"Shall I unpack your cabin case, miss?" the woman said.

She was thirtyish, alertly competent-looking, and very black, much like a female Pullman redcap—which was something her father, brothers, and uncles might well be.

"No, I'll take care of that myself, thank you," Luz said.

When the door had clicked home she locked it—you could shut out the staff with an unbeatable deadbolt while you were in the cabin yourself—and grinned for an instant as she put the brass-strapped leather suitcase on the folding stand. There were things inside that the stewardess would probably have been startled to see. Nothing strictly illegal, not in the United States at least, but she might have talked. The O'Malleys had always had some servants once they settled down in a place for more than a few days. Luz knew how difficult it was to keep secrets from the people who handled the underwear, and how easy it was to forget the constant presence of those ears and eyes.

Germans were usually the world's worst spies, but part of being a good one was not confusing *usually* with *always* and assuming they weren't plugged into the staff grapevine.

One corner of the cabin held a set of drawers where she put her underthings, including lace-trimmed modern brassieres, chemises, and fashionable tight short underdrawers and silk stockings; some rather daring Chinese-styled black pajamas instead of the conventional nightgown; and two sets of shoes as *un*fashionably flat-heeled as the ones she was wearing now. She hung up her outfits in the closet next to it; there were only three, selected for wrinkle resistance, which was much less than she'd have had to take for an ocean voyage. A first-class passenger had to change her dresses at least twice a day on a ship and have a ball gown as well. That *would* have been difficult if she were on her own.

American National Airways tried to make their airships sound like ocean liners of the sky in their advertising copy. So far they were actually more like an airborne luxury train, say the *20th Century Limited*; not surprising, given the numbers of passengers and crew—eighty and fifty-two, respectively—and the fact that ANA was a subsidiary of the new American National Railways. ANR was still working hard on unifying the chaotic mass of North America's rail systems, though already you could travel from Boston to the Yucatan on one ticket, and you didn't have to switch in Chicago to get to the West Coast anymore. They'd had a blank piece of paper to start with a few years ago as far as dirigibles went, but the influence of Pullman cars was evident.

The first part of the secret compartment at the bottom of the suitcase was actually just a *very inconspicuous* flap. When she lifted the concealing cover back, there were six slim books custom-bound in soft leather lying within. One was the inevitable *Kim* by Kipling, which Teddy adored and which was the Chamber's unofficial official novel—she'd had to play that revolting memory game the *pinche escuincle* Kim suffered through hundreds of times in training, but she admitted to herself that the book was a masterpiece. And so popular having it wasn't likely to raise any alarms. *K* by Rinehart, *Life and Gabriella* by Glasgow, both trashy, guilty pleasures. *The Mucker* by Edgar Rice Burroughs, even guiltier because to her it held fantasies of frolicking on the lost tropic isle with that fascinatingly herculean roughneck Billy Byrne and his deliciously refined Barbara in ways that would probably have sent Burroughs running screaming for the hills, poor man. *The Hunt for Villa*, by Richard Harding Davis and a runaway best seller—she'd given the famous war correspondent a few tips on that one, sub rosa; and a copy of the uncensored edition of Baudelaire's *Les Fleurs du Mal.*

She'd included that because she liked it, to help keep her French up, and because the very, very naughty color illustrations by Schwabe would give a customs agent something to be indignant about if he got past the inconspicuous-flap part. Nothing soothed a petty bureaucrat's suspicions like *finding* something, preferably something that made him feel morally superior to the wealthy people who sneered at him every day.

The books' real use were as keys to several ciphers she'd memorized for this mission, and since she was undercover, she'd been able to avoid lugging around her autographed copy of the paralyzingly dull and earnest Party bible, *The Promise of American Life* by Herbert Croly (1914 edition), one of the most-bought and least-read books of modern times. Uncle Teddy *had* read both versions, but then he read two or three books a day and never forgot a word.

As a bonus the Baudelaire was an ongoing revenge on "Specs" McGuire, the codes-section manager in the growing New York station, who was always hinting that she'd only gotten into the Chamber because the president was a friend of her family or that she'd slept with Director Wilkie or both. He was an unbearable prig as well as a woman-hater and had to embarrass himself hideously and publicly every time he took out this illustrated edition to decode a message, and she always tried as hard as possible to have the cipher hit something extremely juicy like *Femmes Damnées.* As an added joy everyone else laughed at him when his ears went red.

The books went by her nightstand, and then she painstakingly unscrewed the *really* secret cover below; the volumes also helped disguise the fact that the suitcase weighed more than you would expect if it held nothing but toiletries and frilly silk unmentionables. Built into the frame of the suitcase was a layer of hard rubber with shaped holders for a number of other things, including money from different countries, identity documents for several different identities, her lockpicks, a magnifying glass and a miniature monocular telescope, several sets of thin black leather gloves with unusual properties, a coil of slender but extremely strong silk cord, a chamois-covered sap filled with fine lead shot, and assorted chemicals in small thick vials.

Right now she removed two items. One was a six-inch *navaja* folding knife, which she'd inherited from her mother's coachman-cum-bodyguard, ancient one-eyed Pedro El Andaluz . . . along with years of the wicked old *barratero*'s clandestine instruction in the Sevillana style of *pelea de navaja*. She tucked it into a loop sewn into her skirt pocket on the right, which left the hooked handle in just the right spot to be whipped out with a single finger and slapped into her palm as it opened and made that demoralizing little *crick-crick-clack* sound when the blade locked.

The other was a small compact Browning FN 1910 automatic, which went into a molded holder in the inside left front of her jacket under a thin silk pad that cunningly concealed the outline from the most discriminating eye; ordinary shoulder holsters didn't go with a bosom. She smiled fondly as she balanced the little Belgian pistol in her palm for a moment before tucking it away. Uncle Teddy kept another just like it in the drawer beside his bed in the White House, and her father had given her this one on her nineteenth birthday. He'd insisted that she and her mother learn to use firearms, just as a precaution given the way his occupation took them to odd places, and Luz had been a crack rifle and pistol shot by her midteens, and a hunter who'd bagged deer and peccaries and jaguar.

Most Black Chamber field operatives used Colt .45 automatics when they carried a pistol, but while she wasn't a small woman—she was a lithely fit five-six—she thought the .380 was easier to her hand and that a lighter bullet that actually *hit* was infinitely more effective than a .45 monster thrown off aim by mule-kick recoil to break windows and kill bystanders.

After all, when Princip shot the archduke with one of these he started the Great War. In a way it's killed more men than the Maxim gun!

Using a pistol was usually a rare desperation move anyway when you were undercover, though when you *did* need one you needed it . . .

Desperately, she mused.

Fortified by that thought she did a little discreet eyeliner and lipstick by Rimmel and paid some attention to her hair.

"Ravishing, as always, *mi corazón*," she said to her reflection. "I fall at your feet and plant kisses like flower petals upon your so-delectable toes."

Then she spent a final moment using a very little spirit gum and a few hairs from the brush to make sure she'd know if anyone searched the suitcase left temptingly on the stand. The door locks were a joke to anyone who knew what they were doing, and the staff had keys anyway. Her handbag was harmless, except for the very compact little film camera that spent most of its time built into it, and a few experiments showed that the noise of the airship covered the soft click when she triggered it by pressing the concealed button in the handle.

The passenger cabins made up the top deck. The crew quarters and baggage were on the bottom; the lounges, kitchen, and dining areas were in the middle. She walked along the corridor past the ladies' toilet and shower-baths and down a spiral staircase of wrought aluminum in sinuous vine shapes into a subdued glow of light. Vast slanting windows stretched along nearly eighty feet to either side, and you could lean on the railing and look directly downward, or sit at your leisure on a chaise longue or around tables set on the polished spruce veneer of the floor and glance out toward the horizon, though right now the view was of the interior of the hangar.

There was even a bandstand, and the brochure promised dancing to Morton's Red-Hot Ragtime Band. Currently it held a single striking-looking young Negro musician—

As a good Progressive, Luz always used the respectful term *Negro*. Besides being polite, it also stuck a thumb in the eye of the Dixie-dominated Democrats, who could barely bring themselves to say *colored* or the mildly insulting *black*.

—in a tuxedo and bow tie who was tinkling out something quick and light that *wasn't* quite ragtime on a surprisingly good aluminum-framed piano, and doing it very well.

Now that's an interesting piece, and I don't recognize it, she thought, pausing for a moment and cocking her head to the side to listen. *I'd dance to that! I wonder if it's his composition?*

Unfortunately she couldn't just go up and ask, since she was here on business and had to keep character.

There's just a bit of tango style there too, sort of a smoky undertone. Much more complex than you'd think . . . four themes, sixteen bars each, four-bar bridges . . . AABBCCA, I think.

It gave a cheerful background to the big bright room. Weight was at a premium on dirigibles, and everything was of light strong construction, wicker and aluminum and cloth, but empty space for the designers to play with was plentiful. Removable eighteen-foot-high fabric panels marked off the dining area, covered in colorful mural-like designs of tropical flowers and vines and parrots. The whole ensemble had a spare, cathedral-like modern elegance.

It's well-designed, and well-designed means pleasing, she thought.

Luz was the daughter of an engineer who delighted in an efficiently crafted spillway or the elegant transfer of forces in an arch. She took one of the last of the small round tables still available and set her handbag on it so that the lens concealed in a fake topaz covered most of the rest of the lounge. A waiter came by, and she ordered a glass of seltzer water with lime; it came at the same time as a trolley of pre-dinner canapés and another with magazines and newspapers.

Let's see what light reading's available, she thought, nibbling on a toast point dabbed with patriotic, nationally sourced but quite tasty Columbia River caviar amid a background hum of conversation. *It wouldn't do to just stare squint-eyed at people.*

The usual periodicals were at hand, starting with the inevitable copies of the *New Republic,* which was Croly's rag and more or less the Party's house organ. She took a quick glance at the table of contents for the August issue and decided she didn't need to know . . .

. . . how wonderful the New Nationalism is. What a surprise dear Croly thinks so, since he gave Uncle Teddy the idea for the name.

She also didn't need to read another puff piece about Secretary Mather's ever-expanding national parks . . .

Or . . .

Her eyes flicked down the list.

Or new sewage plants in the Protectorate . . .

Or cooperative grain elevators . . .

Or universal labor arbitration boards for everyone down to the Amalgamated Chicken-Pluckers . . .

Or a debate on whether the Scouts should be compulsory as a preparation for national service . . .

Which, what a surprise, Croly thinks is a wonderful idea.

Though Uncle Teddy would probably insist that Fred Burnham head up the program, and he'd do it splendidly. The deadly, soft-spoken little bantam adventurer was already running wilderness-scout training for the Ranger battalions and Black Chamber operatives from the camp near his Yaqui Valley hacienda, and Luz liked him a great deal. Besides being able to out-Apache real Apaches, when he did talk about the things he'd done in war and wild places he was among the few men who reduced Uncle Teddy to a listener.

Her eyes went to the last entry in the table of contents:

Or, finally and worst of all, "Efficient Citizenship: How to Taylorize Your Life" by "our editors," which meant the man himself.

Someone had said once that when Croly really got going you could see the homemade lemonade boiling in his veins.

She took the *New York Times* instead and held it up to read while scanning faces around it without being obvious, and also occasionally struggling not to laugh. Reading newspapers was a bit surreal if you were behind the curtain and saw some of the machinery that cast the public shadows. One of the editorials actually seemed to think there was still doubt about the United States declaring war on the Central Powers, for example. As if Uncle Teddy had told the Iron House—the

War Department's monumental new headquarters, shared with the Navy even though it wasn't quite finished—to conscript three million men and federalize another million guardsmen and reservists back in the spring as a just-in-case precaution.

The European news on the front page was, as usual since August 1914, bad.

But there is bad and then there is something rather like a cinema film of an avalanche coming right at you, done with the projector turned to slow.

It started with the perennial French claim that they were going to retake Verdun *really soon now, any day, honest we will!* And Crown Prince Friedrich Wilhelm publicly laughing his Royal and Imperial buttocks off about it, which was fair enough since he'd commanded the Army group that finally took it back in the spring after months of interminable massacre. The Russian offensive against Austria had gone well until the German General von Mackensen smashed it up; and the Rumanians were already saying how very, very sorry they were that they'd joined the Entente and tried to grab off Austro-Hungarian Transylvania just before the aforesaid smashing of General Brusilov. Which had been an act of monumentally shortsighted stupidity astonishing even by the standards of the Great War's participants.

Luz smiled wryly. The Bible said it didn't profit a man to lose his soul and gain the whole world; but getting your head kicked in for the privilege of a three-week stay in . . . *Transylvania?* Now they were begging for mercy from Germany, which was rather like pleading with a shark not to take a second bite.

And mutual slaughters continued on the Somme as both sides tried to turn Picardy into an artillery-sculpted replica of the moon, or of the humid, leprous skin of some monstrous toad . . .

The domestic news was more cheerful, especially if you were a Party member. A lead headline was the Democrats' attempt to filibuster the Dyer anti-lynching bill, doomed under the new Senate rules on closure, since they only had twenty-six seats now and were helplessly split between the southern Bourbons and the northern Progressive wing, which was gradually dribbling away bit by bit to the PR or to Debs and his Socialists. Senator Bankhead of Alabama had invoked states' rights and the virtue of southern womanhood menaced by the *lustful nigra* and accused the president of waving the bloody shirt of the Civil War.

The president had formally said *no comment* but had been heard to say off the record that the senator could have a bloody nose to drip on his bloody shirt if he'd rather stand up in the ring and settle it that way, man-to-man.

Luz grinned. She could just see *him* grinning as he let that comment about the Alabaman drop, while meaning every word of it. To add some *mulato* peppers to the *mole*, she happened to know that in the coming session one of Uncle Teddy's cronies was going to reintroduce a stronger version of the Federal Elections Bill that the southern Democrats had filibustered to death when Henry Cabot Lodge proposed it a generation ago. That would guarantee black suffrage in federal elections; they couldn't block it this time and the Negroes would all vote Progressive Republican in lockstep until the Day of Judgment and instantly send the Party's vote in the Deep South from nothing to at least a third and finally bring New Nationalism to Dixie . . .

Which will have the Bourbons down on all fours snarling and foaming like rabid dogs, which is art imitating life. ¡Ay! ¡Pero que estupidos son esos pendejos!

That was Uncle Teddy to the inch; he was the canniest of all politicians, but he was also the man who'd once leapt off his horse and stabbed a cougar to death with his hunting knife because the dogs mobbing it blocked a shot. He enjoyed life more than anyone she'd ever known, at least anyone over the age of eight.

Luz sighed. She missed him and Aunt Edith and Ted and Ethel and the rest, but she hadn't been to the White House or Sagamore Hill lately. Partly because it wasn't easy to do that without being photographed these days, which wouldn't be professional in her line of work, and partly because he was letting his eugenics bee buzz out of his bonnet lately and kept having Aunt Edith introduce Luz to stalwart young officers he thought would be good breeding stock while dropping hints about the joys of enormous litters. And because Uncle Teddy had been born before the Civil War and was—by her standards—a bit of a prude. She wouldn't lie to someone who'd done so much for her, but she preferred not to hurt him with irrelevant details about her private life.

The official motto of the officially nonexistent Black Chamber was *Ex umbris, acies*. Which meant *From the shadows, steel.*

The unofficial motto, coined in 1913 by a Harvard wit among the original recruits and used much more frequently, was: *Non Theodorum parvis concitares ne perturbatus sit*, often shortened to NTPC. Which translated freely as: *Don't bother Teddy with the details, it'll just upset him.* That was a good rule all 'round.

The *Times*' other main stories were Japan biting off chunks of China for what it swore was China's own good (with Uncle Teddy giving them a warning glare they would be well-advised to heed) and whether the Philippines and Puerto Rico should be put on the road to statehood. Which was starting to look somewhat possible—someday, maybe—for Puerto Rico at least, given the way Hawaii had added a forty-ninth star just this year. You could be absolutely sure neither was going to vote for the Bourbon Democrats, which was a powerful antidote to whatever qualms the Party's membership had about letting so many suspiciously swarthy people into their tent.

Speaking of voting . . .

There wasn't much comment on November's elections, since everyone knew that the Democrats weren't going to carry any state that hadn't been part of the Confederacy, and might well lose Texas too. Luz couldn't even remember offhand who the Democrats had nominated, except that it was some judge from Connecticut. Teddy had been president for twelve of this century's sixteen years, and he'd go right on being president as long as he wanted, or more likely until he died in office. Since he was still in his fifties, robustly healthy, and showed no loss of interest in the game, that might not be for decades;

she'd heard him say the worst mistake he'd ever made was promising not to run for a third consecutive term back in 1904.

She glanced over the top of the paper occasionally while she sipped her soda water, apparently with casual boredom. Some curiosity was natural for a traveler, and the faces were more interesting than the news anyway.

Let's do some analysis.

The passengers included quite a few assorted industrialists and bankers and their emissaries, as you'd expect when each ticket cost twice what a coal miner made in a year even in these times of rising prices and wages. They were from both sides of the Atlantic—she thought two were Japanese, come to that—and a dozen countries but might have come off Ford's new assembly lines at Highland Park otherwise, plump men with cold cash-register eyes or thin wolfish ones with a hungry gaze, in neutral suits with the occasional pinkie ring for the more raffish. The neutrals . . . other neutrals, for now . . . and the Entente powers were both buying everything America could mine, pump out of the ground, grow, or make. And doing it with money borrowed right here in New York; the City of London's position was never going to be the same again.

There were a few Americans who she thought from their expressions of painful middle-class earnestness and dowdy clothes were members of Hoover's Belgian Relief Commission, which was currently feeding millions in occupied Belgium and France and could afford the passage. Several of them were women who looked to be the type she'd seen so often at Bryn Mawr: ones who weren't content unless they were doing someone good whether the someone liked it or not, at loose ends since the suffrage struggle ended with the bang of the Sixteenth Amendment and fanning out to find other causes. Now that Mexico was more or less safe for American civilians away from the real back-country, you met a fair number down in the Protectorate running schools or sanitary childbirth classes or in doomed attempts to convince the locals that bland crème of celery soup was better for you than tripe *menudo* with red chilies.

The Chamber had also found the commission useful as a cover for getting agents into Europe, but if any of these were, she didn't even try to pick them out because she didn't need to know.

There was a clutch of so-called gentlemen of the press, most of whom had perked up at the sight of her as they would have for any pretty unaccompanied young woman. She knew that seedy breed, and would probably have to administer a few crushing setdowns to those who thought it was flattering to be treated like a piece of steak dangled over a kennel. Journalism was also a useful cover, but thankfully not one she'd ever had to use.

It would be like impersonating a leper.

Then there was an obvious Englishman who was also obviously a soldier despite his slightly threadbare Savile Row suit, a rangy auburn-haired man with a military mustache and face burned brick-red by years of tropical suns and expressionless blue eyes.

Marksman's eyes, she thought; the name on the passenger list was Arbuthnot.

His companion might have been a twin brother except for his coloring, turban, and beard; undoubtedly Indian and probably a princeling of some sort, named Singh on the manifest, which was the Indian equivalent of *Smith*. You saw more turbans these days where the British were involved, since Indian troops were all that had kept the Channel ports from falling after the Germans broke the front at Ypres wide open with their massive surprise gas attack early last year.

Here to talk with the War Department in Washington, she thought. *And going home with encouraging news.*

There had already been clashes between U.S. Navy airship and destroyer squadrons escorting American merchantmen and the U-boats of the Kaiserliche Marine all over the western Atlantic. At a second guess they were probably also both attached to the British secret service, either from London or more likely the Raj's older and rather more professional version operating out of Delhi and Simla. Luz had admired the neat way they'd scooped up the German-backed Ghadar Conspiracy in '14, having infiltrated it to a fare-thee-well, and she had been involved in helping collar the California branch of that movement for what the Federal Bureau of Security called *reform through corrective labor.* Something that did indeed involve a lot of labor, bad food, barbed wire, and profoundly unsympathetic guards.

And as for the players from the Central Powers . . . the Chamber had known there would be at least one agent on the airship, but it was standard practice to have one operative buy the ticket and another show up with it at the last minute just as she'd done, so she was going in blind on his appearance. She'd have to spot him on her own, and so . . .

Surely it can't be that *easy?*

All she knew definitely was the code name the real Elisa Carmody had been given: *Reichsschwert,* Imperial Sword. There were a dozen Germans among the passengers, most trying to get home before the eventual declaration of war trapped them behind the wire of an enemy-alien camp. Only three couldn't be positively judged harmless from regular background checks. An obvious white-haired Herr Doktor Professor type with a goatee and pince-nez, deep in a book, *Zur Genealogie der Moral: Eine Streitschrift,* and probably misunderstanding it.

In her experience Germans usually did misunderstand Nietzsche, often willfully, starting with his sister-editor's grotesque redactions.

The next was an obvious businessman, a squat bulging mound of bad manners in an expensively ill-fitting suit, sweating and shoveling vol-au-vents from the canapés trolley into his mouth and washing them down by guzzling beer like the Westphalian hog whose cured ham his flushed red face resembled.

According to reports the British blockade has Germany eating turnips by now, she thought. *Not* this *German, though,* ¡por Dios! *Not when he's back in Essen or Dusseldorf, either.*

Her guess was that his background looked suspicious because he was doing something deeply shady, but *commercially* shady.

The third was the one she instantly suspected; for starters, you could imagine him answering to "Imperial Sword" without your brain undergoing spontaneous combustion and then exploding. He was about six feet tall, hard and fit, and sitting with a leopard's long-limbed ease that held a military erectness as well. Bristle-cropped ash-blond hair, broad shoulders, narrow waist, shapely but large hands, and a square sculpted cleft-chin face that looked very like Manfred von Richthofen's, or possibly the daring Red Baron's slightly older brother. He didn't have a monocle and wasn't brandishing a riding crop, but . . .

¡Qué delicioso! *That's a dueling scar on his left cheekbone, a sip from the soup plate of honor! Yes, Colonel Nicolai, you* have *sent us a pantomime Prussian Junker as a spy!*

The man's name on the passenger manifest was Herr Hans Krämer, commercial agent, which was not only false but transparently so. *Krämer* literally meant "shopkeeper," and apart from the fact that a fit young German would be in field gray now rather than peddling samples, a thousand clues of posture and expression shouted *nobleman* and *soldier.* If this man didn't have a *von* tucked away somewhere, and probably a *Freiherr* or better, she'd give up chocolate and all carnal pleasures and become a Carmelite nun.

Why not a spiked helmet? Or one of those new coal-scuttle steel ones? Unless he's supposed to distract me from someone else? But no. Germans like to think of themselves as cold and rational, but that's only true when they're designing engines. In human matters they're often childlike and romantic . . . childlike and romantic and brutal, *but even so.*

Click-click the camera went as she rearranged the handbag and raised the glass of soda water to bring a steward with a refill. The Junker's eyes met hers for a moment, pale as Baltic ice, and he surprised her a little by smiling and suddenly looking like someone with a sense of humor.

Well, he is *a man as well as a spy.*

Men smiled at her quite often, which could be amusing or annoy-
ing depending on the circumstances, and they didn't need ulterior mo-
tives to do so. Beyond the obvious one.

*Quite a handsome man too, if you like the blond beast look, which is very nice
now and then. Now, what sort of approach from a beautiful lady spy would appeal
to a childlike sense of romanticism and convince him she's the* friendly *anti-
American Mexican revolutionary spy he was warned to expect and not a wicked
ringer slipped in by the sinister cunning of diabolical Black Chamber master-
minds?*

She let her features soften just a bit, not quite a smile of her own,
then ostentatiously looked away, as if interested only in what was going
on outside. Luz was perfectly willing to use seduction as a professional
technique, provided it was someone she'd at least have considered se-
ducing on her own time.

Even as a spy, one must have some *standards.*

The light through the windows brightened as the huge clamshell
doors of the hangar finished opening, revealing the blue sky and drifting white clouds of a summer's afternoon. The great floating building
had already been turned so that the blunt bow of the *San Juan Hill*
pointed into the wind. The engines—ten big Curtis-Martin radials,
mounted five to a side in a row of pods along hull corridors well above
the passenger section—were already turning over. Now they growled
louder and a slight subliminal vibration went through the airship's fabric. There was a bobbing jolt as the tugboats gently took up the slack
and pulled it free of the building, and then a rumble as water ballast
poured from the keel tanks, and a double *chunk* as the towing cables
released.

She closed her eyes for a moment to pay closest attention to her
own sensations. And then . . .

"*¡Que maravilloso!*" she murmured to herself with delight, in the language of her mother, the tongue of strong feeling and unguarded truth.
"We're *floating!*"

Floating *upward*, so gently that she could barely detect the elevator motion. The engines were there, but no louder than a motorcar, perhaps even a little less. Behind their throbbing was a profound stillness, like a slow-moving breeze on a spring day. And a creaking and flexing sound, like but utterly unlike that of a wooden ship under sail.

She opened her eyes, looking out eagerly. The airship was rising in a smooth clockwise circle miles in circumference, the chair beneath her feeling as solid as if it had been her study at university. That path was ANA policy, to give their new craft the maximum possible exposure to the public. It also put the tip of Manhattan below as they swept by at sixty-five miles an hour and rose to their cruising altitude of twelve hundred feet.

The great city spread out below her, with the green rectangle of Central Park surrounded by towering apartment blocks, and people and automobiles and carriages doll-tiny on the streets below. New Yorkers were jaded enough, or prickly enough about their reputation for being elaborately unimpressed, that few could be seen to stop and look at the seventy-first flight. The skyscrapers slid by; the Woolworth Building looked like a model in colored terra-cotta, despite being nearly eight hundred feet high and the tallest solid structure in the world.

Luz felt herself laugh in sheer pleasure. It was a *marvelous* age to be alive, and young, and a woman, and an American.

They turned northeast, and the city fell behind them with startling speed, and the land turned to a distant line of blue. The waters below were thick with shipping. That ranged from fishing smacks to windjammers with sails like poems written in geometry to the usual dingy smoke-belching tramp steamers, the elegant greyhound shapes of liners, and the hulking-sleek menace of a squadron of *New Mexico*–class battleships bristling with fourteen-inch guns and anti-air batteries. A murmur and pointing brought her eyes around; a wing of aeroplanes was passing the *San Juan Hill* in two loose gaggles of four.

They started as dots and then flashed by the airship with a combined speed well over a hundred miles an hour, banking into a curve;

twin-engine biplane Curtiss Falcons with their sharkish look brought out by the fanged mouth painted below the sharp noses. Two Browning machine guns pointed forward before the pilot, and there was another on a ring mount for the observer in his rear-facing seat. A pilot waved, close enough for his teeth to show in a smile beneath the goggles and leather helmet, trailed by a fluttering red scarf.

She glanced aside. The Westphalian Hog was among the passengers who studiously avoided looking out the windows; in fact, he'd turned his broad back on them and was clutching the table, looking as if he regretted the vol-au-vents. The Herr Doktor glanced up from his book and returned to wrestling with the conflict between master and slave morality, writing in a notebook now and then. Handsome Not-Really-Hans, on the other hand, was leaning over and following the fighting scouts with keenly intent eyes.

And knowledgeable ones, por Dios. *So, he's one of Colonel Nicolai's boys; but is he the one expecting to make contact with Elisa Carmody de Soto-Dominguez, that belle of the Irish Republican Brotherhood-Partido Nacional Revolucionario alliance, now looking for the Kaiser's help to resuscitate their respective lost causes?*

Elisa had talked; everyone did, in the end. But the eternal question with what Room 101—named after a chamber in Lecumberri—pulled out of resisting subjects was how reliable the information was, and how complete and whether it was out of date. Parts had been corroborated from other sources; parts had not; some had contradicted other things they thought they knew and put *those* in doubt.

About par for the course, Luz thought.

A really hostile subject wasn't going to tell you anything at all without severe pressure, and they'd lie truth out of creation as long as they could, whatever you did. Anyone still active underground in the Protectorate was probably very tough and determined. On yet another hand . . .

Room 101 works. *But you can never be sure how* well *it works.*

Some of what they'd gotten had enabled them to roll up most of what remained of the Partido Nacional Revolucionario in central

Mexico in a flurry of surprise shoot-outs, midnight arrests, and inter-rogations, which led to *more* arrests and so on, but you never got abso-lutely everyone. They had no idea if the remnants of those rolled-up networks had managed to pass on the information that Elisa and her luggage had simply disappeared from her rooming house one dark night, with the rent money slipped under the landlady's door. Or if they'd linked her disappearance to the bad things that started a few days later; enough bad things were happening to them anyway that they might not have, and simply thought she'd gotten tired of it all and done a bunk for parts unknown.

She and Luz looked alike in a general sort of way, enough to fool anyone who didn't actually know the revolutionary and was expecting to see her, and Luz knew everything the Chamber had managed to find out about her, which was a fair bit. But if any of a dozen things had slipped up, Luz would be walking into a trap the minute she tried to convince someone on the other side that she was Elisa. That made memories of strolling down Anacapa Street to the ocean and sitting and watching the sunset over the Pacific rather more alluring. Of course, after a while doing that she was terminally bored . . .

Not-Really-Hans walked casually nearer and leaned on the railing, looking after the aeroplanes.

"Formidable machines," he said in good but accented English, not exactly presuming to talk *to* her without an introduction. "They are as formidable as anything on the Western Front are."

"President Roosevelt is determined that his Air Corps should be second to none, regardless of expense," Luz said.

She was also not quite talking *to* him; etiquette could be awkward in an age of transition. And she used her perfect German. Elisa had spoken the language too; ironically that was because she'd attended the same finishing school near München that Luz had, though their time there hadn't overlapped.

"But warriors are the true *sword of an empire*," she said.

He started slightly at the words, and the very faint emphasis she'd laid on them. Then she turned and walked into the dining area, as a steward came through the lounge tapping a rubber hammer on a xylophone-style device he held in the crook of one arm, giving off a pleasant little tune that signaled the beginning of dinner service.

A waiter bowed and escorted Luz to her table; they were assigned by cabin. She scanned the menu; another thing that had gone away unmourned with the last century was women pretending they didn't get hungry or need to eat, and she was sharp-set after a hasty boiled-egg breakfast and nothing but a big pretzel from a pushcart for lunch.

Most of the dishes were a Harvey House version of the sort of sub-French cuisine you got at Delmonico's or the better hotels, with American specialties like terrapin or Virginia ham for patriotism's sake; only to be expected, since the Harvey company now had the contract to supervise dining for the whole of American National Railways and its airborne offshoot. She saw some south-of-the-border items—or at least ones with Spanish names—in a special section of the menu. They were fashionable, and a good many veterans of the Intervention had acquired a taste for the real thing as an escape from that oxymoronic vileness known as "Army food," which was even blander than what Anglos normally ate. There were a fair number of war brides, too, bringing their skills and tastes north with them into their new families.

Invasions go in both directions, sometimes.

She looked up at the waiter, who was standing with deferential calm. He was a stocky man in early middle age with a pepper-and-salt mustache, the white jacket of the service staff emphasizing his dark-olive skin, high cheekbones, rather narrow black eyes, and square—almost roundish—face. She wasn't surprised. The long struggle in Mexico and the long boom in the United States had also pushed and pulled a great many workers north of the now fairly theoretical border, the more so as the flood of immigrants from Europe had been cut off in 1914. The Poles and Rumanians, Magyars and Jews who'd once come in endless shiploads to shovel coal and work the looms were busy slaughtering each other in Flanders and Galicia and the Pripet

Marshes, millions of native-born farm boys and laborers were being swept into uniform, and in the meantime the construction gangs, mines, factories, and harvest crews needed willing hands. So did jobs like this.

"*¡Bien, Maestro Tomas!*" she said, reading the name embroidered on his breast pocket.

She pulled on her upper-class Mexico City accent like a familiar pair of gloves, fruit of years spent there as a girl while her father designed dams and bridges and tramways, and then for the Chamber after the Intervention. Languages fascinated Luz and had always come easily to her, and so had the little subtle tricks of their varieties, even before she'd needed them for professional reasons or studied them formally. The unfortunate Elisa had lived most of her life in the Mexican capital and nearby Puebla, being the granddaughter of an Irish deserter in the war of 1848 who'd prospered greatly in its aftermath. Luz continued:

"*¿Alguno de estos platillos valen la pena, o mejor pido de los platillos norteños?*"

The steward hid a delighted smile as she asked whether the Mexican dishes were worth ordering or whether she'd better stick to steak and *pommes frites*, and gave her a quick but respectful second look. She obviously had a great deal less *indio* in her background than he did, but she could easily be criollo of a highborn *raza pura* variety. Which was exactly what her mother had been, of course, just from a different part of the old Spanish dominions.

"*No, Señorita Carmody,*" he said; he'd probably studied the passenger list too.

Her mind's ear instantly tagged him as from northwest of the capital; the Bajío, and at a guess probably Querétaro. And born in a village about the time Porfirio Díaz took power.

"Carmody de Soto-Dominguez," she corrected with her eyes on the menu, as if absently.

An unmarried woman used both parents' surnames in the Iberian world; the Irish-Spanish mixture implied was precisely the fact of the

matter, which made it an ideal cover. He nodded and continued, with a
little scorn for the tender taste buds of the northerners under the professional courtesy of a waiter:

"*Estos gringos, les damos una salsita y gritan por agua . . . el humo les sale por
las orejas.*"

She smiled and nodded with a conspirator's chuckle. Acting a role
aside, it *was* rather funny. She'd heard that anguished howl for water
quite literally, though bread was actually more effective, since the heat
of the peppers cooked out into the oils. And metaphorically she'd seen
that smoke pouring out of shell-like pink ears more than once.

He leaned forward a little and murmured conspiratorially himself:
"*Pero le puedo traer de nuestros frijoles con chorizo y salsa chipotle; con una carne
asada y guacamole y crema acida. Nos dan bien de comer en la cocina, Señorita.*"

Saliva ran into her mouth at the thought of the authentic *carne asada*
he was offering her, and the cook would be working for love rather than
duty. You could eat well in New York in any number of styles since
most of the population were immigrants from everywhere on Earth or
their children, but for weeks she'd been dining with people of deepest
Anglo-Saxon dye, colleagues and good friends but ones who thought
béchamel sauce was hot stuff and a hint of garlic on a steak was a daring transgression risking stomach problems. And the whole exchange
would help establish her cover—it was never too soon to get into character. If her opponent-target was tapped into the grapevine, so much
the better.

"Yes, please, and I am most grateful, Maestro Tomas," she said,
continuing in Spanish.

"It shall be done, Doña Elisa," he said, promoting her respectfully;
that was how he'd have addressed the daughter of his *patrón* back in the
old country.

Not-Really-Hans, she noticed, had ordered lobster Newburg at a
table not too far away and his ears were virtually pricking up like a
wolf listening for a threat or prey.

I'd have thought he was a red-meat man, she thought. *Just shows that you shouldn't make too many assumptions.*

Come back to bed, *meine Süsse,*" Hans, or rather Hauptmann Horst von Dückler said two days later.

She'd been right, and even the Hans was fictitious; he was the third son of a baron with an ancestral *Schloss* near Breslau, too.

"Sweetie yourself," Luz chuckled, also in German, feeling pleasantly relaxed as she fished the bottle out of her cabin suitcase.

She was trying to drop just a tinge of what an Irish-Mexican accent would sound like into her aristocratic but slightly Bavarian-flavored German; his own upper-class standard *Hochdeutsch* had a distinct eastern tinge now and then, with hard *r*-sounds.

Then she raised a brow as he flipped back the sheet to indicate quite specifically what he had in mind.

"It's true what they say about you Prussian Junkers, then."

"I'm Catholic, and Silesian *niederer Adel,* actually, but what *do* they say?"

"That you're men of iron," she said, glancing back over her shoulder out of the corners of her eyes and standing hipshot as she turned to pour two small glasses of tequila.

Men liked this view of double curves, especially when you didn't have any clothes on, which was understandable—she did herself. And it was pleasant to be *admired* so by someone you also found attractive once you'd gotten over being shy. She'd lost the last of that when her parents died and her prayers went unanswered into an empty universe. Though she was ready enough to pretend for appearance's sake, since you had to be careful of the world even when the world was being an imbecile. Oddly enough, on a mission pretending to be someone else she could sometimes be less governed by pretense than she was *as* herself.

Which means we're always playing a role; being a spy has just made me more conscious of that.

She certainly wouldn't have adopted this strategy for putting him off-guard if it had been the Westphalian Hog or the Herr Doktor. Horst had a body like a Norse god, all lean clear muscle and ridged belly and tight backside and long shapely legs, shoulders broad and strong without being bull-massive, and almost translucently pale skin smooth except for a moderate dusting of golden hair and a few scars, from bullets and what was probably shrapnel on his left flank. He even smelled nice, a hard clean musk. And he had all the stamina in the world. Men were dismayingly prone to what she privately thought of as *Bumblebee Disease*, stinging once and dying, or at least falling limply asleep and snoring, but Horst was among the exceptions.

Of course, he is a mortal enemy and I may well have to kill him . . . but that's work, *not personal. Not for me, at least.*

She sighed inaudibly as he preened a little under her regard and turned her eyes back to the bottle of honey-colored liquid; the drawback was that he was vain about it, and like most males inclined to attribute magical powers to certain organs rather than what he did with them. In fact on balance she was rather sorry for his eventual wife. All that potential, and after the play of feint and gradual revelation . . . and then he was actually rather boring, carnally speaking. He seemed to have taken his conception of the bedroom arts from an infantry drill manual, and assumed that a female would naturally fall into worship of his own awesomeness. *He'd* been surprised and a little disconcerted at a woman who wanted to do more than . . .

Throw back her knees and think of Germany while he plunges ahead, Luz thought. *Which was great fun for a while—those scratches on his back are perfectly genuine—but I doubt it's ever occurred to him to do anything else!*

"The iron is better demonstrated than talked about," he hinted.

"Patience, *Süsser,*" she said.

And it would require the patience of a saint *to keep tiptoeing around his fragile self-regard for years, and that's depressingly typical of his half of the human race. Why is it that men seem to think that if you're intimate with them you should be a cross between a worshipping acolyte and a doting mother who's constantly shoring up their feelings? And marriage gives them a license from the government to expect you to do all the emotional work for the rest of your life; it's exhausting just to contemplate! Maybe after the war—which hasn't officially started yet, and which I probably won't survive—I should just find some nice like-minded California girl . . .*

Bryn Mawr had been educational in that respect, too: *gnōthi seauton*, the old Greeks had said, and it meant to know yourself. She had a vague mental image of someone willowy and blond; more importantly, someone quick-witted, with a ready laugh and fond of long walks beside the sea, books and music and gardening and cuddling on hilltops on warm starry nights, or in front of a fire on chilly rainy ones.

. . . and settle down to a Boston marriage with whoever-she-turns-out-to-be.

There was her parents' place in Santa Barbara, which she could love again now that the memories had stopped hurting so much, and that land north of town she'd inherited as well, near Los Olivos. Very pretty amid the golden hills and live oaks, and her parents had long intended it for their retirement; these days with an automobile you could be in town quickly, and catch a fast electric train to L.A. or San Francisco . . .

She'd qualify for a veteran's settlement loan, officer grade. Even better, Black Chamber veterans got it off the books, without paperwork or questions.

Aloud she continued:

"Sure, and it's flattering that the sight of me has you rising to the occasion once more, so to speak, but another drink won't be amiss. We've a little while before we reach Amsterdam and have to get back to work for the cause . . . well, our respective causes and countries."

"What is that stuff?" he asked. "It makes schnapps seem like milk."

"Tequila. It's made from agave juice," she said.

He made a face. "Pulque? Isn't that a drink for peasants?"

"Tequila is made by roasting the heart of the agave *azul*, and it's like any drink—quality varies from liquid sandpaper to liquid gold! This is the genuine article, *añejo* in the barrel, from Don Eladio Sauza's hacienda, which is where my comrades stole it. We sold most of it for the cause, but a few bottles went astray."

In fact Don Eladio gratefully sent her and another Black Chamber operative named James Cheine each a crate of his best every Christmas, since they'd saved his family's life and property from a *revolucionario* plot. That had been three years ago and a bit, when open guerilla raids were still common even near American garrisons—not all the big landowners had favored the Intervention but most had, and you needed to protect your supporters if you wanted to keep any. Some bits of his stock-in-trade *had* disappeared in the fighting before the jaws of the countertrap snapped shut with the gratifying finality of pistols to the backs of necks, which made it plausible for her cover identity to have some of the expensive liquor.

"Now, treat it with respect this time," she said, turning back to him and smiling, letting her glass touch her lips and enjoying the sharp agave bite mellowed with hints of citrus and walnut. "Don't toss it back like schnapps, you only do that with *white* tequila. Sip!"

He grinned back at her and reached for it. "A beautiful naked woman comes to me with fine drink in both hands! The gates of Valhalla have opened for Wotan's warrior!"

"But this time the Valkyrie is doing the riding—"

Their laughter covered the click of the lock, but she was already turning when the door opened. Then she froze and let a long breath flow from between her lips, controlling the sudden leap of heart and flush of blood and the impulse to gasp. The red-haired English soldier came through with a revolver in his hand, a man-killing brute of a .445 Webley, with the turbaned Indian close behind. *He* had a *rumāl* in one big brown hand, a cotton bandana done up Thugee-style with a coin knotted into one corner, and held between thumb and forefinger ready to toss, which meant he knew how to use it.

"Deal with the Fenian slut, Narayan," the Englishman snapped, jerking his head toward her without unlocking his eyes from Horst's. "We need the Hun alive. Quickly, don't let her scream."

The Indian came toward her smoothly, brown eyes like pebbles in his impassive face; she recognized the look, a cold killer who knew his business. She'd been inside that face, often enough. This Narayan outweighed her by fifty pounds and the look of his shoulders and neck said he'd be much stronger, and almost certainly he'd been to the dance before and knew all about dirty fighting. With guns that wouldn't matter at all, with knives only a bit, but she was literally naked and in her bare feet with no weapon available but two glasses of liquor. Quick thought flowed into decision, and that into words; she needed to make him see her as someone to be punished, not an opponent to be fought or target to be killed as emotionlessly as a farm wife snapped a chicken's neck.

"Haan, aao, kadamaboj banchhut!"

That about exhausted her Hindi, but she knew from the episode with the Ghadar conspirators that for his people *sister-fucker* was very, very provocative. Especially from a woman, and an angry man reverted to his reflexes . . . and men operating on reflex always underestimated women, since most had never in their lives faced physical risk from one after their last spanking from their mothers. With her that had been the last mistake several men ever made, and it was working again. The dark eyes flared with anger, and his mouth tightened; he grabbed for her with his left hand, obviously intending to hold her still while he hit. His instinct now was to hurt rather than simply kill.

A snap of her wrists sent both shot glasses of eighty-proof tequila into his eyes. He snarled a curse but with commendable spirit ignored the stinging pain. No amount of willpower could stop it from blurring his vision to a smear, though, or throwing his concentration off for an instant as his attack turned into a blundering lurch. She spun aside and grabbed for his reaching left arm with both hands, striking for the wrist.

Uncle Teddy had been fascinated by certain aspects of Japanese culture for many years, especially their martial arts; he'd had an instructor in them at the White House in his first administration, shaking the floors with the throws and falls. He'd brought more over later for the American armed forces, and the Black Chamber had gotten some of the best. It had certainly been more practical for her than boxing, though not more than the *savate* she'd picked up in Paris.

Kote mawashi simply meant clamping your fingers into the inside of the wrist, pressing on the back of the hand with both thumbs, and using the leverage to twist the arm sharply against the natural direction of the joints; you couldn't use raw power to pull out of that lock, not without tearing your own tendons loose. You *could* just whip your right fist back and punch in the face of the man—or woman—holding your arm locked, which Narayan tried.

Luz wasn't there, or rather her face wasn't where the Indian's knuckles headed. She was already throwing herself back, pivoting on her right heel and drawing the man forward. Her own head just missed the sink as she leaned—this was *crowded*—and her left leg came up, curled back to her chest. Then she drove the heel up at almost ninety degrees, directly into the Hindu's armpit with all the strength of the long muscles of thigh and hip—ballet practice helped with this, too.

The meaty *thud* of impact shocked back through her pelvis and into the leg, driving her down a bit into a one-legged crouch. Narayan came up on tiptoe, breath wheezing out of the wide O of his mouth in a squeal of agony.

Luz twisted at his arm, which didn't resist much now that it was dislocated. That let her land with both feet planted wide in a *kiba-dachi*, a horse-stance. Her right fist touched her left ear, and she twisted her body as she slammed the elbow around into the spot behind his ear. That hurt her elbow and made her hand tingle, and the turban blocked it slightly, but the big Indian abruptly lost all interest in the fight and collapsed to the floor.

The narrow intense focus of absolute effort flared wider, and she was suddenly conscious that she was panting and running with sweat. And that the *other* fight was coming to a conclusion. Evidently the Englishman had been distracted—probably frozen by disbelief—for just the necessary fraction of a second.

Her first glance at Horst had been enough to make her think that he was a very dangerous man, quick and enormously strong and with a streak of savagery underneath. Close contact had made her sure of it.

I was right, she thought.

He had the other man's throat in one hand and was about to club him to death with his own revolver, looking small in his right fist. From the purple shade of his enemy's face, that might not be necessary.

"*Nein,* Horst!" Luz said sharply.

Then she took another risk, grabbing for the Englishman's arm and twisting it into a lock with all her strength; that put her face close to the German's snarling mask of killing fury.

"No, Horst! We can't explain the bodies! *Think!* We'd have to get them down three levels to the keel compartments before we could drop them off the ship and into the water."

That brought humanity back to the wide, ice-pale eyes; he'd looked very much the Norse berserker he'd invoked in jest. When he actually looked at her she shoved the English agent against the cabin wall and spoke rapidly:

"The Dutch police would be all over us in Amsterdam—a Dutch prison would mean death."

Horst grunted. "True, the city's got more Entente agents than it has canals."

"And even if we could get them into the water without being spotted, there's the wireless once they're missed—the crew would report a disappearance and the English would have people waiting for us. If we hold them until just before docking, we'll be able to disappear and *they* will be the ones explaining things to the police."

She could see him thinking, and looking at her with narrowed eyes. "You are a woman of unexpected depths, Elisa."

Luz shrugged. Then he blinked and smiled. "And their compartment will be unguarded now."

He made a swift decision. "You are right, or at least we have no need to do anything irrevocable just yet."

Together they swiftly bound and gagged both men, sitting them side by side on her bed. Horst agreed that it was a good idea to pop the Indian's shoulder back before he started screaming uncontrollably, and they took a minute to do that—it needed two pairs of experienced hands to do quickly, but they were both used to this sort of field expedient.

"Scarcely the use I had in mind for my bed this night," she said.

Horst barked laughter as he finished pulling on dark-blue silk pajamas and a belted smoking jacket. It was perfectly credible for him to be abroad in that on the passenger deck, since the cabins didn't include toilet facilities, and she'd gotten him into this section officially unnoticed by the simple expedient of a massive bribe to the stewardess, probably not the first time someone had paid her to turn a blind eye. He put the Webley in one pocket of the robe, and assorted interesting blades and devices into the other.

"Will you . . ." he began.

She fished her *navaja* out of the loops in the pocket of her skirt, which had been tossed aside over the table amid a scattering of underclothes. Then she snapped the blade open with a flick of thumb and wrist and rolled the weapon across her knuckles before throwing it spinning from right hand to left and back. Snake-quick, literally faster than the eye could follow, a showy *gitano*-style maneuver called *el cambio*. The subdued light of the electric lamp glittered on the honed edge of the Toledo steel and the mother-of-pearl inlays in the bone scales and brass of the hilt. The eyes of all three men followed it.

"Well, yes, you will be able to handle them," Horst said, following the knife with his eyes. "Keep them quiet; I want to do a thorough search of their quarters."

When he'd left she stood glaring at the two British agents, counting to a hundred and then cracking the door enough to scan carefully, while they looked back at her—mostly at the knife. The corridor was dim, with only a single hooded blue electric light, and quiet beneath the muffled throb of the engines. She locked the door and turned back to the two captives. The Indian was still a bit dazed, but recovering enough to turn gray and sweat at the pain of his dislocated shoulder; popping it back didn't magically heal the damage to tendons and muscle, or make it possible to use it naturally. His Anglo-Saxon partner was fully alert, and watching her with lynx-eyed hatred.

"You *idiots*," she hissed. "*¡Estupidos!*"

Then she laid the knife down for a moment, held up her left palm, touched the fingers of the other to it, clenched that right hand into a fist, and bent the other to enfold it.

"Manifest," she said, making two fists and tapping the knuckles together. "Jackson. Rocket."

The English agent made muffled sounds through the gag, and Luz loosened it with the point of her *navaja*, keeping it ready for other action. He knew death when it was cold on his skin and stayed still until she moved back to the chair. His eyes were slitted thoughtfully now.

"Keep it quiet, or I will hurt you," she added.

He nodded, wisely and obviously believing her about *that* at least.

"You expect me to believe Elisa Carmody is a Black Chamber agent?" he said.

"No," Luz snapped in a deadly hiss. "I expect you to believe Elisa Carmody is in Lecumberri wishing she still had toenails—"

That was rhetorical exaggeration; except for emergency field expedients like fists, boots, and pistol butts, for Room 101 interrogations the Chamber generally used a less drastic and more scientific version of the Water Treatment that had been common during the Philippine insurrection back around the turn of the century, which could be repeated indefinitely. The old saying had it that cowards died a thousand deaths, but modern scientific progress meant you could put the brave through the same thing.

"—and that *I* am impersonating her to get next to the man who is our only clue to what the Germans, and their new best friends the Irish Republican Brotherhood and the Partido Nacional Revolucionario, are conspiring to do in the United States now that we're going to declare war on the Central Powers. What it is they plan, we don't know, except that it's very big. Bigger than Dublin."

The Englishman winced. That revolt had been very embarrassing for his empire and far too close to its heart, among people who were in theory at least voting citizens of its homeland. Personally she thought their handling of it had been a ham-handed disaster mitigated only by the commuting of the death sentences to life imprisonment on Uncle Teddy's urging, but that didn't count in the larger scheme of things.

Luz's own father, Patrick O'Malley, had said more than once there was something in the air or water of Ireland that made men demented, and that was one reason he'd never once wanted to set foot on it. He remembered his ancestors and honored them, but his *homeland* was the place where his only child was born.

"And you just endangered our only chance at it with this piece of blundering amateurism! You decided to do this on the spur of the moment, didn't you?"

The Englishman probably wasn't convinced, just open to the thought that she was telling the truth; the code she'd used had been set up some time ago as a fail-safe, but too many people knew it to be really safe.

"I'm not interested in any secrets you think you have," she went on, which made him relax a little. "And Horst couldn't break you in the time we have left—not without making too much noise and leaving marks that would be as bad as having your dead bodies found. Rest assured this idiocy *will* be in my next document drop. You're Indian Secret Service, you two, aren't you?"

Neither of them answered, and their tells weren't obvious, but she could see them—it was very hard to control the expansion and contraction of your pupils.

"Back in '14 after we helped you with the Ghadar business you agreed not to operate on American soil without prior notification. *Don't* insult my intelligence by claiming this airship doesn't count as American soil!"

He started to answer, and she realized she'd been gesturing freely, enough to make certain things bounce and jiggle, distracting his attention. When she was upset, the way she spoke with her hands was very Latin, unless she consciously suppressed it, and while her figure was fashionably slender it wasn't meager, either. The Indian was fully conscious again, but hurting too badly to notice, or perhaps just feeling too humiliated.

"*Men!*" she exclaimed. "Get your mind on business and your eyes off ¡*mis chichis!*"

She took a moment to get into her own pajamas. She did it slightly reluctantly; she hated dressing or sleeping after intercourse without an opportunity to wash or remove the precautions. It was still advisable, since she might have to go out into the corridor herself. The Englishman averted his eyes, which was a good sign.

"Ah . . . well, this will make your cover more convincing to the Hun," he said, flushing.

"No," she said. "It would have made it *absolutely* convincing if I'd helped him kill you and hide the bodies. Now he'll be wondering at least a little if I was saving your lives because I'm not what I claim. Now shut up. I have to do this before Horst gets back."

She turned to the little table, took out the copy of *Kim*—there was no time to be humorous with Baudelaire—and wrote quickly, referencing the necessary words from a mental image of the key. Then she folded the paper and tucked it into the Indian's turban; even if Horst did another search, there was no way he could tell that it wasn't a British code, and coded messages were entirely natural for spies to have on their persons.

"Turn that over to your superiors when you get to Amsterdam," she said. "They can forward it."

Then she smiled. "And we do have to explain why I removed your gag. Ah! *¡Eso es!* It was to stop you from choking to death on the blood from your nose!"

"But my nose isn't—" he began.

Her fist whipped forward and he gave a choked grunt. "There! A bleeding nose!"

THREE

Luchthaven Nummer Één

(Airport Number One)

Amsterdam,

Koninkrijk der Nederlanden

(Kingdom of the Netherlands)

SEPTEMBER 5TH, 1916(B)

The great floating hangar below had been fabricated in New Jersey and sent over to Amsterdam in naval transports during February, heavily escorted by American warships—both for safety's sake and as a calculated thumb in the eye of the Kaiserliche Marine, daring them to do anything about it. The assembly had been completed in the spring, with the hangar resting in a basin dredged off the main canal to the ocean and looking nearly identical to its counterpart in New York except that a giant Dutch flag was painted on the exterior . . . ironically, in the same red-white-blue colors. Originally the hangar had been intended for London or Portsmouth, but the war had intervened and the Netherlands had eagerly bid for the privilege. Not only because of the commercial advantages for which they always had a keen eye, but because they were a small neutral country who desperately wanted the diplomatic support of a large one. They must be dreading the moment the United States declared war on the Central Powers, with the fates of Serbia and Rumania and their own Belgian neighbor before their eyes.

The *San Juan Hill* came into the wind with a long low circle over the Dutch capital, its great teardrop shadow scrolling across a flat sprawl with a glint of canals and streets of high narrow brick houses. Here and there were clusters of larger, newer structures or the church spires that dominated any skyline except in Chicago and New York; avenues and electric trams and thronging traffic; and then a sprawl of warehouses and modern docks and ships from everywhere.

The sun was westering, an hour or two from setting, and the long golden-gray light turned the city into a dream of Old Europe. It made you think of explorers setting forth in big-bellied, well-gunned galleons, and returning—when they did—with their sails beaten to rags, laden with gold and silks, furs and spices and pearls and brags.

Luz sat with Horst on the observation deck, patting her mouth with a gloved hand as she yawned, with a broad-brimmed hat before her on the table and her suitcase and hatbox resting ready to hand. She felt a little underdressed because her knife and automatic pistol were back in their receptacles in the suitcase, under the false bottom and its cover of trashy romances, adventure stories, and naughty French poetry. Not that she was going to fight her way into a neutral kingdom, but . . .

. . . *I've always got me*, she thought with what she considered pardonable pride. *Considering what I did stark naked and armed with two glasses of tequila, that statement covers a great deal.*

The steady throb of the engines changed as they were throttled down until they barely balanced the wind from the west, and the airship sank toward the surface of the water as gas was loosed from the valves along the upperreel. A *thunk* sounded, and out of the corner of her eye she could see the towing cable falling away from the bow of the airship, turning thread-thin and then caught with a long turntable-mounted pole on the aft deck of the tug. Hooking it up took a few minutes, since it had to be done with exquisite care not to damage the fragile frame of the *San Juan Hill*.

When weight came on the line there was a subliminal shiver through the deck beneath them. The motion of the airship changed as the hawsers fore and aft held it rigid, a quicker almost-fluttering feeling and then a stillness as the engines were cut for the first time since they left New York, a noise so accustomed you heard only its sudden absence. A large hose dropped down as well, now that they were within fifty feet of the surface, and a pump throbbed as it drove water into the ballast tanks. The dirigible slid into the cradle and the dozens of ground crew sprang to lash it down with ropes through the eyelets set into the lower ribs. Looking up, Luz could see that there were great blocks of the more expensive incandescents in front of reflective panels, not arc lights of the type usually used for large public spaces or big industrial buildings.

Her parents had both been adults before they lived in a house with electric lights, and she'd seen the world grow brighter every year.

"Our mothers and fathers were born in a world lit only by fire, as it was from the beginning of time," she said. "And we have . . . this."

Horst nodded agreement to the point. "My father only put in electric light at the *Schloss* when we added a power plant for the sugar-beet mill."

Then he looked up into the vaulted vastness of the hangar himself. "That is good practice. Hydrogen goes *up*, and you don't want high-temperature naked arcs there where it's leaked and mixed with the air. Plenty of ventilation panels, too. The Yankees have good engineers, damn them. We have airships just coming into service bigger than this with more lift, built specially for a . . . special mission. But the design is very similar to this."

"You've flown often?" Luz said admiringly—and, mostly, honestly. "This was wonderful, but it's my first time."

Horst grinned, indicating the lounge with a sideways flick of the wrist—she recognized a *mensur*-swordsman's gesture. "The ones I've flown on before are much less comfortable than this—flying at six thousand meters to stay above the ceiling of the enemy's fighting scouts; freezing cold, and sucking on an oxygen tube and still feeling as if you were smothering for hours on end. And in *Flugzeugen*, but those I have piloted myself."

"Ah, and what's that like?" she said enviously.

She could have gotten into a flight school course, since the Chamber encouraged you to pick up any number of skills and some field operatives did fly, but she'd never found the time, and it was harder for a woman to do so without attracting notice anyway. Male operatives could just be dropped into the Army Air Corps training system with cooked papers, but sending her would be like tattooing *dangerous Black Chamber female spy* on her forehead for the duration of her stay, while dozens of regular-Army blockheads memorized her face and then blabbed.

"Flying a *Flugzeugen* yourself," Luz clarified.

Flugzeug translated literally as "flight tackle" or "flight stuff" and meant what in English was called an aeroplane, a heavier-than-air winged craft of the sort invented by the Wright brothers. That had been in '03, but nobody had paid much attention at the time except for a few like her father, not for years afterward. Then suddenly six or seven years before the war everyone was talking about aeroplanes; she'd seen that flight in North Carolina grow more important in retrospect as she grew up herself.

A dreamy look came into the man's pale eyes as he remembered.

"Noisy, rough, dangerous . . . magnificent!" Horst said. "This"—his foot tapped the deck—"is like sailing. A *Flugzeug* is like flying yourself, as close to being a bird as is possible for a man. Like an eagle, like a bird of prey! Like riding a lively, ah—"

Lively woman, Luz supplied with an inner raised eyebrow; Horst had forgotten exactly who he was talking to for a moment, speaking as if to another man, which was even a compliment in an odd way.

We're both very tired; they'd been spelling each other, which meant some sleep—but not enough of it, and frequently interrupted.

"—a good horse, but much better. Louder and with bad smells, but . . . glorious." He chuckled. "My father was a captain of Uhlans when we beat the French in 1870, and his grandfather the same at Leipzig and Waterloo when we crushed Napoleon a century ago. He was vastly disappointed that I would not be a horse soldier, but the day of men sitting on the backs of animals and poking each other with pointed sticks is past, even if some of the elders won't admit it."

"You have a point," Luz said. "The Yankee aeroplanes—and armored war-autos armed with pom-poms and machine guns—have hurt us badly in Mexico, and they have swarms of both now, thousands. They can make it impossible to move in daylight in open country, across the deserts and plains where in the old days the vaquero was lord. The war-autos run down bands of mounted men and kill their horses with exhaustion even before the fighting, and then machine-gun riflemen who can't hurt them except by accident. And the flying scouts pinpoint our bands of fighters and attack from the air with more machine guns and bombs and mustard gas, while motor trucks bring gringo infantry up ten times faster than marching speed. And even in the mountains where vehicles cannot go, the air scouts can see much—they can guide foot soldiers or mounted infantry and bomb and machine-gun the camps of *los guerilleros* unless there is thick forest. We have to move in darkness, make no lights nor show smoke, and hide in daytime like mice from hawks."

Horst asked some keenly specific questions; she supplied a few anecdotes that were convincing because they were true, with her simply reversing the viewpoints. The only problem was that most of the ones she'd been involved in ended with all the *revolucionarios* dead or kneeling with their hands on their heads as a preliminary to a new career turning large rocks into small rocks while helping to build Mexico's first good road network.

He nodded, and for a wonder he didn't act as if tactics were beyond a woman's comprehension without using spelling blocks and crayons and very simple words. When he spoke, it was soberly:

"This is valuable intelligence. We have used motorized fighting vehicles and troops carried in motor lorries in cooperation with aircraft on the Eastern Front, against Russia and Rumania—there is more space there on the great open steppes than on the Western Front. In the West, the French and English have a division for every few kilometers and so do we, both locked in place by barbed wire and machine guns with interlocking fields of fire while the artillery hammers without ceasing—that has gone on since our first attack stalled on the Marne in 1914, though we came so close to Paris . . . The eastern steppes are rather like your Mexican deserts and plains in that respect. The Chief of the General Staff and the First Quartermaster-General understand the possibilities in the East."

That referred to the duo of von Hindenburg and Ludendorff, who'd been running the German Army—and Germany, whatever the Kaiser or the politicians thought—since von Falkenhayn stood too close to a stray howitzer shell at the opening of the Verdun offensive back in February and left nothing to be found but his feet, still in his jackboots. Before then they'd been the hammers of the Russians, lords of Ober Ost and commanders on the Eastern Front. And Colonel Nicolai of Abteilung IIIb was their man.

Horst smiled: "Even horse cavalry can be useful in the East, though the men fight on foot more often than not even if they ride to battle. But we have little rubber and much less petroleum to spare than the Yankees . . . though that may change soon, *Gott sei Dank*."

Aha, Luz thought, sipping at her tea; she'd known about Germany's shortages, but not any hope of bettering them. *That's interesting, isn't it? If true and not just whistling in the dark. Everybody boasts, but Germans make it an art form.*

"You haven't told me precisely what we're doing next," she said. "It's getting to the time where I need to know if I'm not to be a burden."

Horst thought for a moment, then nodded. "Yes. You are no ordinary . . . agent."

Ordinary woman, Luz thought without much heat. *Meaning I'm not featherbrained or hysterical. Thank you so much for making a special exception for me, Horst. I remember Rebecca Grunstein at college with metaphorical smoke coming out of her ears and going literally beet-red once when someone told her she was hardly like a Jew at all. You could see her thinking: So, that's a compliment?*

The basic attitude to her sex was common enough in America, despite Uncle Teddy's well-known liking for *spunky girls* who shot lions and rode their horses like maenads across hill and dale. It was much stronger among central Europeans, particularly the landed nobility. Horst was actually much more flexible than she'd anticipated, but then by Junker standards he was an eccentric and an iconoclast.

"We must go from here to the Fatherland," Horst said. "To a *Schloss* in the eastern marches . . ."

Luz clapped her hands together and made a round-eyed expression of innocent-imbecilic delight, as much to hide the slight stab at the knowledge that soon she would be wholly in enemy territory and in constant danger of death by torture as for the devilment of the thing. But the devilment was tempting enough:

"Horst, darling! You mean you want to take me home to Silesia and introduce me to your mother and father!"

Stark horror greeted *that* statement. Then she dissolved in laughter and put a hand on his. "I'm sorry . . . very sorry, Horst, but the expression on your face . . . oh, *Madre de Dios* . . . if you could only have seen yourself . . ."

The German glared at her for an instant, then laughed unwillingly himself and ducked his head in the seated equivalent of a heel-click.

"Was I so transparent? I am sorry if I offended."

"Transparent as glass, sweetie—I took you by surprise. No, really, Horst: You are a magnificent specimen of Germanic manhood and intelligent as well—"

If rather boring in bed, though with instruction that might change.

"—and I have enjoyed our time together and look forward to working with you, but even if it were possible, which it is not, I wouldn't *marry* you for all the potatoes in Silesia. And if I remember my geography lessons, there are a *lot* of potatoes in Silesia."

"Sugar beets," Horst said dryly. "My family's estate is mostly in sugar beets, and we have a refinery and distillery. But I take your point, Elisa."

She nodded. "I have my own country, my own cause, and my own plans for my life . . . in the unlikely event I live much longer. I'm not a silly girl who swoons over a handsome face."

Horst looked miffed for a moment—it really was a bit deflating to be told your noble blood and cleft chin and youthful stamina were disposable—and then made a gesture that was half a salute. He was probably slightly relieved too, which had been her intention. Besides the sheer artistic pleasure of deceiving someone by telling them the precise truth.

"I have never encountered a woman like you, Elisa," he said. "You are a true warrior, in your way. I shall regret our parting."

Far more than you think you will, dear Horst, probably. And for entirely different reasons than nostalgia about the feel of my legs wrapped around your waist, she thought, and said aloud:

"I thought it best to be honest . . . well, as honest as possible," she said, which, oddly enough, was . . . honest.

"*Die ehrlichkeit der spione,*" Horst said ruefully: *the honesty of spies.* "It is a drawback of intelligence work.

"I *can* tell you," he went on, "that this is a project of vast potential on which you will be fully briefed—and potentially it will give your country a real chance to throw off the Protectorate the Yankees have imposed on it. Ireland too will have a chance to strike for its freedom. Details I cannot yet provide, of course."

"Of course," she said with a smile.

You didn't, until you absolutely had to, for the same reason soldiers didn't get issued ammunition until they were actually going to shoot.

"And Germany will at last have its rightful place in the sun. Our immediate problem is that the Dutch are running only a few passenger trains across the frontier. And all of them start before noon. We must spend the night here in Amsterdam. Trying for the frontier in an automobile would be entirely too risky if the enemy . . . any of six or more enemy intelligence services . . . have any hint of our presence. Autos are not nearly as common here as in America, and less so now with wartime limits on petrol."

"At least we may get some sleep tonight," Luz said. "If I'm going to spend a whole night and the following day awake, I can think of more agreeable ways to do it than watching two English spies watch me with murder in their eyes."

Horst barked laughter. "Are there many women in Mexico like you?" he said.

"If you mean in the Revolutionary Party, no," Luz said. "I like to think I'm one of a kind."

In point of fact the ones she'd met had all been boring fanatic prigs, like their male equivalents but worse; not counting ordinary *soldaderas*, who were often cheerfully carefree. But then, the *revolucionario* women she'd met had all been trying to deceive or kill her or both, and vice versa. It did make her feel more satisfied with her work, considering that she was thwarting such a bunch of pickled puritans. The Protectorate was no paradise, but it was certainly an improvement on the Porfiriato and doubly so on the charnel house the *revolucionarios* and their mixture of vendetta and theory-schooled grudges and sheer bandit lust for spoils had made of whatever parts they controlled . . . And unlike them, Plenipotentiary Henry Cabot Lodge and his people were prepared to let those who didn't want to openly support the Intervention regime just keep their heads down and mouths shut while they got on with their lives and stayed out of politics unmolested.

Now that vengeance wasn't a question anymore, she really rather liked Mexico and most of its people again. Not as much as California, which she loved, but more than, say, the essence of flat, gloomy dullness that was Ohio, or even worse, Indiana, or worst of all, Illinois. Her own particular concept of eternal damnation would be an endless January in Chicago with the wind off Lake Michigan whistling down the Burnham Plan's grand new avenues. Though a sticky summer there when the winds brought the unforgettable scent of the Union Stock Yards north was a close rival.

And the Germans have no conception of how to handle a beaten enemy except to grab them by the throat and squeeze until the victim's eyes pop out; witness

Belgium or Serbia or what they call Ober Ost. I suspect that Mexico and Ireland would find it a jump from the frying pan into the fire in a world where Germany did *have its place in the sun.*

"I hope the Englishman and his Gunga Din don't manage to make trouble immediately," Horst said. "They should be freeing themselves by now; it was fortunate we got them back into their own compartment without notice. I was a little surprised that they did not struggle more when we did—perhaps you had terrified them too much! You would terrify me, I can tell you, if I had my hands tied and you were scowling at me and holding that barbaric Spanish knife."

Luz grinned. "Don't worry, sweetie. I dropped a few hints with the staff when I gave out the final tips."

"Hints?" Horst said, alarmed.

Usually it was better not to attract any notice at all if you didn't have to.

"Yes, I said I'd overheard them having this terrible drunken lover's quarrel, which ended up with them weeping in each other's arms, battered and contrite, so they should be left alone for a tumble of reconciliation. That'll account for the bruises, too, and any thumping and pounding as they wiggle out of the cords."

The German nobleman stifled a shout of Wagnerian laughter. "Oh, Elisa, you are a treasure!"

"I thought it would make it more difficult for them to get much cooperation, or be taken seriously," she said demurely, casting her eyes up innocently. "Technically it could get them arrested, but that's too much to hope."

"And of an Englishman, it will be believed, along with tying up and bum-switching."

Luz nodded, carefully *not* mentioning the terrible scandal that had started a few years before the war when General Graf—Count—Dietrich von Hülsen-Haeseler of the Kaiser's military cabinet had dropped dead of a heart attack in mid-dance while dressed as a ballerina and performing before the All-Highest and his cronies at a remote hunting lodge. It had spread from there in ripples of resignations, courts-martial, and suicide among various high- and well-born military men for some time. The French newspaper cartoonists had had a field day while the English-speaking world's press had merely talked about *unmentionable vices* and made vague references to poor Oscar Wilde.

And Bryn Mawr is more or less a singing grove of the higher Sapphism, starting with President Thomas and Mary Garrett. People are people the world over. It's really absurd the way people carry on about it, she thought; there was the theology, of course, but . . . *Though I must admit the thought of the Kaiser and his generals frantically trying to get the limp corpse of one of their number out of a pink tutu and back into his dress uniform and six pounds of medals* is *rather funny. But it wouldn't be at all tactful to mention it to Horst.*

There were a series of echoing clanks through the fabric of the airship, a rumbling sighing sound—probably the hydrogen being pumped out of the gas cells so they could be thoroughly dried of condensate—and a flicker in the internal lights as the dirigible changed from its own power system to the exterior supply. A steward walked through playing the xylophone-like thing used to draw attention to announcements, and said:

"Ladies and gentlemen—*mesdames et messieurs*—*Sehr geehrte Damen und Herren*—*mevrouws en mijnheers*—"

The multilingual gist was *follow me to disembark.* She took Horst's arm, forcing herself not to snatch her suitcase back when a steward scooped it up, and they strolled down the spiral staircase to the forward ramp, now down and locked to the platform with the ship's first officer making polite good-byes in a Deep South gumbo accent. Everyone who could afford an airship passage was important enough to rate that sort of thing.

She glanced up again at the huge silver-gray bulk of the dirigible and smiled to herself. The shark-fin control surfaces at the rear had the Stars and Stripes on them, the latest version with a forty-ninth star for Hawaii.

My first air voyage. And my first airborne fight and first airborne fornication, too. I wonder . . . no, human beings are human beings; someone must have done that already. Probably decades ago in a balloon. But I may be in the first hundred!

The stewards put their cabin baggage down beside them as the line passed the scowling Dutch customs officials checking documents—and several men in plain civilian suits whose thick necks and beady eyes and bowler hats blared *detective* of some sort for anyone with eyes to see. The uniformed officials examined the passports with meticulous care, sometimes calling in a plainclothesman; one even used a jeweler's monocular on hers while two of his colleagues went through her suitcase, though they didn't turn a hair when they leafed through the books. They probably had her classed as a loose woman anyway, since she and Horst were obviously a pair.

It was a comfort to know that the faked products of the Black Chamber's American documents section used the very same materials as the State Department, and it stood to reason that Horst's forgeries were as good since they'd probably been made up at the German embassy in Washington.

"Between your armies on the frontier and the English battleships off the coast, the Dutch must feel as if they're between a school of sharks and a pack of wolves," Luz observed as Horst dispatched their heavy luggage from the cargo ahead to the railway station.

It would go out on an overnight freight and be waiting for them wherever they were going. There would be inspections here and again when entering Germany, but there wasn't anything in them that would excite suspicion, or at least not in hers, unless the observers were far better than she expected. She managed to see part of the address he scribbled and imprint it on her mind without being obvious: *Schloss Rauenstein, Königreich Sachsen.*

Those endless lessons in Kim's Game did come in useful. The name didn't ring an immediate bell, which wasn't surprising since there were thousands of *Schlösser* in the German Empire, and the Austro-

Hungarian one too for that matter, and even in Baltic Russia where the nobility were mostly of German descent.

The term covered what the English word *castle* implied and more besides: everything from modest manor houses to Mad Ludwig's fairy-tale creations, sitting on Bavarian mountaintops like spun-sugar neomedieval fantasies on a baker's shelves. *Sachsen*—Saxony—meant far southeastern Germany, and at a guess it would be away from the major cities like Dresden and near the border with Austrian Bohemia. Mountains and forests, mostly . . . a very good place to hide things from Entente or American eyes. The fairy tales from those parts were heavy with werewolves, and witches in gingerbread huts eating stray children. A few days farther east and south and it was *leshy* and *vampir.*

Horst nodded a bit complacently at the thought of the Dutch sweating about the German armies on their flat, indefensible border, his smile turning slightly . . .

Wolfish, Luz thought. *He really* is *a dangerous man. He'd be even more dangerous if he didn't underestimate me—or women in general. Not alone in that, alas, but sometimes . . . quite often in fact . . . it's useful.*

"This country is an absurdity, anyway, a bad historical joke," he said. "The so-called Netherlands language is just a dialect of Low German with a flag and a little play army suitable only for walloping wogs in Asia. Logically this place should be part of the *Reich*; the trade connections and colonies would nicely complement our present holdings."

"So is English a dialect of *Plattdüütsch*," Luz pointed out. "With some Danish and a lot of French added. And I suppose the British Empire would nicely complement the *Reich*'s present holdings too."

"That may take a little longer than attending to the Netherlands," Horst granted with an air of deep thought, then winked at her.

"And Austrians are just Germans in three-quarter time?"

He laughed outright at that. *Careful, you could really like this man*, she thought; he had his full share of Prussian military stiffness, but he could take it off when he wanted to . . . and he didn't always take himself seriously, either. *Don't start liking people you may have to kill and certainly have to lie to and betray.*

She was almost sure he'd have added something on the order of *the time of small states is past, this is the century of great empires* next, which was a political commonplace these days what with Mackinder and his geopolitics and Heartland Theory being so popular. Uncle Teddy adored Mackinder and so did the Kaiser and his professors.

That he didn't meant Horst had remembered in time that he was talking to someone who was a Mexican revolutionary who wanted to throw the gringos out and have a social revolution too, and allied by blood and politics to Irish nationalists. It did show a certain elephantine tact on his part. Even an intelligence operative probably wasn't bare-faced enough to pretend that the *Reich* had any interest in promoting national independence for weak countries except as a tool of war policy, the way it had used the Ottomans to proclaim an Islamic holy war against the European colonial empires. Except in Germany's *own* empire, of course.

The Turks must be very trusting sorts.

The area outside the hangar was still a chaos of new construction that would eventually be the aerial equivalent of a major train station, piles of brick and girders and half-liquid soil and half-made pavements and holes full of water and a web of scaffolding and cranes. It smelled of coal-smoke and dirty brackish harbor water and the peculiar scent of glutinous much-used European mud dredged from canals that had received everything you could think of from a great city for generations beyond count. Horst set his homburg on his head, whistled sharply, and flagged a motor taxi—a French-made Renault, boxy and black with an almost comical little ten-horsepower engine under a miniature bull-nosed hood—and the driver sprang out to put their suitcases in the compartment.

Something caught her eye, and she stretched and yawned again, looking behind her casually for an instant. Two men, reading newspapers, ordinary middle-class suits with narrow ties and turnover shirt collars and bowler hats . . . who put the newspapers down simultaneously and moved forward behind someone else.

"Horst, don't look around, but there are two men by the entrance who are following . . . not us, but that fellow who looks like a professor from Leipzig. They're not Dutch, I think, or German."

Horst cursed quietly under his breath—German was a good language for that—and used the window of the cab as a partial mirror.

"You're right," he said tightly. "They're French—you won't see a Dutchman with a mustache like that, and one of them is dark as an Italian. *Schluss mit lustig!* Playtime's over!"

That was exactly what she'd thought, but Elisa Carmody wouldn't be equipped to make that sort of snap judgment of the rather subtle differences between Europeans. Horst went on:

"And that means they will be following us too; he's heading to the same hotel. And he is a professor, but from the Kaiser Wilhelm Gesellschaft."

The ears of her mind pricked at the name. That was an institution in Berlin that served as a central government-sponsored clearinghouse and funding source for pure and applied scientific research in conjunction with universities and corporate labs, founded in 1911 and now working at forced draft on Germany's war effort including dozens of secret projects. Several of them had given the Entente very nasty shocks indeed, and had impressed her own service, like the poison-gas shells that had rained down on the British at Ypres, and the long-range submarines that could recharge their batteries while below the surface through extensible tubes.

Uncle Teddy had imitated the Kaiser Wilhelm Gesellschaft with the American National Advanced Research Projects Institute during the reforms of the famous first Hundred Days after his 1912 victory—a lot of Progressive intellectuals were German-educated and admirers of the German theory of the state and German methods. Only Teddy's Institute was larger and had more money and a more impressive headquarters in Washington; he'd said himself more than once that like most Americans he just liked things *big*. Then the Kaiser had pouted and replied in kind with a further avalanche of money to *his* Institute.

Wilhelm had hated Theodore Roosevelt since he made Germany back down in the Venezuela crisis of 1902 with a blunt threat of war. And he'd had a serious case of Teddy envy for years, since the American president was all the things he wanted to be but wasn't, starting with being a real soldier who'd charged to victory at the head of his troops and working on from there through *great reformer* to *frontier adventurer* and *amateur scientist of real distinction*. It had gotten much worse since Teddy's triumphant return to power. Wilhelm was known to grind his teeth at the mention of the Roosevelt name and to have launched a secret project to find out if the Roosevelts had any German noble or royal blood in their backgrounds. He'd proven to his own satisfaction that they were descendants of the Van Rosevelts who'd been made lords of Oud-Vossemeer by William III, Duke of Bavaria, back in the late Middle Ages.

How Uncle Teddy laughed at that!

"Ah. I thought the Professor was the other strong possibility; you, him, and then the Westphalian Hog. And I couldn't imagine either of them being code-named *Imperial Sword*."

"They haven't spotted us," Horst said, with a slight snort of *Uradel* nobleman's agreement at her choice of nickname for the obese businessman. "But it is crucial that . . . that the academic person makes it safely back to the Fatherland."

Aha, Luz thought. *There were two agents. And the Herr Professor is less likely to attract the eye than Horst, especially with Horst around to attract the eye. I may have underestimated Colonel Nicolai . . . but the French, if that's what they are, have made him . . .*

Made was the term of art for penetrating a false identity.

. . . and not us. Of course, they might well have had previous experience with him. Scientists are very important in this war. It'll be a pity if I have to put a stop to any agents of our prospective French ally, but our operations take priority . . . for us.

"If it's the Deuxième Bureau de l'État-major général they'll wait until night," Horst said. "As a gesture to the Dutch. But they're not going to let a target escape to keep the cheese-eaters happy."

Luz kept herself from nodding agreement by an effort of will; her cover identity wouldn't be as familiar with the workings of European espionage and counterespionage organizations as she was. The Second Bureau of the French General Staff was notoriously proactive when operating abroad, as much so as the Black Chamber and much more so than the chronically underfunded British secret service, whose head had been reduced to traveling around Germany just before the war with a false mustache plastered to his lip.

"Can you call for help?" she said. "Or get us all to a safe house?"

"No. This operation was segregated and kept hermetically sealed from the usual channels. It was managed directly by . . . from Berlin."

"Well." She shrugged. "We'll just have to manage, won't we?"

FOUR

"This is excellent, sweetie!" Luz said, savoring a forkful of the *babi recap*.

The delighted surprise was entirely in character since she'd simply transferred that aspect of herself to the constructed personality of her Elisa cover, and true as well. Like Elisa Carmody, Luz had been through Amsterdam before, several times on her way to and from school in Bavaria or on trips from school to *absorb culture*, presumably on the theory that it was the visual equivalent of blancmange. She liked the city, mainly for the art museums and the history and the stolid sensible *Burger* calm of the people, though she had been profoundly unimpressed with what she'd experienced of Dutch food.

Which was like German cuisine, except without the subtlety and grace, she thought. *But I could have had something like this if the teachers shepherding us hadn't been so stodgy. Who knew?*

There was a covered bowl of steamed rice and six little side plates: skewers of chicken or others of shrimp, marinated in a sweet-spicy peanut sauce and covered with more after grilling; slivers of pork belly braised in its own juices and a soy reduction; hard-boiled eggs in a chili-based sauce; and several types of vegetables steamed or fried with spices and sprinkled with desiccated, grated coconut and flanked by little cups of a red-chili paste.

"And it was a good idea to have it sent up to the room, too."

He beamed across the table at her as if he'd invented the *rijsttafel* that was scenting the air with anise and garlic and mace and lemongrass himself, rather than Dutchmen stealing the concept and most of the ingredients from the inhabitants of their Southeast Asian empire. It had come to Amsterdam along with much else in the ample bellies of the Vereenigde Oost-Indische Compagnie's Indiamen, making their stately six-month passages from here around the Cape to Batavia in Java and back for century on century. Having the kitchens send it up here this late had probably cost a pretty penny, but as Horst said, it was on the All-Highest's account and enabled them to keep a closer eye on the Herr Professor, so why not?

"This is the abbreviated version," Horst said, grinning at her and spooning up some sauce. "The full banquet can have forty dishes, besides six types of rice."

The impassive staff had set it up in the parlor of their two-room suite. The suite had all the modern conveniences, electric lights, and an attached bath and water closet; it was done in pale yellow silk and had a rather ornate plaster ceiling, and the furniture was fussily over-decorated and carved in an old-fashioned way, though the place was only about as old as she was and had been renovated as recently as '06. Luz and Horst had taken advantage of the bath after coupling like stoats in a rain of half-removed clothing—they both found prospective danger made them randy; she thought it a bit disturbing how much they had in common—and each standing a watch while the other caught a few hours' sleep. They were young and fit enough that that made them refreshed rather than groggy, which was fortunate since nobody was fit enough not to lose their edge after enough time without rest.

"The Victoria gets a lot of Dutchmen going to and from their colonies," Horst said, and added with a laugh: "And a lot of spies, these days; I've been here half a dozen times since the war began. They're familiar with Herr Hans Krämer."

They hadn't asked for her papers when he checked her in as Frau Krämer, though she looked about as un-German as you could be unless you were a Zulu or Chinese, but . . .

"You do realize that nobody would think that's your real name, Horst?" she said.

He stared at her, slightly offended. "I assure you the documents are perfect. And there *was* a Hans Krämer, who looked quite a bit like me—he was called up in 1914 as part of the Thirteenth Division—Westfälisches Jäger-Bataillon Nr. 7, in fact. He died on the Marne."

"I'm sure there was just such a man, Horst, and that the documents are perfect. But nobody who knows anything at all about *die Deutschen* is *ever* going to mistake you for Hans-the-shopkeeper-reservist. You should really pretend to be some *other* German *Uradel*. It's much easier to hide *who* you are than *what* you are. Or you might just manage to pass for a Swede—a Swedish nobleman, that is—if you spoke good enough Swedish. If you try to appear as what you aren't unsuccessfully, you just draw attention to an obviously false identity."

He looked at her quietly for a moment, then nodded. "That is a very perceptive remark," he said quietly. "More rice? And some of the satay?"

"Thank you."

It wouldn't do to stuff themselves if they had serious work to do, but a rice table consisted of a large number of small dishes and he'd picked a few, and they nibbled slowly. They had split a single mug of what even Horst admitted was an excellent local beer.

The food was an exquisite mixture of textures and tastes, in a way totally new to her. She'd dined often and marvelously in San Francisco's Chinatown in several different regional styles; you just had to pick the places well-to-do local Chinese went to, rather than the ones making Americanized versions for the *gwai-lo*. And her family had often gone to dinner at the home of a Japanese business acquaintance of her father's in Santa Barbara and been delighted at the subtle combinations and the beauty of the arrangements and colors that Mrs. Taguchi and her daughters produced. But this was a tantalizing glimpse at yet another world. She strongly suspected the actual cook was from the East Indies himself.

Travel is *broadening, even if that's a cliché*, she thought; truisms were often . . . true. *How vast and varied the world is! You could spend lifetimes sampling just the food, and then there's dance and music and art and stories.*

"Ah, now I feel fit to fight tigers, much less *Gabachos*," she said, patting her lips with a napkin. At his glance she explained: "*Gabachos* means 'Frenchmen' . . . but it's not complimentary."

"Perhaps you should dress for it?" Horst said. "Even if they are only *Franzacke*."

Luz laughed, with a hard edge to it. "*Bärchen*, I *am* dressed for action."

She was wearing her pajamas, one of several black silk outfits she had along of vaguely Chinese inspiration and as fashionable as yesterday evening, slightly loose pants and collared jackets with black cablework on the front. Luz extended an arm.

"Feel. This is tough silk, light but stronger than canvas, and there's chamois leather on the knees and elbows. It's street wear in China . . . I'm told their . . . what did they call them, Boxers? They wore something like this as fighting gear; that was where I got the idea, that and Chinese pajamas being fashionable. Nobody can tell the difference between this and simple nightwear."

"The Yihequan," Horst said, surprising her a little by knowing the name. "It means Righteous Fists; *we* said Boxers. My elder brother was with the expeditionary force that marched to Peking to relieve the diplomats in 1900; I was in cadet school then. Yes, I remember he took some photographs of Chinamen in costumes very much like that."

A grin. "Mainly dead Chinamen with 7.92mm holes in them, to be sure."

Kaiser Wilhelm had given a speech to the German troops departing for that messy little conflict, urging them to make a name for themselves in China that would rival that of Attila's Huns for a thousand years. It had been one more example of his chronic foot-in-mouth disease and had given the Germans their modern nickname of *Hun*, but it was just an exaggeration of a common national trait too. They'd issued a commemorative medal for the sinking of the *Mauretania* showing the ship going down on one side and passengers buying tickets from a skeletal figure of Death on the other. That had had blood boiling and teeth grinding from New York to San Francisco, but Horst's people had mostly never really understood *why* it had that effect, or why the British had made thousands of copies. It was an aspect of the same failings that made them such terrible spies, though some could overcome it by sheer application.

"And these slippers"—she ran the toe of one down the inside of his calf under the table—"have buckled tops and woven cord soles. Excellent traction, much better than leather."

"Useful, as long as it doesn't attract attention," Horst said. He cocked his head. "Which it would. Though the ensemble gives you a certain boyish charm."

She grinned and arched her back against the chair a little; her bosom was moderately sized, but definitely there.

"Horst, if it's one thing I've never desired to be taken for—except when I was doing it as a disguise once or twice—it's a boy."

His brows went up. "I thought you had rather advanced opinions on the rights of women?" he said. "Surely as a girl you chafed at seeing boys able to do things you could not?"

That was perfectly true, and so was his supposition about her opinions—and it also fitted her revolutionary cover identity. Ironically enough, the most conservative people in Mexico had backed the Intervention, and had ended up with new laws imposed at the point of American bayonets, including a close copy of the Equal Rights Amendment of 1912–1913, which was far more drastic than the most radical imaginable Mexican government would have passed anytime soon. Even in America it had gone through in that pure a form only because of a complex congressional maneuver intended to derail it, and it had horrified the hacendados and Catholic clergy when the gringo armies brought it with them . . . though there wasn't anything they could do about it since the *revolucionarios* were the only alternative they had. And *they* wanted to kill the upper classes wholesale and take all their property, and the wilder ones burned churches on general principle.

"Yes, I did, but that doesn't mean I ever wanted to *be* a boy, I just wanted to have the same *opportunities*," she said, which seemed to baffle him a bit.

The telephone made its soft dinging; it was a very modern Siemens model with speaker and microphone in the same handset. Horst covered the distance in two strides.

"*Ja*," he said after a moment, then gave her a grim nod as he hung up.

"A party of French gentlemen have arrived," he said. "That little talk with the concierge was worth the money. The Frenchmen have paid extra to be on this floor."

Flush times for the Victoria's staff, Luz thought. *They must be on half a dozen payrolls, not to mention tips.*

"How many?" she said aloud, feeling a taut excitement.

"Four." He grinned. "Ample to handle one old man."

He crossed to the bedroom; she heard him thump his fist on the wall, and presumably pressed a wineglass to it to hear the reply. She hadn't asked what he was doing earlier when he wrote a note and folded it and left the room for a minute; that would have been a gross breach of professional etiquette, though it was a virtual certainty he'd slipped it under the door of the Herr Professor next door. The pajama outfit she had on had a belt loop for her pistol and a pocket for the *navaja* that left them both concealed by the jacket. She thoughtfully slipped an extra magazine into her other pocket, one of the special nine-round ones she'd had made up by the Chamber's armorers, and her cosh.

Horst saw that as he came through. "Shoot if you must, but not un-less you must," he warned. "Our objective is to get out of here tomor-row unremarked, with the Professor alive. His life is the maximum priority if we must choose between those two."

"Will they try to kill him, or take him?" she asked.

Her first priority was maintaining her cover, but it amounted to the same thing in practice.

Though I'm certainly not going to die *for the Herr Doktor if I can help it.* Aloud she added clinically:

"I'd say take from the way this is going, but you'd know better here in Europe."

He shrugged. "Impossible to tell for certain, but I would wager any sum that they will try to take him—and kill him only if they cannot. He knows much that *they* would very much like to know."

"Bad practice to send a man like that abroad," she said absently, thinking very hard indeed about what the Germans were up to. "Don't bet what you can't afford to lose."

He gave her a sharp glance; the remark was a little sophisticated for the agent of a domestic revolutionary group rather than an interna-tional spy. Then he shrugged again.

"It was necessary."

She mentally chided herself for the slip, then went to the outer door and knelt; the door locks were a rather old-fashioned French box style, which meant you could look directly through the keyhole—in America they would have been replaced with Yale types long ago in a major city, but this was convenient and for a seaport Amsterdam was extremely law-abiding. Horst made a motion to follow her, then sat in a chair facing the door—it would be much easier for her to maintain this posture without stiffening muscles she would need at maximum efficiency than it would be for a six-foot man.

The soft sound of the elevator bell sounded from down the corri-dor, and the rattle of the operator pulling back the folding brass screen of the door. Luz made a thumbs-up gesture. Then she drew her eye back a little from the hole as four men came into view. They were all youngish and medium-sized, none of them past their mid-thirties from a quick estimate, and all in unexceptional middle-class gear including overcoats, with carpetbags in their hands. All but one had mustaches, cut rather close . . . which was a little bit sloppy. Though plenty of men other than young French military officers favored that style these days, it still made you mentally superimpose a kepi above it. Two of them turned casually and watched either way as the third opened the door, and then they all entered neatly.

Her teeth skinned back a little as a flush of heat warmed belly and chest. She'd felt like this before . . . and the earliest time had been hiding behind a pungent-smelling bush with her father, the Winchester in her hands, waiting for the jaguar to come down by the water hole where they'd staked out the goat. She put a thumb over the hole just in case and turned her head; Horst was at her shoulder.

"Four of them," she said softly. "Two were definitely the ones we saw at the airship dock. Just right for a snatch team."

Horst nodded, his hard square face expressionless save for a narrowing of the eyes.

"There will be more outside, with an automobile ready to take him to a Deuxième Bureau safe house for interrogation . . . though they might want to get him to France for that. And to put him on trial," he added absently, as his eyes went opaque with thought.

¡Ay! her mind prompted.

Things Horst had said about trips on high-altitude zeppelins coalesced with hints about the Professor.

The May raid? Is that what they want him for?

Ten German airships had raided Paris on May 5th, coming in at night and very high to avoid the fighting scouts guided by searchlights. They'd dropped gas, not explosives—hundred-pound sheet metal containers full of phosgene mixed with chlorine as a spreading agent and a small bursting charge set to explode at three hundred meters up. The carnage had been terrible, since on a short trip from the German bases in Belgium each airship had been able to carry tons of the noxious stuff. Thousands dead and many more blinded or crippled, mass panic and flight . . .

But if Horst and the Herr Doktor were both involved in that, *and they were both in America just now . . . this has to be some sort of project aimed at* us *but . . . maybe related to that raid? Perhaps it was a trial run? Berlin knows we're coming in to the war soon; they don't have any more incentive to avoid angering us . . . but a transatlantic raid would be very difficult with any worthwhile payload. Oh, this really* is *big. It's worth* anything *to get the intelligence on it back to Washington.*

The thought flickered through her mind in an instant, and a cold prickle ran over her skin. Aloud she went on:

"We have to intercept them before they leave this floor with him," she said. "But, Horst . . . we'll have to take them by surprise, unless you want a gunfight right here. They could have anything up to machine carbines in those bags, depending on how badly they want this man."

He winced and bared his teeth. "They will want him very badly," he admitted. "Assuming that they know who he really is, which is a good bet at this point. And from Amsterdam they could consult with Paris on secure lines easily to get orders."

"If we try to play it safe and stop them flat before they reach him we're actually increasing our risk and his, especially since you want to keep this quiet. We're outnumbered, so we need tactical surprise, and it's worth it if they're not going to kill him. And to kill him they wouldn't need four men—one man with a knife or a muffled pistol would do fine."

Unwillingly, he nodded. That meant letting the French agents get into the Professor's room, letting them think they had him secured and nothing to worry about except an inconspicuous extraction, and then hitting them from the rear. The slight extra risk that they'd simply kill him was worth it.

"How long to open one of these doors?" Horst said musingly, as if speaking to himself.

She answered straightforwardly: "Seconds if they have a passkey, and I think they probably do."

"In this whore of a merchant city? *Ja*."

"I could get through one of these locks in about twenty seconds with my picks," she said, tapping her finger lightly on the box lock. "Less, after I practice on this one a bit. And if they don't leave their key in the other side of the lock—if they do we'd have to break in. Or they may not lock it behind them at all, if they're set on speed; they could leave one man on guard in the corridor. That's likely from the way they handled getting set up in their own room. In, snatch the Professor, get him back to their room, and lock his door behind them."

And if he's behind the Paris attack, they'll want him very, very badly . . . for which I don't blame them in the least. Odd I'm going to have to kill them for the greater good defending thoroughly wicked enemies, but there you are. That's espionage for you.

Aloud she went on: "I'd have a much better chance of taking out a guard quietly if they do, so I'd better go out first."

He closed his eyes and thought again. "*Ja*, we will have to do it that way. I do not like it . . . but, yes." A chuckle. "I am going into battle beside a woman, not something I had imagined, and yet I find your presence profoundly comforting, Elisa."

"Not many I'd rather have on my side in a fight either, Horst," she said.

Technically he was going into battle *behind* a woman, but it wouldn't be tactful to mention that.

His eyes went to a clock on the mantel above the hearth. "Ten o'clock. They will not move for some time, at least four hours. Good, we will have time for dinner to settle."

She nodded; the best time for that sort of operation in a large city was a few hours after midnight, which was as close to deep sleep as a metropolis got.

"You should get some more rest, if you can," she said. "I'll wake you in two hours or if they move."

He went out and returned with a comforter and pillow for himself and another for her to kneel on; one of the things she respected in him was that he didn't need to chatter. She settled in to wait, letting her mind drift without words and keeping her eyes a little out of focus as she looked through the keyhole. All she had to watch for was movement.

Hisst," Horst said softly, then plugged the keyhole with his thumb for an instant: "They're moving."

Luz came out of her half doze instantly. Some inner sense told her it wasn't long before dawn, and the air had a peculiar stale stillness. The clock said three forty-five. She rolled to her feet and waited, still loose from her last set of stretches; they looked at each other as the half-minute mark went by, Horst showing his teeth in an unconscious snarl and Luz smiling slightly and letting the cosh slip into her right palm with its loop around her wrist while she undid the collar of her pajama jacket.

He nodded and opened the door, standing behind it as she went out first—though she could see his repugnance at it in every inch of his taut body. There was no way any French agent was going to look at *him* and see anything but a very dangerous German, though, and *gracias a Dios* Horst was smart enough to see that.

Whereas I'm a good-looking young woman in the sort of pajamas a cinema siren would wear . . . or a very high-class courtesan, I suppose.

The doors on this floor were fairly far apart, since most of them led to multiroom suites. There *was* a Frenchman standing mock-casually outside the Herr Doktor Professor's. He came alert as the door opened, and she thought she recognized the knee-forward stance of a *savateur*. Then he saw who she was and relaxed, taking his hand out from beneath his jacket. Luz smiled slightly, putting on a sleepy-sated pouting look and rolling her hips a little more, and saw his eyes drop to the hint of cleavage showing where the top two buttons of her jacket were undone.

Oh, you deserve this so much, François, she thought. ¡Que güey! *Darwin never sleeps!*

Still smiling, she pivoted smoothly on her right heel and drove the ball of her left foot up between his legs as hard as she could. That would have hurt even if he were wearing a cup . . . and he wasn't. The *thump* of impact was followed less than a second later by another as she brought the cosh around and down on the back of his head, which was presented to her neatly as he bent over gasping with his mouth wide open and no sound but a breathy hiss coming out of it. The fine lead shot inside the leather transmitted all the force of the full-armed strike with her weight behind it as it flattened against the bone, and he fell as limp as a puppet with its strings cut.

He might well be dead. She hadn't pulled the blow; it would have been insane to do so.

The first time Luz had killed had been on the night her parents died. It had been one of the *revolucionarios*; she'd cut his throat when he staggered drunkenly by her hiding place to piss out some of the looted pulque, and she'd taken his rifle and bandolier and clothes and horse to escape into the silent Sonoran desert. Pedro's lessons had worked perfectly—hand over the mouth and nose, jerk back in the same motion, drag the cutting edge down diagonally from below the ear to past the Adam's apple.

She'd had nightmares about it for a long time, the sudden smell like wet iron added to the rebel's stale sweat and tobacco and liquor, and the hot flood over her hand, black in the darkness lit only by the last flames of the hacienda's *casa grande*, and the body twitching beneath her until it went flaccid.

After that it got easier and easier. Sometimes she was a little troubled that it didn't trouble her much anymore.

Horst was beside her before the Frenchman had finished slumping into a puddle, moving like a big golden cat. He looked down at the body and pursed his lips admiringly, then put his big left hand on the doorknob. In his right was what they called a trench knife these days, a cut-down bayonet with a set of brass knuckles added to the hilt and a lead knob on the pommel. It looked crude and ugly and effective, which was truth in advertising, and he had a Luger tucked into his belt.

Luz drew in a long breath, let it out, felt her pulse slow a little, and nodded.

He turned the knob—the door wasn't locked—then crouched and lunged through as it opened, going instantly from a standing start to a blur of speed like a charging tiger. The suite was a mirror image of the one next door that Horst had booked, and this was the large sitting room. There were the remains of a meal on the table and four men; two of the Frenchmen were holding the Professor. He sagged between them in his old-fashioned nightshirt, blood streaming from a cut under his thick white hair, and his eyes rolled up as one of them pressed a damp cloth over his mouth and nose.

The third had a Star Model 14 automatic in his gloved hand—with blood on the barrel, so he'd pistol-whipped the elderly German to quiet him for the chloroform—probably a mixture of alcohol and chloroform and ether, since the pure stuff didn't work as well as fiction would have it. He leveled the weapon as the other two dropped the half-conscious academic unceremoniously. Luz whirled the cosh around her head once by the strap and then threw it across the ten feet separating them; the man whipped up his right hand to protect his face, fired, and missed. Horst closed with him.

The first of the two Frenchmen who'd been holding the old German came at her with a pivot like a dancer, his left foot flicking up and snapping around for her head—a *fouetté figure*, a high whip kick. It was delivered with bone-cracking force and dangerously fast; she barely managed to go in beneath it, weight and momentum pushing her down as she let her knees go slack and threw out her left hand to stop the fall. The *navaja* snicked open in her right and she cut viciously at his groin as she rose. He tumbled backward just in time to avoid having the inside of his thigh sliced open and came upright with a knife in his own hand. It was a narrow double-edged blade and he held it point down with his other hand covering it, Apache-style.

Some distant part of her noticed that the Deuxième Bureau were apparently recruiting street fighters from the gangs who haunted the drinking kens of Ménilmontant, or at least using them as trainers.

"*Come to me and die,* puto *Gabacho,*" she snarled in Spanish.

His dark eyes flared as he recognized the blade in her hand and the way she held it, and this time there was no nonsense about her sex—he probably wasn't seeing anything but knife, hands, and feet. Then his covering hand moved in an extravagant gesture designed to distract the eye while the point of the knife lanced forward—Apache-style again. They were already close enough to strike without footwork.

When you are ojo a ojo, *someone is going to die very soon,* old Pedro's voice echoed in her mind. *You are committed. Strike or die, there is nothing else.*

Her blade moved in a smooth swift *floretazo* toward his midsection, point lowered and edge turned to the left. The Frenchman's guarding hand flashed out to grab her wrist and immobilize it while he struck himself. The hand slapped down on her wrist . . . but the blade wasn't there. He had just time enough to realize she'd flicked it into her rising left inside his guard before the point took him beneath the chin.

There was a crisp popping feel as the six-inch blade slammed up through his palate and into his brain, and she wrenched the knife free with desperate speed and skipped backward.

The third Frenchman might have been a bad problem, except that Horst had just gripped his chin and neck and turned his head until he was staring out from between his shoulder blades. The German dropped the body and put a hand to his side.

"The pigdog *kicked* me," he wheezed. "I don't think any ribs are broken, though. Or if they are, just a little cracked."

Luz shuddered and took a deep breath as her awareness flared out again into the harsh blood-and-feces-scented aftermath of twenty seconds of combat. There was no *time* for reaction, or anything but dealing with the consequences. Probably nobody had heard the single shot, or dismissed it.

The first man Horst had gone for, the pistoleer, was lying on his back with the trench knife jammed up under his breastbone and apparently stuck fast.

Close in, knife beats pistol nine times in ten, she thought.

Horst was already returning with a handful of towels from the bathroom, and they wrapped them around various wounds; luckily the blood stopped pumping out like a hose when the heart ceased beating, but there had already been too much from the loser in the knife duel, and she discovered that there was a tiny nick over her collarbone where his thrust had *almost* gone home into her jugular.

Mierda, she thought, sticking a little piece of clean paper over it. *No time, no time . . .*

She stepped to the outer door, checked both ways, and dragged the man she'd coshed over to the French agents' room and through into their bathroom by his feet—it was convenient that this was a first-class hotel, with the luxury of private bathing facilities for most of the higher-priced rooms. She heaved him into it, and helped Horst with the others. The four of them made a mound even arranged spoon-fashion, but with a little effort they fitted well enough into the big claw-footed, cast-iron tub that body fluids and blood would leak down the drain and not drip through the floorboards.

It was astonishing how *much* blood a human being held, and as any-one who'd spilled a bottle could testify, a little went a long way when it got out. The same bathroom furnished towels to replace the ones they'd taken from the Professor's suite. Back there Horst took the half-empty bottle of red wine from the old man's late meal and carefully poured it over the stains on the rug. With luck that would cover the blood and the smell long enough; they only needed enough time to cross the bor-der, and their train left about dawn.

While he did that she examined the Herr Doktor, reflecting that she'd need a name for him. The wound on his scalp was superficial, though it had bled copiously as injuries there always did, and she fixed it with sticking plaster and iodine from Horst's supplies. The bone beneath seemed unaffected, but though he seemed in reasonable shape the skinny old man was at least in his sixties, and he'd been drugged too, with the usual mixture. At least they'd smeared Vaseline on his face to avoid chemical burns.

He stirred as Horst lifted him effortlessly like a child; another thing that lurid fiction didn't mention was that it took a solid three or four minutes of breathing through a pad to really put you out. A hypodermic was much better if you were in a hurry. His eyes fluttered open and he muttered:

"*Loki . . . Hauch des Loki . . . Americans . . .*"

That meant "Breath of Loki"; Loki, the trickster-god of the ancient Germanics, who ended up chained to a rock beneath the drip of venom from a serpent. Her parents had read her those stories, with many others, though her father had preferred the Ulster Cycle and her mother the *Song of the Cid*. Luz carefully didn't react, and the sound died away to mumbles.

"They used a knockout mixture," she said; she'd sniffed at the cloth before dropping it on the bodies. "Risky, but I think he'll wake up fairly soon."

"Good," Horst said; they tucked the old man into the bed in their suite, making sure he wasn't drooling too much or in danger of choking on his tongue. "It's only a few hours until we leave for the train. Lucky that it's right across the square!"

Luz nodded thoughtfully. "Horst, can you square the customs agents on the German side?"

He nodded. "Yes, if I must. We'll be switching to a special train there direct to . . . where we're going. Why?"

"Because if the French are this determined, I'd like some more firepower if they try again. And the *Gabachos* were all carrying carpetbags."

His eyes lit. "Ah! Just-in-case gear!"

They slipped across again to the room the French had so briefly occupied; it might be her imagination, but she thought she could smell death under the sweet flowery odor of the bath oil they'd spilled over the bodies. The four identical carpetbags were all resting on the parlor table.

"*Na, was haben wir denn hier?*" Horst said as he opened one and his brows went up.

Which was roughly equivalent to *What have we here?* Or *well, well, well*, a phrase suitable for opening Christmas presents.

What they had here was an arsenal: two sawed-off shotguns, ammunition for them in the form of heavy buckshot and slugs, a half-dozen hand grenades shaped like miniature pineapples—

"English. Mills bombs, not as good as our *Stielhandgranate*, but a sound design," Horst remarked.

"The gringos use a similar one lately, but what's this rifle?"

Horst laid out the disassembled weapon, clicked it together, and took it apart again after running his hands over the join. Luz was familiar with it from briefing papers, but she let the German explain; in her experience most men derived considerable pleasure from explaining things, particularly to women, and it wouldn't be in character for Elisa Carmody to be completely familiar with European military exotica. Luz liked a well-designed weapon as she did any other tool, enjoyed hunting, and was very competent with them for that or a fight, but she'd never derived that semi-sensual pleasure from guns that she'd seen often in others and of which Horst showed every sign.

"It's a Meunier semi-auto rifle," Horst said. "A specially made one for taking down and putting in a small case and assembling again rapidly."

"Semi-automatic? Like the gringo Colt-Browning? Those have caused us hard problems."

"Very much like, though it's recoil operated rather than gas. A good weapon, much better than the Lebel, and a much better 7mm rimless cartridge too—which they stole from Mauser-Werk—though the action is a little delicate for the trenches. The French started producing it just before the war, but they never had enough for general issue. They give it to elite units and marksmen and raiding parties. And ten clips of ammunition, fifty rounds. Can you use a rifle?"

"Yes," she said flatly. "Quite well."

He nodded, taking her at her word. "Well, let's take our gifts. Ah, and a coil of rope, always useful."

They put the brass *Do Not Disturb* signs on their little chains around the knobs of the French agents' door, and the Professor's, with a one-guilder coin bearing Queen Wilhelmina's rather plump face left in the helpfully provided slot in each for emphasis. The signs were recent inventions and the mark of a first-class hotel in a sophisticated city, but the thriller writers had already begun to note how they aided skullduggery.

When everything was packed they sat on the sofa together in their own suite to wait the remaining hours; Horst decided that they would ask for an invalid's wheeled chair if the Professor hadn't fully recovered by then. Luz shivered a little and leaned against the man's shoulder. He gave her a surprised look and put a gentle arm around her.

"I don't like killing men who've never done me harm," she said. "I will if I have to, but . . . I don't like it. Better them than us, but there may be children who can't understand why their fathers aren't coming home."

After a moment he said with clumsy goodwill: "They were men fighting for their country and people, as I do for mine and you for yours. This was honorable war, with equal chances for us and them, blow for blow and shot for shot."

"Yes," she said, and they waited in silence.

FIVE

Maatschappij tot Exploitatie van Staatsspoorwegen
(Netherlands State Railways)
Eastern Gelderland Province
Koninkrijk der Nederlanden
(Kingdom of the Netherlands)
SEPTEMBER 6TH, 1916(B)

It was supposed to be six hours from Amsterdam's *Centraal* to Cologne in Germany. Judging by where they were, across the Rhine and past Arnhem, just beginning to head south, it was going to be at least two hours more; in fact, they'd be lucky to make the customs house at Emmerich-am-Rhein by two o'clock. Horst grumbled, his tidy Teutonic soul offended by the irregularity; Luz thought he'd probably have gone mad if he had to live in Mexico or Guatemala or any of a number of places her father had built things.

But he allowed that it was probably the result of the war and the shortages of good coal in the Netherlands, which had to import every lump from combatants who needed it themselves. The engine up ahead was wheezing and making asthmatic noises now and then; even at the peaks between stations they were doing distinctly less than the fifty miles an hour a passenger express should, which meant there was probably duff and shale in every shovelful going into the firebox. The locomotive had looked like a toy to her anyway. European engines always did, compared to the massive brutes that roamed American railways.

At least the first-class passenger compartments were joined along the side by an interior corridor, what Europeans for some mysterious reason called the American Plan, despite it not being all that common in the United States. A lot of trains here still used the other, older type that had nothing but the exits on the side, showing the design's descent from a string of stagecoaches stuck on a flatbed, which meant you could end up dying to pee while the train crawled between stations and no place to do it but the floor.

She'd left for the ladies' toilet an hour out of Amsterdam at a hint from Horst, and when she came back the Professor—technically, he was Privatdozent Ernst von Bülow—was still chilly and aloof but at least minimally polite, mostly ignoring her. Luz assumed that Horst had explained to the older man how she'd helped save his wrinkled backside from the French, though he'd still been surprised, or seemed to be, when she spoke excellent upper-class German.

She assumed from the slight but detectable edge of a rough Brandenberger accent that he was a genuine Prussian and not one by historical accident and Frederick the Great's ambition like Horst the Silesian. But then, nearly all Germans had *some* sort of regional tinge even when speaking the standard tongue, which had been more or less made up in the Reformation era and wasn't something anyone sang lullabies in or shouted in play as a child. From the combination of an academic title and the nobleman's *von* he was probably also the non-inheriting younger scion of a family with a minor entailed estate out among the pinewoods . . . an estate that in America would qualify as a biggish farm. In England only the eldest son of a noble had a title and the rest were commoners, but in Germany all the children were of the *Edel* caste, and they bred like rabbits.

His head probably feels like it's going to explode, between being pistol-whipped and drugged, she thought with an attempt at charity by the young and healthy. *It takes longer to spring back at his age.*

They were into the eastern part of Gelderland now and had turned south, closer and closer to the German frontier, and the land passing by outside their windows was no longer pancake flat. By Dutch standards it was mountainous and thinly populated, meaning there were occasional wooded ridges or even low hills, one towering as much as two hundred feet into the sky. Wooden fences surrounded the fields, reaped and yellow and some with sheaves of grain still in pyramidal stooks, or bushy with root crops or green pasture thronged with fat-looking brown cattle with odd white bands from top to bottom in the middle of their bodies, like broad belts. Scattered farms stood with brick nogging between their half timbers under steep red roofs, and now and then a small castle or stately manor house dreamed amid formal gardens. The occasional, inevitable windmill clacked away, probably grinding the newly harvested grain, and the air through the half-open window smelled warm and sleepy-green and somehow had a hint of *first frost soon*, under the coal smoke. You could imagine a cotillion in one of those manors, and Mozart lilting softly out the French windows, or a mother in a lace cap spooning cheese soup out of a tureen for eager tow-headed children in a farmhouse kitchen of scrubbed wood and shining tile.

Hard to imagine it's the edge of a continent tearing at itself like a mad wolf eating out its own guts, Luz thought.

Horst seemed to catch the thought. "There has been war here often enough," he said. "This is where my ancestors broke the Roman frontier fifteen hundred years ago, and Charlemagne fought his long campaigns against the heathen Saxons and Frisians. Viking ships came far up these rivers with their dragon heads to burn and plunder and carry off captives. War in the Middle Ages, war in the Eighty Years' struggle against the Spanish, war against the French of Louis XIV. And against Napoleon, in the time of our own grandparents and their parents."

Luz smiled rueful agreement. "There is war where there are human beings," she said.

"War is the locomotive of history," von Bülow said a bit sententiously.

Luz was tempted to argue the point simply because she didn't like him, though in fact the statement was pretty much true as far as she could see and a rather striking phrase. Instead she looked at the book beside him, *Also sprach Zarathustra*, and said:

"That bit with the old woman talking to Zarathustra is metaphorical, you know, Herr Privatdozent."

Privatdozent meant an independent scholar with at least a doctorate who wasn't formally appointed to a university post. It was often somewhat more prestigious than a regular academic position.

"And often misinterpreted," she added.

"Which part? You have read Nietzsche?"

He sounded slightly indignant, as if she'd checked the book out of a library and kept it beyond the return date. She smiled sweetly and fluttered her eyelids.

"Well, of course. Hasn't anyone who actually reads read the most influential philosopher of our time? I mean the part where the old woman says to Zarathustra: *Du gehst zu Frauen? Vergiss die Peitsche nicht!*"

Literally that meant: *Thou goest to the women? Forget not the whip!* If it wasn't his favorite pair of sentences in the book, she'd stick jalapeño peppers up her nose.

"Metaphorical in what sense?" von Bülow said, his eyes lighting up despite himself; like most of his breed he simply couldn't resist word chopping, or textual exegesis if you were feeling charitable. "There are many levels of interpretation possible, of course; this I grant."

"Well," Luz said, opening the Hotel Victoria's lunch basket and handing around the sausage-and-cheese sandwiches, pickles and apples and bottles of flavored seltzer water. "Notice that the old woman has just given a wise reply to Zarathustra's first statements about women in general. And that she addresses him with the familiar *du* as if he were her child, and the word she . . . which is to say, Nietzsche . . . uses for women is *Frauen*, not *Weiber*."

Frauen and *Weiber* were more or less precisely equivalent to the English distinction between *ladies* and *females* . . . or between ladies and women-in-general. With malice aforethought she added:

"Possibly it helps not to have been born a native German speaker to appreciate exactly what he's trying to do there."

Luz continued as the professor sputtered:

"With Nietzsche precise word choice always matters crucially; he's a poet as well as a philosopher, a philosopher who speaks in poetry—he says things that can't be summed up in a simple declarative sentence, the way you can the price of apples. Hinting at truths whose meaning can only be approached allusively, recursively, because language itself creaks beneath the weight. Each word is surrounded by a penumbra of possible meanings that must be considered together rather than one being chosen and the others dismissed."

Horst was leaning back, with a straitened expression on his face, as if he were fighting down a delighted grin.

Yes, there are times when it's a bit of a struggle not to like him too much, she thought.

Luz spread a napkin across her knees. Von Bülow did likewise and took a bite of his sandwich and chased it with the fizzy water, frowning. Luz bit into hers; inside the crusty roll was *ossenworst*, a raw-beef sausage made with pepper, cloves, mace, and nutmeg and then slow-smoked at low temperature.

That, I have to admit, the Dutch do very well. And this Gouda is excellent.

Von Bülow looked past the wall of the carriage. "Granting the general principle of the allusiveness of Nietzsche's prose for the sake of argument, particularly with respect to this work, what is your *specific* interpretation?" the academic said challengingly. "Can there be a new one of so seminal a work?"

"My interpretation would be twofold. First, the old woman is reminding Zarathustra of the whip the *woman* holds—her role as the maker-into-human of the wild-beast boy-man whom she mothers—and how more generally she uses the whip of restraint, of culture, to tame the male; so Zarathustra should take care when he goes to the ladies, lest they tame him with *their* whips. *Him* in this case, of course, being not merely Zarathustra in this passage but that screaming child he carries, the child of his mind surely, his *truth* that he fears is too loud."

"Outrageous sophism!" von Bülow said. "Why so contradict the first reading . . . oh."

"Oh indeed; and note that she does not say *forget not* your *whip*; she says *forget not* the *whip*. It's a complete *reversal* of meanings, which is the theme of the work, isn't it?"

"The inversion of *morals* is the theme! Well, that and eternal recurrence."

"So shouldn't we examine each statement in it in light of that? A reversal of both morals and meanings? And secondly of course the 'whip' is an expression of *distance*, of the *Pathos der Distanz* to which Nietzsche so often refers. With the whip, the woman requires that Zarathustra—the male Prophet—maintain a wary distance . . ."

"Superficially striking, but surely—"

Bless you, Miss Lucy Ganz, Luz thought, recalling her philosophy teacher kindly as von Bülow began his indignant refutation.

Twenty minutes later they were crunching the last of the apples and going at it hammer-and-tongs about the meaning of *over* in relation to the concept of the *Übermensch* and Luz was pointing out the fact that *über* could as easily mean "transcendent" as "superior," and that *mensch* was used rather than *man*, conveying the more general sense of human being rather than specifically a male. Von Bülow wasn't a professional philosopher any more than Luz was; she gathered from some casual remarks that he was a scientist, probably a chemist, and they were contending on nearly equal ground.

Horst was silent except for a little helpless wheezing, and had a hand clamped firmly over his mouth. She thought she saw a tear trembling at the corner of one pale gray eye.

Then his head came up, the amusement vanishing. "Quiet!" he barked in his officer's voice. "Something's wrong!"

Von Bülow did fall silent, for a wonder, with his index finger in midpoke toward her in the air. Luz listened too, and heard the scream of steel on steel and felt the swift hard lurch as the train's emergency brakes locked. She stuck her head out of the compartment window in time to see rooster tails of sparks from the six driving wheels going into full reverse as the engine turned into a curve before a small bridge. She didn't have time to check that the dark gap in the rails her first glance saw was really there . . .

But the locomotive driver certainly thought so, and he had a much closer view; she'd just seen him and the fireman jump for it.

"Sabotage!" she shouted, grabbing the leather straps above the seat and slamming her feet against the seat opposite her. "The train's going to derail, brace for it!"

The engine started to take the curve, and then there weren't any rails beneath the foretruck and then the driving wheels were biting uselessly into gravel and dirt. The sixty-ton weight of the locomotive plowed down the embankment and into the water of the little river, and there was a deafening, roaring *bang* when the cold water struck the boiler and firebox and the riveted seams yielded, then ripped open as the flaying steam within escaped in a huge whistle. Screams echoed in their wake as passengers were thrown across cabins, breaking bones and faces, and rivets and fragments flew like shrapnel.

Luz gave a shivering grunt as the impact wrenched at her, but the springs she made of knees and thighs and back held, despite the savage wrench of the forces trying to turn her into a tumbling mass of organs wrapped around fragile ceramic sticks and the strap that felt like it was cutting through her wrist. Horst managed too, and he had one iron arm braced across the professor's chest. The carriage they were in was the fourth back from the coal and water cars, and it came off the rails and almost immediately rammed into the one before, twisting until it lay three-quarters over with the outer door of the compartment pointing down toward the damp ditch beside the track. The screams of humans seemed slight after the shriek of tortured metal.

"Out!" Horst snapped. "They'll be here any moment; this is an ambush."

He tried the door that led from the compartment to the outside, but the frame was jammed. Then he went down with his back on the canted floor, drawing his long legs up and slamming his boot heels downward and out into the door over and over again. The doors held for five impacts hard enough to rock the carriage and then screeched open with a sound of tearing metal.

He really is *Siegfried Fafnir's bane come again*, Luz thought. *Only not stupid and not hip-deep in a sea of aunts.*

While Horst's boot heels hammered, Luz was moving quickly; she slung her suitcase over her back by its strap, opened the Frenchman's Gladstone bag, extracted the rifle, and fitted it together as Horst had demonstrated. It made a satisfying *snick* as the joints clicked together, and then she had four feet of automatic weapon, very much like the Colt-Brownings she'd used before. A moment and she pulled the operating knob on the side to the rear and pushed five rounds from a stripper clip into the magazine with her thumb and let the bolt drive the first into the chamber. The rest of the ammunition went into the pockets of her skirt, and two of the grenades into those of her jacket.

By then Horst was helping von Bülow down the five-foot gap to the torn damp earth, making nothing of his weight.

"Come along, Herr Privatdozent," he said cheerfully. "The French are very determined to make your acquaintance, but this time I think they'll settle for killing you rather than kidnapping you for the Sorbonne."

"Putting my stuffed and mounted corpse on display at the Sorbonne, perhaps," von Bülow surprised her by saying. "Like that lunatic Bentham at London University."

Bright sun, Luz thought as she dropped through into a crouch with the rifle at port arms across her body and squinted around; it was bright for northern Europe at least. You forgot how much farther north Europe was than the parts of America with similar climates—without the Gulf Stream this would be like Hudson Bay.

Just the time for the local climate not *to be sodden and wet and misty and easy to hide in!*

There was a dirt road to the west, then a wooden fence enclosing a broad field of something bushy—potatoes—and then woods of oak and beech with a few hints of color in the leaves about three hundred yards from the tracks.

A flicker of movement between the car and the one to its rear—more nearly upright—showed a man in rough laborer's clothing climbing through with a shotgun in his hands, not more than thirty feet away. There wasn't time for anything but reaction; Luz swung the muzzle of the rifle around and squeezed off three shots from the hip, the hard *bam-bam-bam* cutting through the chorus of screams and moans of pain as it bucked in her hands, shouts and the crackling crunch of metal contracting and buckling . . . and the growing crackle of fire from the coal truck and the crumpled lead wagon.

The first round kicked up gravel from the track bed by the man's feet, the second sparked off the frame of the crumpled rail car behind him with a wicked *pinnng,* and the third took him in the shoulder. He fell backward with a scream—she thought she heard *merde!* in it—and both barrels of the shotgun went off, with buckshot whining uncomfortably close.

A few people noticed, several of them idiotic enough to point and exclaim rather than hit the dirt, but several others were running . . . and they'd inform the authorities fairly soon. There was a village named Stokkum south of them, just in sight across flat open country.

Horst had slung the professor over his broad shoulder but was hesitating. Luz tossed the carpetbag with the rest of the grenades and the shotgun and its ammunition to him and snapped:

"Horst! *I* can't *carry him!*"

Or at least not at any speed, she didn't need to say. He nodded, the momentary irresolution leaving his face.

"To the woods."

"I'll cover you and then fall back."

He sprinted to the fence, hit it running, and vaulted over, with one board creaking dangerously as the combined weight of the two men went on it. Then he was running across the field of potatoes, which was easier said than done—they were in hills parallel to his westward run, which meant there were little furrows and ridges just right to catch the foot, concealed by the knee-high plants. He bounded across the field at a dead sprint anyway despite the carpetbag and a hundred and thirty-odd pounds of scientist, jinking irregularly from side to side as he went to keep from presenting a zero-deflection shot with what looked like an experienced infantryman's reflex.

Horst said I was one of a kind. I certainly hope he *is, or Germany really will rule the world!*

Luz followed through the grass of the verge between the railroad right-of-way and the road and then over more grass to the fence; with European tidiness and reluctance to waste an inch of ground everything green had been grazed, probably by tethered sheep, which was good. The American equivalent would be a wild tangle of waist-high weeds only hacked back a couple of times a year at best. Her skirts were cut with hidden pleats that allowed a full range of movement to her legs, but they were still more likely to catch on things than trousers.

There were situations where a woman could wear trousers without attracting too much attention these days—on a wilderness hunting trip, or in advanced circles when riding astride—but traveling on a respectable first-class train was *not* one of them. The only alternative was to dress and pass as a male, which she'd done when necessary; it was amazing what people *didn't* see. That would probably have stressed Horst too much, though.

She reached the fence—which was board-and-post and about chest high on her—hopped up and did a roll-over using it as a fulcrum, and let herself drop to the ground, cushioning it a little by leading with the butt of the rifle.

"Ooof!" she said, as things in her pockets gouged her.

The things included two grenades, and rough handling *might* dislodge a pin, but there was no point in thinking about that . . .

There was a ridge of soil beneath the fence, thrown there over the years by plowing around the edge of the field, and it gave her a little cover. The dirt smelled damp, with the sharp dusty smell of mature potato vines over it, and the scent of things burning that shouldn't from the train as wafts of smoke drifted by—the coal in the tender had all caught, for starters, and that would burn hot enough to make metal slump. She squirmed around to lie facing the train, licked her thumb, and wet the foresight of the rifle, which had a simple adjustable leaf backsight; she was about a hundred and fifty feet away now, and with a fast-shooting round like the 7mm that meant a flat trajectory or near as no matter. Assuming the weapon was properly zeroed in with the sights in the lowest battle setting . . . which she just *had* to assume.

And die if it isn't. Here I am, risking my life to defend a mass murderer from justice at the hands of people who'll be American allies in a few weeks, she thought whimsically. *And using their own rifle to do it.*

Though the Deuxième Bureau hadn't hesitated to wreck a train full of neutral civilians. Still, compared to dropping poison gas on Paris . . . well, war was war. The train was still swarming with people, pulling the injured or trapped out of compartments, helping others away to lie still or groaning on the ground, or standing and talking to each other. A few pointed to Horst running across the potato field with an elderly chemist slung over his shoulder . . .

Ignore details. Look at everything. Purposeful movement will catch the eye, or weapons. There!

A man's head and shoulders appeared over the edge of the roof of the rail carriage she'd been in. The way it was canted made it awkward for him, since he couldn't lie on the top without sliding down; he was probably being boosted from below, and he braced his elbows on the roof and leveled a rifle like the one she was carrying at Horst's fleeing figure. Still less than two hundred yards away, easy for a good shot firing from a brace. She came up just enough to rest the forestock of the rifle on the lowest board of the fence, let the sight fall down on the triangle of head and shoulders, breathed out, held it, squeezed . . .

Crack. Crack.

Two more brass shells spun off to her right and the bolt locked back. The black silhouette—the man—jerked and toppled backward, probably with the ones below him trying to catch him; the rifle fell from his hands and slithered across the slanted top of the carriage and fell to the ground.

Crack, and it fired as it landed, the bullet going who-knew-where; hopefully not into someone's six-year-old Anneke off to visit her grandma, but things were as they were.

Luz was already on her feet, sprinting west and trading safety for speed by doing it in a straight line. She managed to reload as she went, shoving the charger clip in and pushing down to strip the rounds out and into the magazine, but the bolt nearly mashed her thumb as it ran forward, and the potato bushes caught at her skirts.

Meunier, you hijo de puta, *why didn't you use a detachable magazine like Browning when you designed this thing? Colt-Brownings have twenty rounds and you can just slap a new one in when you're in a hurry!*

For thirty seconds there was only her own panting breath and footfalls and the rustle and catch of vegetation against the hem of her skirt, and Horst dwindling in front of her . . . was he powered by steam? Then a *crack-crack* from behind her, and a sound like *ptow* to her left and a ripping echo following it like silk parting, *ptow* again to her right.

Those were rifle bullets going by, and far too close. She'd been bracketed, which meant the next one—

Luz threw up her arms and collapsed forward, letting her body bounce flat with the rifle still loosely clasped in her left hand, and there was another *ptow* and the ripping sound right above her just as she fell.

No scream, no thrashing, don't overdo . . .

More often than not a couple of hits to the center of mass just made someone drop down limp as the body cavity flooded and blood pressure dropped. Hidden by the potato vines, her right hand went into her skirt pocket; the suit she was wearing today was a russet tweed for the jacket and skirt, and it should fade into the background of slightly wilted potato vines and brown dirt well, disguising details. She let her bobbed black hair flop over her face and controlled her breathing by an effort of main will, the urge to gasp in air almost overwhelming—but that would make her move, and with the loose sandy dirt of the field so close it would mean breathing it in and then coughing, and the weedy scent of the crushed potato vines tickled her nose . . .

¡Madre de Dios! *To die because I sneezed!*

She lay and pushed it out of her mind. Pushed out everything but sounds. The slow thick wind of this country through the rustling vines, the distant noises of the wreck . . .

"Marcel! We're getting in range of the woods, we should spread out. The rest will come in from the other side in a few minutes if we signal," a sharp voice said, speaking with a nasal Picard accent, full of *k*-sounds at the beginnings of words where most French-speakers put *sh*.

"*Ta gueule, Pierre!* I want to make sure of the *Boche* bastard I shot, the one who killed Etienne. And get that other Meunier rifle back, the shotguns are useless in open country."

Cinco, she thought. *Cuatro . . . tres . . . dos . . .*

"*¡Uno!*" Luz spat aloud.

She pulled the grenade out of her pocket, brought her left hand across and jerked the pin free with her thumb through the ring, came up to her knee and threw, and let the motion spin her flat again, shoving her face down into the dirt between two rows of potatoes.

Pierre was right, she thought. *They should have spread out. And Marcel is an idiot; he should have remembered we'd captured grenades with the rest of the snatch team's gear.*

The three Frenchmen were standing about ten feet from each other, the one in the center with a rifle like the one she carried, the other two with shotguns, all of them in coarse workman's clothes and flat cloth caps. The little clump was a hundred feet from her and she was fairly sure the grenade would land right where Pierre was standing with his rifle. Luz was good at throwing things—her father had been a baseball enthusiast since he'd grown up in the game's New England home and had played catch with her as a girl, and she'd trained with grenades specifically since joining the Chamber and since the Great War had shown they were necessary. A field operative wasn't an infantry soldier, but you needed some of the same skills sometimes . . . as in situations like this.

The problem was that the Mills bomb was a defensive fragmentation grenade, meant to be thrown from places where you could duck down behind cover after you sent it toward the enemy; jagged shards of the cast-iron shell would almost certainly hit anyone standing within fifty feet of the point of impact and *could* go as far as two hundred. These miserable six-inch ridges of loose earth were a very poor substitute for a sandbagged trench, and she very much did not want a piece of cast iron pinwheeling into her skull.

Someone started to shout *grenade* in French, getting as far as *grena*—

There was a loud but unspectacular flat *bumpf* sound, followed by a pattering as dirt fell back to earth. In the same instant a man began to scream, a high wailing sound that didn't end. Luz winced inwardly a little as she snatched up the rifle and dashed across the field; a single backward glance had told her she didn't need to worry about those three Frenchmen again, though some of them might live.

This is beginning to get ridiculous, she thought. *I'm decimating the Deuxième Bureau's operations in the Netherlands! And if I* don't *get the information out of Germany, whatever it is, I'm helping whatever German plan this is succeed!*

Intelligence work was full of paradoxes and could astonish you with flights of what was supposed to be logic and wheels within wheels, but this . . .

She didn't stop when she came to the edge of the woods; they were open in the European style, tended like a garden, with none of the litter of deadfalls and outer screen of saplings and underbrush she was used to in the American equivalents. Instead she ran another twenty yards and plastered herself to the other side of a beech tree four feet thick. Luz was just trying to work up enough spit to whistle when Horst's voice called from *above* her:

"Very well done! You are welcome on any trench raid I lead! That was extremely impressive, *meine Süsse!*"

"So was the speed you ran at, sweetie," Luz replied.

Luz felt a rush of relief mixed with paradoxical pride; he *was* an enemy, more or less, even if fate had put them on the same side in this fight, but he was also someone whose praise was worth having.

"If they revive the Olympics after the war, you should enter the pentathlon," she finished sardonically.

Horst and von Bülow were on a broad branch more than forty feet up. The younger German pointed westward.

"There's a country road that way pointed toward the border, I can just see a bit of it," he said. "This is the southernmost neck of these woods and it's narrow."

"Probably a country road with *Gabachos* on it," she said. "I overheard them before I threw the grenade and they were expecting help from that side."

"Ach, so!" Horst said, an all-purpose remark in his language.

He had the coil of rope from the snatch team's bag over one shoulder like a bandolier; now he undid it, put a loop he'd already tied under the academic's arms, and lowered him effortlessly hand over hand to the ground, which must have been the way he got him up there. Luz steadied him, feeling the bird-fragile lightness of the elderly man, and sat him down so that he could lean against the trunk. Meanwhile Horst slung the carpetbag over his shoulder, dropped the rope, then dropped himself from branch to branch, agile as an ape. The last one was ten feet up and he caught it casually in one hand, slowing himself so that he could drop into a crouch, smiling and breathing deeply with a light sheen of sweat on his face and his neck where he'd torn off the tie.

Suppress that impulse to rip his clothes off and throw him to the ground! she told herself; it was good to smile again amid the deadly tension.

"I'll scout the road and return," he said. "When I do—"

He whistled a tune; it was the opening bars of *Ride of the Valkyries*, which he'd also done in an intimate moment back at the Victoria, and an appropriate one. She had laughed so hard then that she'd almost done herself an injury *in media res* since things had just gotten to the point of no return for both of them.

His jacket pockets bulged with the grenades. She handed him the rifle and the ammunition for that as well, and took the shotgun in exchange. Luz had no doubt Horst would do the scouting at least as well as she could, particularly in something close to his home environment; these probably weren't exactly like the woods of Silesia, but they were closer to that than to California or Jalisco. With a nod he padded off westward, and Luz sank down into a crouch.

On a thought she looked in the carpetbag and found one of the Codd-neck bottles of soda water still intact. She opened it, took a sip— her mouth and throat were paper-dry with reaction to the surge of action in her blood—and offered it to von Bülow before she went to one knee and braced the shotgun across it, trying to watch in every direction at once. That was mostly a matter of not looking anywhere in particular; you were trying to see and hear and feel things that *didn't* fit the background and letting everything else flow through you. Patterns and gaps, gaps and patterns.

The principle was the same as hunting, except that you were the stalker and the prey at once. Insects hopped and buzzed, but more quietly than in the autumn woods she was used to; squirrels were that spectacular fire-red you got on this side of the Atlantic, blurring in streaks up and down the trunks and occasionally pausing to curse at her; a fox went trotting by, intent on getting away from the noise and trouble and doing a double-take and sideways jump when it saw her. Birds fluted or squawked.

Von Bülow took the bottle, lifted it in salute, and surprised her again when he spoke softly:

"Vielen, vielen Dank, gnädiges Fräulein."

Which was not only *thank you*, but a very formal thank-you indeed, and he'd called her *gracious miss*, as well. His voice had been a bit of a croak until he moistened it.

"Gern geschehen," she said; you're welcome. *Though if there was some way to keep you alive* and *kill you . . .* "Quietly please, if you speak."

"Ja." After a moment: "You are of mixed nationalities, are you not, miss?"

She spoke—quietly but not in a whisper. Whispers carried. "Yes. Irish and Criollo . . . Creole Spanish-American."

She didn't mention that there were almost certainly Arawak girls in there many generations back, and it being Cuba the odd much-diluted and officially denied African too, though the Aróstegui family would have rather been racked and burned alive than admit it.

Von Bülow muttered under his breath; Luz thought she caught *Vandal* and *Visigoth* in it, and suppressed a grin at the mention of Germanic tribes who'd settled in Iberia back in the *Völkerwanderung* after the Roman Empire fell. The good professor was looking for reasons to account for her in the mental categories he was accustomed to, like his monarch's genealogical research project to prove Uncle Teddy was really a German *Uradel*. Which was sort of sad and funny for Queen Victoria's grandson, especially when you considered that his idol Frederick the Great had thought German an uncouth language where you had to read a whole page to get to a single verb, mainly suitable for speaking to servants and livestock. In Frederick's day much of Berlin's population had been French, Protestant refugees he'd welcomed to give the dowdy provincial city some culture.

If you go back to the Visigoths . . . or even just medieval times . . . everyone is descended from everyone, including Charlemagne and Genghis Khan, she thought but did not say. *You can prove that with some simple mathematics. I prefer to think of myself as a purebred American mongrel. As Uncle Teddy says, if you subscribe to the Constitution and speak the language and call yourself American, you're an American. And if you say I have a man's spirit I will clout you, Ernst von Bülow, or at least wish I could.*

Something prickled at her, a sudden silence in the wood. She went flat and leopard-crawled through the soft moist duff of the forest floor for a few yards until a big knotted root gave her cover, then leveled the shotgun over it.

"*Wer da?*" von Bülow called . . . which made him a useful decoy.

The *Ride of the Valkyries* answered. Horst came through very quietly indeed and went to one knee as she rose to hers. He was all business despite the puckish choice of recognition signal.

"They're on the road," he said, clearing the duff and drawing a quick sketch map in the dirt with a stick. "Two automobiles, large touring cars, but only three men guarding them. About a thousand meters from here."

"Only two vehicles?"

"Only two in sight." He shrugged; they had limited time to scout around.

Which *might* kill them, but delay *certainly* would.

"How far can you throw a grenade, Horst?" she asked.

"A little less than fifty meters accurately with these egg types," he said, which was impressive. "But the autos would burn."

"*One* of them would burn, hopefully," she said.

"And the other could be very useful, *ja*," he replied thoughtfully; she'd relied on his being quick on the uptake. "Risky, but much must be risked in war. The frontier is only six kilometers away, very little time by motor."

"And more than a lifetime by foot," she said, which prompted a grim smile.

"I lead, you cover," he said, as they exchanged rifle for shotgun again. "Start shooting when I throw the first grenade. I prefer it this way."

"So do I, Horst, so do I," she said with feeling—and truthfully.

Not being concerned with proving my manhood, ¡gracias a Dios!

Not for the first time, Horst disconcerted her a little by saying before he turned away:

"And perhaps your courage is more pure than mine, eh, *Süsse?*"

S tay here," Luz whispered. "Come as fast as you can when we finish the Frenchmen."

Von Bülow sank down behind a tree, looking tightly calm. "God go with you," he said.

Closer to the edge of the wood the beeches grew shorter, squatter, thicker and branched more. One with a divided trunk would give a good view at about the right distance; she pushed the rifle ahead of her, jumped, gripped knobs through the smooth gray bark, and climbed, as agile as the girl who'd played chase with a pet raccoon through the live oaks of their Santa Barbara home until her mother called her down. Fifteen feet up, the trunk branch split again, and she edged up to that; there were leafy branches right behind it, so her head wouldn't be out-lined when she raised it into view. The road was just ahead, stretching north-south in two rutted sandy strips with scruffy grass between them, from the look of it made by nothing more elaborate than forest-ers' carts and farm wagons, cows and sheep, and generations of blond peasants in wooden shoes whacking out anything that tried to grow enough to block it.

The two dark-green automobiles with black trim were there, both parked heading south; Renault 40CV touring cars, big open-topped brutes that could carry seven passengers, with massive V-6 engines that could push them very fast indeed, better than sixty miles an hour on a good flat road. They'd been expensive before the war and unob-tainable since with the Renault factories making other things, but she supposed the French secret service would have first call on what was available. At a guess, the French agents had parked them there and then crossed the woods she'd just traversed to remove the rails before the train arrived. It would have been a rushed, improvised operation, which was all the better—people were always more likely to make mistakes when they raced the clock. They might have gotten all the gear necessary and all the men she'd seen here in those two, if they'd started out around the same time the train did . . . and by then it would have been obvious they'd lost their snatch team.

Less than a hundred yards from her, the three Frenchmen were waiting, one in each car—those would be the drivers; it wasn't a common skill anywhere, and less so here in Europe than back home—and one man taking a knee between them, with a rifle in the crook of his arm. Luz lowered her head and looked down; Horst was behind a tree and looking up at her. She held up three fingers—remembering to use her thumb and the first two in the German fashion—and then folded a fist with the thumb inside and tapped it against the tree in the gesture for "good luck"—the American thumb-and-forefinger *OK* symbol meant something entirely different and very rude here.

Horst took a grenade in his right hand, pulled the pin, and dodged forward, moving in smooth darts from tree to tree with the shotgun held at the balance in his left. Luz edged back up to just below the fork in the tree, making herself breathe deeply and slowly—the Japanese combat instructors Uncle Teddy had imported for the Black Chamber emphasized the benefits of that, and it did help.

I am getting very tired of this, occurred to her; then she suppressed it. *Millions of soldiers all over the world are probably a lot more tired of it than you!*

And they were doing it knee-deep in mud saturated with bits of corpse, trying to breathe in the claustrophobic closeness of a gas mask and watching obscenely fat rats run by, not dining in the Hotel Victoria or taking first-class trains. A moment of waiting, controlling her breathing, not looking at anything in particular. Then a loud but muffled *bumpf!*

Luz surged back up to the fork in the trunk of the beech tree and leveled the rifle. The northernmost car had been thrown a little to one side and there was a trickle of smoke—the grenade must have gone off right under the body. The driver was out but staggering with his hands to his head. She ignored him for now. The kneeling rifleman had gone prone and had his weapon leveled, waiting for Horst to expose himself to throw again. Fortunately she was twenty feet up, which gave her an excellent field of fire.

Crack.

Crack.

He shot and she did in almost the same instant. Her round kicked dirt out of the roadway beside the Frenchman, and he rolled frantically backward. Luz dismissed self-blame—it was a clout shot and she should have made it—and squeezed off the rest of the magazine at the moving target. By the time the bolt locked back and she reloaded, he'd gotten into the ditch on the other side of the road. When she put the rifle back through the crook he was shooting at *her*, and his third round gouged right through the two-foot-thick beech a foot above her head in a shower of splinters that stung the left side of her face. Her belly tensed where it was pressed against the slightly—very slightly—thicker main stem. Amateurs tended to underestimate what rifle rounds could penetrate . . .

Just then the Frenchman seemed to levitate out of the ditch and roll frantically away. The *bumpf* of a grenade came less than a second later, and dirt shot upward from the ditch near where he'd lain. He sprang up and aimed for the woods Horst was throwing from, apparently more worried about another grenade than a bullet.

Crack.

This time she hit, low in the pelvis or thigh, and he started to crumple. There were no second prizes when people shot at each other.

Crack. Crack.

The French rifleman went still, and Luz was freed from the peculiar focus of a marksman's duel. Two more grenades went off at almost the same time under the first Renault, and this time there was bright fire and then a big soft *whump* of expanding flame. Enough gasoline had spilled and vaporized to really go up. And to splash when the tank ruptured; the dazed driver caught a gout of it, and rolled on the ground screaming and beating at himself.

The driver of the intact car was standing, firing a Star automatic at the woods, presumably at Horst, which was futile, unless he was one of the rare really good pistol shots. Then he jumped down and ran for it across the road, the long yellow chauffeur's duster he wore flapping around his ankles, a cap on his head, and goggles pushed up. She swung the rifle's muzzle toward him, but he staggered and clouds of dust burst out of the back of his coat as she watched. Then his knees buckled and he fell flat, hitting the ground with his face full-force and not moving. Horst walked into view breaking open the shotgun and sliding two more shells into the breech and snapping it closed. He walked over to the other Frenchman and fired both barrels into his struggling, smoking body, which was an act of soldier's mercy.

Luz slid backward in a controlled fall and landed on the ground crouched, her skirt flaring up for a second. Von Bülow was already hurrying toward her.

"I knew you had disposed of the enemy when the firing stopped," he said.

"Or they had disposed of us," she said, jerking her chin toward the road.

He fell in beside her as she walked quickly, seeming spry enough, and gave a pinched smile.

"In that case, I would not be losing much. I am . . . it has been a very long time since I was a young *Fähnrich* serving my King and Fatherland against the Danes."

At her well-hidden surprise, he chuckled a little. "Yes, gracious miss, I was not born such a dry old stick as I am now. Though even in my youth in the Wars of Unification I was never such a Siegfried as the good Hauptmann von Dückler, nor so fortunate as to fall in with a beautiful and fearless shield-maiden."

They came out onto the road and met the unpleasant stink of burning gasoline and the worse one of burning flesh. Von Bülow's nose twitched and he finished softly:

"And there are some things one never forgets. There was a barn full of injured men . . . we could do nothing . . ."

Well, that's the fuel for the locomotive of history, Luz thought. *And plenty of bad dreams.*

"Are you injured?" Horst said sharply, turning as they came up.

Surprised, she brushed at her cheek and saw a little blood on the wrist. "No, just scratches—splinters from a near-miss in the tree I was using. He was too good, I should have gotten him with the first shot."

"Many shots, few hits," he said, shrugging, and sliding in behind the wheel of the remaining Renault. "You're alive and he is not and that's what counts. Let's go. That burning car is marking us for all to see."

The black smoke was already fairly high in the sky; the larger pyre of the train was to their east. She helped von Bülow in, feeling a bit less inclined to *throw* him in than she would have been yesterday, and rolled into the backseat herself, kneeling and facing to the rear. Acceleration threw her breasts and stomach against the cushions instantly, and nearly blew the hat off her head. She removed it and tossed it to the floor; that reminded her to unstrap the suitcase she'd been carrying like a soldier's pack since they left the train and let it fall too.

"You are attached to your underwear," Horst cast over his shoulder as he manipulated clutch and shift.

The big engine roared smoothly, well kept and still warm from its drive from Amsterdam. It probably didn't have all that much fuel, but they didn't need to go far.

"Only to the parts next to my skin right now," Luz shot back without turning. "But I have deathless works of literature in there," she went on.

"Trashy popular fiction," he called back, and they both laughed.

Then . . .

"No, no, no! *¡Mierda!*" she swore. "We keep killing these *Gabacho* pigs and they keep coming!"

Three motorcycles came through the smoke of the burning auto, crowding the eastern edge of the road to avoid the flames and swaying back upright as they followed. Sand spurted from under their rear wheels as they accelerated. Luz loved driving autos and motorcycles herself, work aside, and recognized the model—Alcyon's dispatch-rider type. Not faster than the Renault car on a good hard road . . . but with much better acceleration and much better at any sort of rough country. Perfectly logical to bring along on a mission like this, an ambush in the countryside; you could take those anywhere a horse could go, and most places that a man on foot could, and much faster.

She hadn't even realized what language she'd mostly been yelling in until both the Germans laughed.

"Now you know how we feel all the time, *Süsse*," Horst called over his shoulder.

"You don't have any more grenades?"

"No," Horst said; she hadn't thought so from the count, but it was easy to miss things when you were fighting.

She thought, juggling times and distances as the driver concentrated on making the best speed he could. It wasn't necessary to tell Horst to slow down; the cycles were going to catch them anyway, and too soon. Luz leveled the rifle and emptied the magazine at them, not expecting to hit moving targets from the bouncing, lurching platform of the car, just to keep them away for a moment. She used it to pull a ribbon from the band of her hat and tie it around her brow to keep the wind from behind her putting hair in her eyes, something that wouldn't have been as much of a problem if it were longer and up.

But the Frenchmen were brave men and rode well, and they'd be desperate now. All three of them wore leather jackets and leather helmets and goggles. As she watched they all drew pistols . . . which was something of a relief; she'd been worried that one of them would have grenades too, and get close enough to toss one into the car.

"Five-second delay on the Mills grenade?"

"Four to six," Horst said, then added pedantically: "English quality control is not up to our standards."

Oh, wonderful, she thought, shooting again, the rifle hammering at her shoulder; it was impossible to keep a proper cheek weld with the car doing better than forty on this surface, and the muzzle wavered no matter what she did.

What I need for this is a Thompson gun, something I could spray like a hose. ¡Por Dios! *They'd turn up their toes at* that.

The Frenchmen were counting her shots. At the fifth they all gunned their cycles, the one in the center firing his pistol, the other two spreading out to come up on either hand. She reloaded with the rifle down and out of their sight, probably faster than they thought she would, but then pulled the second grenade out of her jacket just as they broke out of the shadow of the woods into bright sunlight.

"¡Estoy hasta la madre de harta, aqui! ¡Toma esto, Gabachos estupidos!"

She'd grown up speaking English and Spanish interchangeably, sometimes from sentence to sentence, and often didn't even notice which one she was thinking in. But for some things Spanish was just more *satisfying,* particularly some words and phrases she'd learned from the staff and in the markets rather than from her mother.

Luz pulled the pin on the second grenade, hoping that between aiming their pistols and keeping their motorcycles upright one-handed they wouldn't worry what she was doing, or would just think she was still reloading. Making her hand relax enough for the spring-loaded lever to fly off and set the grenade's fuse going was hard, but flipping it out was much easier, as if hidden hands were guiding hers. The one coming up on the left had just enough time to show a gape of surprise beneath the goggles before she lobbed the grenade at him and instantly ducked.

Bampf!

The explosion came so fast that she was very, very glad of that quick flip and could feel sweat running down her flanks. Right on the heels of it there was a sharp metallic *tink-tink* sound, and Horst cursed mildly.

"Der Teufel!" Then he shouted on the heels of the oath: "That hit something! The brakes are not working!"

Luz was back with the rifle leveled as she called out with a wild laugh: "So what? We want to go fast!"

The man she'd tossed the grenade at was alive; his motorcycle had gone over in a long slide, and he was lying clutching at one leg, just a glimpse through the dust plume the car was kicking up. The other two came charging forward again as soon as they saw she didn't have another grenade, but it was taking them longer now that the heavier vehicle had had time to build speed. They fired their pistols and she replied and nobody hit anything. Then they abruptly pulled up, slewing their machines sideways in rooster tails of sandy dirt. One of them sprang down and went to one knee, firing with his automatic braced over his left forearm; the other tore off his leather helmet when he dismounted, dancing on it in a frenzy of rage, which was about as effective. They'd both have to leave, and quickly, if they didn't want the Dutch police to add them to the mysterious strangers who'd sabotaged their train and killed their citizens. The man firing got up and started trudging, pushing his motorcycle back toward his injured comrade while his companion still jigged and screamed oaths.

"Heads down!" Horst shouted—almost screamed—himself.

Luz looked around just in time to duck frantically as the big touring machine struck the leveled pole of the customs barrier at more than forty miles an hour. There was a massive crack as the striped ashwood shaft splintered and went by in a shower of fragments, then a blurred glimpse of figures in field gray leaping aside. And a scream of tortured metal as Horst stopped the car the only way he could, downshifting brutally as he cut the throttle. Luz yelped as she was thrown backward into the middle seat and then tumbled as the car pinwheeled four times in complete circles before coming to rest with smoke leaking out from under the hood and cooling metal *ting*ing and *click*ing. The silence was enormous for a moment, before thudding boots and panting breath surrounded them.

A dozen bayonetted rifles were leveled at them amid glares and curses. Old-fashioned rifles, Gewehr 88's, in the hands of men in their middle years or midteens, gray beards or beardless chins under out-dated spiked helmets. Luz carefully raised her hands and was glad she had before the noncom in charge of the Landsturm squad limped up and barked:

"Hände hoch, Schweinehunde!"

The limp, the missing two fingers on his left hand, and the three thick scars that ran down the left side of his face beneath the brimless field cap to the edge of his small black mustache showed why a veteran *Obergefreiter* in his twenties with the ribbon of the Iron Cross First Class through a tunic button was commanding a bunch of fourth-grade re-servists on a minor border crossing with a neutral country, though he also had a curious accent, more upcountry-village Austrian than Ger-man. The way he held his Luger and the flat, expressionless look in his blue eyes, like glass marbles, told Luz that three more deaths would be nothing to this man. Less than the bother of telling his men to bury the bodies . . . or filling out a report.

Horst and von Bülow stood and carefully raised their hands as well. "All can be explained, Corporal," the young nobleman said genially, in his officer's command tone.

Then, grinning, to Luz: "Welcome to the *Reich, Süsse*! We're safe!"

Luz smiled back, as the noncom's face showed doubt and the begin-ning of a brace that would end with something on the order of *Jawohl, Herr Hauptmann! Zu Befehl, Herr Hauptmann!*

And thought behind her answering grin:

No, you're *safe, Horst. I'm in the belly of the beast.*

SIX

Königlich Sächsische Staatseisenbahnen
(Royal Saxon State Railways)
Pockau, Kingdom of Saxony, German *Reich*
SEPTEMBER 8TH, 1916(B)

There are special trains, and then there are special trains, *Süsse*," Horst von Dückler said patiently.

At his gesture the orderly cleared away the remains of a rather skeletal breakfast, which the two Germans had wolfed down with good appetite: boiled eggs, heavy coarse bread with a suspicious taste of potato, and tasteless margarine rather than butter. At least it was difficult to do anything very bad to a boiled egg.

"We are on a special train. That is a *special* special train."

He nodded out the window of the lounge car at the one chuffing by as they waited on the siding; he was looking relaxed and more natural in the uniform he'd resumed as soon as they crossed the border. The priority train was pulled by a big—by European standards—4-4-2 superheated locomotive; behind it was obviously a headquarters on wheels, with office and map rooms, kitchens and sleeping quarters, and probably a message section with wireless and ready attachments for telegraph and telephone wherever it stopped. And just behind the locomotive tender and at the end were flatbeds with breast-high steel bulwarks. Each mounted an antiaircraft gun—twin-barrel pom-poms, Maxim machine guns scaled up to fire 37mm light cannon shells and mounted on X-shaped high-traverse beds.

That meant the train went places where Entente aeroplanes were conceivable, though the storm of shells would also be a conclusive argument against partisans, and they had sloped steel shields for ground work. Their crews and the guard details weren't boys or superannuated Landsturm; their gray-green uniforms were clean and newish, but they wore the simplified loose style now used in action, and topped with beetling gray-painted coal-scuttle steel helmets. Many of them carried the drum-fed machine pistols the Germans had copied from the American Thompson and had stick-grenades slung through loops on their harness or crewed the light Lewis machine guns they'd also duplicated.

If you steal, steal the best, Luz thought. *And they* came up with that quick-change barrel and we copied *that* and so it goes. Isn't progress grand?

She added thoughtfully aloud: "Those aren't play soldiers."

"Real *Frontschweine*," he confirmed.

That was German military slang for actual fighting soldiers as opposed to bureaucrats and storekeepers in uniform, meaning literally *front-line pig*. Horst could claim the title himself; he'd let slip that he'd been wounded leading an infantry company in the first months of the war before going back to intelligence work. He hadn't gone into details, but even nobly born officers didn't get the awards on his tunic from behind a desk, nor the puckered bullet and shrapnel scars on his torso.

The American forces had an equivalent slang term, picked up from their enemies during the Intervention and turned from an insult into wry self-identification and an ironic boast: *sicario*, killer, the ones who actually took and gave death.

Horst went on thoughtfully: "Given this duty as a rest, I wager, but you still don't see guard details like that for just anyone. This conference is important, I tell you, to draw this sort of attention—particularly just now."

"I need to get at my trunks," Luz said. "And send off some laundry."

And find out what this precious mission is!

Horst chuckled indulgently and went back to reading his morning newspapers. He'd been chortling over them since they got on this train, laid on for the three of them in Emmerich-am-Rhein. She could understand why; the headlines were banner-sized in that angular Fraktur script Germans tended to use when they wanted to be solemn and historic and nationalistic or all three at once. Von Bülow was handling them reverently, like some sort of footnotes to Scripture.

She could read them easily enough, and if accurate, which she thought depressingly likely, they certainly justified the fuss: BUCHA-REST FALLS and RUMANIAN ARMY SURRENDERS UNCONDITIONALLY TO GENERAL VON FRANÇOIS had been there the first day, followed by VON MACKENSEN PHALANX DRIVES BRUSILOV'S ARMY IN UTTER ROUT and VINNITSA FALLS TO OUR TROOPS.

Yesterday they'd added: TSAR ABDICATES and GRAND DUKE NICHO-LAS TO BE REGENT FOR TSAREVITCH and RIOTS IN MOSCOW, MUTINY IN ST. PETERSBURG GARRISON. This morning it had been: RUMORS THAT GRAND DUKE ASKS FOR ARMISTICE BETWEEN RUSSIAN EMPIRE AND CENTRAL POWERS TO SAVE ROMANOV DYNASTY and excited variations on that.

When that *rumor hits the Russian armies, it's Katie-bar-the-door,* she thought. *Who wants to be the last Ivan Ivanovitch to die for the* former *Little Father in a lost war? Do they have enough cohesion left to stop men who've decided they'd rather go back to their villages? How many men have the Russians lost al-*ready, *since the Germans cut them to pieces at Tannenberg right at the beginning and then broke their bones at Gorlice-Tarnow and Grodno last year? At least four or five million, counting prisoners, after the pincers closed at Brest-Litovsk. They've won battles with the Turks and Austrians a couple of times, but that doesn't really count; it's like trying to make up for a beating by kicking your opponent's dog and assaulting his elderly aunt.*

"These are events of world historical significance," von Bülow said, wiping up the last of his egg.

In that annoyingly sententious tone he used when in his Germanic Sage persona, as if he'd mentally added a long white beard and a gray robe and staff and a mystic crystal ball, and possibly Wotan's eyepatch and floppy hat.

Don't underestimate him, there's a first-rate brain under that white thatch. And one full of romantic yeast. He's an evil man but oddly innocent about it; it's not because he takes pleasure in cruelty or is greedy for himself.

"Soon we will be in possession of the Heartland! Who holds the Heartland, rules the world-island; who rules the world-island, commands the world."

Yes, yes, Herr Privatdozent, I too can read Mackinder. Who's an Englishman, remember. ¡Dios me libre de un hombre de un solo libro! *Though I admit if I were German I'd be breaking out the castanets and dancing a flamenco too . . . no, actually if I were German I'd be swilling bad wartime beer and yelling:* Hoch! Hoch!

"Soon we'll have all the food and petroleum and raw materials we need," Horst said a bit more practically. "Rumania is backward but rich in grain and livestock; they were a major exporter before the war, and now we'll get their harvest for this year. Germany's cities won't be eating turnips when winter comes, we'll press them like beet pulp in a mill to make sure of that."

"Or take them by the throat and squeeze until their eyeballs pop out," Luz said helpfully.

"Exactly," Horst said with happy unself-consciousness. "And Rumania has some of the world's richest oilfields, which, from the reports, we've captured mostly intact, because the Rumanians ran so fast. I have heard that there is a regulation in the Rumanian Army forbidding officers under the rank of major from using rouge and eye shadow on duty, and I can believe it!"

Von Bülow chuckled dryly. Luz raised an eyebrow.

"I use rouge occasionally, Horst," she said. "And eye shadow. And sweetie . . . I never found it slowed me down much."

She remembered a Black Chamber operative who'd been so swish he'd publicly asked to borrow her compact powder-puff.

And he crawled into that revolucionario *camp at night, the one I got the location of down in the jungles in Quintana Roo, and slit every second man's throat with a straight razor so the others would have a surprise when they woke up. Even the Philippine Rangers were impressed.*

And those little grinning brown devils from Mindanao didn't impress easily. Horst gave her an odd look, and then an acknowledging nod, and went on:

"Though of course you are not a Rumanian . . . There's more wheat and cattle and horses in the Ukraine, and coal and iron and manganese, and if . . . when . . . now that the Russians have collapsed, the Caucasus are open to the Turks and they . . . which means Germany . . . will have copper and cotton and bauxite and half the petroleum in the world in Baku. Now the English can take their so-vaunted blockade, which they thought would strangle us and starve our children, and ram it . . ."

He glanced at her out of the corner of his eye and continued after a slight pause: "Somewhere sensitive, wrapped in barbed wire."

"Much good their battleships will do them then," Luz added, which was precisely what Elisa Carmody would think; and true, if short-sighted. "But the gringos . . ."

"Yes!" Horst said, slamming his fist down on the table, the blow a bit muffled by the papers but making the remaining chinaware bounce and rattle.

Ernst von Bülow nodded. "Exactly," he said. He glanced at her. "You have summed up the next great challenge facing the Fatherland, gracious miss. And that is why we are here. Drastic measures must be taken, ruthless measures to grasp this opportunity to consolidate our hold on the Heartland while it is within our reach."

She didn't expect them to say anything more in detail yet, and didn't ask, which she thought they appreciated. Instead she sipped at the last of the coffee, or at least what the orderly running the little kitchen annex in the rear carriage claimed was coffee; there might be some actual *Coffea arabica* in the brew, or not. She'd diluted it heavily since at least the cream did come from a cow, and recently. Horst caught her slight grimace and chuckled sympathetically—Germans *really* appreciated their coffee. As if to confirm her thought he sang a children's tune:

"C-A-F-F-E-E, trink nicht so viel Kaffee!
Nicht für Kinder ist der Türkentrank,
Schwächt die Nerven, macht dich blass und krank,
Sei doch kein Muselmann, der ihn nicht lassen kann."

"I picked up a couple of kilos of beans from Java in Amsterdam for my chief," he added with a laugh, acknowledging the vileness of the roasted chicory mixed with burned, powdered mystery vegetation. "And it will be appreciated!"

On her previous visits before the war she'd much preferred the way Germans made coffee, slowly and meticulously, to the usual weak or burnt American fashion, though Viennese style with whipped cream was even better. Austrians were still the patron gods of baked goods, café culture, and music even if they weren't much in geopolitical terms these days.

Soberly, and looking into her eyes, Horst added: "Please be careful with Colonel Nicolai, *Süsse.* A very able man, he rose by sheer ability from modest beginnings, but . . . hard. Not overly concerned with gentlemanly scruples. A *very* hard man. And very powerful these days."

Which accords exactly with our own briefings, Luz thought. *Except merciless bastard is more the way they put it. And deeply involved in German politics now that his patrons von Hindenburg and Ludendorff are running things—in charge of their censorship system, for starters. And there were rumors about his helping organize this new Fatherland Party they're talking about; I'll dance the flamenco naked in Times Square if the Herr Privatdozent isn't involved with the Pan-German League too. Von Bülow wants Germany to be great and would like to have power so he could bring that about; I think Colonel Walter Nicolai wants Walter Nicolai . . . General Walter Nicolai . . . to be powerful for Walter Nicolai . . . which means making Germany great.*

The orderly came through and snapped to a brace with true Middle European *Ordnungsliebe*.

"We will proceed to the *Schloss* now, Herr Hauptmann, I am informed."

The train chuffed slowly into motion and off the siding onto the winding main line up the narrow curving valley of the little Flöha River, which was just a bit too big to be a creek by American standards. Pockau was a pretty village of farmers and laborers and small workshops making toys and lace and glassware, surrounded by sloping pastures and fields and forested hilltops, with old churches and steep-roofed cottages showing they got a lot of snow in this region. It would have looked more picturesque a few years ago, when there wasn't a creeping shabbiness born of shortages of everything, and when the population hadn't held so few healthy adult males and so many women in the deep black of mourning garb, and everyone hadn't looked underfed and overworked.

This part of southern Saxony lay in the foothills of the Erzgebirge. Non-Germans called them the Ore Mountains for the minerals that had once made them famous, though they hardly qualified as more than massive worn-down hills by most American standards, with an occasional sandstone cliff. The geography reminded her of the Appalachians, or parts of New England, but more of the land was cleared than would have been the case across the Atlantic: mostly in faded green pasture, but often for fields of oats or rye or potatoes. Heights rose higher and wilder to the south, where the Boehmerwald loomed at the edge of sight when breaks in the hills allowed, to mark the Austrian border.

"Not many horses," she said, looking at the passing scene and comparing it with previous visits to this general area in peacetime.

Women in headcloths and drab skirts were cutting the last of the rye with bent backs over flashing sickles, or carting off huge bundles of it on their backs, or digging potatoes with thick-tined pitchforks and tossing them into wicker baskets or tattered burlap sacks dragged away by children. More children went behind the reapers, gleaning up every single grain of rye that had fallen out of the stalks. The only animal-drawn cart she could see was pulled by a pair of skinny oxen, if you didn't count one little thing drawn by a large but discouraged-looking black dog led by a little boy.

At least nobody's hungry enough to eat dog *yet,* Luz thought; she liked dogs, who were more honest than men in her experience. *Apart from the railway, there's nothing in sight that might not have been here five hundred years ago, or a thousand.*

Horst sighed, taken out of his happy daze of victory. "Yes, the farm horses were mostly called up like the young men, to draw guns and transport wagons, and more since. It is hard for those who remain, especially on the small farms of the peasants as you see now—there are plans to use more prisoners of war for farm labor here, though it is more difficult to manage on small holdings than on the large estates like my family's lands. We employed migrants before the war for the harvest, Poles mostly. Almighty Lord God knows we have plenty of *prisoners*, at least; we took a million and a half just around Warsaw last summer, and a million in the Bialystok pocket a little later. And they all have to be fed anyway."

"It is only right for the under-man to serve the purposes of the higher," von Bülow agreed. "And for the defeated to serve the victors."

They passed into forest again; spruce plantations on the higher ground, oak and beech and other leaf trees lower down, and then a steep narrow riverside clearing with a little stone-built railway station that had probably been put up a generation ago to serve the *Schloss* and its dependent villages but already looking old. They climbed down and stood amid an orderly bustle of men in uniform, motorcars and horse-drawn wagons coming and going, and a very pink young lieutenant who strode up to them looking at a clipboard, his wispy mustache trained up into sad little points in what he probably thought was his monarch's style.

"Hauptmann von Dückler?" he said, exchanging salutes. "Yes, we have transport and quarters in the *Schloss* laid on for you and the Herr Privatdozent and this Mexican who is expected. You are lucky! We're quartering people as far away as the resort hotels in Marienberg!"

He looked down an aquiline nose at Luz, screwing in a monocle as he did so. Junkers used them the way ladies had wielded fans in the old days, to express emotion without words.

"Ah, there may be some difficulty finding space for your *friend* . . ."

Luz gave him a smile of poisonous sweetness. She hadn't long to wait; Horst barked:

"My *colleague* the good *Fräulein* whose name you are not cleared to know is an important intelligence source who has come here, at considerable risk, from the Western Hemisphere to provide data crucial to the operation being discussed . . . which *she* is cleared to be briefed on, and *you*, I would guess, Lieutenant, are not. I am *under instructions* to bring her as rapidly as possible to Colonel Nicolai . . . Lieutenant, and I would be surprised if there was not documentation to that effect."

The young man went from pink to pale at the name of the much-feared intelligence chief. The German concept of military rank was surprisingly flexible, in some respects; authority attached as much to function as title. Nicolai's functions were manifold, mostly secret, and occasionally involved sending people to the Somme front where an in-experienced junior officer pitchforked into a strange regiment had a life expectancy that averaged about four weeks. Or just ordering that some individual disappear, now and then.

"You will act accordingly," Horst finished.

Tone and inflection joined in a way that suggested gross inferiority on the lieutenant's part and desperate consequences if he didn't obey sometime in the next few seconds; German was a wonderful language for telling people what to do in fine shades of who-is-boss.

The lieutenant's respectful but man-to-man demeanor shifted to ramrod stiffness and a heel-click as the flat, cold words continued. Von Bülow stared at him silently with a look like an entomologist about to pin a specimen to a corkboard for eternal display.

"*Jawohl*, Herr Hauptmann! At once, Herr Hauptmann!" the young man barked, eyes staring rigidly ahead, then departed with a brisk stride.

"German discipline is a fearsome thing," Luz said, and laid a hand on Horst's arm; he was virtually bristling. "You have a knightly soul, dear Horst, but don't cut him into dog meat with your *Glockenschläger* just yet. I don't want to attract too much attention. It might have been better to simply let him assume I was your mistress."

Orders were called, and a blocky businesslike Stoewer staff car with a driver pulled up. Horst handed her in, laughing ruefully.

"I would have been gentler if that well-groomed puppy had showed any sign of front-line service," he said. "Ones like him give the *Edel* a bad name, like a spoiled apple spreading rot in a sound barrel."

Von Bülow nodded. "One such helps the Social Democrats more than a dozen dirty Jew agitators with egg in their beards ranting Marx-gibberish on street corners."

"*Ja*," Horst said. "I may be misjudging him, but considering how many platoons and even companies at the front are commanded by NCOs now, I do not think so."

"I do not think so either," von Bülow said. "The *Fräulein* is twice the soldier he is and has done the enemies of the Fatherland more injury, as I have seen with my own eyes."

Luz felt a slight stab of guilt, of the type you couldn't avoid in under-cover intelligence work unless you were a complete reptile. Which many people in the business were, of course.

But I really don't want to start to hiss cheerfully at my reflection in the mirror every morning with a flicker of a forked tongue to groom my scales.

"Thank you, Herr Privatdozent," she said as she settled into the seat. "But please bear in mind that what I have done, I have done in my own country's service, not that of the German *Reich*, to which I owe no na-tional loyalty beyond our present alliance. I am willing to fight French-men or Englishmen, or Italians or Russians for that matter, in the service of *my* country, but if—hypothetically, of course, *¡Dios me libre!*—Germany were our enemy, I would fight Germans too."

"*Aber natürlich*," he said and nodded respectful acknowledgment. "You are a true patriot, Fräulein."

Which is true, but not at all the way he thinks it is. Sometimes in this line of work irony becomes more pervasive than air.

Then he raised a hand as they turned south and west to cross the Flöha on an iron bridge.

"Schloss Rauenstein," he said, pointing across the narrow valley and falling into an academic's lecture tone. "First recorded here at the very beginning of the fourteenth century, but parts may be older; built to command the crossing of the Flöha and the road between Frieberg and Annaberg. The estate is currently a possession of the von Herder family, who have given the building over to the *Reich* for the duration of the war."

The *Schloss* stood on a low hill flanked by more wooded heights on the western bank of the river. It didn't have the naked stone or high curtain wall and multiple towers the idea of *castle* evoked in an English-speaking mind, but the lower parts were on an elevated terrace cut out of the hill crest and were made with white stucco over walls of either stone or brick that looked formidably massive and were pierced only by a few narrow slits.

Above, sitting on the older and grimmer part like a striped cloth cap on an armored knight's head, was a rambling half-timbered country mansion, with white plaster over the noggin between the black oak beams and topped with steep slate roofs. One square tower rose from the central roof, but nips and tucks and little protruding bits showed centuries of building and rebuilding, as means and fires and wars allowed or changes of ownership demanded. Off a little and still mostly hidden was an annex, a biggish building in its own right, whose larger and symmetrical windows and hipped roof and yellow stucco showed that it had been built in a later age, evoking powdered wigs and minuets rather than *Raubritter* in bearskin cloaks feasting coarsely with their thuggish retainers.

Even that newest part was old by the standards she'd grown up with, probably older than the first of the California missions. She shivered a little; knights in chain mail had dwelt here, and might have left on

Crusade—to the east, or to the wars against the Baltic pagans. Vastly bearded *Landsknecht* pikemen had marched by in puffed and slashed finery with two-handed swords across their backs, and cuirassiers with plumed helmets and wheel-lock pistols had trotted off to rescue Vienna from the Turks; those walls would have seen the mercenary hordes of the Wars of Religion, pigtailed musketeers of the Age of Reason when Germany was a maze of little courts and free cities . . . and all that time the lords of this place had held the surrounding lands in thrall.

We've had less time in America, but done more with it, she thought stoutly. *Though* . . .

"Is that a power line?" she said; wires looped up from the river through the woods on tall poles that were visible here and there amid the trees.

"Yes, the von Herders modernized extensively a few years before the war," von Bülow said. "There is a small electrical station on the Flöha."

"And we have put in more communications, of course," Horst added.

The automobile swept up a forested gravel road and suddenly confronted a towering wall, real stone this time; she realized it must be the retaining wall that secured the platform on which the *Schloss* was built. An arched tunnel pierced it, leading up to the surface the actual buildings occupied. No doubt there had been iron-bound doors and a portcullis once, which would have looked more natural than the sandbagged Maxim machine-gun nest and moveable barbed-wire obstacles that did the duty now, or the electric lights and their cords stapled to the stone. A polite but implacable sergeant with the silvery gorget of the *Feldgendarmerie* around his neck checked their credentials; then the car swept up through the tunnel and on to a courtyard. That had a fountain and statue, and more windows showed on the inner side of the buildings.

Another aide was waiting, this one looking rather more businesslike.

"Colonel Nicolai will see you and the Mexican agent immediately, and the Herr Privatdozent," the man said after exchanging salutes with Horst and a heel-click and bow with the scholar. "Everything is moving very quickly now, Herr Hauptmann, as you will understand from the news."

Like most of the men in uniform he looked almost indecently cheerful, under his stiff propriety. He was also looking around for the Mexican agent he'd been told to expect.

"There seems to be some error, the agent is listed as being assigned joint quarters with the Irish—"

Probably expecting a barefoot, sinister indio *in a serape with a tattered straw sombrero whose crest is two feet tall and a machete between his teeth and a long droopy mustache. Or possibly a dashing vaquero, dressed* charro*-style with lots of buttons and holding a lance, or a somber Don in a short embroidered jacket and long black cloak flourishing a rapier. Germans all read those adventure novels by Karl May, like our western penny dreadfuls but worse; I don't think May ever crossed the Atlantic. He got his ideas* from *the penny dreadfuls. At least Edgar Rice Burroughs actually* was *a frontier cavalry trooper and a cowboy and a prospector.*

"*I* am the Mexican agent, Herr Lieutenant," Luz said flatly. "The name is Carmody De Soto-Dominguez? You'll have it there, I suspect."

This time Horst was simply amused. The aide did another expressionless heel-click at learning that the glamorous and stylishly clad young woman was a revolutionary emissary and led the way.

And apparently Horst and I are in separate quarters. That will be useful. Fun and frolic and putting him off-guard are one thing, but a spy needs to do night work, which is hard if someone on the other side is sleeping on the next pillow or fondling your buttocks.

The interior of the *Schloss* was crowded with uniformed Germans from staff officers down to messengers and orderlies, bustling about and carrying papers and talking earnestly with each other or into telephones whose lines were looped along brackets on the walls, or huddling together over tables and eagerly pointing out advances on maps that were a tangle of curving black lines ending in arrow points. Seemingly they were divided into those who'd been here for some time and those who'd just arrived in the train—literally—of some extremely exalted panjandrums.

Otherwise Schloss Rauenstein lived up to her expectations; whitewashed walls, lots of antlers and stuffed heads of bear and boar and wolf, huge gloomy halls down below and huge somewhat less gloomy ones above, and fireplaces big enough to walk into or roast whole oxen in or both, though apart from the ancestral portraits and suits of armor and the bits and pieces of animals the lords of Rauenstein had killed over the years, the furniture had mostly been removed and replaced with office gear. There was a continuous rattle of typewriters in the background, a smell of ink, ozone, tobacco and boot polish on leather, wool uniforms and clean male sweat, and the odd whiff of scented mustache wax used to make the points turn up in Kaiser Wilhelm's style.

Though fewer of those than there used to be, I think, Luz noted. *Perhaps that's intelligence too.*

"Colonel Nicolai's office is currently in the top room of the central tower," the aide said.

"So I would expect. Best for security reasons," Horst agreed. Then, sotto voce to her: "And to prevent people of high rank wasting his time by dropping in."

That location involved leading them up interminable narrow turning stairs; Luz and Horst and the aide, who was in his late twenties and wore spectacles, all took them without effort but waited courteously on several landings to let von Bülow catch his breath. Heavyset generals with gray hair might indeed find it a little inaccessible. Two of those landings involved pairs of hard-faced guards with machine pistols who insisted on seeing papers for all three of them, despite knowing the aide. *Their* uniforms showed no *Waffenfarbe* or unit designations at all, much like the Rangers who worked with the Black Chamber in the field sometimes.

Tsk, Luz thought, irritated but unsurprised. *Everyone carefully following procedures really is inconvenient for a busy spy; it complicates everything and slows you down. Which is why procedures are important for security, of course. They don't make things impossible, but they do make them a lot harder.*

Colonel Nicolai rose from behind his desk as they entered, a considerable courtesy, and answered Horst's salute; his office had probably been a study of some sort, since it was lined with bookshelves. Those mostly held document files and scrolled maps and reference works now, and the large desk had several telephones. Light slanted in from four small windows, one in each wall, but more came from a brace of electric lamps. The windows were open slightly, letting in a draft of mild early-fall air scented with forest, and also with horses and automobile exhaust.

There was another person sitting beside the desk, surprisingly a woman, but tensely silent in the intelligence chief's presence.

That's odd, Luz thought. *And if it's odd, it's significant.*

The American armed forces had uniformed women's auxiliary corps now, volunteers handling noncombatant and clerical jobs, including things like driving field ambulances, to free up men for combat. So did the British. As far as she knew, the Kaiser's army didn't. The woman was in . . .

American clothes, Luz thought.

There were a dozen minor differences of cut and sewing technique that shouted that out immediately, and fabric of that quality hadn't been available here since before the war. Rather full, frumpy ankle-length skirt and jacket and shirtwaist, made at home and not very recently, but made skillfully and skillfully repaired since. Straw hat with a ribbon and a silk flower, over long hair done up in a rather old-fashioned way and held with several amber-headed pins that were the most expensive things she was wearing.

She's American too, Luz thought. *Lower-middle-class, big-city.*

Ways of sitting and holding yourself were as distinctive as clothes. Strawberry-blond hair, natural from the pale Celtic complexion and bright turquoise-blue eyes. The face was innocent of cosmetics and distorted by tension, but with the big eyes and snub nose and pointed chin probably had a cheerful open golliwog prettiness normally; her figure was fuller than was fashionable these days but perfect for a Gibson Girl a decade ago.

Nicolai gave Luz and von Bülow another of the inevitable little half bows, his rather ordinary-looking face expressionless; he was a man of medium height in his early fifties, with close-cut graying dark-brown hair and mustache, and his eyes were of some mixed color that might be hazel in better light.

"*Gnädiges Fräulein*," he said to her. "You will pardon a necessary discourtesy," he went on, and it wasn't a question.

"Is this indeed Elisa Carmody?" he asked the woman sitting beside his desk.

Luz's eyes had flicked over her as part of her scan of the room. Now they snapped back in horror, and she controlled her expression just in time. The one thing she couldn't talk her way out of: someone who actually *knew* her cover identity's real face.

Her first impression had been a woman of about thirty. Now she saw that the other was younger than Luz's mid-twenties if anything, but under some tremendous stress she was concealing well. There was a slight shock as their eyes met and locked for a long instant.

If I get Horst's gun—

It was a Luger P08 parabellum, with an eight-round magazine.

I might be able to take them all, I know he carries it loaded but no round in the chamber, Luz thought with icy detachment as the blue eyes studied her solemnly; her own face bore a slight inquiring smile. *Or at least make sure they don't take me alive. Horst first, of course, I'll draw it with my left hand and put two rounds through the body with the muzzle touching . . .*

"Well, I seen her for years have not, six no seven," the young American woman said, in fluent but slightly clumsy German. "And myself was a young then in among a crowd at a function of social, so she would not me probably know."

American-born, the ear of Luz's mind said automatically. *Big-city, East Coast, Irish neighborhood. Boston, probably. Book-learned German, but also being around someone who spoke it . . . spoke it like a Bavarian peasant from half a century ago.*

"Please think carefully, Fräulein Whelan," Nicolai said. "This is of the very first importance."

The other woman stood up, walking closer and studying her carefully. Then she smiled and stepped close, opening her arms.

"Elisa!" she cried, and went on in English. "I was just a brat then, but I'll never forget you!"

Luz returned the embrace and felt a stab of thankfulness that she'd spoken in that tongue.

Which I am in turn glad Nicolai doesn't speak well, because that is the most welcome and one of the least convincing lies I've ever heard! She knows perfectly well I'm not Carmody. It won't matter with Horst; he knows I'm who I say I am, poor man.

She could feel quivering tension in the arms that gripped her, and heard a single whisper:

"Talk later!"

The girl turned to Nicolai and said in her slow German: "It is of a complete certainty the Miss Elisa Carmody, Colonel. She older of course is, but the face the same remains and the eyes remain, and the little nick below her right ear, that remains also to be."

Which nick Luz had gotten two years ago, from a rock fragment peened off by a bullet from a sniper, and hadn't really noticed until later. It was embarrassing; a spy didn't want identifying marks, contrary to popular fiction, which was full of one-eyed, scar-faced agents with limps, missing ears, or dramatic stripes in their hair, but it was also something that could only have been seen at very close range. The girl was improvising, but fortunately Horst hadn't noticed the mark and so she hadn't supplied him a story which would contradict the little detail.

She'd probably have given the truth, just modified to fit her cover—it was much simpler to keep track of things that way. *Al mentiroso le conviene ser memorioso,* as the old saying went: A liar needed a good memory.

There was a palpable relaxation in the room as they all sat, and Horst was hiding a smile behind the ramrod machine stiffness he could put on.

"Fräulein Elisa Carmody, of the Mexican National Revolutionary Party; Fräulein Keera Whelan, our liaison with the Clann na nGael," Nicolai said, as the two women shook hands briefly in the double-handed clasp ladies often used.

Calluses, Luz thought. *Strong fingers. Did some work with her hands, but not just laboring—something with fine tools, artisan's work. And a few burn marks. One from acid. People who handle laboratory equipment get those. And she's still tense, but less so. She knows I'm not Carmody, and that makes her feel* much *better.*

Clann na nGael meant the Irish Republican Brotherhood, and did probably mean Boston.

The name would be spelled Ciara, Luz thought.

Though pronounced with a sharp *k* at the beginning and a long vowel, *Keera.* She couldn't remember anyone of that name in the briefing papers, which had said the IRB operation had been thoroughly pulverized by the Federal Bureau of Security after the Dublin thing, when the embarrassment with the British became more important than not offending a constituency that mostly voted Democratic anyway. Luz tended to think the FBS was a bit pedestrian and unimaginative, and apparently the Brotherhood had been *almost* absolutely smashed. Which, as the saying went, was not the same thing as *absolutely completely* smashed.

Still, an almost absolute smashing might account for why they were using a woman who might or might not be old enough to vote. And who also just happened to have once seen the woman Luz was pretending to be, but that sort of thing happened more often than you might think. Generally speaking, people weren't more than ten degrees removed from anyone else in the same country, and if you added a common interest like revolutionary politics it became more likely still.

And she was willing to lie truth out of creation about it, thus saving me from probable torture and certain death. And look how she flushes! I am once again glad that I inherited Mima's complexion, not Papá's, so that isn't such a problem for me.

Ciara Whelan's face was lightly freckled across her snub nose, and otherwise pale as milk, and right now there were spots of near-crimson on her cheeks and her ears glowed. Luz's father had been what they called *black Irish*, black of hair and dark-eyed and relatively swarthy by the standards of that damp misty island full of extremely pink people. The natural olive of her skin and control of her breathing was keeping Luz from going corpse-pale at the sudden brush with death and the lurching emptiness in her stomach. She didn't flush with the giddy-nauseous rush of relief either. Luz didn't think Colonel Nicolai's eyes missed much normally.

I don't show every passing emotion like a book written in blood below glass, and *I don't burn and peel with a little sun.*

Nicolai tapped a set of papers on his desk. "I have read your report on your return from America with interest, Captain von Dückler," he said. "Most stirring. A pity we cannot release it to the popular press; the Fatherland is in need of heroes, but until after the war . . . probably long after the war . . . they will have to make do with the *Stoßtruppen* and the pilots of the fighting scouts. Like this new one, your relative the, ah, Red Baron."

"A very distant relative, Colonel." Horst tucked his head. "A certain degree of . . . flamboyance could not be avoided, sir," he added apologetically, and then with perfect sincerity: "That I have served the Fatherland is reward enough. Fame is nothing."

"Certainly it could not be avoided after the French identified the Herr Privatdozent," Nicolai agreed. "Probably the English on the zeppelin were merely acting opportunistically; typical amateurism. I would like to go over certain details."

They seemed mostly to be concerned with Luz, or more precisely Elisa Carmody. Horst confirmed the written report he'd telegraphed ahead; von Bülow added a little on the bits he'd seen himself. The actions did seem a little . . .

Dramatic, Luz thought.

Ciara Whelan was staring at her, with eyes going wider and wider as the catalog of beating large Indian *rumāl*-wielders into submission, identifying French agents, pursuits and ambushes and rearguards and high-speed chases by pistol-wielding enemies on motorcycles went on.

I really didn't have any choice, though. If I hadn't given it everything I had, we'd all have died. ¡Por Dios! Most importantly, I would have died!

Horst left out the naughty bits, but Luz thought that Nicolai had probably deduced that anyway. The head of Abteilung IIIb brought out a cigarette in a holder, looked at her for a nod of permission—but not Ciara Whelan, she noticed—and lit it.

"So, Captain von Dückler, you judge this . . . gracious miss to be capable?" he said, exhaling smoke.

Bulgarian tobacco, or possibly Turkish, but very high quality, Luz thought absently.

"Very capable. Frankly . . . astonishingly so, sir. I would not have believed that a woman could do any of it, if I had not seen it with my own eyes. I must reconsider certain assumptions."

"I also," von Bülow said. "Furthermore she has an excellent education, and a good if unorthodox grasp of our German culture."

Which was nice of him, though *Kultur* actually meant something subtly different and much more all-encompassing than the English cognate.

"Yes. I bow to your direct experience. She is very good; in fact, a little implausibly good. For a member of a revolutionary group. Not, perhaps, for a trained international spy of the new type, now that intelligence work is no longer simply a matter of blackmail of homosexual staff officers or slipping a few marks to seedy Balkan adventurers and *grandes horizontals* and the doorman at a foreign embassy. Yet now we have a direct confirmation of her identity, which is . . . most reassuring. She will be useful in the Boston operation, since she is known there; the other agent may not be up to the needs of the matter."

Luz smiled very slightly and inclined her head. "Those of us who have survived the Black Chamber are often very good, very lucky, or both, Herr Oberst."

Or just hid in a cave and didn't come out, she thought.

"Indeed." He turned back to Horst. "You would say then that she is strong-willed? Not squeamish?"

Horst actually chuckled. "No, Colonel. Quite the contrary. Very strong-willed; not bloodthirsty, at least not to those other than the occupiers of her country, but with a true soldierly ruthlessness when necessary."

"Good. You will all attend the demonstration, then. Of the, ah, Breath of Loki."

A slight grimace of distaste, either at the thing itself or more likely at the name, which to Luz bore von Bülow's mental fingerprints. His type of romantic pan-German nationalist often insisted on plucking terminology out of Wagner or the myths the composer had drawn upon, as if they were spiritually bellowing at some Rhenish dragon or brooding on a misty rock in a forest all the time. Nicolai didn't strike her as that sort of sentimentalist.

The intelligence officer went on: "Then there will be a conference with the Chief of the Great General Staff and the quartermaster-general, at which you and the Herr Privatdozent will be present and required to summarize your observations. You will understand that this plan, far along as it is, must still be given final operational approval at the very highest level before we move."

"The very highest, Colonel?" Horst murmured.

The three Germans looked at each other. Nicolai cleared his throat and said rather formally:

"It has not been thought advisable to bother the All-Highest with . . . tedious operational details."

Meaning, the Kaiser is an idiot who's the creature of whoever talked to him last, and his generals don't tell him anything if they can avoid it, Luz thought, her mind working smoothly once more. *Amazing how quickly one can recover from the shadow of the Death Angel's wings.*

Kaiser Wilhelm still had the constitutional power to appoint men to the highest posts and dismiss them at his pleasure, like the chancellor and the Chief of the Great General Staff, but nobody outside Germany was sure how much actual authority he retained these days. Von Falkenhayn had been more or less his man, or vice versa, but von Falkenhayn was dead now, and von Hindenburg and Ludendorff in the ascendant—because of the victories they'd won, but also because they had a much better grasp of modern politics. They were popular with the masses, whereas Falkenhayn had been a product of the traditional court system of favorites and camarillas and Chancellor von Bethmann-Hollweg was a colorless bureaucrat. They'd be much *more* popular when the latest series of victories had sunk in, too, and the booty flowed in to make Germany less hungry, dark, and cold come winter. High morale produced victory . . . but you needed victories to keep high morale. Everyone had a breaking strain, even if this war had shown it was often much further away than anyone would have thought.

"The All-Highest is attached to . . . possibly outdated humanitarian scruples," von Bülow said, as if that were some sort of mild vice. "He was . . . unhappy with the experimental raid on Paris in May when the details became public knowledge. I was not altogether sorry to leave Europe then."

"Things are no longer as they were in May, Herr Privatdozent," Nicolai said, contemplating the end of his cigarette. "The crown prince, I might add, was *not* unhappy with the May experiment, which he regarded as a suitable coda to his great victory at Verdun, and has been kept briefed on this operation, which has his enthusiastic support. Of course, he is more militarily active, as a man in his prime actually commanding forces in the field and doing so very ably."

"Ach, so," Horst said, with much meaning and little expression, and von Bülow nodded.

Before the war, Kronprinz Friedrich Wilhelm Viktor August Ernst of the House of Hohenzollern had been mainly noted for chasing—and catching—society women, driving fast cars, wearing fantastically extravagant uniforms running to fur busbies with silver death's-heads attached, and in general being even more of a deranged parody of a Prussian militarist than his father. Since then he'd commanded an Army group on the Western Front; doubtless his chief of staff had done most of the actual work, but he'd shown considerable talent and had made some crucial and successful changes to the plan for the Verdun offensive in the confused period between Falkenhayn's sudden death and the new Chief of the General Staff really settling in, particularly in driving forward positions that enabled the Germans to use their artillery to interdict French resupply of the fortress town through the narrow neck that was all that connected it with their main positions. That had led to the final chaotic collapse of the position into a pocket that was starved and battered into surrender, despite frantic attempts to break out and even more costly attempts at driving relief forces through the encircling German positions.

The crown prince had also had the usual German relationship of a royal heir to his father; they detested each other, which meant he detested his father's favorites and favored the new team. With his status as a victorious field commander, that meant a great deal; all the *Uradel* and military elements who'd worried about his father damaging the prestige of the monarchy were rallying around him.

All useful intelligence, Luz thought. *And Horst and von Bülow and Colonel Nicolai are all contemplating futures as members of the new, triumphant group under the benevolent rays of to-be-imperial favor, achieved by bringing glory and power to the Fatherland. Anyone who thinks monarchies don't have politics doesn't know much about politics or monarchies. Or hasn't seen some of the stuff that goes on around Uncle Teddy these days, come to that. And speaking of monarchies . . .*

All four of President Roosevelt's sons were in the U.S. Army as of this spring. They were all hard-charging, able, and ambitious young men, and she knew Ted Jr. was brave to excess, and would bet his younger brothers would be too. If any of them came out of the war trailing the sort of clouds of glory their father had in Cuba and went into politics . . .

Though Alice would have a better chance at making herself empress of the world, if merit were the only consideration.

Luz shuddered mentally at the thought, even now. Alice Roosevelt Longworth was a force of nature in a very decorative package, the only one of the president's children to inherit every scrap of his wits and willpower, and with much less of his Victorian-era scruples.

Von Bülow continued in his Germanic Sage voice, and the other two nodded agreement: "The crown prince accepts the stern necessities of modern *absoluten Krieg.* The days of cabinet wars with limited means for limited aims are past; this is the era of war between whole peoples, for stakes that are without limit."

"And so," Nicolai said, standing and taking up his peaked officer's hat. "Now we will see the practical demonstration of the Herr Privat-dozent's inspiration."

Horst nodded. "Many reports cross a high commander's desk; reading them is one thing . . . but seeing something in practice, another," he said. "Come . . . *gnädiges Fräulein."*

Luz was glad Horst had enough social sense not to call her *sweetie* in this context, and to offer an arm to them both. But from the grim look on his face, and the way Ciara Whelan had gone paler than milk, the demonstration wasn't going to be anything she'd be happy to see.

Absoluten Krieg meant *absolute* war, though the usual English translation these days was *total* war. It had become more and more popular to describe what the Great War and the twentieth century were doing to Europe, and to the United States, for that matter. It wasn't an accident that the Germans had been the first ones to come up with it, though.

And people generally use either version when they're about to do something totally, absolutely *beastly.*

SEVEN

Schloss Rauenstein
Kingdom of Saxony, German *Reich*
SEPTEMBER 12TH, 1916(B)

A bout a thousand men," Luz murmured to herself—and to Ciara. They were to one side of the group of German officers who'd disembarked on the hilltop two kilometers from the castle, and, apart from a single glance and nod from Horst, unacknowledged once they arrived. Colonel Nicolai and his two subordinates had immediately been swept near to Germany's warlords and de facto rulers.

It's as if we had some peculiarly virulent and female form of head lice, Luz thought. *Or possibly just contagious girlyness.*

It wasn't a novelty, but it was irritating, amusing, and in this context, useful.

Whatever Ciara Whelan's doing, thinking, and thinking of doing, I need to know and quickly. She holds my life and the mission in her hands—she could always change her mind and at the very least make them do checks that would have them lock me up and eventually break my cover. She's an interesting case. Quick thinking, to keep Colonel Nicolai in the dark like that. ¡Me salvé por un pelo de rana calva!

The Boston-Irish girl nodded tightly, holding each of her elbows with the opposite hand. She was wearing a sleeveless calf-length cloak-jacket with a rabbit-fur collar and slits for the arms, good quality but altered to fit her and at least six or seven years old, and of a brownish color that clashed with the blue of her skirt and jacket. Like everything else about her it virtually screamed solid lower-middle-class respectability, of the sort that didn't go hungry but had to watch the pennies relentlessly to keep up appearances.

Luz had on a camelhair trenchcoat, a female-styled copy of what British officers wore in the actual trenches, and for a wonder sturdy and useful as well as stylish—one of life's little nuisances was that women's clothing, while prettier than men's and these days sometimes more comfortable, was usually less solidly made. It was moderately coolish on the top of this hill, with a steady wind from the north and patches of cloud in that peculiarly European whitish-blue sky. She estimated that they were at nearly two thousand feet, and autumn would come early to these upland valleys. The road to this location had been good graded dirt but also something hacked out recently along an old sheep track, possibly by the very men they saw in the enclosures below.

"Mother of God, but I wish I didn't have to see this. The animals were bad enough," Ciara said softly, as if to herself, and in English.

American-born, Luz confirmed to herself. *But first-generation, with Irish parents, and raised in a neighborhood with plenty of other immigrants in it.*

"Courage," Luz said equally quietly: something perfectly in character . . . and necessary. "What will happen, will happen; it's not in our power to change it."

Who does she think I am? Logically, she must think that I'm someone impersonating *Elisa Carmody. And logically, that would be an American government agent; a Black Chamber operative, in other words. ¡Ay! But I certainly can't tell for sure . . . I think she's intelligent, too, but she's a civilian and under terrible pressure. Not out of the woods yet there,* mi corazón. *But best of all, she needs me to be her hope in a desperate hour, and people see what they need to see, if you give them the slightest help. Fortunately I'm usually very good at getting people to like me, but . . .*

The question hammered at her, and she pushed it down with an act of will. It was utterly impossible to find out right now, and she had other business.

So concentrate on what you can *do.*

She could observe.

The hilltop was crowded with about a score of German military men, von Bülow and Ciara and her; she had a distinct impression there would have been more hangers-on were it less secret. Von Hindenburg was unmistakable, a massive bemedalled figure with an even more massive square Baltic head on a bull neck and broad shoulders, graying blond hair cropped an inch long showing when he lifted his spiked helmet for a moment, and a huge gray handlebar mustache. There was a wart over his left eye, and with a different expression he could have been a plump indulgent grandfather; the one he had on now, and the context, made him a good model for a statue of the Archetypical Prussian Military Brute.

The Iron Titan, she thought. *The hammer of the Russians and savior of East Prussia and conqueror of the Baltic and Poland and White Russia and the rest of Ober Ost.*

He pointed downslope with his walking stick. "These men," he said. "They are not prisoners of war? That would be entirely unsuitable!"

"No, Herr General," Nicolai said, prompted by a sharp glance from the *other* general.

Erich von Ludendorff—the *von* was a courtesy, since he had noble connections but no title of his own—was younger, shorter, and slimmer than the senior of Germany's ruling pair, in his fifties, and according to reports the brains of the partnership, the supreme military technician. He'd taken the citadel of Liège in Belgium by cool bluff, back in the opening days of the war, walking up to it and hammering on the front door with the hilt of his sword. His eyes were among the coldest Luz could remember ever seeing, and she had met some exemplary specimens.

Nicolai filled in the details: "They are Czechs who killed their officers and allowed themselves to be overrun at the beginning of Brusilov's offensive, and then went over to the Russians—enlisting with them to fight against the Central Powers for separatist reasons."

Which turned out to be a very bad bet by these Czechs, Luz thought. *And letting themselves be retaken alive . . . even worse.*

Brusilov was far and away the best of the Czar's commanders, and his attack had gone well for almost exactly two weeks of chasing unenthusiastic Austrian troops taken by surprise amid what were for once meticulous Russian preparations. Then it had run into a force the Germans had been preparing for an attack of their own, under General von Mackensen, the victor in Russian Poland last year and in Serbia in 1914, when a German commander had been Bulgaria's price to enter the war on Austria's side. The result had been rout and massacre.

Whatever this mystery Loki weapon is, I hope it's quick.

The German faces all went bleaker as Nicolai told the tale; the Czechs had violated their military oaths to the Austrian emperor as soldiers, something the breed around Luz took very seriously indeed.

"Ach, so," von Hindenburg said. "Traitors and rebels, their lives forfeit. Condemned?"

"To death, General," Nicolai said. "By Austrian summary field court-martial before being handed over to us."

"Very well." Von Hindenburg sighed mountainously. "This is not a knightly struggle, but we do what we must for the Fatherland. Proceed."

He peered a hundred yards down the slope, to an apparatus simple to the point of starkness; a steel platform with an adjustable, pivoting rod of steel two inches thick jutting up from it. Troops with the black *Waffenfarbe* branch of service of Pioneers—combat engineers and likely to be tasked with any technically demanding job or new weapon—were, with extreme care, sliding a shell-like object onto the rod, which went into a tube in its base; there was a ring of fins around it as well. That meant a spigot mortar, with a charge in the base of the shell providing the propulsive force. Von Hindenburg peered with interest at the procedure.

"That shell the *Pioneer-Versuchskompanie* have set up is only about twenty kilograms," he said. "It does not contain enough gas to affect such a large target."

"This would not be a sufficient quantity of chlorine or even phos-gene, no," von Bülow said, and cleared his throat. "But it is more than enough of the Breath of Loki agent, even mixed with some chlorine as a dispersant."

There were a few quiet snorts at the code name. Von Bülow flushed and added:

"This *Vernichtungsgas* . . . annihilation gas . . . operates on entirely new principles. The previous war gases burn and scald, essentially, particularly the mucous membranes of the throat and lungs. Their ac-tion is . . . mechanical. This one is derived from a fortunate accident while experimenting with organophosphate compounds for killing in-sect pests in our African colonies under the Kaiser Wilhelm Gesell-schaft. A laboratory accident in early 1914 showed its extraordinary effects on human subjects, though fortunately only on the clumsy na-tive laborers who dropped the equipment."

"You are saying the new gas does not cause direct damage to tis-sues, then?" Ludendorff said; he had a reputation as a patron of new technologies. "A true poison, systemic?"

Von Bülow nodded eagerly. "Its action is directly on the nervous system. Concentrations as low as five parts per million are lethal for any mammal and need not be breathed—a touch anywhere on uncov-ered skin will do."

There was a murmur of awe and horror at that. Commanders lived by numbers, and they were all mentally calculating the amount neces-sary to kill . . . which was one minuscule droplet too small to see, too light to be actually felt. A single shell could carry the death of a thou-sand men, if it was dispersed evenly enough.

"Essentially it functions by turning off, blocking, the operations of the nerves that govern the heart and lungs. Smaller concentrations can cause permanent paralysis, dementia, and other symptoms. The agent is colorless, odorless, not very volatile in pure form but divides readily into very fine particles, and highly persistent on cloth, wood, brick or stone structures, vegetation, and soil."

"How persistent?" Ludendorff asked sharply.

You could see that von Bülow wanted to say: *as was outlined in the technical reports you were sent!* He didn't, merely continuing:

"From days to months even on exterior surfaces, depending on how high the temperature, how much exposure to sunlight, and how much rainfall. In a cool sheltered space that is not detoxified with steam or very hot water and chemicals such as hydrogen peroxide, indefinitely.

"Or at least," he added pedantically, "as long as we have had the time to test. Up to a year. Decontamination workers require full protection: sealed rubber suits and air filters."

The quartermaster-general's brows went up. "An ideal weapon for denying the use of an area to the enemy. And of very great effect on morale, particularly when first employed and unfamiliar. A terror weapon of extreme frightfulness."

Colonel Nicolai clicked his heels. "Exactly, Herr General. There were many problems with full-scale production, problems of purity of materials and quality control, but these have been solved. The shock and frightfulness is why it is important that the effect not be frittered away by piecemeal introduction as we did with the other war gases, but saved for one massive, decisive blow."

"Yes, yes," von Hindenburg said brusquely. "Carry on."

Luz made herself look down to the hollow at the base of the slope more than a thousand yards away. The men there were sitting and standing or wandering aimlessly within a barbed-wire enclosure marked by guard towers at its four corners; within were crude board barracks, looking even from here as if you could stick your fingers through the gaps between the planks. There were German machine-gunners in the towers, but even as she watched they dismounted their light, easily carried Lewis guns, went briskly down ladders leading outside the encampment, and joined the men at the gates in clambering into a Benz motor truck—itself evidence of the priority this had, given how short of such transport Germany was. They left quickly with an engine growl audible even more than a thousand yards away; they probably hadn't been told what was about to happen, just to get out of the way without wasting time . . . and they probably also suspected something ghastly and were leaving just as fast as was physically possible. In their situation she'd have done exactly the same thing.

The Pioneers came up the hill, leaving the spigot mortar alone, which surprised Luz slightly. Ciara spoke softly:

"Electrical detonator," she said, and pointed. "The wire leads up here, see?"

Luz did, and looked back at the younger woman with a raised brow.

"I'm interested in mechanical and electrical things," she said, blushing and mumbling. "My brother was too. I studied his textbooks and took correspondence courses and we used to work on things together."

"Good for you!" Luz said sincerely, and thought she saw surprise at the praise.

The sergeant in charge of the Pioneer detail saluted an officer in his branch of service, who used a field telephone before turning to Colonel Nicolai.

"The meteorological office still predicts a consistent strong wind from the north for the rest of the day, Herr Oberst."

Nicolai looked at the switch in the man's hand. For a moment Luz thought he was considering offering his commanders the honor of pressing it, then probably wisely thought better of the notion.

"Please take your observation stations, gentlemen," he said instead.

Then turning his head toward Luz and offering his own field glasses, which she took: "And ladies."

There were half a dozen tripod-mounted instruments, like binoculars with eyestalks that also acted as range estimators. The senior officers took them, while their subordinates used their own binoculars. In a formidable display of cool self-command—his reputation and position would be riding on this—Nicolai simply stood with his arms crossed, waiting.

"Ready?" he said. "Very well, Lieutenant. *Now.*"

The combat engineer did one last calm meticulous visual check that the area around the spigot mortar was vacant; it should be safe there anyway, and he'd done it before, but there was something to be said for an infinite capacity for taking pains. Especially when you worked with deadly things every day . . . though rarely as deadly as this.

The man's hand clenched the pistol-grip-like mechanism at the end of the cord, and his thumb came down on the button atop it.

There was a sharp but not particularly loud metallic *bamp!* sound. The bomb from the spigot mortar flew up in a long arc, just fast enough to be blurred, leaving a donut shape of dust behind on the ground. Luz didn't try to follow it, focusing instead on the camp. The binoculars were fine Zeiss models and didn't need much adjustment for her; evidently Colonel Nicolai still had excellent vision, though not as good as her twenty-ten. The shell burst about two hundred feet up, fine fusing but not very hard with plenty of time to adjust and a known range to target. Tendrils of green shot out in every direction, and she remembered von Bülow saying that they used chlorine to help disperse the heavier Loki agent.

The Czechs were unremarkable-looking men still mostly in ragged pike-gray Austrian uniforms, though with bits and pieces of Russian gear and the odd blanket roll over the shoulder. Most of them had been relieved of their boots and had rags around their feet instead. You couldn't tell a Czech from an Austrian-German to look at anyway, both being mostly generic Middle Europeans. The most notable thing about them was that they looked distinctly underfed, but that wasn't very extraordinary these days either. They were alert enough, though: When the spigot mortar went off plenty of them hit the dirt with veteran speed. They recognized the green of chlorine gas immediately too. Despite shouts of rage and fear, nearly every man had a wet cloth over his mouth within thirty seconds, some taking the direct approach and peeing on them . . . which actually worked with chlorine, since urea helped neutralize it.

The invisible stuff von Bülow had christened the Breath of Loki fell, drifting downward in tiny droplets through the air. One man fell over, twitched, and went limp as his heart seized after a contraction. Others tried to gasp and found that their lungs weren't working and choked. Another, farther toward the wire, twitched and then went into convulsions, his head nearly touching his heels in an arc that must have broken his spine. Others dropped and purged and vomited and frothed as if their bodies were trying to expel every drop of fluid from every orifice as they writhed. One ran into a guard tower's post . . . over and over and over again. More and more near the center of the camp simply fell, struggled to breathe for a few seconds, and died. Terror spread outward like the unfolding of a malignant rose, but few had enough time to run far.

The sound of screaming was audible even on the hilltop, but only for a little while.

"Let me have those," Ciara said quietly.

Luz lowered the binoculars. "They're dying, Miss Whelan," she said flatly. "Badly but quickly. You don't need to know any more."

"I do. I came here. I volunteered to come here, though I didn't know . . . I should see, deserve to see."

Luz sighed and handed them over. She took calming breaths, holding them for a second and then letting them go. She was feeling light-headed and more than a little nauseous herself, and she'd seen violent death in many forms for years now.

The memory that prompted was one that made her wince even now; the *revolucionarios* had taken a Chamber operative and staked him out over an ant heap with his skin slashed in sensitive places to start the process of being eaten alive. They'd found him about two days later.

So this is just . . . bigger. But it's all new for her and I suspect self-punishing Catholic guilt added in, she thought.

Luz was technically Catholic herself, of course, but neither of her parents had been more than formally and unthinkingly religious, confessing and attending Mass when those about them expected it. She'd gone through a fervent phase at about twelve when she'd been full of the presence of God and the Virgin and sure she wanted to be a nun, specifically a Daughter of Charity, but it had worn off gradually. Her mother had seemed to expect that, as if it was something girls went through, and had humored her. What faith was left after time and education hadn't survived her parents' deaths.

This Ciara probably has a more serious case, grew up in a neighborhood under the thumb of strict Jansenist Irish priests where everyone or at least everyone female confesses and goes to Mass every single week. And I doubt she's ever seen anyone killed before, much less a massacre. But it's her decision.

Ciara leveled the binoculars and gave a small gasp. Her hands were shaking; she lowered the instrument, then raised it again and held the view by main force of will.

"Holy Mary, Mother of God, pray for us sinners, now and at the hour of our death," she said.

Then she dropped the binoculars—Luz caught them just before they hit the ground—ran a dozen paces, and dropped to her knees behind a tattered bush, bending over and retching uncontrollably. None of the German officers spared her even a glance, but then, they were pointedly ignoring one of their own number who was doing exactly the same thing, with the addition of sputtering curses between the heaves, and *he* was a middle-aged veteran with a Merit Medal.

Luz handed the binoculars back to Colonel Nicolai, smilingly courteous: "*Vielen Dank für alles, Herr Oberst.* A most interesting demonstration, and everything that the Herr Privatdozent promised. A weapon of great power."

That seemed to leave him a little impressed, and amused. Then she walked quickly over to where Ciara was kneeling, stopping only by a younger officer to snap:

"Your canteen and your flask, please, Oberleutnant."

The man handed them over automatically, only starting to think about it once she had them in her hands. Then she knelt by the younger woman, holding her with an arm across the collarbones and with her other making sure her long hair didn't come down into the way of the heaves. Those subsided to dry retches, and Luz wiped her face with a handkerchief—she always carried at least four clean ones, good practical sea-island cotton and of substantial size—and then let her hold it against her lips as the retching turned to quivers.

"Here," she said, opening the canteen. "Rinse your mouth out with this, and spit. Now sip some of the liquor."

She sniffed at it herself; it was pear brandy, and good quality; the sweet-strong scent cut through the sour stink of vomitus.

"Be careful! Now a little more."

Ciara obeyed, took a swallow, and coughed, then took one more, successfully blinking back tears.

"Thank . . . thank you," she said. "Thank you very much. I'm being such a noodle."

Luz handed her a second handkerchief, sipped a little of the brandy herself, then helped her rise and sat her down on a trunk full of equipment, quelling an orderly with a glare and giving him the containers to hand back to their donor.

"I've seen some very bad things, Miss Whelan," Luz said quietly. "And that was as bad as any of them. The more credit to you, in fact, that you can't look on it unmoved."

The officers had seen enough too; there wasn't any more movement from the camp, except for a few figures hanging on the wire and going through what looked like epileptic seizures and one man crawling out of a barracks door, rising for two steps, and then falling on his face. His legs kept running in that position for twenty strides, as if moved by some unseen machinery.

Luz walked back and waited until Horst had a moment to spare.

"That was bad," he said. "No more so than a battalion's worth of artillery catching the same number of troops in the open, just easier to do, but . . . bad."

Luz nodded; objectively he was perfectly correct. When human beings fought to kill, there weren't many good ways to go. She'd seen a man take a bullet just behind the eyes once, and have them both pop out of the shattered sockets and hang there while he ran screaming *Mama! Mama!* and bouncing off walls and doors until someone on his own side gave him a mercy shot in the back of the head . . .

. . . but it didn't *feel* very true. And if they were planning on using it as she suspected . . .

Horst's eyes went to Ciara Whelan. "That was kindly done," he said.

Luz shrugged. "She's young and very naïve," she said. "She'll learn to deal with it. We do, *ja?* And then we go on. I'd better stay with her. I can't attend your conference, after all."

"*Ja*, it was decided that only military personnel should be present."

She dropped into English for the American saying: "No girls in the tree-house."

Horst nodded, missing the point. "I'll get you transport . . . and tell you about the conference later. It'll be just like being there, but without the boredom."

EIGHT

Even with the presence of the two great warlords and their entourage, Castle Rauenstein had some empty space within the rambling pile built and rebuilt and burned and built again over the last eight centuries in a dozen different styles. Ciara led her to the *new* wing after they'd been dropped in the courtyard, which had probably been a generation old when Mozart was born.

"They've put us in together," she said, still looking a little shaky, as they climbed the stairs past what had been the main public rooms to bedchambers and suites. "We're lucky at that, most of the men are six to a room."

We're both working hard at not thinking too much about the details of what we saw, and each helps the other with that just by being here. The last thing I want now is solitude.

The bedroom was large, and had probably been uncluttered in the Biedermeier style of three generations ago before the von Herders turned their country estate over to the government; there was a faded but excellent Shiraz rug on the floor, catching early-afternoon rays from the two square-paned windows. Now, besides a large four-poster bed, it held a great piano shining in burnished ebony, one small battered trunk that was probably Ciara's, the two large yellow Vuitton ones that belonged to Luz, and more miscellaneous items shoved in here to get them out of the way. She thought the small pile of English-language volumes and magazines beside the bed were Ciara Whelan's own; the books had titles like *Principles of Wireless Telegraphy* by someone named Pierce, and the magazines were similar.

Not my idea of light travel reading, but there's no accounting for tastes.

"I hope you don't mind sharing?" Ciara said, being polite, and possibly a little wary of the glamorous, deadly stranger.

She *didn't* sound as if she expected Luz to be upset. In a family of her background it would be rare for daughters to have their own individual bedrooms, or beds for that matter, and unmarried guests would share sleeping quarters with their own gender and age. Luz had been the sole child of affluent parents, starting out upper-middle-class and moving on to borderline-wealthy before they died. But she'd spent enough time as a guest at her father's clients' houses, at finishing schools—European ones often had startlingly primitive ideas of what was appropriate accommodation for young ladies—and in college digs not to be picky.

Not to mention time with the Chamber since, when sometimes privacy meant the men looked the other way while I squatted.

The thought made her take a quick look, first at the water jugs and basins and towel sets on a bureau, and then under the bed after she stowed her suitcase and hatbox; yes, it was back to a chamberpot, and baths might mean a towel, a tin tub, and having buckets carried in. She sighed a little, but that wasn't any novelty either; not all that many places were as modern as the house her engineer father had built in Santa Barbara.

At least it's a clean *pot and has a good tight-fitting lid. In fact, apart from a little dust and . . . that* old *smell you rarely get outside Europe . . . the room's very well kept.*

"There's a lavatory one floor up," Ciara said helpfully. "But it's usually full of men and I don't fancy waiting in line with them. There's an orderly who comes by twice a day for the pot, and you can reserve the bathtub for an hour if you ask a day ahead . . . I will say for these Germans, they're *clean*. Much more so than I'd expect for men together on their own, which usually is like bears with furniture or pigs in the parlor, not human beings at all."

"It must be a bit difficult, being the only woman here."

"Most of them have just ignored me, and the rest mostly act decent." She flushed. "Colonel Nicolai, though . . . he's a masher and a cad!"

Luz raised her brows sympathetically; that was a revoltingly common problem, always getting in the way of things when you least expected it. People said you *had* to expect it, but she'd never met anyone who could give her a convincing explanation of precisely why. Except *they're like that*, which was a circular argument if she'd ever heard one, and she'd never found *just because* very logical.

"You had . . . problems with him? He tried to give you insult?" she said, which was a phrasing any woman would understand.

Ciara smiled; it was brief, but she was getting a little color back. Her teeth were white and slightly uneven, a generous smile in a large full-lipped mouth.

"Not anymore . . . well, not *that* problem. I gave him a good slap with my shoulder behind it when he couldn't understand plain-spoken language in English *or* German, which hurt my hand some and his face more. Then I showed him the business end of a pin when he gave signs of thinking that was just a love-tap."

She touched one of the amber-headed pins through her hat and piled hair; they were nearly a foot long and would be like an unrebated fencing foil in the right hands, or at least an Italian stiletto. From the momentary look of steely determination in the turquoise eyes, Ciara had probably been absolutely ready to use it. That was another sign of courage, and Luz felt a glow of approval.

I'm quite taken with this girl, and not just because she saved my life. Though possibly she didn't understand exactly how *brave it was here and now.*

Germany wasn't the sort of place where powerful men could just carry young women off or openly have their way by force, save perhaps on some Junker estate far from the cities where the local police were the lord's creatures and he was the magistrate himself. That sort of thing would be more likely in Hungary, and common as the rain in Rumania or Andalusia or Sicily. But nobody in wartime would have said much if a nameless foreigner disappeared.

Though I don't think Nicolai would actually endanger a mission out of pique at getting put in his place by a woman. He's far too much of a cold fish. If Ciara wasn't useful to him, though . . .

Luz felt a little surprised at how strong the flush of answering anger was and decided that the ghastly demonstration had thrown her emotions off-balance.

"And just what he deserved," she said firmly. "No woman's a piece of meat to be snapped at by hungry dogs."

In an ideal world you wouldn't have to do things like that. But then, in an ideal world people wouldn't be plotting to massacre each other with nerve gases, either. You make the best of what you have.

"Yes, but try and convince a lot of men of that!" Ciara scowled and glanced aside. "That was probably why he made me . . . see that thing today. To punish me."

Luz nodded. "Undoubtedly. But I wouldn't think you've much else to fear from him. He needs you for this . . . thing, and my judgment is that he'll put everything aside for that."

That is a very strong *hint that you must not balk openly at cooperating with this mission, or he will kill you or worse.*

"You think so?" Ciara asked, flashing her a grateful look.

"I'm fairly sure of it. Mind you, I'd avoid him afterward, were I you," she finished. "By a continent or an ocean."

"Thank you!" Hesitantly. "And thank you for . . . for comforting me."

Luz waved a hand. "We're in this together."

She's lonely, far away from home and friends and kin for the first time in her life, absolutely isolated among enemies and desperate for help. She wants to like me and trust me. And if I say so myself, I'm fairly good at getting people to do both . . . whether they should, from their own points of view, or not. Fortunately for Ciara

Whelan, trusting me is just about her only hope of getting out of this alive. And I hope she does; she's made the right decisions and she's . . . rather charming herself, in a naïve sort of way.

Luz looked around the room again, this time with security in mind. The clutter and the upheaval made it impossible to tell if there were any listening devices; it wasn't *probable* that someone had gone to the trouble of installing the bulky and expensive gear that was gradually revolutionizing clandestine surveillance . . . but it was entirely *possible*.

"Do you feel like a rest?" she said. "I wouldn't blame you a bit."

Ciara shuddered. "I'd not like to lie quiet just now, and sleep still less," she said. "Climb the walls and shriek like the Woman of the Barrows, perhaps."

Well, that's understandable. Distraction, then; I could use some myself.

She was keeping the precise details of what they'd seen out of her mind with a practiced effort of will, but it wasn't easy. She moved to the piano and sat, testing a few keys, surprised to find that it was in tune. There was a tall mahogany rack of sheet music beside it; a quick glance showed all the usual favorites, including a lot of arrangements for piano solos, or piano and violin.

It wouldn't do for us to rush out, though. If there are listeners, that would arouse suspicion.

"Do you play, Miss Whelan?" she said, which was a soothingly conventional thing to ask.

"I do that. I love music, though my voice is middling at best, but the good sisters taught us piano, and my aunt Colleen has a rare talent for it and tutored me more. Ours was an upright, of course, a Steinway, not a great concert grand like this!"

There was pride behind that, as well as gratitude at talking of anything else but the horror they'd seen. One of the first signs of middle-class status was a parlor and a piano to put in it, a luxury families would scrimp and save and do without to achieve. Not that it didn't bring a breath of culture into settings otherwise bare of it, which could be well worth making the winter coat last another year.

"Someday people will have all the music they want, the best performances from the great orchestras in recorded form," Luz said, caressing the satiny wood.

"True! But there are problems to be solved first, which won't be until they use electrical recording and not just acoustic. In the meantime even a good Victrola sounds like the music was filtered through a tin bucket."

"This doesn't," Luz said, touching a key and letting the sound reverberate through the room.

"Sure and it's a very good piano, the best I've ever set fingers to," Ciara said. "Though it took getting used to. Ninety-seven keys! And in tune, for a wonder, rather than knocked about by the soldiers, though I think the man they had in here before me may have worked it up. He left some music in his own hand. Couldn't make head nor tail of it, though—no melody at all, all these clashing chords."

"Modern music, and I can't say I like it. This is a Bösendorfer Imperial 290," Luz said, stretching her hands to supple them. "Viennese, and you won't get any better instruments in Europe, though the French would dispute that. I've never liked the metallic tone they prefer, myself. I've played on Bösendorfers before, though not this model, and always wanted one, but they cost the Earth, and you can't carry a piano around with you. They started making these back around the turn of the century, because Ferruccio Busoni wanted it for his transcription of Bach's Chaconne. The von Herders must love music; you don't often see these in a private home."

"Maybe they should have taken it with them. Though this is a *private home* in the same sense and way as saying the King of England's family lives above the shop!"

Luz laughed. "It weighs five-eighths of a ton, too!" she said, which got an answering chuckle. "And you'd have to disassemble it to get it out of the building."

She let her fingers drift into a piano solo arrangement of *Eine Kleine Nachtmusik*, the bright carefree sound like gleaming strings of gold and silver through the still air of the room. Perhaps not appropriate on this grisly day . . . or perhaps perfect, for reminding you that there were things in the life of humanity other than war and the breaking of nations.

After a minute she let the tune drift off, and Ciara sighed. "You play very well, Miss Carmody; I always loved Mozart, but I've only heard that piece performed once by a full orchestra."

"That's a pity. Though personally I think a chamber group is just as good; it's what he usually wrote for. I'm actually better with stringed instruments."

"There's a fiddle here . . ."

She rummaged and pulled out a violin case from behind a stack of crated books. "But I've never gone beyond the beginnings with these."

Luz took the case and opened it, then blinked. "*¡Ay, qué bonita!*" she said. "Now, leaving *this* here goes beyond carelessness; either the von Herders are criminally negligent or their servants are. This would disappear eventually if it hadn't been out of sight, military discipline or no! I'd be tempted to steal it myself, if the circumstances were right; it's a lot easier to walk off with than the piano."

Ciara chuckled—though Luz had been perfectly serious about taking it—and said: "It's an ancient and venerable violin, then?"

"Not all that old—just over fifty years, twice my age—but Viennese too, and very good quality. See?"

She held the case so that the light revealed the label inside: *Gabriel Lemböck Anno 1862.*

Reverently she lifted the instrument free, turning it to enjoy the lustrous sheen of the oil varnish and subtle *craqueleur* on the distinctive one-piece back.

"I've never touched one of these before, but I've heard them."

She took out the bow, checked it and the condition of the strings.

"Pitch?" she said, putting it under her chin and looking at Ciara.

The other woman leaned over and tapped the D and F just below A on the piano, then the C just above, to give a starting pitch for the A string on the instrument. After a minute Luz had the violin ready and tested it with an arpeggio. The tone was dark and velvety but with a light and easy response; it filled the room effortlessly, projecting without harshness, pure and buttery at once.

"Oh, that is pretty!" Ciara said, her strained face lighting up. "It makes most of the ones you hear sound like a cat in a hurdy-gurdy."

Luz nodded. "I'm tempted now to steal it just to see that it gets proper treatment . . . except that I couldn't guarantee it. I doubt I could get the Germans to let me mail it home!"

She stood and ran through a tune her father had liked, an old Irish planxty called "The Raggle-Taggle Gypsy-O" that had meant something special to him and her *mima*; one of her first memories was of him singing it to her, while Luz rested in her arms.

After a moment Ciara sat and began to echo it on the piano, singing the words in a voice that was a little thin but true:

"What care I for house and land?
What care I for daddy's money-o?
I'd rather have a kiss from my gypsy lover's lips
I'm away wi' the raggle-taggle gypsy-o!"

Luz stopped with a laugh at the trailing last note. "Do you want to try that Mozart piece, but for piano and violin, Miss Whelan? I think there's sheets for it there in the rack by your elbow."

It does help when you have interests in common.

"I'd love to; I've heard it done that way."

They set up the music—Luz put hers flat on the top of the piano—and Ciara began, not sophisticated playing, but adept and full of spirit, the sort of style someone developed if they'd played a good deal alone, for their own pleasure and probably hearing an ideal instrument in their mind.

After a moment Luz closed her eyes and let out a deep breath to expel everything else from her consciousness and began. Mozart had been a repellent human being, by all accounts, but his work had been touched with the finger of something from beyond the world of common day, and deserved all respect. It was the art that mattered, not the artist. They followed each other through the long quick dance; when she looked up again the last notes of the coda were dying away.

Luz gave a long sigh, her eyes half-closed with pleasure. It had been a good while since she'd been able to give herself to the music so completely, or enjoyed playing with someone so on first acquaintance.

"Oh," Ciara said. "That was lovely! Thank you, Miss—"

Her face changed slightly as she realized she didn't *know* the real name, and Carmody was someone else's. Someone else who'd probably come to a bad end, at that. Luz shrugged and smiled wryly.

Not quite singing in harmony yet, she thought. *But give us time.*

"Please call me Luz," she said. "You can say it's a childhood nickname. Pardon me if I'm presuming on brief acquaintance, but . . ."

It was a little quick for first names, even for two young women in these informal days, but the time since their meeting had been rather intense. And they were the only Americans here, though Ciara wouldn't be certain of that yet.

"Do call me Ciara, Luz," she said shyly. Then, more firmly: "We need to—"

Luz leaned closer and spoke softly, but without the sibilance that carried: "We need to talk, but not necessarily here."

She glanced around the cluttered room, then picked up a copy of *The Electrical Experimenter* from the bedside dresser; the June 1916 issue, price twelve cents, editor Hugo Gernsback, with a rather gaudy but fundamentally accurate cover about electrical guidance of aerial torpedoes launched from above that should *never* have been allowed to leak to the civilian press. Skimming through it she found an illustration advertising Murdoch Complete #55 headphones for six dollars each. Luz held it up in one hand while pointing to it with the other, then glanced around, putting a finger of her free hand to her lips and finally tapping an ear. Ciara looked puzzled for a moment, then shocked.

Luz shrugged and made a palms-up, maybe-yes-maybe-no gesture. Ciara spoke brightly . . . and very slightly artificially and a bit too loud, though Luz found it a creditable performance for an amateur.

"Let me show you around, Luz!"

They went down a floor, and then through a hallway. "They were taking things out of here yesterday, so it's probably . . . yes!" Ciara said.

The near-empty ballroom was well lit by a long string of windows giving out on a view of the forested Ore Mountains, a mirror-lined space impossible to eavesdrop on invisibly, and unlikely to attract some staff aide busybody. The windows were open, letting in air still comfortable with September but damp and fresh and pine-scented, and cool enough to hint at what the central European winter would be like once the weather broke in these remote uplands still haunted by wolf and boar. It was exactly the sort of room Mozart had written for and performed in, too; probably the piano's original home.

Ciara sank into one of the spindly-looking chairs ranged along the wall, all carving and gilt, and folded her hands together in her lap, fingers working on each other. She was still pale but determined.

"We need to talk," she said after a moment's silence, looking up sharply. "After what we saw . . . I'm certain I'll have no part of this horror the Germans are making for our country. You're an agent for the government in Washington?"

"Yes. The Black Chamber; you've heard of it?" Luz said.

And you shouldn't have assumed that was the truth because it was mostly likely, but still . . . perhaps dancing around it wouldn't have helped either.

Ciara's eyes widened; the name was frightening, from her perspective, but now reassuring as well. A name of secret power, reaching out into an enemy citadel.

"Yes. Oh, thank God!"

Then: "How do I know you really are? You might be working for the British!"

Luz smiled wryly. *That's a* bit *of healthy skepticism*, she thought.

Aloud: "Welcome to the world of the intelligence operative, where everything depends on trust and nobody can trust anyone."

Ciara put her hands to the sides of her head. "It's like a hall of mirrors!"

"Let's put it this way: You know for certain that I'm *not* working for the Germans and *do* want to stop this. And this morning I saw you lie to them, so I know you're not working for them either. Besides, do I *look* English?"

"No," Ciara said, her head slightly to one side. "You might be Welsh, though, or Black Irish . . . but I'd have said Italian or French or Spanish, or even Greek. So tell me who you really are, then."

Ciara's voice challenged, and their eyes met.

Luz thought for a moment, pursing her lips. *She wants to believe me,* she mused. *But she knows that and she's fighting it. The odd thing is that I'm telling her the actual truth, mostly . . . Is she any good at picking up on that?*

"All right," she said, decision firming. "I'm going to do something dangerous, but you did save my life when you confirmed my cover, and we need to work together. I'll tell you the truth. Not all of it, because what you don't know you can't yield if they interrogate you, but what I *do* say will be true."

Ciara nodded, obviously reserving judgment. "Who are you? Really? What's your name?"

"Luz," she said. "It means—"

"*Light*, in Spanish. I speak Spanish . . . well, I can read it and speak a bit."

Luz smiled a little. "Luz O'Malley Aróstegui," she said.

There are times when the main problem is remembering which one I'm using. Knowing that wouldn't help the opposition.

"Thank you," Ciara said. Then as a thought struck her: "That's not too much of a risk?"

"Names are the small change of intelligence work at this level. The crucial thing is that they think I'm Elisa Carmody de Soto-Dominguez.

If they discovered I *wasn't* her, I'd be dead anyway regardless of who I really was."

Then the red-gold brows went up. "You *are* Irish? And part Mexican, like Elisa?"

"Not Mexican. *Cubana* on my mother's side, Irish on my father's. Boston Irish, that is, three generations from Erin."

"Oh? And you were born on the South Side, I suppose, two blocks over and up one street from myself?"

Well, that's a little more *healthy skepticism!* Luz thought. *Not bad, when you must want something to cling to like a life-ring after a shipwreck. This one is nobody's fool, just vastly inexperienced.*

"Nothing so convenient," Luz said in reply. "I was born in California, in the house my father built in Santa Barbara—that's a town . . ."

"Just north of Los Angeles, by the map," Ciara said.

"The Irish get around, don't they?"

"Well, that we do. How did that happen?"

"His grandfather, Pat O'Malley, came over in the first famine year. From Kilmaine, in County Mayo, with nothing but the rags on his back and the lice in his hair and very much of nothing but hunger in his belly. He worked carrying a hod full of mortar, then laying the bricks, then built a little contracting business with a pair of wagons and a few men and boys working for him. His son built it bigger until he was a man of substance . . . as such things went for an Irishman and a Catholic in Boston in his day . . . and sent *my* father to MIT—class of '87."

Ciara's face thawed a little. Luz had thought it might; though every word of the story was true, she couldn't have made up anything better to appeal to someone from the Irish enclaves of the Bay State. It wasn't impossible for those who'd landed hungry and in bug-crawling rags from the coffin ships to better themselves in America, but it wasn't easy either beyond getting what a strong back and willing hands would bring, enough to eat meat with the potatoes five days a week and buy shoes and put a roof over your head. The streets of Boston in particular hadn't been paved with gold for the sons of the Gael, being at the time the most purely English and Protestant place on the western side of the Atlantic Ocean. Though nowadays Irish political bosses ran it, to the vast chagrin of the likes of the Lowells and Cabots and Saltonstalls, and the Irish themselves felt the Italians and French Canadians stepping on their heels.

Then the younger woman frowned, in thought rather than anger.

"That wouldn't be . . . wasn't there an O'Malley who helped build St. Agnes on Fourth Street, wouldn't take anything but his costs for it? I remember a plaque, when I went to school there."

"I think so," Luz said. "Though I couldn't swear to it without looking through Papá's papers in the trunks in the attic at home."

"Well, then," Ciara said, less suspiciously. "How'd he meet a Cuban lady?"

"Papá met my mother in Cuba in '91, but her family were . . . are . . . hacendados, sugar barons. Owners of plantations, and of slaves by the hundred in the old days—which in Cuba means 'before 1886.' Old family, richer than God and prouder than Satan as the saying goes, and they didn't much fancy plain Patrick O'Malley, the bricklayer's son, at the table of an evening or fathering their grandchildren, even though he was laying out their new cane railway and mill, so he and Mima eloped. There was also the matter of a man they did want her to marry, without consulting her wishes very much."

That brought a shyly charming smile, one that made Ciara look more like her twenty years.

"And you?" Luz said.

"My father was Irish-born," the younger woman said. "He came over in '85 with his sister Colleen, him on the run from the English law. She had nobody else to look to and was crippled in one foot besides. He had enough to start a bookstore in south Boston. We might have met, perhaps!"

Luz returned the smile and felt her shoulders relax slightly. That was sincerity if she'd ever heard it, and profound relief at not being alone among malignant strangers, and desperate hope that an ally had been found, someone who knew what they were doing. Luz would very much have regretted having to kill this naïve well-meaning youngster who'd wandered into waters much deeper and more shark-infested than she could have imagined.

"Probably not," she said. "My father was the only son of an only son . . ."

"The poor man!" Ciara said. "There was only me and my brother, Colm, in my family too; my mother died when I was born, and Da never took another. Being ill by then, and saying he was no use to a woman."

Luz nodded; that made them both children of unusually small sets. She went on:

"And my father was almost as glad to leave Boston as his granddad had been to board the coffin ship out of Galway; he said he preferred to live where he could be just an American, not a jumped-up bogtrotter beneath the feet of the Back Bay snobs."

That brought a flash of understanding. Luz went on: "We lived in California when we weren't on the move from project to project, mostly in the Latin countries, or the West when we were in America. No kin in Boston when my grandparents had passed, and no sister or brother for me, and so not much reason to visit. And you?"

"Just my brother, Colm."

For a moment the bright blue eyes went narrow and very hard.

"The Sassenach killed him in April, in Dublin; he'd gone back to fight for Ireland as our father had in his day. Da had been ailing for a long time, and that news was the death of him, as sure as a bullet. A stroke. I sold the bookstore and volunteered for . . . well . . ."

"Courier work for the Clann na nGael? Which means the Irish Republican Brotherhood, too," Luz said.

A quick nod. "I thought it was revenge for my Colm," she said.

Luz's face went bleak. "I understand. I joined the Black Chamber because my parents were killed in Mexico by the *revolucionarios*. I was in the room when it happened, hiding . . . five years ago, now, so I'd have been about your age then."

Ciara gave a small shocked gasp but didn't venture any offensive stranger's sympathy, just a quick nod.

"I thought . . . I thought this was for Ireland," she said. "But it's not. They're going to use that stuff we saw on *us*. On America. I won't help with that, even if it means my life. In Boston I felt very Irish, but here in Germany I've realized that it's American I am, at seventh and last."

"*Sí*," Luz said. "That's well put! At a guess, they're planning to use it on our port cities—as many of them as they can, though I don't know how. Yet. That's an incredibly deadly weapon, far worse than chlorine or phosgene or even the new mustard gas. There were only a few pounds in that mortar shell, and it killed them all; killed or crippled or drove gibbering mad. One twenty-pound shell, a thousand men. Imagine tons of it released on a city."

Ciara blanched and crossed herself, swallowing hard and obviously imagining it on *her* city. "Mother of *God*!"

"Exactly. I'll have to get the details out of Horst, or otherwise; that's why I'm here. We caught wind of some plot, but only vague hints. They were reckless sending von Bülow . . . the white-haired man, he's a chemist . . . to America with all that in his head, but at a guess he was picking the sites for the attacks in full detail, so they needed someone fully briefed. There'll have been factions in the government and military here who didn't think it would work, or even had scruples about it, so he needed to make it convincing. He and Colonel Nicolai."

Ciara took a moment of frowning thought. "What . . . happened to the real Elisa?"

"Were you close?"

"No, we only met once, for a moment, and that when I was fifteen and she about the age I am now. I wasn't *altogether* sure you weren't her; people change fast in those years and you've much the same hair and complexion, until I saw your eyes close—hers were light hazel-brown, and yours are that blue that's almost black, something you won't forget."

Luz pursed her lips. "I did say I'd tell you the truth, so what happened to her was . . . very bad things, probably followed by death, after we caught her. That's not my side of the job, but I won't pretend I don't know about it. There's no Hague Convention for spies; we're vermin without rights if we're taken by an enemy. That's how this game works, and those are the stakes we're playing for here, you and I. It's harder than going for a soldier."

Ciara winced a little, but Luz could see she'd gained a little more confidence by her frankness.

"What can we do?" she said. Then she dropped her head into her hands. "Oh, God, I keep seeing those men—"

Then she raised her face and said fiercely: "They only wanted to be free!"

Luz laid a hand on her shoulder for a moment, before she stepped back. "That's natural. That was a . . . hard thing to see."

"You're used to . . . such things," Ciara said. "I'm not and I feel . . . empty inside. And I keep imagining it happening to my friends and my neighbors."

"I'm not used to things like *that*," Luz snapped, then controlled the flush of anger; it was part of the reaction.

She took a deep breath: "Not a thousand men gassed like rats in a cage to prove a theory! And I've seen hard things, yes, but it always . . . does something to you. You can shove it away for a while, but it comes back later."

Ciara looked up, met her eyes for a moment, then nodded. "I thought about what to do . . . but I don't know anyone in the American government, even if I could get away from here. And who'd believe a girl with such a tale anyway? Half the time men don't listen to you when you try to talk to them about anything but themselves or the weather or what's for dinner, if you know what I mean. It's as if they don't *hear* what you're saying unless you're saying certain things."

Luz gave her a wry smile. "Yes, and I do know what you're talking about, as one *girl* to another! But I'm a Chamber operative, I'm trained for this work, and I *can* get people to listen."

And if it came to the last piece to play, I can talk directly to the president, since

I played Bear with him and his children at Sagamore Hall. As long as I don't waste it on trivialities . . . and this is definitely not trivial.

"Precisely how to get the information out once we've got it . . . that we'll have to improvise."

And I'm certainly not telling you anything about codes or drop boxes!

Aloud she went on: "I'm here under deep cover. First we need solid intelligence: numbers, places, times. This would have to be closely coordinated, however they plan to do it. An overwhelming onslaught attack, probably coordinated with a massive offensive on the Western Front."

"I need to think," Ciara said. With a shudder. "Though not about what we saw. I wish I didn't have to think about that!"

Wait until you see the faces in your dreams, Luz thought grimly but did not say. *Or in that hour when you lie wakeful before the sun rises.*

Instead she went on: "We're supposed to be known to each other, so it's natural enough that we talk. See this?"

She ran her right finger behind her right ear, as if dealing with a mild itch. "That's the sign it's *safe* to *really* talk. Do *not* say anything that you wouldn't say to the real Elisa unless I give you that sign, right? Remember that!"

Ciara nodded, though Luz wasn't very confident she *would* remember, especially under stress. Consistent falsehood was hard for amateurs, but you did what you could.

Then she went on: "In the meantime I'm going to practice a bit, if you don't mind."

"Practice?" Ciara asked.

"A physical drill. I need to settle my nerves too, and it'll seem in character to Horst if he happens by."

Luz stood and made each muscle of her body relax. That itself helped calm the mind. Then she flipped the *navaja* from her pocket into her hand and snapped it open—the thumb stud that let her do that one-handed was the only modification she'd made to it, and it would have offended old Pedro's purist soul. As the *click-click-click* of the blade locking sounded she dropped lightly into *guardia* stance, crouched with right foot forward, right hand at waist level with the curved hilt held in a saber grip and the cutting edge down and to the right, left hand open in front of her navel and moving fluently in graceful sinuous curves.

The quick darting movements took her out of herself, a dance with the invisible . . . until she took one final deep breath, imagined her enemy coming in with a thrust to her face, and threw herself forward under it to land on left knee and left hand in the *pasada baja*, body bowed, right leg straight back and knife hand flung forward with her weight behind the lunge of the point into his gut just below the breastbone. After a moment's stillness she swept her right foot around slowly, using the change of balance to sway upright again.

"Faith," Ciara murmured, looking a little wide-eyed. "And do they teach you that in the Black Chamber?"

Luz blinked back from the state of absolute concentration. Her body felt purged, loose and balanced, cleaned of the poisons the morning had brewed as the music earlier had cleared her mind. She controlled her breathing and rolled her head and shook it, then sank into a chair. She was sweating a little, but it was worth it.

"No, I learned that as a girl, oddly enough."

"Can I see it? The knife."

Luz flipped the weapon and offered it across her palm. "Careful! It's sharp."

"It's . . . well made," Ciara said with a slightly queasy fascination. "And heavy."

"Heavy for a knife, light for a sword," Luz said. "About the best of its type I've ever seen."

It was old and finely crafted and the hilt use-smoothed, a pound of Toledo steel and brass and bone and mother-of-pearl. Luz took it back and closed it—there was a ring on the back at the join of blade and hilt; you ran your middle finger through that and pushed up. That pulled the pin free and unlocked the ratchets and it snapped shut like the folding straight razor it had originally been named for.

"This saved my life the night I was conceived," she said as she slid it back into her skirt pocket and sat again.

"It did?" Ciara said.

Her voice held a little of a child's appetite for wonders, or someone who'd always loved tales of the faraway and strange.

As I do myself, Luz thought, with a smile; and this was one of the oldest family stories her parents had told her. *And it will appeal mightily to this romantic youngster, who very much wants to be somewhere else right now.*

"I told you my parents eloped? In the middle of the night, and rode for the coast—my father had a boat waiting there. There was a full moon, and my father stood on the saddle to help Mima down from the balcony, as I was told, and carried her before him on the saddlebow through the fields and woods, hotly pursued."

Ciara's eyes shone at the image, imagining starlight and the lovers' hair mingling in the rush of speed. "Pursued? Her family sent men to bring her back?"

"After them yes, but more likely to kill them both, to avenge the Aróstegui family honor, you see. *Certainly* to kill Papá. So, old Pedro El Andaluz . . . the Andalusian, that night he brought the horses, and followed along behind. He was born in Seville, a deserter from the Spanish Army who'd gone to work for the Arósteguis long before. As a coachman, in name, and he was superb with horses, but really as my mother's bodyguard from the time she was a little girl."

"She needed a bodyguard?"

"A rich girl in Cuba in those days? Oh, *por Dios*, yes. Bozal runaways and *mambises* in the mountains when they were in the country, *hampas* in town. There wasn't much law in Cuba even between the rebellions, except what the strong made for themselves; not like today when there's an American-run police force and the gendarmerie the Marines trained. Pedro wasn't the only armed man in their employ, and God have mercy on the common man my mother's *papá* took against. He'd be lucky to get off with a beating."

"But Pedro helped your mother elope?" Ciara said eagerly.

Luz nodded. "He said it was time for her to have a man and children of her own, and a real man, not a eunuch in breeches, which is what he thought of the one her parents had picked. This *navaja . . . carraca*, it's called too, or *la Sevillana . . .* was his. He left it to me, along with his guitar, the only two fine things he owned. So, they got away from the *casa grande* without raising the alarm, but after a while Pedro could tell they were being tracked through the jungle; this was not far from Santiago de Cuba; the Aróstegui estates are mostly there, south of the Sierra Cristal, in the good sugar land of the valley bottoms. My father agreed with him; they thought they'd be overtaken before they got to the cove, and they didn't want my mother exposed to a gunfight, but they couldn't leave her alone either."

Ciara clapped her hands together. "And what did Pedro do?"

"Sent my mother and father forward, saying he'd catch them up. They waited at the boat, more and more anxious; there were a couple of shots, and silence . . . and my father told me later he was feeling torn in two but would have pushed off in another instant for his beloved's sake, except that Pedro *did* show up. Strolling, and wiping the blade on the seat of his britches; he always wore *estilo andaluz*, even after thirty years in Cuba."

At her questioning look, Luz said with a fond smile at the memory that rose up before her mind's eye:

"Think of a matador, but scruffy instead of glittery, and with a sash, and a black silk bandana tied around his head and knotted at the back. And a patch over his left eye, which he'd lost years before, and a gold ring in one ear; like a pirate in a pantomime, except it was no act. And then he bowed and said, *No need for hurry, they will not trouble us any more, Don Patricio, Doña Luciana*, and my father said: *How?*"

"And Pedro just smiled and said: 'La Sevillana los beso. *They kissed the girl from Seville, and she left them too breathless to pursue the matter.*' La Sevillana is *a Seville girl*, but it's a nickname for that type of knife, too."

It was a literally murderous pun.

"He . . . well, he sounds sort of appalling," Ciara said, torn between delight and horror. "Brave and loyal, to be sure, but . . . a bit wicked?"

Luz grinned reminiscently. "Oh, he was. A *barratero*, a killer and a rogue and no mistake. He drank and gambled and chased girls—caught quite a few, too—and was bone-idle about anything that didn't involve horses or fighting or betting money. Papá was always getting him out of scrapes, or jail, or both, which he took as nothing less than his due from *el patrón*. In the old days he'd have trailed a pike behind Pizarro or Cortez."

"Still, I can see why your parents put up with him!" Ciara said.

Luz nodded. "When I was about six, playing in a garden while my parents took the siesta in hammocks—we were in Mexico, Durango, Papá was laying out an irrigation project on an estate in the Laguna district—I heard this buzzing sound and my mother gasped and made this little shriek. I looked around and there was the head of a rattle-snake not a foot from my face with Pedro's hand around its neck; a big one longer than a man's leg, and he snapped its spine with his thumb. He'd seen it coiling while I played at scratching the soil with a stick, and he'd glided in and caught the thing, faster than the snake itself."

She gestured to show the motion, a flicking snatch. "My father went white as a sheet when he saw the snake, for in the hammock he could never have gotten close enough. He called it a brave deed of Pedro's, though."

"Indeed it was brave!" Ciara said. "A rattlesnake with his bare hand! The man was a hero, and must have had no nerves at all. Brave and loyal indeed, to do that for another's child."

Luz chuckled again. "*¡Verdad!* Pedro smiled a little and said: 'De nada, *Don Patricio*, estas viboras Mexicanos *always give themselves away before they strike. Whether they walk or crawl they brag with every breath.*' I do still remember the pink color of its mouth, and the drops on the ends of the fangs."

Ciara gasped. "The poor child you were, I'm surprised you weren't shocked into convulsions!"

Luz shrugged. "I was young . . . I just said: '*Can you show me how to catch snakes like that and can I have the rattle and a bracelet from the skin, Abuelo Cabo?*'"

"What did he say to that?" Ciara said, laughing.

"Laughed long himself, and told me I could have both, as befitted a princess."

"You called him . . . Granddad Corporal, that would be?"

Luz nodded. "It sounds right in Spanish; he *had* been a corporal in the Army, which is how he came to Cuba. Enlisted because it was that or the public garrote, and left the King's employ in Havana over a little matter of stabbing a sergeant who wanted too big a cut of his winnings with the dice. Mima called him *Tío*, Uncle, or sometimes *Cabo Pedro*, Corporal Pedro."

"Was that when he showed you how to use the knife? It strikes me it's not something you could learn overnight."

"It started a little after that. I asked him to teach me after I saw him practicing, the way I did just now. I think he liked that I didn't flinch at the snake, and that I loved the look and feel of the *navaja*. Though he had high standards, sometimes when we'd gotten on beyond the basics I'd end a session with tears running down my face from tiredness and pain in the muscles . . . that was part of the teaching, you see, to learn to work through pain and see if I really meant it."

"And your mother didn't mind?"

"Mima didn't know about the lessons . . . officially. She'd have had to disapprove if she admitted she knew, like when Father started teaching me to ride man-fashion and taking me on hunting trips."

Though she didn't disapprove very loudly or long about that, Luz thought. *Perhaps because she always felt a little guilty he'd have no sons, about which he said not a word nor glance nor sigh, though the lack of more children was a grief to them both.*

More cheerfully she went on: "Pedro said his sister had always carried a *navaja* tucked into her garter, a little one, so that anyone who raised her skirts without asking got *a little something*, but *not* what he was looking for."

Ciara chuckled; her face looked charming when she did, not just pretty but keen and interested.

"It looks . . . very graceful," she said. "Like a dance. And so quick!"

"It is a dance," Luz said. "One that makes you quick. *Flamenco de la muerte*, Pedro called it. When he handled a blade . . . suddenly he wasn't this scruffy skinny old man with two days' white stubble and a cigarillo hanging out of the corner of his mouth anymore; he was a dancer, a toreador, quick and quiet as a cat. He taught me all three styles of *pelea de navaja*. The *barratero*, which is street fashion; *gitano*, for the flash and fancy and for *el duende* . . . the demon, the spirit; and then *Sevillano* for the art. By the time I was sixteen he allowed I was quite passable."

"Well, I'll call him a grand old man for saving you that way," Ciara said. "What happened to him?"

"He fell off a horse one night and broke his neck, in Santa Barbara," Luz said, lightly, but remembering the bitterness of not being there, since it had been during her first year at Bryn Mawr. "Probably drunk and probably on his way back from an assignation with a cook at the Potter Hotel. He must have been . . . at least seventy then. Better so. My parents were killed the next year, and he couldn't have saved them. Nothing could."

She shook herself a little. "Your father owned a bookstore, you said?"

"Indeed he did! Or rather, we did; in an old house, and then two we knocked together. I helped him with it from as early as I could remember, and ran it after he was too ill. There was hard work to it, and I learned the buyer's part too, which meant traveling about a little, even to New York once!"

There was an innocent pride to her voice, and Luz hid a smile. There was more than a little respect in what she was feeling anyway. For a girl to succeed at a hard-bargaining trade like that required more than brains; it needed plain grit, and in large quantities.

And I don't suppose she'd have ended up here in Castle Rauenstein if she were a shrinking violet, Luz thought.

"But it was a grand education, even better than going to high school! A quiet life, but I loved the books; reading them, and cataloging, and the smell and feel of them, and finding just the right one a customer wanted. And the way it felt like a thousand friends were always waiting for me to drop by. My brother didn't want it, and started doing more with motors and electrics—though I helped him with that too, when I got the chance."

"You have a knack for that?"

"Oh, yes. I—" She blushed. "Well, I know it's not ladylike, but . . ."

Luz grinned and patted the pocket over the *navaja*. "Ciara, do I look as if I grow pale when a young lady doesn't flutter like a helpless butterfly and swivel her eyes about for a man to help her? It's the twentieth century; women have the vote! We can *fly*, and speak instantly across continents, when in our grandparents' time the fastest way to send a message was on horseback. I'm good with guns and horses because my father trained me and it was fun, and I can keep an engine running because I had to learn that, but if you've the natural talent for machines, I admire it."

"I don't see why most people think it's hard," Ciara said, frowning a little in puzzlement. "It's . . . seeing how things flow, the structure of them, how they fit together. Like mathematics, or music. It's *patterns.*"

Luz blinked in genuine admiration. *I can make figures work for me, but it's like digging a ditch—digging a ditch if you were blind and had to do it all by rote. I can see the patterns in people's faces and hear it in their voices or see a fight or a dance as a whole thing, but numbers? A language I have no ear for. Speaking of which . . .*

"How did you learn German?" she said.

"From books mostly. It's very important for the sciences, you know! And Auntie Treinel had it, her mother and father having been from a little place called Lermoos, in Austria, and she spoke it at home as a child. Though what she speaks isn't much like the books."

Luz raised a brow. "You have an aunt from Austria?" she said. The name Treinel was regional, not just German, very much like Ciara's accent in that language, in fact, which was sort of a hyper-Bavarian-Tyrolese.

"Oh, she's not really my aunt, not by blood. My father's elder sister—Auntie Colleen—and she are both spinsters. Auntie Colleen was thirty and still unwed with no prospect of it when she came over with Da, she having no inheritance and a clubfoot, too. And in Ireland these days it's common for folk to stay unwed anyway, unless they've a holding or a trade. Or a good dowry, for a lass. The which is a big reason so many leave."

Luz nodded. It was, even if you didn't count the huge number of Irish who were celibate religious, and those who did marry did so late in life. The Emerald Isle was full of younger brothers of farmers who were still bachelors at forty living by themselves in a loft, or with their spinster sisters; it was a habit that had come in with the Famine, and the fanatical fear of splitting the family's possessions it had bred. Few actual farmers had perished in the great hunger, whether tenants or freeholders. It had been the landless men unable to rent a holding and depending on day labor who had died by the hundreds of thousands, or the little cottars with a quarter-acre patch of potatoes who held as subtenants of a farmer in return for their labor, and their wives and children. Those with just a little more money or luck had fled wearing all that they owned. Only abroad in lands where work and food were more abundant could the Gael keep up their old habit of early marriage and big families.

"Auntie Colleen kept house for Da until he married, but by then she and Auntie Treinel were fast friends. They've shared a flat not far from where I live . . . lived, ever since then. With never a quarrel and happy as a pair of cats in a basket, with *their* cats, and cage of birds, and books and knowing everyone in the neighborhood and they so well liked, for being such good neighbors always ready with a hand for those who need it from sickness or ill-luck. Auntie Colleen was like a mother to me and a good sister to Da in his illness, and Auntie Treinel helped too. Helped me with the German when I started on it as well, and with other lessons too, the way Auntie Colleen helped me with the accounting. That being how she makes a living. Auntie Treinel teaches school, but she, Auntie Colleen, since she's lame and has a talent for the numbers, she has account books sent in and cleans them up for folk. More than one crooked bookkeeper has confessed or run for it at the mention of her name!"

Ciara frowned and went on quietly: "That's how I knew there was something going on with the bookstore. When I started doing the accounts, a few years ago. Money flowing in and out that didn't belong there—always balancing, but more than there should have been, and more by a good bit. The bookstore made us a fair living, until the doctor's bills were very bad—thank the saints for the new National Health Insurance; I don't know what we'd have done otherwise! Never a fortune, you understand, just an honest living for honest work. That other money, it was too much. Enough to frighten me."

"Ah," Luz said, her ears pricking up. "Not my specialty, but I've had specialists describe it to me. Money's the fuel and grease of organization, and an underground one has to tap into conduits to move it around and account for it and store it places where it can't be stolen but won't attract attention. Especially these last few years, with income tax and currency controls and official channels for bullion transactions."

"Yes! I knew friends came and visited my father . . . some of them from the Old Country . . . and later with Colm. They didn't talk much about it with me. And hard men, some of them. There's one named Sean McDuffy who sent me here . . ."

"Ah, now there's a familiar name," Luz said. "We never had enough on him for an arrest . . . He organized this?"

Ciara nodded, and her face went bleak. "He didn't tell me details, but what he said made me *think* that what this was . . . that it would be some sort of arms smuggling, from here back to Boston, and then from there to Ireland on neutral ships, since it's too dangerous for U-boats to try."

"Mr. McDuffy keeps bad company," Luz said thoughtfully.

Ciara nodded. "Gunmen, killers. There's a look about the eyes, especially when they think they're alone."

"Oh, yes," Luz said. *I've seen it in the mirror at times.* "Does this Mr. McDuffy know Elisa Carmody, do you think?"

"I wouldn't know. He might, but probably not—he only came to Boston about . . . three years ago, to my knowledge."

Ciara's own face went hard and furious for a moment. "And when Colm left and then he . . . was killed . . . and my father had his last stroke, I tracked McDuffy down and made them let me help."

She bit her lip. "I was *stupid!*"

"No, you weren't," Luz said, her tone clinical rather than sympathetic, which was more helpful.

Ciara looked up. "You needn't flatter me. I ended up here, didn't I? And not because I was so clever."

"I'm not in the habit of flattering. You had inadequate information," Luz said. "It happens all the time in intelligence work. Making decisions based on outdated information, or incomplete, or worse: corrupted, poisoned—what the Czar's Okhrana call *dezinformatsiya*, dis-information. Then it doesn't matter how clever you are, for the cake can't be sweeter than the spices."

"Dis-information? Now, there's a devilish thing to brew up!" Ciara said with a born scholar's indignation at someone deliberately fouling the well of knowledge.

"And devilishly effective. Did the *Protocols of the Elders of Zion* ever cross your bookstore's counter?"

"Oh, yes," Ciara said. "Henry Ford put out that edition and it was everywhere. I read it . . . it didn't seem very sensible. There's Mr. Silverberg who has the antique store who we did business with on old volumes, and I mentioned it to him, and he said some very . . . high-spiced things . . . in Yiddish. He didn't know I spoke German, which is nearly the same . . . and then he said that if the Jews ruled the world from behind the scenes they would get a good deal more practical use out of this dreadful secret power! Which is a good point, when you think about it. If there's any tribe who get the sharp end of the stick poked in their eye more than the Irish or even the blacks, it's the Chosen People."

Smart girl, Luz thought. *Remember not to confuse formal education with brains. Though I must find a gentle way to say* Negro *is much more polite than* blacks.

Only about a tenth of Americans finished high school, though the new Department of Education under Secretary Jane Addams was prodding and poking, shaming and subsidizing the states and localities hard to make it more. The cartoonists always showed her as the schoolmarm-in-chief with a switch in her hand, but at least you could be sure the girls wouldn't be scanted.

"That's an example of dis-information—and of the way people will always believe something they want to believe. The Russians came up with it because the pogroms against the Jews were hurting them in the Western countries, making it more difficult to get credits."

"So they flung some fake dirt to make up for the real smut on their own faces!" Ciara said. "I call that shoddy behavior and no mistake."

Luz nodded. "You would not believe how much trouble Henry Ford has caused by spreading that damned thing—he has a bee in his bonnet about Jewish bankers, and people listen to him because he makes all those Model Ts and raised his workers' wages to five dollars a day."

"A good solid family wage for a laboring man, near as good as a machinist or locomotive engineer makes," Ciara said, in the tone you used when making yourself be fair. "Unless he drinks it up before his wife gets her hands on it, that'll keep the house clean and warm and good food on the table, shoes on the children's feet and clothes on their backs, and enough left over for some savings against misfortune and the odd treat. And a glass of beer with dinner, no harm in that."

"Yes, Unc . . . the president was quite pleased at least one of the big boys did it without being pushed the way he had to with the steel barons and the mine owners . . . and the railroads provoked him until he nationalized them outright. Though that was also *pour encourager les autres*, a nice early example to keep the others reasonable and tell them the days when they ran Congress were well and truly over. But if only Henry would stick to making autos!"

"And the Clann na nGael told me what they knew *I* wanted to hear, after Colm and Da died," Ciara said bitterly.

"Yes," Luz said. "If it's any consolation, they thought they were doing it for a good cause. And they probably didn't know all the details of what we've seen, just that there's a weapon and an attack planned."

"Nothing good could come of that . . . that *horror* we saw," she said; Luz nodded, knowing what she meant. "And I'm sure as sure they knew the Germans meant America no good, if not precisely how much bad."

"Well . . . Ciara, did you ever read any H. G. Wells?"

It was a good bet, given her interests. "Oh, yes!" Ciara said enthusiastically, thinking she was changing the subject. "*The Time Machine*, and *The Food of the Gods*, and *The Island of Dr. Moreau*, and *The War of the Worlds*. Even"—she blushed at the mention of the *advanced* book—"*Ann Veronica*. How I envied her attending the Imperial University! Though . . ."

She frowned. "This free-love thing . . . it seems to me that it wasn't that free at all for *her*, and would have ended fine for him and badly for Ann, in the world as it is. Also he's too old for her."

"I suspect that's more of a daydream by Mr. Wells," Luz said, agreeing with every word. "That man she throws herself at is suspiciously like the author, cleaned up a bit, and Mr. Wells has an eye for young ladies, I hear. I don't doubt he'd be pleased to have them throwing themselves at his feet, saving him the risk and work."

"Men!" Ciara said, rolling her eyes. "The other books are fine . . . though now you mention it, in *The Time Machine*, doesn't the time traveler take up with that Eloi girl named Weena? And she pretty but stupid as a monkey, having no speech of her own, and altogether too much like a little girl in a woman's body, sort of a pet with a bosom? Which is revolting, when you think about it."

"No young man of your own, then, I presume?"

"Oh." Ciara made a dismissive gesture. "Spotty young tykes, the lot of them, and interested in a girl for only one thing—not one to hold a candle to Colm or Da. A husband off to the saloon three days in seven, wanting his corned beef on Sunday and a cradle filled every eighteen months, I do not think. Not yet; someday, perhaps, if I find one I could abide. One I could *talk* to about real things."

"Ah," Luz said. "Now, the reason I mentioned Wells . . . well, my father and mother read *The War of the Worlds* with me . . . when I was ill, back when I was fourteen, a bout of malaria. And something my father said then struck hard and stayed with me: that if the wilder sort of Irish Brotherhood type had been around in the book, they'd have made common cause with the Martians in an instant, if only they promised to eat the English first, and them last of all. This is not altogether different."

Ciara gave an involuntary snort of laughter. Then she looked down. "It . . . what we saw today . . . makes me think the worse of . . . what I was brought up to love."

"Ciara, there's no country on Earth that doesn't have great good and great ill to its credit, according to its power to do either, because different as countries may be, they're all composed of human beings at the last, and there's a devil and an angel in all of us. Everyone should love their country, and love and respect the memory of their ancestors; there's something wrong with anyone who doesn't. England's treated Ireland badly . . . but it was Diarmait Mac Murchada first sold his kin to Strongbow for help against his personal enemies. There's bad, and then there's worse."

Ciara nodded in easy recognition of the name of the King of Leinster who'd called in armored Anglo-Norman mercenary knights and their retinues from the marcher lordships to back him in a feud, and sworn fealty to London to get their fierce and greedy aid. The Gael had always had long memories. Luz went on:

"And I'm not going to say you shouldn't have wanted to avenge your brother, or that you wouldn't have been justified in fighting the English. I crawled through my parents' blood, and that night I killed the first of those who murdered them—slit his throat in the dark and took his horse and rifle. I killed more of them with my own hands over the next couple of years, during the Intervention—three of them were kneeling in front of the graves we made them dig and I shot them in the back of the head. I helped hunt the others down and watched them die. Some well, like Villa, whose followers the killers were—he walked to the wall on his own and scorned the blindfold and shouted *Viva Mexico!* into the muzzles of the rifles as he ripped open his own shirt. Others badly, wetting their britches and whimpering for quarter, or their mothers; but they all died and it was my doing. So I'm not going to judge you, not me of all people on Earth."

"I've been thinking . . . today," Ciara said. "That Colm died, yes, but he died as a soldier with gun in hand, fighting openly for Ireland against his enemies who were doing likewise for their country. That's a hero's death, death with honor, to be remembered with pride. This, what's going on here, there's no honor in it at all, only shame. That my brother would turn his face from me, if I had any part in it."

Luz patted her hand. "And you've had the good sense to turn back when you saw it was leading you . . . some place you really didn't want to go."

She looked at the sunlight; it would be dinnertime soon. And after that she could get the results of Horst's meeting out of him, one way or another.

NINE

H orst von Dückler thought he knew why the conference started in a grim frame of mind, for all that the room was large and bright with afternoon sunlight and smelled pleasantly of coffee . . . real coffee . . . being handed around to the participants. And for all that the talk was mostly of victories won after a long hard struggle.

They were all men of war, and even Privatdozent von Bülow had seen combat in his youth. And they had all seen weapons grow steadily more deadly. The oldest among them had watched while the Dreyse needle-gun replaced the muzzle-loading musket, and the younger had seen U-boats and airships and aeroplanes, machine guns and cannons that could throw shells the weight of an elephant twenty kilometers. Then clouds of poison gas drifting across the ghostly, cratered tangles of barbed wire on the Western Front among the millionfold rotting legions of the unburied dead.

But a regiment being obliterated in minutes by a single mortar round . . . that is something else altogether. And so is the thought of whole cities destroyed by the same means. Almighty Lord God, even to think of what a few battalions of heavy artillery could do with those shells is enough to make you blanch, much less a zeppelin fleet or . . . what we have planned for the Americans.

Horst put it from his mind; he had work to do. Various aides to the supreme commanders used maps and summary reports to outline the war situation, and he carefully stored the precise data. For once it was even more encouraging than the newspapers, which was probably a unique event in the history of war. That put him in a better mood, exhilarated and keenly anxious at the same time. After two years of titanic effort and terrible sacrifice from Belgium to the Pripet Marshes, from the Baltic to the Persian Gulf, the glittering prize of victory and safety for his Fatherland and *Volk* was so *close* . . .

And he was uniquely placed to know how grave the danger was of it being snatched away at the last moment.

Von Hindenburg spoke at last: "So. The Russians we have broken; they have agreed to send emissaries to Brest-Litovsk to negotiate a separate peace. But in the meantime our advance continues and their forces melt away from desertion or mutiny."

"We tore their hearts out when we trapped their main armies in Poland last year," Ludendorff said, obviously proud.

Justly so, Horst thought.

It had been Ludendorff's plan to drive for a double envelopment from north and south on a huge scale instead of just pushing them back as von Falkenhayn had wanted, a risky gamble that had paid off a hundredfold when the Russians' frantic retreat failed by a hair to prevent the hard-marching pincers from closing in their rear. A *Kesselschlacht*—cauldron-battle—was the ideal to which German commanders always aspired, and that had been the largest in all recorded history. Germany had brought off a number of encirclements since the war started, mostly in the east: The original attack on France had been intended as an even larger cauldron, but it hadn't . . . quite . . . succeeded. Verdun had, though at terrible cost.

Risky. But oh, the triumph when it works! That is how armies are broken and nations beaten into dust.

"This offensive of Brusilov's was their last throw of the dice. An act of desperation—*der Mut der Narren*, the courage of fools. When it was crushed and the best troops they had left with it, what remained of their will to fight evaporated," Ludendorff finished.

"It has become almost comical, in the east," Colonel Nicolai added. "We send a battalion and a few field guns down a railway line, they take the station and make prisoners of the Russians who have not run away, and then we repeat the whole process."

Von Hindenburg nodded, ponderous and implacable: "There will be no real negotiations, only our *Diktat* imposed with the point of a German sword to their throats. Russia will be thrust back to the borders of four centuries ago, to those of barbarian Muscovy, and within those they will be our vassals and pay tribute as and when we demand it. The rest, all her rich possessions, the Baltic, Poland, the Ukraine, and the Caucasus—perhaps even central Asia—we will dispose of as we see fit."

Which means either annexation to the Reich *or German colonial governors or puppet governments we control under new monarchs taken from our nobility, as seems most convenient to us,* Horst thought. *We lost millions of our best to the United States in the last century, because we could not give them homes or bread here in Europe. Now for our* Volk . . . *lands to settle, lands to rule, lands to exploit for what we need without depending on the seas the Anglo-Saxons control, all without leaving the shelter of our German flag or the protection of the German sword.*

"And France bleeds to death from the wound they took at Verdun, and still more their attempts to retake it," Ludendorff said. "They no longer have any offensive capacity against us. I did not like General Falkenhayn's butcher strategy there, but I must admit it worked. With the crown prince in command, of course."

Colonel Nicolai spoke: "Our latest reports indicate widespread refusals to advance among the French troops in Foch's present attack against our positions on the Chemin des Dames line, though they will still fight hard on the defensive. The death of General Petain was as great a loss to them as Verdun itself; now there is no one who has the confidence of the soldiers. Joffre they have come to hate as a blind fool who spends their lives to no purpose, but there is nobody to replace him in supreme command."

Ludendorff inclined his head to the intelligence chief. "Any peace we grant France will ensure that they too can never threaten the *Reich* again; they must acknowledge our hegemony in Belgium, give up the Briey ore fields and the coast down to Dunkirk and most of their African colonies, do no trade with the English, and pay us indefinite yearly reparations that will leave them nothing for an army or navy of their own. And which will pay much of the cost of ours.

"It will take them a little time to realize they have no alternative but to accept these terms," Ludendorff went on. "Meanwhile the English still strike us heavy blows on the Somme, which is the only reason we have not crushed the French altogether, but we have hurt them even more badly in return. They are paying the price for the small army they had before the war. We destroyed that army in the advance to the Marne, and at Ypres, leaving few to train their rush of volunteers."

He inclined his head to von Bülow. "There the help of the Institute's special munitions projects was crucial. That we had thousands of gas shells ready, even the crude early ones, enabled us to eliminate the Ypres salient and drive forward to the edge of the Channel ports before they could develop countermeasures. The English armies that confront us now are brave and numerous and not too badly equipped, even their Indian sepoy mercenaries fight with savage determination, but their volunteers are clumsy and ill-taught, and our U-boat blockade chokes them ever more tightly."

"Yes, Herr General," Nicolai said. "But that leaves us with the Yankees. They have been determined on war since the spring. Rather, Roosevelt wished war from the beginning, and now has manipulated their public opinion to the point where most support it, and now he feels he is ready for it."

Tactfully, he didn't mention the sinking of the *Mauretania*; Horst thought that the Americans would have entered the war even without it, but possibly—crucially—later than this year. He'd been there when the news came through. It had been fantastic arrogance on their part to imagine that their citizens could blithely sail into a war zone on a British ship carrying military contraband and be immune from attack, but the ugly wave of hate and thirst for revenge had been real enough to raise the hair on the back of his neck. With enough wealth and power you could afford such arrogance, and make others take it seriously too.

We accepted that our invasion of Belgium would bring in the English, but counted on it allowing us to destroy France before they could intervene in force. Then our U-boats were to choke the English before the Americans enraged by the sinking of their ships could intervene in force. There is a pattern here and it is one we must break. Our Project Loki will not enrage or frighten any other Great Power into war against us . . . but only because we are already fighting every other Great Power on Earth except the Austrians, who are not greatly powerful. Germany is very strong, but are we strong enough to make war on the whole world at the same time?

Then he shook himself mentally.

But it's not the whole world, not anymore. As the general said, we've broken the Russians; they're out of the fight and we can take what they make and grow and use it for our own purposes. The French are broken too, or nearly so. England bleeds, and totters and chokes. We can crush them one at a time. Frederick the Great did the same thing when he took Silesia—it looked as if Prussia would be ground to powder between France and Russia and Austria, but then there was a change of Czar in Russia and it came out right in the end. Otherwise I would be an Austrian. Brrr!

The head of Abteilung IIIb continued, giving Horst his cue:

"I will let my agents on the spot outline the difficulties and possibilities there," Nicolai said. "Hauptmann von Dückler will begin; he has been surveying the United States and its preparations in person and through subsidiary agents since the spring, at great personal risk."

Horst rose and saluted, and went through the necessary honorifics. He wasn't . . . overly . . . intimidated by reporting to Germany's supreme commanders. The German Army had always had a tradition of leaders listening to and learning from subordinates closer to the actual action, just as it had always encouraged the officer at the front to interpret orders flexibly—to take the knowledge of the commander's intentions and fit it into the context of the ever-shifting variables of war. Blind obedience was for peasants or Russians.

"The problem we face is that the United States is both inherently stronger than the English, our only other remaining unbroken foe, and better organized. We fight this war in order that Germany may be unassailably strong for the great trials of the coming century through the domination of resources on a continental scale."

Or at least that has turned out to be what the war is about, not least because you and General Ludendorff so decided. How long ago August of 1914 seems!

"But the Yankees *already* command a continent and have had generations to develop its resources. It is one thing to read statistics, another thing to see. I have ridden the railroads across that continent, from the Atlantic to the Pacific and back, half a dozen times. For thousands upon thousands of kilometers nothing but fat black earth rich with wheat and maize, maize and wheat and potatoes and cotton and cattle and pigs—farm after farm, tilled by men of Germanic or kindred stock with the most mechanized methods, only possible on such large farms with broad acres. Raising not only food but strong sons to work and fight for America. Grazing lands running day after day as well, forests of fine timber equally vast. Enormous manufacturing cities, as if Essen had been multiplied by the score, belching smoke into the sky as they pour out steel and explosives. Mountains of metal ores of every type, mountains of coal, oceans of petroleum, all harnessed to a most formidable industrial machine with efficient management and abundant skilled labor. If these are all deployed against us, we face a struggle without limits and with . . . no foreseeable favorable result."

"Resources and population are one thing, even industry capable of using them; their timely deployment as actual military power another,"

Ludendorff said. "As witness the English. Their empire is vast and their manufacturing capacity still fairly considerable if technically inferior to ours, but . . ."

"With respect, Herr General, the cases are not comparable and the reason is President Roosevelt," Horst said firmly but politely.

There was an unconscious stiffening. The Kaiser envied and emulated President Roosevelt. The rest of the German leadership took him very seriously indeed.

Von Bülow spoke: "With iron hand and iron will, he has mastered the chaotic energies of the Americans, and given them discipline," he said. "Particularly in the last four years, when he has led an organized movement thoroughly inspired by our theories and methods. In some areas they have gone beyond us, as with their Ministry of Public Health and Eugenics."

Horst nodded, though that appraisal of the Progressives was . . . not exactly untrue, but more than a little self-flattering from a German perspective. He spoke to add precise detail:

"More particularly, when he took office four years ago, the Americans had a hundred and fifty thousand volunteer soldiers and a militia."

"Comparable to the strength of Bulgaria," Ludendorff observed dryly. "Bulgaria before it mobilized."

"A joke of Bulgarian proportions, yes, Herr General, though in his early terms of office he had seen to the foundation of a General Staff modeled on ours and planning for larger things. But by this spring, the Americans had *six* hundred thousand men in their standing army—nearly equivalent to our peacetime strength in 1914—and a million and a half trained reservists, besides a very powerful navy. He used the conquest of Mexico to increase their army, and did so—together with General Wood, Chief of their General Staff and a very able man—in a way calculated to provide cadre for a *further* rapid expansion. Roosevelt is not only a clever devil with a broad knowledge of history, statecraft, and war; he is good at picking able subordinates and knows how to delegate."

"They concentrated on training staff officers, technical specialists, the organizational framework in general?" Ludendorff said. "These were prepared in numbers beyond what was strictly needed for operational reasons in their Mexican war?"

"Exactly, Herr General. Far beyond. The parts of an army that *cannot* be improvised rapidly, and their Reserve Officers' Training Corps was also cleverly conceived. Now with conscription the recruits flow in to put flesh and muscle on those strong bones, and already they have three million men under arms, though many are still in the training camps. And it is not as it was with the English in 1914, with men in civilian clothes drilling with broomsticks and sleeping in barns and taverns. Everything was ready, from barracks and boots to heavy artillery; or the factories and plans and machine-tools were ready. Good weapons, often excellent ones, in abundance. In some areas, such as motor transport, equipment in quantities that we simply cannot match, all in the hands of fresh, eager troops drawn from a population larger than ours. We face a power as vast as Russia, but with European or better-than-European standards of development and efficiency, one which has carefully studied the lessons of this war."

Colonel Nicolai took over smoothly. "We must strike before this strength can be deployed against us. The Breath of Loki, as you have seen, is an ideal weapon to deny an area to the enemy. We will use it to strike massive blows from the air against the English and the French, and tactically via guns and *Minenwerfer* on a large scale at the front. What the operational plan turns on, though, is our ability to use it to bottle the Americans up on their own continent. High-capacity ocean ports are yet another thing that cannot be improvised. They require both favorable geography and heavy investment over many years; hence each is a potential choke-point, far more so than any single railway line or bridge. With the help of the Navy, especially the secret capacity developed over the last year, we can do this long enough to establish our hold on all Europe. Then . . ."

"*Festung Europa!*" von Bülow said. "Against such fortress walls, even the arrogant and reckless *cowboy* Roosevelt will hesitate to throw his troops. Behind that wall, we can consolidate our strength and prepare for the day when we can break out to control the World Ocean."

The naval representative nodded sagely; it was the newly ascendant Admiral von Hipper, in charge since Tirpitz's fall.

"And here another of the Institute's programs, that of the Hülsmeyer group and their Project Heimdal, seems certain to bear valuable fruit this year or early in the next. The North Sea after the white nights turn to the short black days is a murky place to fight. If we are able to see and the enemy cannot . . ."

Silence fell. Ludendorff caught von Hindenburg's eye; the older man nodded with a Jove-like somberness, and then the younger spoke:

"Project Loki is hereby authorized to proceed to full operational status, then."

The admiral spoke: "If we begin immediately, L-Day can be set for twenty-two to twenty-six days from this date. The first part of October. Those vessels intended for the most distant targets will sail first, of course. Immediately, in fact, if word is sent after this meeting. The final attack order can be broadcast."

"Now is the moment to drive home the sword," Ludendorff said.

"Agreed," von Hindenburg said. "You are authorized to execute the attack."

The discussion finished with detail work; Horst remained mostly silent, as that was the Navy's bailiwick and as everything was apparently at a high state of readiness. He wasn't surprised; this was the Kaiserliche Marine's chance to do something decisive, even if not yet with their so-expensive battleships. When the generals had left and the gathering broke into knots, Nicolai took him aside.

"Captain von Dückler, I am tasking you with the northernmost element of the attack on the U.S., against Boston and its navy yard and port facilities. Yours will be the responsibility for guiding the crew to shelter with our local allies after the devices are planted, and seeing to their evacuation along the paths you previously established."

"Thank you, Herr Oberst!" Horst said joyfully.

Given his familiarity with the country it was also a job he was fully qualified to accomplish.

There would be ten separate but simultaneous attacks. Halifax, which was in British Canada; then Boston, New York and its associated harbors, Philadelphia, Baltimore, Hampton Roads, Charleston, Savannah, Mobile, and New Orleans in the United States. If most of them came off as planned, the United States would be effectively cut off from Europe for six months or more, its plans completely disrupted. If all of them did . . . the prize was dazzling, and the glory unlimited.

"Saving the crew is of high priority, Captain von Dückler," Nicolai said. "They are picked men, brave men, volunteers specially trained, and you yourself are a valuable agent, a weapon in our hand. But neither they nor you are the highest priority, not in a war in which thousands of brave men die every day."

"That is understood, Herr Oberst," Horst said gravely. "If I must, I will trigger the launching mechanism with my own hand. Victory is never cheap, not a great victory such as this."

And I will cry long live sacred Germany *as I do it*, Horst thought. *Or perhaps just* Scheisse *. . . but I will do it in either event, and that is what matters; then I must trust that the merciful Lord God and His mother will not deem it suicide. But if I must lose Heaven for Germany . . . that too.*

Nicolai stood silent for a moment. "This woman, Carmody, will be useful in moving your party overland to Mexico, and in arranging the arms shipments to revitalize the guerilla war against the Americans . . . you have not allowed yourself to become infatuated, I hope."

"Of course not, sir!" Horst said indignantly . . . and with a stab of guilt he thrust his hand down firmly.

Entranced, yes, but not infatuated. Elisa was right; we could no more make a life together than a tiger and a shark could.

"Is she?"

Horst sighed, still feeling a tug of wounded . . . *yes, vanity, I should admit that.*

"No, sir. She is . . . extremely self-contained and does not allow personal matters to interfere with her mission."

Nicolai raised a brow. "Unusual in a female; more often they are preoccupied with petty personal concerns. Perhaps she will also be useful in keeping the Whelan girl from collapse; it will be convenient to have the two females on the same ship, less disruptive, since we must make use of them at all. Whelan is naïve and wedded to childish scruples, but some use may be gotten from her for the Fatherland; and hers are the contacts in Boston itself. That will be a delicate matter. They must evacuate the crew quickly, and before they realize what the nature of the Loki weapon is. They might balk if they realize that the effects . . . cannot be contained strictly to the naval installations, which is their current impression."

When they realize it will destroy their city and presumably their families, Horst thought. *And the extent to which we have deceived them. Though they were most willing to be deceived!*

Nicolai continued: "It may well be necessary to silence the girl at a crucial moment. She knows too much."

Horst couldn't altogether hide his distaste but answered stolidly: "I understand the military necessities, Herr Oberst, you may rest assured as to that."

After all, I am going to be killing thousands . . . no, certainly tens of thousands, possibly hundreds of thousands of women and children. What is one more?

You do have to eat, Ciara dear," Luz said gently, noticing that the girl was merely pushing things around her plate. "Think of something different. Something that gave you pleasure."

That meant not thinking too much about the food itself: thin potato soup that might once have been frightened by the corpse of a chicken waved above the pot, followed by rubbery schnitzel encased in limp dingy crumbs, gray noodles in nameless sauce, excessively boiled potatoes and cabbage, and something that disgraced the name of apple strudel. All accompanied by that suspicious bread and margarine that someone had tried to make without using animal *or* vegetable fats. You needed fats to make glycerin, and you had to have glycerin to make explosives.

It all represents German cooking about the way an accordion man with a trained monkey represents Italian opera. Though there is enough of it, at least, so stop whining, Luz—you remember sucking on pebbles because there wasn't even any water, por Dios.

It was seven now, and the sun was touching the western hills. Long golden spears shot through the high narrow windows of the hall that served as the officers' mess, catching on a gilded antler now and then as they lanced across the high spaces, or the halberd of a motionless man-at-arms in a niche. She had to admit there was a certain melancholy magic to the long northern twilights.

Either the food situation in Germany was very bad, or the high-ranking here were being ostentatious about not escaping from the tribulations of ordinary folk, or both. She suspected it was both, from the way everyone else was tucking in as if this were better than their ordinary fare. From overheard bits of conversation the visiting heavies would be leaving tomorrow morning, doubtless off to approve of some other evil plot.

Tomorrow I'll have an opportunity to pump Horst, Luz thought. *Probably in both senses of the word, which will be fun. Nothing like that for taking your mind off something unpleasant.*

Right now he wasn't all that far away, but he was deep in conversation with Colonel Nicolai and the Herr Privatdozent, kept to a level lost in the buzz and clatter off the high roof. The two women, and one extra man, were at the end of one of the long trestle tables. Luz was keeping an eye on the civilian; he was unmistakably an American, of a particular sort, which meant that she should learn more. There was no way on God's green Earth he could be up to any good in this company.

"Did your Auntie Colleen tell you stories when you were a girl?" Luz asked. "My parents did, one or the other or both, nearly every night.

That was always my favorite time of the day; it was how I learned to read."

"Stories? That she did!" Ciara said, a little more cheerfully. "She'd often come over and cook for us, and tell us stories later in the parlor. Or we'd visit at her flat, lying on the rug before the coal fire with the cats, and she'd read to us—there was this book by a man named Curtin, when we were small. *The Shee an Gannon and the Grugach Gaire* was my favorite of those, and Colm most liked *Fin MacCumhail and the Fenians of Erin in the Castle of Fear Dubh*. She had Hans Christian Anderson too, and Peter Pan, and others . . . And Auntie Treinel had this lovely book of Grimm's tales, it must have been forty years old even then, and she'd read them to us—translating as she went. Odd and bloody and exciting they were, not the version like boiled potatoes with no salt you see today."

She added scornfully: "Thinking the little ones will be scarred for life at a fright."

"Treasure Island?"

"Oh, yes, and I wanted to be Jim so badly! And then we moved on to Twain, *Huckleberry Finn* and *Tom Sawyer*, reading them together and talking about them. I reread them again a little while ago and for all the games and make-believe and boys' naughtiness they're deep and sad."

Now that's very perceptive, Luz thought, and went on aloud:

"Twain knew his business and no mistake. He's wiser when he's showing boys at their foolishness than many a solemn man is with a thousand ponderous pages of conversations in parlors and ballrooms. Henry James, for example."

"Oh, *him*," Ciara said, and rolled her eyes. "But still, that raft trip down the river is like a happy dream in some ways . . ."

Ciara paused with the fork halfway to her plate. "And that was cunning of you. I've actually eaten half of this. Not much of a treat, but I've had worse and I feel better for it."

"What's more, I ate half of *mine* without noticing either. Thanks!" Luz said.

She'd managed to get the schnitzel down, gristle and all, and the rest was mostly just dull. When it was finished she felt . . . not hungry anymore, which was the minimum basic function of food, after all. Like all those locomotives being fed bad wartime coal, she could get the work done.

"The mind and the body can't really be separated, you know," she said. "The one affects the other equally. You were hungry; it was just that your mind was getting in the way."

"Auntie Treinel is a splendid cook," Ciara said, smiling fondly at the memory. "Her sauerbraten of a Sunday was fine, and her *Schwein-shaxe*. So it's not that we're in Germany that makes the food here so dreadful."

"They're short of everything, ladies," the man said; he'd moved a little closer after pushing away his plate. "Hungry as my people were in sixty-five. More credit that they don't let it stop them."

He inclined his head and mimed lifting the hat he wasn't wearing. "Robert Edward Daubigny, of South Carolina, happy to be at your service," he said. "Pardon my forwardness in introducing myself, but we've been thrown together by circumstance. And in a common purpose."

Luz and Ciara both inclined their heads slightly and shook hands warily; no matter the circumstances, you always had to be a bit cautious about friendliness with an unknown man. His grip was firm and strong; the hand didn't have a workingman's calluses, but Luz judged he was a hunter, and rode a good deal, which accorded with the outdoorsman's complexion. From the slight dent in his nose, he'd probably played college football too, or possibly boxed as an amateur.

"You're an American, sir?" Luz said coolly.

"A Southron," Daubigny said. "Here as a representative of a brotherhood struggling for liberty for my people, as you valiant ladies are."

He was a slender whipcord-tough man in his late thirties, deeply tanned, with a rather archaic-looking pointed chin-beard and mustache of dark brown, longish hair cut above the ears, and hazel eyes. His well-styled beige linen suit was bespoke and probably comfortable where he came from but would be chilly here soon enough, and he wore it with a black string tie; the whole effect was almost comically regional, like an illustration of a Kentucky colonel in an adventure novel. The accent was definitely southern, but not the *hush-ma-mouf* gumbo one you usually heard, nor the hard upcountry hill-and-holler rasp that was so common in the Army: He said *heppy* for happy and didn't drop the *r*-sounds except after a vowel. In a way it was reminiscent of a very, very old-fashioned English way of speaking, with an overlay of modern British public-school speech as well.

South Carolina low-country. Charleston, she thought. *Upper-class Charleston, old family.*

What was it Lincoln had said about the state of South Carolina? She'd learned most of his sayings, not least because Uncle Teddy considered him the greatest of all presidents.

¡Ay! *That was it! "Too small for a country, too big for a lunatic asylum."*

"I understand that the lovely young lady from Boston represents the Clann na nGael," Daubigny said. "Fellow sufferers from the hand of the descendants of the Roundhead Puritans, with their insufferable meddling and unwillingness to leave anyone alone to live as they please. And you, Miss Carmody, are of the Mexican Revolutionary Party."

"And you, Mr. Daubigny?" Ciara said, unexpectedly bold.

No, thought Luz. *I should* have expected it. *She may have led a sheltered life by my standards, but she also ran a bookstore. She had to talk to anyone who came in, and deal with salesmen who develop faces of brass as a professional necessity.*

He inclined his head. "I, Miss Whelan, am an emissary of the brotherhood which fought the northern occupation of our lands until they agreed to restore at least a minimal degree of community self-government and the protection of white womanhood. The noble Knights of the Ku Klux Klan."

Ciara stared at him blankly. Then . . .

"Oh. That was after the Civil War . . ."

"Properly the War of Northern Aggression, Miss Whelan, but yes."

"There was a cinema last year about it," she added.

That was D. W. Griffith's masterpiece, *Birth of a Nation*, a drama-tized history of the Reconstruction period that was just slightly biased, full of leering Negro rapists, corrupt northern carpetbaggers preying on the bones of the fallen South, evil scalawag collaborationists, and the heroic defenders of Dixie in those rather comical outfits of white sheets—which had a striking resemblance to the pointed hats and masks *penitentes* wore when parading through the streets in Holy Week in the Latin countries.

Luz had heard Uncle Teddy cursing a blue streak and damning the film and its creator comprehensively in that way of swearing he had without using obscenity or scatology—and not knowing she was in the Director's waiting room in Washington. The irony was that it *was* a masterpiece, the first one she'd seen that really convinced her that moving pictures could be an art form like drama on the stage.

Like much great art it was causing no end of political trouble, though, and there was enough of that down in Dixie anyway. For all that his mother had been from a Georgia planter's family and that un-cles of his had fought for the Confederacy, Uncle Teddy had been loathed there ever since he'd invited Booker T. Washington to dinner at the White House, and refused to let Jim Crow into the federal civil service—when he'd had some Negro civil servants and their wives to a White House social along with their white colleagues, the screams of outrage and defilement had been deafening. They'd have hated him for nominating a colored man as chairman of the 1884 Republican Con-vention in Chicago, if most people hadn't forgotten that he'd done it.

It had gotten worse lately, with the rumors (which she knew were perfectly true) about a new Federal Elections Act to enforce the post–Civil War amendments . . . especially since these days the federal gov-ernment had the power to *actually* enforce laws whether the locals liked it or not, and a formidable patronage and presence everywhere. But reports from the southern division of the Chamber headquartered in Atlanta hadn't been her specialty—she'd operated in the Protectorate, and then retrained for Europe in New York. She hoped the specialists *were* on top of it, and the FBS was ready to act.

Because even if this R. E. Daubigny represents nobody but a few lunatics mumbling slogans and stories about befo' de woah *at each other over their mint juleps on the verandah of some decaying mansion amid the moonlight and magnolias, it's still a few lunatics ready to commit outright treason. In which case, Dixie will be getting a taste of what we in the Black Chamber, and the FBS, and the Army did in Mexico.* ¡Y justo el jodido que esos cabrones se merecen!

"The Klan has been revived," Daubigny said. "Secretly, for the most part. But we have powerful friends and allies in many of the state governments and National Guard units."

Luz recognized his tone and the gleam in his eyes; fanatics were something she had long unpleasant experience with. Unfortunately he didn't seem to be technically stupid, something else you could usually tell quickly. And he was obviously an educated man. Intelligence, education, and fanaticism were a dangerous combination; it made for people who could convince themselves they were right in doing absolutely anything, and who could think up quite ghastly things to *do*.

The Herr Privatdozent, for example, will do quite literally anything *for Sacred Germany, and use all his technical brilliance and organizational skills to do it. He's a monster, but he wouldn't be a bad old* abuelo *if it weren't for that, and the bees planted in his bonnet by misunderstood Nietzsche. Greed and cruelty can be satiated, but idealism never tires. It's bad* ideas *that make for the great crimes, not bad character in individuals. Not that I should take too lofty a tone. I'm perfectly willing to do almost anything* for America, *after all.*

She remembered standing unmoved as the figures in their ragged clothes were pushed toward the edge of the trench and the machine guns brought up.

It's a narrow path to salvation, almost is, *but it's what I've got.*

"The tyranny in Washington that crushes Mexico and Central

America—that conspires with the British oppressors of Ireland—that tries to tear up the bargain that ended Reconstruction in our own country—"

Daubigny seemed to realize he was getting a little loud. With a shy smile he ducked his head.

"Let me just say that there are patriots all over the South ready to resist to the last drop of blood the threat of mongre—"

He stopped, cleared his throat, and went on: "—threat to our cherished honor and way of life. We've taken up the name of the first Klan, to show that we aspire to the heroism of our fathers and grandfathers."

Aspire to take on someone who outnumbers you three to one and go down to heroic defeat? And he was probably about to say threat of mongrelization. *Then he realized on the fly it's not the most tactful possible thing to say to a purported Mexican revolutionary, who's probably a mestizo herself. Which I almost certainly am in fact, even if the Arósteguis would rather face the Inquisition's rack than admit it. The really ironic thing is that this gentleman's ancestry almost certainly includes some Negroes too, given the number of octoroons who moved a few hundred miles, changed their names, and blended in over the centuries. I saw that old book from the fifties at Bryn Mawr, the one that the abolitionists published, full of escaped-slave notices from southern newspapers with descriptions like* blue eyes, blond hair, freckles, will attempt to pass himself off as a white man. *There's nothing more amusing than watching a man run faster and faster in an attempt to escape his own sweat . . . except when he's willing to kill to do it.*

"And did you see the . . . demonstration . . . this morning?" Luz asked.

"I participated in the cleanup operation afterward," he said.

"You went *into* that stuff?" Ciara cried, shocked and impressed.

"In a sealed protective suit," Daubigny said casually, obviously not averse to mentioning he'd done something that took nerve. "Gruesome work, but educational. A few of the German naval officers I came over with were there too. We arrived just too late to see the actual use."

"You didn't miss anything worth seeing," Luz said, and mentally gritted her teeth at his patronizing smile that made allowances for the squeamishness of women. "Not unless you have very odd tastes."

"When you've thought as long as I have about revenge, miss, the prospect of finally achieving it strengthens the sinews."

"Revenge?" Luz said. "I have . . . personal reasons for what I do, but an American?"

Daubigny flushed. "My father lost his leg at Fort Wagner when he was sixteen years old. All four of his older brothers died, at Second Manassas and Antietam and Gettysburg, and one of hunger and disease in a Yankee prison camp. Sherman's bummers, scum disgracing the name of soldiers, burned our home on the Pee Dee where six generations of my family had been born and buried, shot my grandfather down like a dog—an old man, helpless and unarmed—when he tried to stop them, and threw my grandmother out in the clothes on her back. She died by the road of hunger and despair. That was what my father came home to, he himself all that was left of our family. Three thousand acres of the best rice land in the world, and now it's gone back to the swamp it was before my family spent two hundred years reclaiming it—"

With just a little help from the slaves, solo un poco, *but I see your point,* Luz thought. *The Aróstegui family would probably put it exactly the same way.*

"—good for nothing but hunting as it was to the Indians. Yes, Miss Carmody, I have *personal reasons* too."

Then he paused, looking down at his hands. "I must admit . . . the bodies . . . it did remind me of some things in Poe."

Luz felt memory stir, but it was Ciara who quoted: "*And the Red Death held illimitable dominion over all,*" she said softly.

Luz decided to switch to something a little less inflammatory, not to mention depressing; "The Masque of the Red Death" was far too good an allegory for the picture her mind painted of the Breath of Loki unleashed on a city of humankind.

"You arrived by U-boat?"

"How did—" Daubigny began, then nodded with a smile and tapped a warning finger alongside his nose. "I won't say a word to that, except to note that you are as clever as you are beautiful, Miss Carmody."

"It's still very difficult to detect a submarine that doesn't attract attention by attacking," Luz said. "We have strong allies, now, *gracias a Dios!* Ones who can sail into the enemy's very ports undetected."

That's it! she thought, smiling at him as he nodded again. *Somehow they intend to deliver the Breath of Loki by submarine!*

She was making progress. Not enough, and getting the information out would be somewhere between difficult and . . .

Between difficult and very *difficult. There is no impossible. Not with this!*

TEN

Ciara Whelan straightened up from where she'd been kneeling by the baseboard. "That's the last of it," she said. "No microphones in our bedroom."

Luz frowned. "You're sure?"

"This wall is solid stone," Ciara said, and thumped it with the heel of her hand. "It's load-bearing. So are the other three. There's no microphone made will pick up significant sound through these oak floorboards. With a very large horn collector and one of the very latest Siemens thermionic-valve modulated signal amplifiers you *might* be able to pick up some by using the ceiling, if there weren't any background noise and you could put the horn directly on the other side of the plaster. Except that directly above us is the water-closet and bathroom, and the piping is twenty-five years old and groans and rattles all through the night."

"So, you're sure?" Luz said; as if to emphasize the point, the plumbing did rattle and gave a wheezing choke like a grief-stricken whale with pneumonia.

"No, I'm morally certain, if you want to be persnickety," Ciara said. "To be *sure* I'd need to go into all the rooms to either side and above and below. Well, not below, that was where we were this afternoon and there was nothing there."

"You're the expert," Luz said. "Good, we're reasonably safe talking here."

I'm not *an expert on electronics, but I know enough to recognize someone who really is.* ¡Ay! Las paredes oyen, *but not all of them.*

Ciara had been standing rather belligerently with her arms crossed over the laced front of her nightgown. Now she looked doubtful.

"You're not going to argue?" she said, as if unaccustomed to being taken at her word.

"No, that would be silly," Luz replied. "I asked you because you have knowledge I don't, and I'd be *una boba* if I didn't listen to you when you use it, wouldn't I?"

The room had a pleasant glow from the low coal fire. Ciara had laid it, and skillfully; half a newspaper ripped up, three sticks of kindling making a triangle to contain it, another three on top at an angle, then the larger pieces of coal around the edge of the bottom triangle. With that she'd lit it, adding the smallest pieces of coal with the tongs gradually as the kindling caught, then larger ones placed to give plenty of paths for air and fire. They'd pushed things around to open out a space around it, and the orderly who'd brought water and changed the pot for a fresh one had been perfectly willing to scrounge some fuel for a few pfennigs tip; Luz would have been surprised if some wasn't available even in wartime, with a military-priority train station a quarter mile away. The night had grown a bit chilly, the weather on the verge of changing.

Her Vuitton trunks acted as armoires if you opened them wide, and they had a number of individually designed pockets. Luz took out a bottle that Horst had slipped to her after dinner—her sharing it with Ciara was not what he'd had in mind, but that was his problem—and set it and two glasses on the little table between the chairs, along with a jar in a padded holder that she unscrewed. She was already comfortable in the black silk Chinese pajamas, which had gotten her a shocked but admiring look.

"You confirmed what *I* thought after I'd had a look. *Good* electrical wizard! Have a *coquito!*"

She held out the jar; within limits the little pastries improved with age, if you kept them from drying out. Ciara took one and sniffed curiously as Luz worked with the corkscrew and poured two glasses of the amber-golden wine.

"Mmm!" the younger woman said, after a nibble, sinking into the other chair. "Coconut?"

"*Sí*. This is Mima's recipe, it's *Cubana*. She called them a taste of home because she'd loved them as a girl. Shredded coconut—real coconut, mind—butter, sugar, eggs, pastry cream, a touch of vanilla extract, some cornstarch. And an apricot glaze. I made these myself in a friend's kitchen a day before I left America, and left her half. Which her children will have finished off that very day. A pity, because they're better a few days later."

"*Mmm! Very nice!*" Ciara said. "Sweet and nutty and . . . this rich dense taste. I didn't realize coconut tasted like that at all!"

Then, curiously: "If your mother was a great lady, wouldn't she have had cooks to do the kitchen work?"

Luz nodded. "When she was a girl in her parents' home, certainly. After that . . . usually we did have a cook of sorts, but Mima always said that you couldn't supervise work you didn't understand. And she meant understand through your hands, something you could do and do well yourself, so she spent time in the *cocina* of the Aróstegui family's *casa grande* when she was young, learning, and doing some of the fancier things herself, for saints' days and such."

She gave a rueful chuckle. "From what she said, it was a relief. You don't know what boredom is, apparently, until you've been raised like a well-born *Cubana* girl a generation ago. They usually wouldn't let her even read anything but saints' lives and other *improving* literature— newspapers were bad for female minds, for example. And later, I can remember that sometimes it was just the three of us, when we were traveling."

Softly: "And sometimes she liked to do things like these *coquitos* with me, just for the fun of it. I can remember standing on a chair to chop things, and her laughing at me because I was squinting and had my tongue out of a corner of my mouth."

"Do *you* like cooking?" Ciara said, curling up in her chair.

My, that's an interested look, Luz thought. *Pupils a little dilated, lips parted . . .*

She smiled back, head a little to one side, considering the other in a new light. Ciara Whelan was extremely pretty now that she'd relaxed, pretty in a way that had little to do with the conventional, fashionable canons.

Appealing, Luz thought. *Very appealing, with those big eyes and snub nose and that air of intelligence and wounded innocence.*

Her hair hung down over one shoulder, a thick shining fall in the firelight, and the cerulean eyes were bright with thought and feeling. What really made a face . . . or a person . . . attractive was that sense of how the being inside dwelt, though the package certainly helped.

Helps quite a bit, to be honest. And her hair probably smells like strawberries. That is a girl asking to be kissed, if I've ever seen one, and eminently seducible . . . even though she has no idea of what she's feeling. A little wine, a little music, some gentle talk, maybe a waltz . . . about an hour to the whispered poetry and then the horizontal part . . . I'll bet she has very sensitive earlobes and would turn bright pink in the most interesting places, and she'd give this little shocked gasp when . . .

Luz laughed ruefully, even as her toes curled a little at the thought and the prickling heat it brought.

"What's funny?" Ciara asked.

"The way my own nobility sickens me at times," she said, which brought a puzzled smile.

The fact is that it would be taking advantage of the circumstances, and of you, Ciara. You're all alone and need my protection, and that might hurt your feelings later, and I like you too much already to risk that, she thought. *I must be devel-*

oping the finer sentiments. Ah, well, probably not a good idea for practical reasons either. You have Virgin in Every Possible Sense of the Word *written on your lovely funny face, my dear, and I couldn't be sure how you'd react in this pressure cooker.*

"And yes, I do like to cook," she went on aloud. "Sometimes you just can't face another restaurant, even a good one; I travel a good deal, you see. It's even better with an audience to appreciate it. Back in California we have a thing called a *barbecue* I like to put on sometimes, but that means pit-roasting and it takes a lot of preparation, and you need at least a dozen guests to make it worthwhile. Great fun when you're all around the trestle tables under the pepper trees, passing the jug of red wine and playing the guitar and getting sauce on your face and fingers. You?"

"Oh, I *can* cook—I did for Colm and Da, for years—but it was always a bit of a chore, and of course you have to shop every day and that took time from everything else needing to be done, especially after Da was too ill to sit at the cash desk and Colm was off doing mechanic's work, or at night classes. Auntie Colleen would come and fill in for me at the desk in the shop sometimes, and then I did her shopping too when Auntie Treinel was too busy with her lesson plans or whatnot to go to market, since the walking was harder for her with her poor foot."

Luz blinked. *Well, yes, shopping every day would swallow a lot of time,* she thought. *Not everybody can have what they need sent over with a message or by telephone, or store the non-perishables in bulk, and even iceboxes are still expensive.*

"Though I did it well, I'd say; not fancy cooking, but proper solid meals a man wouldn't turn up his nose at as the aunties had taught me, and a nice apple cake with custard sauce to follow, or whiskey cake or barmbrack. We had Father Flandry in sometimes, and he never complained, and you could see that he liked a meal from the way he filled his cassock! Now, Auntie Treinel is an artist with the pots and pans, as I said, the best in the family. Auntie Colleen, she's more with the baking—her oatmeal scones with raisins are a treat on a cold winter's day when the snow is at the window and a good cup of cocoa's steaming beside them."

She chuckled. "I must admit that the *eating* part appeals to me much more than the cooking. Can I have another of these . . ."

"*Coquitos*," Luz said. "And try a sip of the wine with it."

Ciara looked at the liquid glowing in the glass dubiously. "I can't say I've liked wine much, the few times I've tasted it—never envied the priest at Mass, you might say. Not for the likes of me, perhaps? Though books I've read with pleasure do go on about it and all the types and the flavors they're supposed to have, and then it tasted like spoiled grapes with spirits in it to me, and sour. Quite the disappointment."

"That's probably because you were tasting near-vinegar, or paint-thinner, or what someone made in the cellar out of Concord fox grapes. This is a dessert wine from the Moselle and quite a good one. *Trockenbeerenauslese*, and it's made to be taken with sweet things. Just let a little of it over your tongue for a moment, swallow slowly, and then wait a bit for the rest of the taste to come out."

She sipped a little of her own and sighed; notes of citrus, honeyed apricot, spice, honeysuckle . . . Luz nibbled at the *coquito*, sipped again. Ciara was making inarticulate sounds of pleasure in the background, and visibly forcing herself to sip slowly.

"That's splendid . . . and it does go with the *coquito* . . . so, I was misjudging wine?"

"Sweet wines are more accessible for a beginner," Luz said, and smiled. "Perhaps sometime I can introduce you to the drier types."

"I'd like that. I'm a bit surprised you'd like it, cooking, that is."

"Why?" Luz said.

"Well, you're . . . you're so stylish and elegant and beautiful, and so . . . so dashing and adventurous and modern, and . . ."

Another fiery blush. "So very much a New Woman," she said—something she'd obviously always wanted to be. "Like a hero . . . heroine . . . in a book, really!"

"Why, Miss Whelan, you've put me to the blush!" Luz said, accompanying the old-fashioned phrase with an even more old-fashioned gesture that put the back of her hand to her forehead. "You wouldn't by any chance be *flirting* with me, would you?"

Ciara looked at her open-mouthed for a moment, then joined in her laughter at the absurdity of the notion.

Though the thought's there now, joke *or no,* Luz mused. She said:

"And the point of being a New Woman is that we get to do what we have the talent for. If I *like* cooking and I do it well? Why shouldn't I do it, then? Just as there's no reason you shouldn't be a second Tesla."

"No, no, there's only one Tesla! Though working in his laboratory, that would be a dream and no mistake!"

Luz chuckled. "Don't underestimate yourself. I've met Tesla a few times—"

"You have?" Ciara said, awe in her voice.

¡Ay! *Did I just grow a halo, or start to glow with an electric-blue crackle?*

"What's he like?" she continued eagerly. "I've heard he's elegant but eccentric."

"The most brilliant mind I've ever met, and an impeccable dresser with a gentleman's manners to boot, but mad. Quite mad, mad as a hatter," she said. "He's not living in the same world as the rest of us, most of the time. But he brings extraordinary things back from the one he *does* live in . . . and often, they work here too."

And sometimes they don't. Mad's not the half of it. If he weren't *a genius nobody would say he was* eccentric *for falling in love with a pigeon or seeing tongues of living flame giving him visions, or . . . He'd be locked up somewhere with soft walls! And I really can't tell you too much about him, given what he's working on for the Black Chamber and the Iron House.*

The latter was the nickname for the great new headquarters of the consolidated War and Navy Departments, standing like an exercise in neoclassical geometry around a courtyard. Uncle Teddy had used his National Advanced Research Projects Institute to give Tesla all the toys he wanted and turned him out to play in the flower meadows of applied science. Without the stress of patent fights and money worries and dealing with businessmen, the Croatian scientist had . . .

Blossomed, Luz thought. *Into something passing strange. Like Prospero in the play, but* with *his book.*

She went on aloud: "Where was I . . . cooking . . . But I couldn't get the salary a French man-chef does for it, or his job in the fancier places, be I never so good."

"You couldn't?" Ciara said, her puzzlement turning to indignation. "And why not?"

"Why do you think?" Luz said.

"For *cooking*, of all things, men get paid more and get the best jobs?"

"The Constitution may say we're equal now, but putting flesh on those bones isn't the work of a year, or two or three, alas. Not that I want to *be* a chef, you understand, but there would be a wall in front of me if I did. Women are well enough for *cuisine bourgeois*, but the *haute* evidently requires a . . . um . . . set of whiskers. Which makes you wonder exactly what they do in the kitchen, no?"

"Oh. Well, it's a shame and an outrage."

"Another thing I'm not going to argue with you on. One more *coquito* each," she said. "And another glass of the wine or two. It's been a hard day and I can use some if I want to sleep. This takes me back—it's like the old days at digs in university, when we'd get together and talk about all the woes of the world and how we'd solve them, until lights-out."

"Ah, now that I would enjoy," Ciara said; then her voice dropped to a dreamy croon: "University! Though your father's alma mater, MIT, that would be my choice."

They sat and watched the flames flicker over the surface of the coals for a moment in companionable silence.

"What I'm really worried about," Luz said musingly, "is how to get into Colonel Nicolai's office."

Ciara choked a little; she'd been upending the wineglass for the last drop. "Past those guards with machine pistols!" she said. "There's a post at the bottom of the stairway and another one level below him! And no other way up! The guards are changed every six hours, four times a day, so they're always fresh!"

"Now, that's very observant of you," Luz said with delight. "What hours?"

"Starting at noon for the ones on the bottom of the stairwell, and four hours later for the ones on the landing below the office, from what I saw," Ciara said. "It would be suicide! Luz, even if you were Scáthach come again, the warrior-woman who trained the Hound . . ."

"I'm a Black Chamber field operative, not a soldier: I'm supposed to be capable of subtlety. It would certainly be suicide to try to *force* my way past," Luz agreed. "They'd shoot me into dogmeat, and any attention would be fatal anyway."

Ciara winced slightly. Luz shrugged: "It's my trade, *querida*, I have to think in those terms."

Then she closed her eyes and sipped more of the sweet wine. "No, the way to do it would be to go over the rooftops and up the side of the tower late at night; I'll have to observe when he turns out the light and leaves, which fortunately is in line of sight from *this* room. The problem with towers and stairs is that people think the only way to get into the top of the tower is *by* the stairs, and they focus their precautions on that."

"You *could*?" Ciara said, wide-eyed. "It's . . . very high and steep."

"Oh, yes, it's not as difficult as it looks if you're fit and you've had some practice, which I am and have, and if you have the right gear . . . which I do. The problem would be to get in, get the information—the precise targets, locations, timing—and get out undetected, without leaving any sign that his security had been breached. Information only stays fresh if the other side doesn't suspect you have it; the least hint it's been blown on and it's as useless as fish three days in the sun. That means I have to do it *muy, muy rápidamente*, and like a ghost. Nicolai has one of the German virtues—he pays attention to detail. If anything's out of place he'll notice . . ."

"Could you copy that much, quickly?"

"I've a little camera along that can do wonders in that line, courtesy of our technical office . . . and yes, you can see it, tomorrow, after the wine's worn off."

Ciara laughed, but turned serious again. "Then there's the alarm system," she said.

Luz turned her head and looked at her. "Alarm system? Ah, more *progress*," she said, pronouncing the last word as a vile curse.

"You didn't see it?" Ciara asked.

"No . . . I was more or less focused on Colonel Nicolai. And you, and whether I was about to die or be carried off for torture," Luz said . . . lightly but truthfully. "And my relief when you saved my life."

Ciara nodded soberly, then brightened. "It's not very complicated. There's a circuit of wires around the windows, with a little switch at the lower right hand of each window frame, running up to a master line around all four sides of the room at the junction of wall and ceiling. I'd give odds that when he leaves the office for the evening he makes sure the switches are closed. If the window's opened without the switch being thrown, the circuit's broken."

"What happens then?"

"Well, that depends on what's on the other end, you see. Possibly a loud bell . . . or any number of things."

¡Me cago en Dios! Luz swore silently; it seemed to be what God was doing to *her*. On the other hand it was miraculous that she'd gotten an observer with specialist knowledge who'd had access to the office and had used the time to observe. She very much doubted Nicolai was going to let either of them in there again.

I think she may have saved my life again. And my life is valuable here, because this mission looks more and more crucial the more I learn.

Her mind raced: "At a guess, a quiet bell somewhere that will send a squad pounding up the stairs and others covering the windows with automatics," she said. "Thus neatly trapping any intruder. I'm going to have to think about this . . ."

Ciara frowned. "But, Luz . . . if they think we're working for them, won't they just tell us what they're going to do?"

Luz chuckled ruefully. "Not unless they're idiots, and they're not *that type* of idiot. They'll tell us in very general terms; any specifics will be no more than the absolute minimum we need to do the limited things they want us to do, and that will be given at the very last moment. I may be able to get a little more—"

No need to shock you with exactly how I can get a little *more out of Horst. But only a little; he'd smell a rat immediately if I tried to get the things that a double agent would be looking for.*

"—but nothing like the detail we need. We need what's called in the trade *actionable intelligence.* Data we can give to the military so they can stop this."

"Yes! Stop this . . . this *horror.*"

"And now, let's get some sleep. We have a few days."

L uz woke. The sobs from the other side of the big bed were strangled, but they showed no signs of stopping.

She sighed, silently. *Being wept on was never something I liked much*, she thought. *Especially if there's a running nose involved too. But really, she's been holding up remarkably well; she's entitled to blubber a bit . . .*

"Bad dream?" she said softly, extending a hand cautiously—you could be startled into fits if a nightmare was interrupted too abruptly.

There was an inarticulate sound of misery and two damp hands grabbed hers with almost painful force.

"Faces," Ciara gasped quietly. "I keep seeing their *faces!*"

"Shhhh, it'll be all right. Come here."

Luz had just enough time to grab another clean handkerchief before the streaming face was crammed into the angle of her shoulder and neck. She put an arm around Ciara's heaving shoulders and rubbed her back soothingly with a slow motion, like stroking a cat.

"It'll be all right," Luz said.

That's a lie, I'm afraid, she thought. *You get used to things but it's never really all right. Still, bleak realism really wouldn't be what you need at this point.*

"Sshhhh, cry all you need to. You're not alone anymore. Shhhhh, shhhh, there now."

Eventually the sobs died away into hiccups, and Ciara used the handkerchief loudly. "Sorry," she mumbled sleepily. "Tha . . . feels nice."

"That's all right. I have bad dreams too, sometimes. See if you can sleep now."

"Mmmmm . . ."

Well, at least her hair does smell like strawberries, Luz thought.

She hummed very softly:

"Aruru mi niño, arrurú mi amor

Aruru pedazo de mi corazón

Este niño lindo que nació de día

Quiere que lo lleven a la dulcería . . ."

Even if she seems to be part octopus, she thought.

Besides a head firmly on her shoulder, Ciara had an arm around her stomach and a leg over her knees, and though she had gone limp she still shifted and clung if Luz moved. Luz slowly squirmed over onto her side, then let herself fall into a bottomless well of darkness. Nothing seemed to be waiting there but sleep, this time.

ELEVEN

T his is my friend from America, Fräulein Carmody; Elisa, Herr
Karl Böhm," Ciara said brightly.

The electrician—a civilian, and so probably a von Herder em-
ployee left in place when the military came in—wiped his hands on a
rag before he shook with her. He was in his fifties, with a gingery
handlebar mustache whose formidable proportions made up for the
way his hairline had retreated under his cloth cap, but the hard dry cal-
lused hand felt as if it had formidable, controlled strength. One of his
assistants was big-nosed, thickset, and bald as an egg. The other looked
to be about twelve, or possibly an underfed fourteen, with a mop of
straw-colored hair. All three of them looked tired, and their dungarees
were stained and worn.

*They look like two middle-aged men and a boy doing four men's work, or
maybe five men's,* Luz thought. *It's amazing how good everything looks, considering. Say what you like about Germans, most of them know how to keep their
noses to the grindstone.*

The same tiredness showed in the little power generation station
with its stone walls and timber roof, for all their efforts. It had probably
been a simple watermill of some sort originally. The engineers who'd
put in the power system for Schloss Rauenstein had used the same

mill-dam and water-race, and now there was a bank of dials and switches in a frame of cast iron and walnut. There was a bitter smell of metals and ozone, as well as of cold fresh water and damp rock, and one end held workbenches and mounts and racks for tools.

Papá would have nodded in approval, I think.

"Is the *Fräulein* also a student of electricity like our gracious Fräulein Whelan?" the mechanic inquired, giving the younger woman a beaming look like a prideful uncle's. "She has told us many interesting things of electrical machinery in America! And she knows her way around an armature and a winding!"

He had a thick Upper Saxon accent, with extra umlauts where most German speakers would put a simple short vowel, and used *dereelnz* for "tell" rather than the standard *erzählen*. That probably meant he'd been born within a day's journey of the *Schloss*, and had acquired his skills by a combination of technical school and learning-by-doing while apprenticed and self-education. His sort were the indispensable NCOs of German industry, and a large part of the reason for its prowess.

"Alas, no, I'm a complete amateur," Luz replied. "But I try to keep current with developments. Electricity is the master technology of our century, as steam was to the nineteenth, after all! So flexible in distribution and division, and with so many uses—light and communications, of course, but also mechanical power in industry and transport and even homes, and then all the electrochemical applications, and more uses are being discovered all the time. Obviously, tomorrow belongs to electricity!"

From their looks she obviously couldn't have offered better praise from all the world's store of flattery, the more so as it was well-informed praise directed at the thing they loved rather than themselves. Even the genuinely humble were vulnerable to *that*. Herr Böhm's whiskers bristled happily, and he produced a bottle and small glasses of some fiery local plum brandy for a ceremonial toast to the spirit of electrical progress—though his own glass was not merely small, but the amount in it was *entirely* ceremonial. So, under his eagle eye, was that of his bald attendant who would obviously have liked a good-sized tot, working hours or not. The shock-haired apprentice simply blushed without daring to speak, obviously struck dumb with an agony of adolescent admiration for the two comely young women. Luz gave him a nod and a smile, at which he almost hid behind his superiors, then remembered himself and gave a half bow in return, shapeless cloth cap clutched in his hands.

A tour of the little plant followed, replete with terms like *Voith-made Francis turbine,* and the names of the manufacturers of the generator and transformer, Siemens & Halske—which she did recognize simply because you couldn't read any military intelligence about Germany without running across the company—and details of how the water intake had been modified.

"We have a two-hundred-fifty-kilowatt capacity, which was ample, when the *Freiherr* had the plant installed for the *Schloss* and the village six years ago," Böhm said. "Our good *Freiherr* is very progressive! Then it was almost all for lights, the *Schloss* first of course, then the church, clinic, and school in the village, and the pastor's house. We were due to add another turbine generator set in 1914; there is enough water flow, but . . ."

He shrugged; a Frenchman would have done that more broadly and murmured *c'est la guerre.*

"Our problem now with the additional demand is that we are simply at the maximum capacity. So when there are surges . . . well, we have been running short of fuses, and there are so many complaints when the fuses blow, we *tell* them to try not to put more load on the circuits than it will take, but so many people still think electricity works like magic . . ."

The bald man muttered something like *Piefkes* and cast a resentful glance in the direction where the military-occupied *Schloss* would lie from here. Luz hid a grin behind the bland incomprehension of someone who hadn't caught the mutter or that of a foreigner who spoke very good German but didn't know the little idiosyncratic bits that never got into the books. In fact she'd heard that term before fairly often, in

Austria and Bavaria. *Piefke* was a personal name, and the best known bearer was the Berlin-born composer of some well-known imperial German military marches. But in a southern German's mouth it also meant either *pompous stuck-up ass* or *Prussian* or more commonly both.

"Trees," the young apprentice said, and retreated behind more blushes. "Falling branches."

Böhm nodded and tugged angrily at his whiskers. "*Ja, ja.* The grounds and garden staff, and the woodsmen, are very shorthanded. With the war, you understand . . . there is simply not enough careful trimming in the forest where the line runs up to the *Schloss.* In heavy weather we have had problems *there*, too—and we lose more fuses if the line shorts. Never has it taken us more than half an hour to restore power after an overload, often as little as twenty minutes, but each time we lose fuses, wire, everything is in short supply these days . . . and damage to the line itself in storms is more serious. I *told* the Herr Ingenieur that it would save effort in the long run to re-route the power line along the road even if it was longer, but there hasn't been time . . ."

Ciara and he went into a technical discussion of base and maximum loads, the meters-per-second capacities of the flue and how it was altered to balance the load and the best way to keep flotsam out given how careless the woodsmen and peasants upstream were, the difficulties of getting sufficient high-quality lubricants for the bearing races . . .

Böhm frowned again when the discussion was over. "Our *Ingenieur* was a most capable man, with plenty of practical experience with this system in particular as well as the rest of his responsibilities. But he was recalled to the colors with a *Pioneer* battalion—he has a reserve commission—and now there is only the young man from Marienbad, who comes in occasionally with many other responsibilities. He has his degree, yes, but . . . sometimes these recent graduates . . ."

He sighed and shrugged. "We manage. When all these extra people are gone, perhaps we will have fewer interruptions!"

The tour of the plant was interesting; it usually was, to see an expert doing things he really knew and cared about.

"Thank you very much for your time, Herr Böhm," Luz said. "I know you are extremely busy. Please accept this as evidence of my gratitude."

She handed the three of them each a bar of chocolate, ones she'd packed in a recess of her trunks. Money might have offended him, but three pairs of blue eyes lit at the sight of the treat, unobtainable in wartime but, like coffee, dear to the German heart. Even more so, if possible.

"Thank you, gracious miss," he said, as the youngster stripped off the paper and tinfoil and crammed some of his into his mouth with muffled sounds of joy. "I will save my portion for my children—the little ones have not had chocolate since last Christmas."

As they walked back to the *Schloss* along a footpath used by the maintenance crew, Luz's eyes followed the looping path of the power line. Someone had taken considerable trouble to keep it inconspicuous; the poles were creosoted pine logs about eight meters tall, the bases buried man-deep and often braced with a ring of rocks and taking an irregular path uphill.

"So fallen branches are a problem?" she said meditatively.

"Yes, particularly in bad weather, Herr Böhm says."

Ciara chuckled a little. "Evidently the von Herder family, progressive or no, didn't want too much of an unsightly path cut through their forest or spoiling the view from the castle windows. They mostly lived here in the summer, and in their town place in Dresden in the winter except for hunting trips. And just before the war they laid up their carriage and got an automobile. A Mercedes 37/90 touring model—a very fine car."

Luz looked around. The yellowing leaves of the beeches rustled overhead with a tattered autumnal loveliness, but add in six feet of snow and a blizzard . . .

"Yes, I can see them living in town in the winter," she said. "This estate would be yokeldom's homeland once the snow fell, hardly anyone to see or talk to except the villagers even with the railroad. With the car they could visit in the neighborhood in good weather, but not once the blizzards begin."

Ciara snorted with a democratic American impatience, and Luz nodded. Though in fact the two groups might simply not have much to talk to each other *about*, except for the weather, rents, Lady Bountiful charity by the squire's wife, and a little extramural frolic and fornication by the von Herder menfolk now and then.

"I'd guess the lords lived here year-round except for some attendance at court or service in war before the rails came through," Luz said. "Now they winter in Dresden, which is a truly lovely city; they call it the Jewel Box of Germany for the buildings. The Frauenkirche, the Church of Our Lady, I had a tour through once and it was far too short; you could look at it for days."

Ciara sighed. "I've traveled only in my books." A wry smile: "Well, except for this! That was a boat to Copenhagen, and right on to the train for here. Seeing a genuine castle is something, I suppose. I envy you so, having seen all these places."

"Travel by book is the best preparation for really doing it, so that you understand what you finally see," Luz said. "And there are a lot of places I haven't seen yet . . . not Spain, oddly enough, nor much of Italy, just a flying visit to Venice. And only London in England; never Yorkminster or Stonehenge. Nor Constantinople, nor Egypt . . . Well, something to think about after the war's over. But it is great fun to travel just for its own sweet sake, especially in the right company."

"Oh, yes!" Ciara said. "Auntie Colleen and Auntie Treinel and I did go to San Francisco for the Panama-Pacific Exposition last year; they got the Party discount and managed to sneak one for me too. And oh, that was lovely, to see so much of our country. And the mountains, and the bay was so pretty, and the Jewel City. You?"

"*Claro que sí*, several times. It's only an afternoon from Santa Barbara to San Francisco by rail."

"It made me sad, to think that those beautiful, beautiful buildings would be torn down, and I cried with happiness when the president said they'd be made to last in that great speech he gave. I read the whole text, three times."

Luz chuckled; that had been a typical bit of Uncle Teddy's approach to life. She'd applauded his impulsive decree that it all be rebuilt for real too, even though some of the buildings had been a bit *too-too* as the English said, or possibly not *quite-quite*. But the Court of the Universe was exactly the way Teddy and the École des Beaux-Arts and the City Beautiful movement—and hence the Party—thought a great city's core should look, anyway, Tower of Jewels and all. The opportunity to bring it to lasting life had been too much for him to resist.

"The Palace of Fine Arts is certainly lovely, as fine as anything I've seen that was built in the last half century," she said aloud. "It would have been a sin to let that vanish, and it's perfect for an art and design school, which is what they'll be using it for. The three of you had a good time?"

"Oh, yes! We saw all the art, and we had a wheeled chair for Auntie Colleen when her foot started to hurt—and those little electric carts . . ."

"The Electriquettes?"

"Yes, such dear things—and I went on all the rides in the Joy Zone. And we came back in the evening twice to see the light shows, the Scintillator, and those lovely glowing pillars in the Court of the Universe and the dome of the Palace of Horticulture. It was like something in the sidhe-mounds then. And oh, the Palace of Machinery had the most fascinating things . . . particularly from Westinghouse and the Institute. They had one of the new turbo-alternators for the Twelve Dams project on the Colorado River, and it was amazing! The degree of transmission loss is amazingly low with voltages like that, and Tesla solved the insulation problem. The three-phase poly—"

"I was impressed," Luz agreed, before it could get more technical. "And with the big scale model of the Panama Canal. *Shhh!*"

Luz put her left hand on the other's arm and her right went inside her coat to fall on the pistol, and they halted. She used her eyes to indicate the source of the rustling she'd heard; it was a boar, black and bristly and low-slung, rooting about for the fallen acorns the pig breed loved. His long curling white tusks clattered and champed as he caught their scent, glowered at them out of one wicked little eye, then trotted off.

I really wouldn't like to have had to stop four hundred pounds of armed porker with this popgun. A nice Remington bolt-action with the new .338 high-velocity magnum round, maybe!

"Not much like a farm pig at all!" Ciara said, a bit breathless. "Sure, and *ripped up by the boar* in the old epics makes more sense now!"

"They're good hunting, and good eating," Luz said. "But taking one on with a spear . . ."

Her eyes went skyward. The early-afternoon sky was thickening with cloud in a rippling, undulating pattern.

"*Un cielo empedrado,*" she said. At Ciara's look: "A cobbled sky, that means."

"Mackerel sky, in English," Ciara said.

"*Schäfchenwolken,* as the Germans put it; sheep's sky."

"Weather moving in, whatever it's called."

"What a pity," Luz said with a brief feral grin. "Falling branches will probably mean another power interruption."

"My head feels a bit heavy," Ciara said. "And there's a barometer we can take a look at."

She looked halfway between frightened and excited, but she'd switched back to the subject of just how Schloss Rauenstein's power—and Colonel Nicolai's alarm—might fail without prompting.

Smart girl, Luz thought; she felt both, but she grinned at the clouds.

"I'm very glad you cultivated Herr Böhm, Ciara," she said.

The younger woman nodded. "He's a nice old soul, and far more fun than the soldiers. Safer, too! Young men in uniform, if you give them the slightest encouragement, just ordinary friendliness, honestly you'd think you'd thrown up your skirts over your head and were doing that scandalous French dance while you wailed like a lady cat wanting a tom . . ."

"The cancan?" Luz said, and then said it again using the English pronunciation with the hard *n*.

"Is that the way the French say it, then? Yes, that's what I meant."

Then Ciara looked thoughtfully at the tower that stuck up from Schloss Rauenstein's highest roof.

"You know, really there ought to be a way to have an alarm system keep functioning despite a power interruption . . . chargeable batteries perhaps? But they're so heavy and require so much attention it would be easier just to keep a man standing there every hour of the day! Edison never did solve the battery problem . . . perhaps Tesla?"

"Perhaps if you could focus on getting me in safely?" Luz said, smiling a little to take any sting out of it. "Rather than perfecting the alarm to keep me out . . ."

Ciara nodded seriously, and they walked through the damp duff of the forest floor, holding up their skirts a little. Once or twice Luz had to catch the other by the arm. She wasn't naturally clumsy, but she was much less used to walking through forests and broken ground, and the higher, narrower heels of her shoes weren't as adapted to it either. At last Ciara nodded and pointed.

"If that branch there fell, it's heavy enough to take the line down—take it right out of the insulator set on that pole, I'd say."

The twisted oak limb was about twenty feet up, overhanging the line of poles where they made a switchback to avoid a clifflike piece of stony steepness that seeped water from its reddish sandstone. The problem was that the branch looked fairly sturdy; the tree wasn't a giant, given where it was growing—she could see roots where they'd driven themselves into the rock—but it was healthy. Still, limbs did break off in storms, and anyone who'd done any forest work knew that an oak that *looked* healthy might have any number of internal problems that could set branches dropping, sometimes on your head with no warning. The clouds had thickened, the wind was still out of the northwest, and the temperature had been dropping since noon.

"Watch out for anyone else coming this way," she said.

It wasn't likely, since this path along the power line's right-of-way looked a bit overgrown, but it wasn't impossible that one of the officers would find time to commune with the ancestral spirit of the forest— Germans did things like that if they'd been in the Wandervögel movement, or just liked taking a stroll the same way anyone might.

Ciara responded by swiveling her head both ways. "No," Luz said, and took her by the hand. "Here. Stand with your back against this rock, in the shadow. Now you can look both ways up and down the trail without turning your head much, and if you don't move, chances are nobody will see you. Plus you'll be visible to me while I climb. See?"

Ciara squeezed her hand before she released it. "And did they teach you that in the Chamber?" she said, obviously fascinated.

"My father did when we were hunting," she said. "The Chamber sort of refined it."

And didn't add aloud: *And later, experience ground it in when I was hunting men, who were hunting me too.*

"Ah, and I wanted to be a Girl Scout and learn woodland lore so badly," Ciara sighed. "There was a troop in my neighborhood before I was too old. But there was never the time to spare from the shop, and some of the Clann na nGael didn't like it, because it was started by an Englishman."

"A very worthy organization, the Scouts," Luz said, more or less sincerely.

Back home people were just starting to talk about making the Scouts compulsory for girls too, or at least free and heavily encouraged and subsidized through the Party, as part of a scheme to extend a less military form of national service to young women before the courts forced the issue. Some disgruntled male conscript would have the money and connections to get a case all the way to the Supreme Court, and the wording of the Sixteenth was very, very unambiguous.

So that's probably going to happen eventually, even if it makes a lot of people unhappy, she thought, with a brief flicker of *Schadenfreude.*

Those were people whose suffering she positively enjoyed, rather like a form of bear-baiting you could watch with a clear conscience. They included, in fact started, with the people who had tried to kill the Sixteenth Amendment by pulling a fast one in committee and altering the wording from a simple extension of the vote to full equal rights for women. They'd bet that even the triumphant Progressives in 1913 couldn't or wouldn't pass *that*, but wouldn't dare offend their more radical supporters by walking it back, either. They'd regretted it immediately when Uncle Teddy and his congressional supporters had taken up the gauntlet and rammed it through in the changed form by a razor-thin margin and gotten it accepted by the states along with the other half dozen going up for ratification at the same time, mainly because everyone was too excited to really notice that it had been radically changed.

Stupid of them. When did Teddy ever back down from a challenge? He is like a bull moose! And he made speeches for full legal equality for women back when he was a freshman at Harvard thirty-odd years ago; they could have looked that up.

The Inadvertent Sixteenth had been spinning off unforeseen consequences ever since, usually ones that elevated the vocal misery of its actual authors to hilarious proportions.

On balance Luz supposed she approved of the idea. Conscription would have been a bloody nuisance for *her*, but few had the advantages she'd grown up with. It would get more girls out of the house and mixing with people from other classes and backgrounds in the fresh air, and the scholarships and settlement grants that went with national service were valuable enough that she'd be very glad not to see them limited to men. There would be unintended consequences from *those*, too; she didn't know what all of them would be, but it would be entertaining to watch and find out.

Ciara was looking at the sandstone cliff. "How will you get up there?"

"Oh, the rock face doesn't look too steep, and it's not raining yet. I'd better be cautious, though. It's leaving sign that's the real danger here, either on the ground or on the tree or on me. People see what they expect, but not if you poke them in the eye with it. Stealth is the spy's best friend."

She had a pair of her gloves in a pocket. She pulled them on, the smooth soft leather dusted inside with talc fitting like . . .

A glove, she thought, said it aloud, and got a gurgling chuckle in response.

They looked like an ordinary lady's glove, specifically a two-button day glove for walking out, slightly old-fashioned but still wearable. But they were much tougher than those fragile creatures, essential if her hands weren't to be suspiciously battered or worn after something like this. She looked up the slope, carefully noting cracks and unevenness, then sprang.

"Huhhh!" she grunted softly as the weight came on her hands.

Then she brought her right foot up and found purchase on the knob she'd seen. A warning tug at her groin reminded her to be more careful to keep up her stretching exercises—now that she was sleeping in the same room as Ciara it would be easier, since she wouldn't have to worry about Horst wondering why a Mexican revolutionary was using an Asian-based limbering routine before coming to bed. She'd thought of passing it off as exotic Hindu sexual preparations from the *Kama Sutra*, and some of the positions in that *did* require you to be limber as a snake, but that would be a bit much even for male wishful thinking to swallow.

Besides which, Position Ninety-Nine is exactly the same as Position Ninety-Eight, but with your fingers crossed.

Careful pressure, and the weight came off her arms; left leg up and braced, and she was hugging the rock, resting an instant until her arms felt relaxed again, reach for the next hold, test that the rock wasn't going to crumble . . .

It went slower than it might have if climbing were her only care, since she was also being careful of her shoes—which were also much tougher than the standard street wear they otherwise resembled, but might be noticed before she could repolish them if they were terminally scuffed. There was only one moderately difficult part right at the top, where she had to reach up to an overhang, take her weight on her left hand and arm for an instant, then swing across and slap her right hand onto the sharp rock edge too and chin herself and throw a knee over and lever herself up.

That left her panting as she crouched on the edge for a moment, exhilarated. Climbing rock faces was enough fun that she thought it might be a sport by itself someday, not just as part of being an Alpinist.

There was a squeak of alarm from Ciara as she made the lift, and it had been plainly audible. She looked down; the other was standing looking up with her hands pressed to her mouth and her eyes wide. Luz made a vigorous shushing motion and then pointed both ways up and down the trail, and finished with an admonishing finger shake to keep the attention on essentials. Then she examined the branch, estimating weight and distance.

This must weigh nearly as much as I do, she thought.

A glance over the edge of the rock showed that Ciara was right and if the limb *did* fall it would certainly hit the power line, and would hit it right where the ceramic insulator was held on a bracket on the pole. Ciara had had an excellent idea of exactly how robust the mounting was—fruit of her conversations with Herr Böhm as well as her own knowledge—and that would short out the power line. Which in turn would cut the load to the *Schloss* for at least half an hour, or twice that at night in bad weather . . . and the weather would be bad. If it cracked the insulator, that would have to be replaced as well, which would take more time still, and first the hard-worked staff at the power station would have to wake up and dress and wade through the inky darkness and wet to *find* what had gone wrong.

Pity to get that nice old Herr Böhm out of bed beside his mattress of a Haus-frau, *but* c'est la guerre.

The problem was that the oak limb looked disgustingly healthy and sound. It would be easy enough to cut it partway through, but she couldn't risk leaving the mark of metal on it. Another power outage because high wind brought down a limb would just be a matter for curses over extra work and lost sleep. One that looked to have been arranged would produce a fit of murderous suspicion. The German military here were on a knife-edge between triumph and disaster, and whoever had come up with that image of them as stolid and unemotional hadn't met many of the breed. They were actually rather given to hysteria, but they—or rather, some of them by class, caste, and profession—controlled it very tightly.

She stood and reached up, putting her hands on the branch about six feet from its junction with the trunk and gradually increasing the weight until her feet were off the ground and her whole lithe but solid hundred and thirty-five pounds of body and clothes and gear were hanging from it. Luz's mother had loved gardening and had accumulated a fund of knowledge of what her husband had called failure modes among branches and passed it on to her daughter, the more so as the grounds of their house in Santa Barbara included a good many live oaks that had been growing there when the only inhabitants were the Chumash tribe. Luz had picked up more while climbing trees herself, which had been her passion for a long time as a girl. It bent, but only a little; she jounced up and down and watched narrow-eyed as the limb flexed.

Oak's strong, she thought. *Now, how would the grain go in a fork like that? Where would it split if the wind whipped it too far and torqued it beyond the breaking strain?*

The shape was a lopsided Y. *So, logically . . .*

She swung up easily onto the top of the branch and bounced a little more. More sway . . . it would be easy to overdo . . .

Luz moved out to get more leverage, which put her over a twenty-foot drop onto a charged power line, and began to rock the limb until each sway went a little farther up and down, pumping more kinetic energy into the oscillation in exactly the same way a child did on a swing. She was watching the fork, but mostly she was *listening*. After a while it began to creak, and then there was an ominous crackle in the middle of the downswing. More creaking, and popping sounds, and then there was a warning mushiness beneath her feet and lack of spring-back. She used what there was to launch herself back to the trunk, hit it fairly hard, and clung laughing for a moment.

Beneath her the branch had split from the fork in the trunk of the oak, heartwood and sapwood blond and white and bristling with splinters, drooping down about halfway to the line. Luz worked her way around until she could look at it carefully, then braced a foot against the section beyond the break and pushed. There was a slight creak and crackle, and the tip of the branch fifteen feet out shivered and bent farther.

¡Bueno! she thought. *Now I just have to hope that it comes down at the right moment.*

I miss you, *meine Süsse*," Horst said.

"Don't make puppy eyes at me, Horst. It looks ridiculous when someone your size with scars on his face imitates a six-year-old whose mother won't give him a piece of *pan dulce*," Luz said briskly. "Fun is fun, but duty is duty. Besides which, there's no real privacy here and if I want to be taken seriously . . ."

They were standing in a corner, with plenty of traffic streaming by; the two visiting warlords and their entourage, many of them considerable Pooh-Bahs in their own right, would be leaving in the morning. All the paraphernalia and documents they'd brought up to the *Schloss* had to be stripped down and packed up again, with suitable security precautions. She still thought rumors of what had gone on here would spread . . . which meant the Germans intended to strike *soon.*

"I hope you're not enjoying sleeping with the Irish girl more than you would with me," he grumbled, probably half-serious.

Luz laughed. "Sleeping in what sense?" she said. "So far all she's done is cry on me, and anyway, you've got equipment she lacks."

Horst chuckled the way you did at a mildly bawdy joke. *My, but literal truth really is the best way to deceive*, she thought, and went on aloud.

"But seriously, sweetie, she needs to be kept up to scratch . . . up to the mark," she amplified when the remark didn't translate well. "She needs reassurance and someone to help her over her doubts. She's an amateur political enthusiast with a grudge who ran a bookstore, not a professional as we are."

"Well, we don't have much time," Horst said. His face went from play-petulant to wholly serious. "We will be . . . on our way, fairly soon."

"In a U-boat?" she said.

She chuckled at his alarm; also it would keep his mind off feeling randy, if anything could do that for a healthy young male. In her experience very little could, even the threat of death.

Especially after the transcendent experience which is rolling around naked with my own glorious and exquisitely sensual self. Which can be una jodienda, she thought, punning mildly. *It's one of my favorite things, but there's a time and place!*

"Oh, come now, Horst, how else? Zeppelins would be at the extreme edge of their range with any sort of useful load, even going one way. And this Breath of Loki is very deadly, but to cause sufficient damage to big areas it's still going to need tons per target. Albeit not *many* tons. How else to get it across the Atlantic when the American and English fleets control the surface? Though how you plan to deploy it *from* the U-boats *to* the target I cannot guess, I'm just presuming you have that thought out."

Horst looked either way down the corridor. "That is a brilliant deduction . . . and would cause great trouble if it came to the wrong ears."

Luz nodded. "Which is why I'm saying it to you, sweetie, and not to anyone else. And you and I and she are headed for Boston—also deduction."

Horst winced. "Yes, and I admit that this Whelan girl may need . . . very careful shepherding when we get there. Possibly disposal."

"Well, if you need someone to finish her off if she balks at the crucial moment, it might be easier for me, being a woman, to . . ."

He exhaled with relief. "Thank you, Elisa. We will need her, though. Not so much for the mission, admittedly . . . but I would like to survive the mission if possible, and she can help a great deal with *that*. I do not think the Yankees will be in a mood to take prisoners after this."

"No need to say more," Luz replied. "You can rely on me . . . though the thought of what we're giving up for our respective countries makes me wish there were a medal for it. Think of how it would be, about the size of a soup plate and sculpted in gold and ivory . . . One version for women, another for men . . ."

Horst gave another of his laughs, like a carefree boy this time. "I like your imagination, *Süsse*."

Luz put down the violin, and a little reluctantly closed the case. "This *is* a marvelous instrument," she said.

"And not that I haven't enjoyed the duet, but hearing two people playing for such a long while makes a good . . . alibi, would you say?" Ciara said.

"Not quite. If it ever comes to a serious suspicion, there won't be any beyond-reasonable-doubt formalities. But it does establish that we were both *here*, which may prevent suspicions from arising in the first place. I doubt even Colonel Nicolai's twisted mind could suspect you of being able to play a Bösendorfer Imperial 290 with your toes, lithe and delicate though they are, while you lie on your back on the floor sawing away at the violin."

Ciara laughed aloud. "Luz, your sense of humor is completely *mad*!"

"So is the rest of me, dear, or I'd be in Santa Barbara swinging in a hammock on the terrace of my house, watching the ocean with no worries except whether to put grilled shrimp in the luncheon salad. I suddenly feel an abundance of *la añoranza* for California."

The noise of the rain on the roofs and windows was a white hiss.

Luz opened one and extended a hand out. It was raining hard, all right; and it was *cold*, just a little this side of being sleet. A gust flicked stinging drops into her face, and she slid the window closed again. Apart from the watery gleam of electric lights from various places in the *Schloss*, the night was as dark as the inside of a closet. One by one the lights vanished as she waited; the one in Colonel Nicolai's office had gone out promptly at eight, as it always did. She cocked an ear at the sound of the wind.

"Rising," she said. "Good. More likely to bring the branch down, and the worse the weather, the less likely people are to move around. And the more sentries tend to find someplace dry and light a cigarette. There's nothing more futile than a sentry at night with a lit smoke in his mouth; *no sirve para un carajo*, but you'd be surprised at how many do it."

Ciara pursed her lips. "The books of adventure are full of useless sentries. Faith, they're there to be hit over the head or made to look foolish or to run about bumping into each other and shouting *turn out the guard!*"

"That's exaggerated, but a lot of them *are* like that—spear carriers. I suppose because sentry-go is so *completely* boring most of the time. It's a real strain staying alert hour after hour when you know that probably nothing will happen. Though I've worked with people who took it very seriously indeed, generally ones who knew their lives depended on it."

The Philippine Rangers came to mind, and the specialist regiment of Regulars who'd revived the name of *Roger's* Rangers, complete with carrying tomahawks; they didn't pace around on guard advertising their presence; they hid instead . . . and listened and watched and even smelled the air very carefully indeed. She'd learned a number of useful tricks from them.

She turned to the two customized trunks and began removing bits and pieces, putting them on the table behind her or into a small rucksack of oiled black leather. The last was a much longer length of the knotted silk rope, disguised as a woven net for holding garments but easily stripped out and shrugged over her shoulder in a coil. When she turned around Ciara was examining the metal parts she'd removed with interest, then fitted them neatly together, using her hands and the little socket wrench. Luz opened her mouth to object, then held silence when her fingers moved unerringly and everything went in the right order on her first try.

"Why, that's a clever piece of work!" she said with delight, holding up the result. "And this part with the jointed lever is an air pump, I do believe."

The result looked like a skeletal metallic rifle with a bulbous tube acting as the forestock, and as Luz checked it over she realized it had been assembled at least as well as she could have done it.

"It's an air rifle," she explained. "For throwing grappling hooks and line, among other things."

The other things included quietly driving short pointed metal rods into human bodies, usually the skulls. Luz wouldn't be using it that way here in any case. She was here for stealthy work.

"Designed to be quiet," she finished.

"And all the little pieces made to look like something harmless when they're in the trunks," Ciara marveled. "Very clever indeed."

Then: "But you're going to go in those pajamas? They're thin for this work."

"They're actually designed for this, and to *look* like pajamas," Luz replied. "It's not going to be comfortable, but there's no way to climb around in cold rain in complete darkness and make it a pleasurable experience. Still, it would be less so in a wet wool skirt."

"What . . . what if you don't come back?" Ciara said after a moment, and took her hand.

Luz sighed and met her eyes. "If they capture me or kill me, I'd advise you to jump out of the window when they come for you," she said, squeezing Ciara's fingers and then releasing them. "I'm sorry I can't say anything more comforting, particularly since you're in this situation because you took a risk to save me, but that's the fact of the matter."

Ciara smiled; it was a forced expression, but gallant. "Thank you for not padding the truth, Luz, and I did get myself into this. I'll try to be as brave as you!"

A genuine chuckle. "You'll just have to succeed for *my* sake too, then, won't you?"

Luz nodded, smiling herself. "There are times when only gallows humor suits . . . but it's then you most need to laugh."

Luz ate a bar of chocolate for the energy and slid on a hood that covered her head except for an eye slit, and lacework across the ears so as not to block sound. She looked at her wristwatch, fashionable enough to be unremarkable now, since military men had taken to them. Especially this type with the radium numbers and the hinged snap-on cover that was also a compass. Then she concentrated on keeping relaxed and waiting in that peculiar hunter's state of mind where time passed quickly without dulling your perceptions.

At one point a shocked giggle and the sound of a book snapping closed made her look around. "What—"

Ciara was reading a book; specifically, *Les Fleurs du Mal.* "Luz!" she said, pressing a hand to one cheek. "This book . . . it must be on the Index!"

"It most certainly is," she said, and her smile was wry behind the mask as she went on: "But remember what Mark Twain said."

"What?" she asked, distracted.

"*No young girl was ever ruined by a book,*" Luz said. "Also, Monsieur Baudelaire wrote some very sad poetry there, if your French is good enough to see the finer points."

"Ummmm . . . I'm not sure. I can't speak it, you understand, and . . . well, I don't recognize some of the words."

"It's great poetry about some very unhappy people," Luz said. "Sinning, but not getting nearly as much fun out of it as they should. I doubt anyone fair-minded could consider it an advertisement or celebration!"

Ciara laughed at that, a little unwillingly. "Father Flandry did say once that envy is the only one of the seven deadly sins that doesn't even give you momentary pleasure when you commit it."

"You'd probably need to go through the Baudelaire with a dictionary and then hear someone read it aloud to get most of the benefit of it," Luz said. "Reading poetry properly in another language is altogether more difficult than prose, and that's hard. Just being fluent isn't enough. It took me a long time to appreciate German poetry even though I had the language well enough to pass for a native. It all felt rather *thin*, until something clicked a couple of years ago."

She looked at her watch again. A little after one o'clock and the wind rose to a wail . . .

"Lights out," she said quietly; all the remaining electrics had gone out at the same time, leaving their own room in dimness relieved only by the low glow of the coals in the fireplace.

"That'll be the branch." Ciara nodded. "Good luck to you now, and I'll keep the fire going!"

TWELVE

Schloss Rauenstein

Kingdom of Saxony, German *Reich*

SEPTEMBER 15TH, 1916(B)

Luz opened the window again with the air rifle slung over her shoulder. The middle of the silk rope went around the back of a heavy chair, and she went out into the hard rain and wind with a length in either hand to slide down the doubled line in a controlled fall, pushing off from the wall of the building with her feet and landing in a crouch as the flagstones of the court met the cord soles of her slippers. By the time she was on the ground even the tight-woven silk she wore was sopping, and the chill began to work its way inward, no more than forty degrees and dropping.

Now it's a race against the clock and the cold, she thought as the rope fell and she coiled it again. *Strength and agility and endurance are all downhill from here, and eventually Herr Böhm's German sense of duty and industriousness will get the power back on.*

The bulk of the old castle loomed to her right, with only a dim candle light or two waveringly visible through the night and rain . . . the same silhouette someone scouting it would have seen two hundred years ago, or five hundred, when the guards would have been carrying spears and crossbows, not Mausers and machine pistols.

Ah, modern war, she thought mordantly.

First, across the courtyard. She simply walked, firmly suppressing any impulse to dodge or skulk; everything she was wearing or carrying was dark and nonreflective, there weren't any powerful lights to silhouette her, and so she was very unlikely to catch the eye. And if she did she'd be an indistinct figure in this hissing wet. Someone running or crouching would *look* like a spy or intruder. If you walked upright and briskly but not too fast, ninety-nine times out of a hundred people would simply assume you were part of the human landscape, with a perfect right to be there. It was a modification of the technique you used on a crowded street.

I'd probably be even less inconspicuous with an umbrella, some part of her thought whimsically. *And I'm wearing trousers, so anyone would simply assume it's a man.*

She came to the corner of the curved main block of the castle and slipped the air rifle off her back and slid in one of the grapnel arrows—the prongs at the tip were heavily padded with coarse rubber, and spring-loaded to open once shot. A loop at the end of the silk rope clipped on just below the prongs, and she crouched to feel and make sure that the coil at her feet was free of tangles . . . and free of her feet, remembering a memorable training accident she'd seen where someone had inadvertently tried to shoot their own foot over a roof when it was caught in a loop. The silk was invisible beneath her fingers, black in blackness, like a tactile memory.

She stood and looked up. Rain spattered steadily into her eyes, interspersed with fierce gusts; that mattered less than it might have, because the wall faded into invisibility about ten feet up anyway, even though it was white-painted. She'd have to rely on trained memory, and on the grapnel not getting caught in a flurry of wind and twisting aside and landing on a sentry's head. She raised the rifle to her shoulder, aimed up, corrected a little, waiting until the shoving pressure of the air slackened . . .

Bumpf-hiss.

The recoil knocked at her shoulder. The projectile vanished instantly; the coil of rope whickered upward smoothly, visible only as a quiver in the darkness. If she'd aimed too high, it would disappear over the roof and be hanging there tomorrow for someone to see and go:

Ach, so, a rope and grapnel! My God, what can *this mean?*

Too low and it would bounce off the wall and fall back . . . or smash into someone's window, and the alarm would go up . . .

Goldilocks, I am counting on you now, mi pequeña ladrona! she thought. *Not too hot, not too cold* . . .

The thought of the Breath of Loki went through her mind; only now those poisonous green flowers were opening over New York as she had seen it from the observation gallery of the *San Juan Hill.* The vast morning or evening crowds looking up, and then the green blossoms of poison, and the screams . . . millions screaming . . . and the invisible torrent pouring down into the subways . . .

A tense moment, and then the rope stopped with a quarter of the coil still on the ground. She waited, pumping at the lever of the air reservoir, but the shaft and grapnel didn't fall back to thud at her feet . . . or on her head, which would be impossible to dodge in time with the rain covering all faint sounds.

¡Ay! The fearsome Black Chamber secret operative, found dead of exposure in the morning with a grapnel sticking out of her head . . .

Nothing. She slung the air rifle and gave a slow pull at the knotted silk cord; not a tug, you did that when you *wanted* to get something to come loose. Luz wanted the prongs at the end of this to catch. Catch in something nice and sturdy that wouldn't tear loose halfway up, or leave a big pale easily seen mark tomorrow.

In fact, I want that . . . ¡Con mucha pasión!

The slack came off the cord as she drew it in. A stronger pull held no sense of give beyond the slight natural elasticity of wet silk; then she hauled with all her strength and let her weight come onto the cord, with no sense of movement. The rope hung straight down, clearing the wall by about a yard, doubtless the distance the eaves overhung far above. She slung the last of the coil from the ground over her shoulder and pulled herself upward, bringing her legs up and crimping the rope between her crossed ankles. The knots weren't big enough to stand on, but they did simplify the inchworm progress; legs up, straighten the knees to push the body upward too, slide the hands up, repeat. All done reasonably quickly, but smoothly and not so fast that she'd start rocking from side to side.

Which would be the best possible way to get the grapnel free of whatever it's caught on.

Ten feet up she paused to loop the slack into the coil over her shoulder, moving quietly and extending a hand occasionally to the wall to damp down the natural tendency to sway in the wind, even though the bulk of the castle blocked most of the storm bearing down from the north. It wouldn't do to leave a loop of the rope right where someone walking by would . . .

Below her, the iron heel plates of jackboots clicked on the flagstones of the courtyard; they were practical footwear, except when they announced *here am I, a German soldier, coming to kill you,* Hoch! Hoch! every time you took a step. There was just enough light from the hooded lantern one man carried to catch the gleam of wet helmets and rain capes; and a hint of other things . . . perhaps a bayonet. Luckily most of the illumination went straight out ahead.

"*Scheisse,*" a voice said quietly. "They march us here, they march us there, we go to fight the stupid Russians, the stubborn English, the tricky Frenchies, and *always* it is raining. And cold. Everything but cold rain and stinking mud has been canceled for the duration wherever we go. The war has created a whole world of wet and mud and rats, and then they march us here into the middle of Germany doing make-work where nothing can happen and there is *still* cold rain."

He said mir gangat *instead of* wir gehen *for* we go, she thought, while remaining absolutely motionless . . . though the loop of the rope was only two feet over their heads, and it was still moving as gusts of wind caught it. *Must be a Swabian. Which is totally useless information but at least my ear is still in.*

"They haven't marched us into the middle of Germany, they've marched us into Saxony," his friend said in the same *schwäbisch.* "Marched us up the arsehole of Germany."

"Arsehole of the universe, and there's still cold rain, like every-where else."

"*Nei, nei, Baba,*" his companion said, equally softly, barely audible under the rain even directly below her. "At Verdun it was snowing. Po-land was heat and dust. And here, there is no mud."

"At Verdun the shells from the French seventy-fives fell thick as raindrops *and* it was snowing *and* there was mud," the first man said.

They both chuckled, the sound of their voices trailing off into the background whistle and hiss of the storm as they switched to discuss-ing women—specifically, the differences in the size of the breasts of Polish and French girls and which was better.

Luz let out a long breath softly and closed her eyes for a moment, making her arms stop trembling. Then she brought up her feet again, crossed her ankles on the rope, pushed . . .

A muted light grew, flickering behind wet glass. The rope ran be-side a window and she arched her body so that as little as possible would cross in front of the glass. From the inside the candle's light would make the outside darker still and she would be black against black, but motion might pull the eye. Slowly, slowly . . .

The man inside was seated at a table with his back to her, smoking a cigarette and writing, his head crop-haired on a thick bull neck, his jacket off and suspenders showing on broad sloping shoulders as his hand went out to dip the pen and returned to the paper. A framed photograph was propped up on the table before him, and the candle on a saucer be-fore it, almost as if it were a shrine; she thought it held a picture of a woman holding a child. Then she was past the window, resting for a mo-ment with her toes on a sill just above it, coiling up more of the rope.

The rain was harder if anything, leaching away the warmth of her body's core, like blood flowing from a wound.

I'm a tropical bird, she thought. *I really do not want to leave my bones in this country of pale troll people and wolves and snow.* No va a ser más fácil si espero, *so let's go*, mi corazón, *and if I make it I'll try to stick to places that grow pomegranates and oranges.*

The thought of her family's house in Santa Barbara was bitter, warm nights with the moon on the Pacific and the scent of Cashmere Bouquet flowers thick and sweet below her bedroom window, and she suppressed it with an effort of will. Another spell of climbing, and then her reaching hand hit something. It was too dark to see what—it was too dark to see her own hand in front of her face, though admittedly she had a black glove on it. Luz flogged her memory and saw the mental map of the *Schloss* and where she probably was.

All right, I crossed the courtyard and went up the south-facing wall of the old section of the castle, just over from that bay-window part. There's a pitched roof and a chimney on top of that. And then there's the section where the half-timbered buildings were built on top of the original castle.

That meant the grapnel had hooked somewhere above, along the roof ridge or the chimney. The roof was too steep to crawl up unsupported, and the rope would be lying flat against its slope. She supported most of her weight where her ankles crossed on the rope and felt along the edge of the roof. No metal guttering, and the roof was at an eighty-degree angle, slippery slate that felt as if it was splotched with moss.

Luz pulled upward as hard as she could on the rope, until her arms shook. Then her feet came up, crossed on a knot . . . an explosion of effort, mentally pouring strength into the muscles of her thighs, and her feet must not slip now of all times . . .

With a soft grunt of effort she propelled herself upward and forward and half her body lay on the slates, with everything from the hips down dangling over the sixty-foot drop to bare stone below. Slid one hand up the rope, underneath, between it and the roof. The other. Then pull again, pain in her arms, biceps, triceps, her teeth bared behind the mask. Squirming forward, elbows scrabbling for traction . . .

Must not pull the rope upward away from the roof. That'd unseat the grapnel and it's a long way down. Keep the pull parallel, straight against the slope.

Panting and shuddering she lay on the roof, with her limbs splayed to make as much friction as she could on the dismayingly frictionless surface of the wet mossy stone. Even the rows of slates were irregular, sloping across the surface of the roof and varying in size; the only consistent thing was that they were slate, held on to the sarking beams beneath with little copper nails, and that each overlapped the one below.

And they are all wet and cold and slippery.

Then upward inch by inch, the rope her lifeline against the lurches backward that threatened with every movement; it was like trying to climb up the side of a giant witch's hat while someone poured endless buckets of ice water over her. At last her hand touched something else; brickwork, square, faintly and blessedly *warm.* The grapnel was next, jammed between the ridgeline of the roof and the chimney's rectangle. She closed her eyes—it made only the slightest difference—and thought about the lines of the roofs as she came erect and hugged the wet brick.

They had no pretense of regularity either; like most domestic architecture before the Age of Reason they'd just slapped on another bit at any angle that was convenient without bothering about symmetry.

Sí. This one has a kink, and then the ridge turns at right angles . . . nearly at right angles . . . along the roof of that single-story half-timbered section. That runs into that thing like a big black wooden shed on top of that rectangular stone part that's a little higher. That has an eaves section below the windows to catch the fall from the roof and direct it outward. Go along that, and at the end the roof of the shed-thing is within reach. If I can just get along that section of roof—it isn't nearly as steep as this—there's another section of roof run out to the north face of the tower, sort of like an abutment.

"How I hate you, Colonel Nicolai," Luz murmured. "And here is another reason for it."

Working by feel she freed the grapnel and collapsed the prongs and tucked it away, then left the rope with a coil around the chimney stack, and the air rifle braced within it; she could retrieve it on the way back. She pressed her hands to the brick between her body and the chimney and rested against it for a minute by the count; she was going to need every little bit of suppleness she could coax into her fingers. Speed was essential now too, but only as fast as she could go and still do everything perfectly.

Then she turned and stood, her feet feeling outward in the darkness, the flexible cord soles gripping as well as anything could on the rounded tile of the roof ridge. One long breath, another, and she walked forward. Ten paces, stop and feel forward for the kink in the roof, turn *left* and a heart-stopping lurch when she nearly unbalanced as a foot slipped. She went down into a crouch and slapped both hands on the curved tile that topped the ridge of the roof, then blew out her breath and the shakiness that accompanied the flash of terror with it.

If this is what it's like to be blind, I sincerely hope I die before I lose my vision.

Along the longer section of roof ridge, feet toes-out like walking a tightrope—though at least it didn't sway as much as those did. The Chamber used circus acrobats as instructors sometimes, which had been fun, both for what they taught and because they'd been interesting people with fascinating stories to tell. By way of compensation for the extra stability underfoot she didn't have a balancing pole in her hands, it was raining buckets, and the wind was only *mostly* predictable—sometimes back gusts caught at her when she'd started leaning into it.

Plus there's no net.

She did the last ten yards in a half crouch, shuffling in small steps that put her left foot forward each time. Her hand was outstretched. It ran into a steady drizzle of cold water, about like that from a half-on domestic tap over a sink, and she halted.

Now that she knew the building was there she could half see, half sense its presence looming in the dark, and hear the steady drum of rain on the slates of its roof. The short section of sloping roof below the windows was nearly awash; this particular addition on top of the thick stone of the old castle wasn't even half-timbering, but outright wood planking. Oak planking, black with age, and wide—whenever it had been built, they'd cut old-growth trees to saw for this sheathing. She remembered from her careful study of the *Schloss* in daytime that there were four small windows, one at either end of the flat end of the structure and two in the middle.

More careful feeling—or as careful as it could be when the tips of her fingers were numb—showed that the slanting section of slates projecting from the base of the wooden wall was at about forty-five degrees. She planted her hands on it—it was about chest high—and did a straight lift, wheezing a little with effort as she brought her feet up and set them between.

Then she stood and leaned forward against the surface of the oak planks, arms stretched wide and body plastered to the surface. There was nothing to keep her from falling backward if she slipped.

So don't slip, she thought, and began inching rightward.

Moving one foot at a time and sliding her body, keeping it in contact with the wood every moment. Except when she came to the two central windows, which were utterly black; she could just get a grip on the frames with her fingertips but had to bow her body out slightly as she passed them, the lower sills bumping at her knees. Then the downslope of the roof above, as she came to the last of the gable end.

This section of roof sloped down to about her breastbone level, and it did have guttering. The half-timber addition had been built on top of the original stone structure, giving the whole thing a mushroom-like organic quality. It all reminded her of illustrations from books of European folktales, for the excellent reason that those artists had used buildings just like this as their models.

Copper, I think, she thought, testing the metal of the guttering with her hand. *Thin and it's only pegged on the underside into the ends of the roof beams. It'll rip free if I try to put all my weight on one spot.*

It was times like this that she wished she could still pray with any conviction; a good useful saint would be a relief right now.

Instead she took another deep breath, put her right hand on the slates just above the guttering, her left a bit higher on the edge of the roof, bent her knees, and jumped. Her body came down on the sloping surface of the roof, and she used the momentum to swing her legs over too. The tips of her toes came down on the guttering, spread wide in a frog stance and she moved as slowly as she could. Thin sheet metal buckled a little but did not give way.

Another long shaky breath; now she regretted the lack of anything to *thank*, except good fortune and those acrobats.

Muchísimas gracias, Flying Corelli Family, she thought.

One thing she could *not* let herself think about was doing all this in reverse, only by then she'd be even more chilled and exhausted. The impulse to beat her brains out against the slates would be too strong if she did. One inch at a time . . .

She worked her way rightward, squirming her entire self against the slates, digging her fingertips into the slightest irregularities in the stone, never letting her palms come out of contact with it, trying to think of herself as a sort of organic pancake creature out of Wells or Burroughs just *oozing* along.

Her right foot touched something: the junction of the two sections of roofing, one heading back eastward to the tower. That would only be about twelve feet long, and the guttering would continue around the corner. But the ridgeline would be much closer, less than six feet up. Six feet up wet slick slate, a jump and mad scramble . . .

When her hands closed on the ridgeline she paused for three minutes, every muscle in her body quivering in relief—the relative relief of having a handhold that she could actually squeeze hard, instead of relying on nearly nonexistent friction from keeping her away from a brief scrabbling and a long fall. A few tears squeezed out from between her clenched eyelids, and then she pushed sensation away again, making herself operate like a machine. You could do that . . . but sooner or later the price had to be paid.

A pull and scrabble and she was astride the roof. The white stuccoed stone of the tower was ten feet away, and just visible, if you also used the eyes of faith. She hitched herself forward rather than getting up and walking; she had a feeling that it wasn't time to tempt fate right now. When she came to the spot where the roof ran into the side of the tower, rising to her feet was almost a luxury.

The windowsill was exactly where she expected it—a little below breastbone level while she stood on the roof ridge. The latch was just at the practical limit of her reach; nothing as convenient as having it at chest height, of course. She slid her right hand up the side and identified the spot she'd have to work on—entirely by touch and memory.

She undid two of the buttons on her pseudo-pajama jacket, gritted her teeth, and ran her hands up under it and the shirt beneath to warm them against her body under her armpits. It was very much like being groped by an animated corpse while locked in a cold-store closet, and her torso wasn't exactly toasty by this point either, but it was the best she had. When some sensation had returned to them she brought them back out and pulled up the mask far enough so that she could grip a little pencil-shaped electrical torch in her teeth; for this she *had* to risk a little light, and she had something from the Chamber's secret labs—advised by Tesla—that was much handier than anything the world in general could get. The windows were the old-fashioned type like a miniature door, with four panes of glass in a metal frame, fastened on one side by a simple lever that pivoted its catch into a U-bracket.

Her lockpicks contained a very thin section of spring steel like a flattened wire, covered in a sheath of oiled rubber that kept it from scraping things. Luz's teeth clenched on the trigger of the electric torch, and even the feeble light of the little shielded bulb was almost blinding for an instant. She squinted upward through the rain—luckily now mostly coming from behind her since she had her back to the northeast—and carefully, gently, despite the pain of working with her hands over her head and racking the overstretched muscles of her shoulders and arms—began to work the strip through between the window and its frame just below where the handle would be.

And at this point the alarm would have silently gone off except for my new good friend Ciara. Who is really amazingly clever.

Not only had she recognized the alarm system and analyzed it, but despite the ugly stress she was under, from the situation and Nicolai personally, she'd thought to *look* for it. That argued for a clever mind, and a basically alert one too. Even clever people were often too focused on themselves to really take in the world around them.

"*Bendita seas, muchacha,*" Luz said softly. "You were right. I have to do this for you too. Not only, but too."

The strip was through, and she relaxed her teeth on the torch. The light went out, but the darkness was so complete that she could see the glow of the cooling filament inside the bulb for several instants. She slowly pressed the strip upward, fractions of an inch at a time; it was just as essential not to mark the paint visibly as it was to get the window open. The information was only valuable if Abteilung IIIb *didn't* know anyone else had it.

Resistance. Luz pushed upward again, steadily, gently. A little yielding, disguised by the spring steel's flexibility. Rain was making even the roughened surface of the leather on the fingertips of the gloves slippery; she corrected her grip and pushed upward. Bit by bit . . . and then the window started to swing open. She halted it instantly, lest water get in and leave traces. The strip went back into the pouch at her waist, and she brought the haversack on her back around. What was on top beneath the buckled flap was mostly cloth sheeting from Castle Rauenstein's stores. Luckily nobody was going to miss it, with a major exodus tomorrow morning.

Or rather, when they miss it they'll know *exactly what happened to it; those thieving bandit bastards in von Hindenburg's HQ company special train stole it.*

If there was one universal constant of military life it was foraging, including the view that stealing from people in your own immediate unit, your uniformed family, was unforgivable, but robbing strangers in the same uniform was simply showing soldierly initiative and only slightly worse than taking things from civilians or the enemy. Your friends were what counted.

Luz opened the window, and warm air struck her like the forgiving breath of the God she didn't believe in. Slide a hand beneath the flap of her haversack, grab the edge of the sheet, flick it through the window and open, toss the haversack after it. Jump and catch the stone and keep the momentum going and through in a forward roll. Turn and swing the window shut again . . .

She collapsed to the sheets, teeth chattering, retching dryly. The room *wasn't* warm, not by any sane standards, well under sixty degrees, but it *felt* warm, without making her feel any less miserably cold. Gradually she won back her self-control, pulled off the hood and the rest of the pajamas and dropped them to the sheet. Then she pulled the second, smaller cloth of actual toweling out of the haversack and used it to mop herself until she wouldn't drip, working up a little circulation with the scratchy-soft surface as she did. For a small mercy the hood had kept her hair merely damp rather than sopping.

The windows had blinds, and it was the work of a moment to pull them down; it wouldn't do to have anyone seeing lights. Even heavy rain might not hide a glowing window. She set the electric torch on Colonel Nicolai's desk, pointing upward, and turned the dial that surrounded the bulb. That opened out in mirrored segments and the light grew brighter, enough to cast her shadow gigantic on the wall. It would drain the battery more quickly, even the incredibly compact, powerful products of the secret labs, but she wouldn't be needing it for long. Then she unpacked the rest of the haversack. That contained the business part of the camera that had been in her handbag, and the very latest development from the labs: miniature lightbulbs containing fine filaments in an atmosphere of pure oxygen, ready to yield a moment of intense light for taking photographs in darkness. The rest of the world used a trough of magnesium powder, which worked but was impossibly cumbersome for this. She supposed that eventually the little bulbs would become commonplace, but it was good to have the best toys first.

"And here are good Colonel Nicolai's map racks," Luz murmured to herself. "All still set up from your last conference with von Hindenburg and Ludendorff and the admiral. How fortunate we had good luck with the weather before everything was packed away. There *is* a special Providence that protects children, drunks, and the United States of America, and also this *Cubana*-Irish-American standing freezing in the altogether."

She did a quick search for the usual tricks of the trade, hairs kept in place by minute dabs of spirit gum and so forth, but there weren't any.

Any that I can detect, Luz reminded herself, as she fixed the exact position of everything she planned to touch in her mind . . . using *Kim's Game* again, and very useful it was too. It was surprising how much actual spy work borrowed from fiction.

Colonel Nicolai, I do believe you're overconfident of the security of this eagle's nest of yours. And probably you're very picky about who you let in here, so you'd have to do all the little chores yourself. Tsk. Bad balance-of-risk assessment.

The maps—they were U.S. Coast and Geodetic Survey issue, and recent ones—were of the harbors of the cities south from Halifax; she whistled silently as she flipped through the stack and saw how many there were. This attack was no piker, no case of doing an enemy a small injury. It would hit every major shipping point on the East and Gulf Coasts; probably it would cut the cargo capacity down to a small fraction of what was necessary to sustain an army across the Atlantic and keep it down for months if not years, besides the carnage and panic. Most of the ports were assigned a pair of U-boats, but not all; New York got six. Savannah, Georgia, had only one. The location of each was carefully marked, with notes on precise distances to landmarks and the orientation of the submarine when it was put on the bottom in attack position.

A cryptic notation, *Auf/u/Ang* . . .

It's an abbreviation, I think. Auf/u/Ang. *That would be something like* Aufstieg und Angriff. *Rise and Attack. Or . . . come to the surface and attack? The number . . . that's time in military twenty-four-hour reckoning. All of them set to catch the maximum number of people going to work to kill off the skilled labor.*

The haversack included an aluminum frame for holding the camera when she was photographing documents. She set it up, locked the camera itself in place with a set of wing-nut fasteners, and centered the first map beneath it. The little bulb screwed into a socket near the camera; she stopped and blew on her fingers and worked them until they were supple enough to fasten the delicate connections to the battery. Then she covered the whole with a folding cloth of dense stuff.

A tube and squeeze bulb set the camera and flash off simultaneously. She squeezed her eyes shut and glanced away each time she triggered it, but the flash from beneath the edges of the cloth was still bright. A dozen times, and just the maps; it would be lovely if there were engineering drawings of the specialized U-boats they were planning on using, but there wasn't time. Then she stowed the camera and frame and put the haversack back on the sheeting with her clothes and used the electric torch to examine the desk, wiping carefully with a cloth and making sure that nothing was disturbed—pen, inkstand (evidently Colonel Nicolai didn't use a newfangled reservoir pen), telephone stands.

The maps were more delicate still; each had to go into its original pigeonhole in the wall rack, and then she had to use the memory game to recall exactly how each had been rolled, which edge had been uppermost, which had shown a slight bit of corner because it was rolled unevenly . . .

Closing and locking the window behind her would require a slip-knot in a very thin strong cord; she set that up before she raised the blinds again. Then she had to re-don the cold, clammy-wet silks and use the sheeting to remove any trace of moisture from the floor. Out into the rain again, and the window; the beat of the cold sluicing drops on her back seemed to make something heavy settle in her stomach.

I have a million American lives in here, she thought, reaching back to touch the haversack, now mostly stuffed with sodden sheets but also carrying the crucial roll of exposed film.

And possibly the outcome of the Great War. Get going, mi corazón. *It's a voyage of discoveries and firsts. How often do you get to save the world?*

Luz was only vaguely conscious of Ciara's frantic hands pulling her limp body through the window. She *wanted* to say, *Pull up the rope, there's stuff tied to the other end*, but she was barely aware that the other woman did it anyway. Strong hands under her armpits pulling her toward the fire, pulling off the sopping pajamas and undergarments, toweling her down, and wrapping her in heated blankets.

That's right, she thought absently, disconnected from her limp body. *She looked after her sick father for a long time. She's used to dealing with invalids.*

A cup against her lips; she gulped strong sweet wine mulled until it was just enough below boiling point to be drinkable, coughed, gulped more. It was a terrible thing to do to a first-class Moselle dessert wine, but that didn't bother her now as heat exploded in her midsection. The gray at the edge of the world drew back a little, but that made her more conscious of the utter misery of her body, and she started to shake uncontrollably. The blankets were ruthlessly pulled away and another set wrapped around her, almost painfully hot. Luz clutched them and managed to choke out, "*Muchísimas gr-gr-gracias, querida,*" between chattering teeth.

"Oh, Mother of God, don't try to talk," Ciara said. "Here, eat some of this chocolate."

Luz managed to get several mouthfuls down and keep them from coming right back up. She sighed deeply and collapsed onto her side as the shaking subsided into shivering, feeling the heat of the coal fire on her face. Ciara knelt beside her in her nightrobe, eyes wide and hand moving out uncertainly.

"Toes," Luz said, sighing again as something unclenched in the center of her body.

Ciara looked down; her own bare feet were not far from Luz's face where it lay in a cocoon of blankets.

"What is it, Luz dear?" she said anxiously.

"You . . . have . . ." Luz said slowly; sheets of darkness were descending, warm as the fire or the blankets, and there seemed to be no difference between thought and words and the world. ". . . such . . . lovely toes."

Blackness.

THIRTEEN

Schloss Rauenstein

Kingdom of Saxony, German *Reich*

SEPTEMBER 11TH, 1916(B)

T he secret is to exclude light," Luz said as she set the roll of exposed film that was the fruit of last night's efforts in the depres-
sion and pressed until the studs at each end of the cylinder clicked
home in the built-in guides. "Then it's just a matter of machinery that
can pull the film through the chemical baths at set intervals."

"The devil is in the details," Ciara said, looking at the device with
fascination. "Someone paid attention to them!"

The room itself was dim; the day outside was overcast and wet and
cold. Luz had slept ten hours and woken ravenous, which was a good
sign, and with a splitting headache, which wasn't. Aspirin and the very
late breakfast that Ciara had fetched and the last of her hoard of *coquitos*
had helped, but she still felt *heavy*.

Heavy and slow. You were pushing yourself very hard there, mi corazón.
*Heavy rain just above freezing can kill you almost as fast as going into the drink
off the* Titanic. *You'll need a couple of days of rest to be at your best again.*

Now that she was near a good coal fire and she'd eaten, that didn't
seem quite so depressing. She certainly hadn't felt ready to confront a
room full of cheerful German officers a few hours ago, unless she absolutely had to, and thanks to Ciara she hadn't.

Perhaps I'm still mentally *cold; or even soul-cold*, Luz thought. *It's no wonder, considering what's in these maps.*

The metal tray she had removed from her trunk spent most of its time cushioning vials and packages of cosmetics, scented soap, and personal hygiene products; they gave the room a pleasant odor of lavender and verbena, and with the coal fire built up they also gave it a summery contrast to the steady cold rain outside. Now the tray's true function was revealed.

"I see!" Ciara said, kneeling beside her on the floor by the bed with the bottom half of the photo-development kit before them.

I have found the route to Ciara Whelan's heart, Luz thought with what she recognized, slightly startled, as genuinely fond amusement. *It isn't flowers or poetry or even my own radiant charm and sensual animal magnetism. It's a really well-designed piece of machinery.*

"The clockwork pulls the strip of exposed celluloid through the chemicals," Ciara said, instantly analyzing something that had taken Luz days to fully master. "Only this length of strong paper follower comes out, and then the perforations engage before you put the cover on and wind the spring and set it going! Like a Kodak, but for individual developing, with these timer mechanisms keeping the period in each solution precise. Building the skills into the machine."

Luz had brought together the various parts from items in her trunks, all carefully designed to look harmless. For instance, the power for the whole system came from the spring and wind-up train of a—perfectly functional—alarm clock, which was something quite commonly found in an affluent traveler's baggage. Amused, she watched as Ciara deftly identified each and started to install them in the slots and screw holes of the base with the tools in a little Swiss Army knife. Luz only had to correct her once, and that was a matter of which of two pieces of gearwork to put in first.

Luz tucked her hands in the wide kimono sleeves of her coat against a phantom chill that still seemed to pain them. Besides her best winterweight *tailleur* suit she'd put on a knee-length coat she'd picked up in

New York on impulse and that always lifted her spirits, French-designed but inspired by Bakst's paintings for the Ballet Russe that had made such a sensation before the war. The fabric was an orange corded merino wool and lined with green satin, with a high soft collar and cuffs of black velvet trimmed with black fur. There was a jet-colored cloud-form pattern in the Chinese style embroidered with curled wool yarn and outlined with black silk cord in mirror images on the shoulders at the back and in strips to either side of the middle down to another outburst at the front bottom hem, and more on the sleeves.

"And here's the top," Luz said, lifting it from the bed's duvet.

"So, you put the distilled water in here, the developer bath here, the stop bath here, then the washing bath and then up here to dry," Ciara said. "It's a darkroom in miniature! And of course developed negatives are far safer to carry."

"¡Verdad!" Luz said grimly. "And a very great deal is riding on these pictures."

They were both silent for a moment, thinking of what the information on the roll of film meant.

"I've heard that there are new sonic devices for detecting submarines," Ciara said thoughtfully. "Besides listening with hydrophones."

Then she put her hand to Luz's forehead; it felt warm. "No fever! Saints, but I was deathly afraid you'd get pneumonia, after last night."

"I'm tough as an old root," Luz said. "I only *look* pale, ethereal, and delicate."

That got her a startled laugh; unclothed what she actually looked like was one of the Flying Corellis, taut curves and long straplike muscle. Form followed function.

"And yes, there are devices . . . they're called *Echels*, echolocation systems, now. But only a few specialist destroyer squadrons have them, and they don't work well in shallow water yet. Still more if the target is on the bottom. With these maps—or just the coordinates—the Navy can probably destroy all the U-boats, if they're reasonably alert. Without them, even with warning they'd be lucky to get a small share. This Loki plot is complex, but not so much so it'll fail completely if everything doesn't go perfectly for them. And the weapon itself is a horror, but it's an *effective* horror."

"We'll just have to get the information through, then," Ciara said stoutly.

She was silent as they snapped in the various bits that would operate the little automatic developer, then lowered the cover on and secured it with wing-nut fasteners that pressed the grooved rubber light seal around it home.

"Luz . . ." she said thoughtfully. "The Germans were the ones who started using the other war gases, chlorine and phosgene and the one they used on Verdun, mustard gas they call it . . . but the other powers, the British and the French, used them right back, didn't they?"

The cover plate had been part of a watertight compartment that held packets of the very latest pre-packaged disposable menstrual pads, the ones that had a removable strip on the bottom that covered an adhesive surface that held them in place in your drawers without a belt or loops. Ciara had been very impressed, since she'd heard of them but never seen any—and also grateful when Luz offered to share. They'd both be needing them in a few days, and the Boston girl had been planning to scrounge rags and face the prospect of hand-cleaning them in the room's basin.

Ciara hadn't packed nearly as much gear when she left her home on what she thought was a mission of vengeance against the Sassenach who'd killed her brother.

And of that, only the prospect of death is the same, Luz thought, then scolded herself for pessimism. *You're just still feeling* no poder en tu alma *about things.*

"*Verdad,*" Luz said. "The Entente powers couldn't *not* use them, not if they wanted to fight back; the Russians never could produce much of it, and look what's happened to *them.* I know we've got plenty stockpiled, and gas masks and so forth too, and our troops are training to use them."

"But doesn't that mean that we'll have to use the Breath of Loki too? That everyone will? Once they learn how to make it, and that won't take long."

"It won't?" Luz said, disappointed but not surprised.

Secret weapons didn't stay secret once you started using them, unless you were fighting savages without a modern industrial base. You usually only got one or two chances to surprise people with them before they came right back at you, often improved in the process.

"No," Ciara said flatly. "The Germans have the world's best chemists and chemical industry, but they're not *that* much better. And from what the old man said, they stumbled across this by luck . . . if you call it luck. Six months, a year at most, and we'd be able to make it too. The British and the French, maybe the same, maybe a bit more."

While they spoke, Luz had let Ciara help assemble the system, but she reserved pouring the chemicals through the built-in valves for herself; they were the only ones she had and there was no room for the slightest error.

"I suppose so, and once everyone's making it everyone will use it," she said. "Just a minute, I can't talk now."

After she'd finished and stoppered the valves she took a deep breath, pushed the whole unit slowly and carefully fully beneath the bed, and flipped the little lever. With a whine it began to work . . .

And if it doesn't *work, what do I do?* ¡Sepa la Bola! *Damned if I know! Not much use in praying. Mima's old* tía *told me those stories . . . I could sacrifice a goat to the appropriate Orisha, Ogún I suppose . . .*

They rose, dusting off their hands and packing away the bits and pieces back into harmless anonymity in her trunks.

"Well, that's going to be very bad," Ciara said, resuming the conversation. "Because you're right, Luz. This is a really, really powerful weapon. Masks don't work with it and one tiny little drop will kill you and it stays around *waiting* to kill you. You can't even touch someone who'd been poisoned to help them . . . or even give them decent burial . . . because enough may be on their clothes or skin or hair to kill you or cripple you or drive you mad. Even the Germans don't have any counter-measures yet, except those rubber suits—and you couldn't put everyone, or even very many people, in those. Luz, you could destroy whole *countries* with enough of that horrible stuff. Even bomb shelters wouldn't help—they'd be death traps unless they were hermetically sealed."

Luz opened her mouth, then closed it again. "You're right," she said simply.

And if you mixed it in with explosives and incendiaries, even a little of it, the effects would build on each other because people would be too terrified to take shelter from the bombs or fight the fires. Usually I'm all for progress—I'm a Party member and it's the Progressive *Republican Party, after all . . . but this time . . .*

Aloud she went on: "But I don't know what on Earth we can do about that, so there's no point in worrying. The president will have to decide about that one. Let's stick to things we can do something about and not occupy our minds with things we can't affect."

They worked in silence at rearranging the trunks so the changes were undetectable to a casual eye. Then Ciara cleared her throat. Luz glanced at her and saw that she had her hands pressed together, something she'd already noticed meant nervousness.

"Ah . . . Luz . . . can I ask you something?"

"*¡Ay!* That always sounds ominous!"

"Wha . . . what did you mean when you said I had lovely toes? Last night? It was what you said just before you went to sleep."

"Before *me caí . . .* went out like a light."

Luz laughed and took up the violin and began to check the tuning on the strings; they were going to play to cover the faint whine of the little spring-driven motor from the alarm clock, though that was probably unnecessary. Although they'd get to enjoy the music, which made it worthwhile in itself. From everything she'd heard travel by submarine was fairly hellish, so they might as well enjoy things while they could.

"*Ay,* at that point I was saying the first thing that came into my head."

"Oh, I understand! You were . . . you looked like you were on the edge of death!"

"There's no quicker way to die of exposure than being sluiced with running water just short of freezing. I *was* on the edge of death. Another fifteen minutes out there and I would have been over it," Luz said feelingly. "That wasn't the first time you saved my life, but it counts."

"So if you were just babbling . . ."

"Not exactly. Just not guarding my tongue. Do you really want to know?"

"Ummmm . . . yes. I mean to say, I've never really thought about my, my *toes*. Except when I stub them or someone steps on them."

"Well, *querida*, everyone should be allowed a few eccentricities of their very own. One of mine is that I like toes."

"You like . . . toes?" Ciara said, looking baffled, intrigued, and apprehensive at the same time.

"You know how someone will say: *She has such nice hair*, or *She has wonderful sparkling eyes*? Not that I have anything against hair or eyes, and yours are striking, but one of the things I notice about a pretty girl is her toes. Except that you usually don't get to *see* someone's toes on brief acquaintance, of course, more's the pity. And yours truly are lovely; I noticed the first time I saw your feet bare. I said it aloud last night because I was nearly delirious; sorry if I presumed."

I will spare you what I actually like doing to, and with, pretty toes. Not that those are so very startling or unorthodox, but they would certainly sound . . . a little lascivious . . . as things are right now.

Ciara sat at the piano; Luz suspected that was as much for the opportunity to stare at the keyboard as for the arpeggio she sounded out.

"And you do think I'm pretty? Really?"

"Devastatingly so," Luz said cheerfully and sincerely; that was a lot more pleasant to think about than cities laid waste by the Loki horror-weapon. "Especially when you smile. Or when you blush, and better still when you smile *and* blush."

Ciara did both, made an attempt to speak, cleared her throat, and then went on: "I suppose . . . I suppose I was flirting with you the other day, wasn't I? But I didn't mean to . . . I mean, I didn't know . . . I don't want to hurt your feelings . . . I do like and admire you so much, but . . ."

Luz laughed aloud and leaned an elbow on the piano and tapped her on the shoulder with the bow of the violin, which brought her face up.

"Ciara, yes, you were flirting, yes, you didn't know it, yes, I realized that and I shouldn't have teased you, that was wicked of me, and no, this is not the time or place. We're alone among enemies, in constant danger of death, and contrary to what the books say that is usually *not* very romantic. It certainly . . . distorts your emotions. Why don't we settle for being good friends and comrades for now? And when it's all over and the day is saved and we can relax and be ourselves . . . *¡Al fin, estaré harta de esperar!* We'll see what we shall see!"

"Oh, yes!" Ciara said. "And I do *so* want to be your friend and help you, Luz."

"*Bueno,*" Luz said briskly. "You've shown you're a very good friend to have."

Then she leaned closer and whispered: "But just before we drop the subject, you do have such lovely, *lovely* toes and they will haunt my dreams. And to seal the agreement—"

The kiss was quick and soft. Luz straightened up and began to turn away with a smile:

Really, you are *rather wicked at times,* mi corazón, she thought with satisfaction. Pero así está la semilla antes de cosechar, *as the saying goes. No harvest without a seed. Let's see how that grows . . . assuming we live to get back to America, that is.*

. . . and then a knock sounded at the door.

"Play!" Luz said, snapping to alertness.

Ciara was staring blindly and touching her lips with a wondering finger.

"*Play!*" Luz said again, more sharply.

The younger woman came to herself with a start, snatched some pages from the music rack, and began to peck out something that segued into Dvořák's Romance in F Minor, Zubatý's B.38 arrangement for piano and violin. Luz joined in—the violin part was the core of the piece, and she could do it from memory—and their playing gained strength as the weaving structure built. The knock wasn't repeated until the final high trill.

Luz went to the door. "Yes?" she said, opening it with the violin and bow in the other hand.

Horst and the Herr Privatdozent were there. "Ah, you are feeling better!" Horst said with relief. "We did not wish to interrupt your duet, which was so lovely."

Oh, Horst, sweetie, if you only knew, Luz thought, and sighed.

"There will be little time for the things of *die Kultur* in the weeks ahead," von Bülow agreed solemnly.

And that is so true as well, Luz thought, and managed to look solemn.

"And for me this will be farewell," von Bülow said. "My duties will call me elsewhere. It has been a great honor, *gnädiges Fräulein*."

"Fräulein Whelan said you were ill when she came to fetch your meal from the officer's mess," Horst said. "We were worried."

"Ah, well, not precisely ill," Luz said. "Cramps and chills and a blue mood."

She glanced over to the chair that held the piled blue-and-white packages of menstrual pads, clearly labeled: *Johnson & Johnson's New Adhesive Sanitary Napkins*, with *Clean, convenient, discreet—freedom of motion for the freedoms of the New Woman!* in smaller print beneath. There were times when she loathed her homeland's advertising mania, and others when it was a source of innocent merriment. The claims were more or less true, in any case; it was a brilliant invention and far ahead of its time.

She could refer to the pads—not in words, of course—with reasonable if not perfect propriety, since the men had entered a ladies' bedroom on their own initiative and without prior invitation. There were times when the code of manners that was so confining could be used as a weapon, rather along the same principles of redirecting force she'd discovered in jujitsu. Ciara was examining the upper wall opposite her and obviously wishing the castle would vanish, or possibly be carried away in a flood.

In *her* world of Catholic Irish–shopkeeper respectability it would all be something you only mentioned with female relatives and friends.

Luz could see both the German men read, mentally translate into their own language, then translate the idiom and context. Von Bülow actually blanched, but he'd been born deep in the Victorian period and had been a man and soldier, albeit a very young one, around the time of the Civil War. Horst flushed, averted his eyes, and forced himself not to mumble.

"Ach, so," he said, that singularly useful phrase. "Ah . . . we will be leaving tomorrow, I'm afraid, so everything will have to be ready to depart by dawn. I can arrange help if you need it."

"That's very considerate of you, Horst, but I'm feeling uncomfortable, not crippled, and discomfort never stopped me from doing anything I thought essential."

As witness last night, poor boy, she thought, and finished:

"Everything will be ready."

"Then we will leave you ladies to your preparations, and see you at dinner. I understand the cooks managed to, shall I say, acquire some surplus supplies from the Great General Staff headquarters train. They will attempt a *Sächsischer Sauerbraten*."

"See you then, Horst, Herr Privatdozent," Luz said, and the men both clicked their heels and half bowed.

The Black Chamber operative burst out laughing when they were safely gone, keeping it as quiet as she could but chortling until she was hiccupping.

"Oh, I needed that! Did you see their faces! The trembling effort of will not to bolt! ¡Ay! The horror, the horror!"

"Luz!" Ciara said, scandalized.

"I can't help it, *querida*," Luz wheezed. "You know, Horst is a prime fighting man, a hardened killer who's gazed unmoved on terrible things. And the Herr Privatdozent is the author of one of history's most monstrous crimes. Yet what is it put them both to flight and protected our whirring little device beneath the bed from their attention and questions we couldn't answer?"

She stepped over, snatched up one of the packages of Johnson & Johnson's finest products, and fell into a fencer's pose with it pointed toward the door, then advanced thrusting and cutting like a *sabreur* on the mat of a *salle d'armes*, or someone playing one on stage.

"Aha!" she said. "Flee, flee, mighty Teutonic warriors, pale with terror before the bloody, awful power of the bloody, dripping—"

"*Luzzzzz!*" Ciara wailed, and then dissolved into helpless giggles mixed with wincing embarrassment.

"*¡Ay!*" Luz said, and sighed. "Mind you, it would have worked just as well at home. Amazing what men can be squeamish about, isn't it?"

She flourished the violin's bow. "Let's do something just for fun!"

Ciara put her head to one side. "Vivaldi? Vivaldi is fun in musical form."

"The Concerto in G Major? It's been done for piano and violin. As a matter of fact, I think I saw a copy . . ."

She rummaged in the sheet music and put it down on the piano's music rack.

"Ah, I know that arrangement!" Ciara said, and they began.

FOURTEEN

Königlich Preußische und Großherzoglich Hessische Staatseisenbahn
(Royal Prussian and Grand Ducal Hessian State Railways)
Lehrte, Province of Hanover
Kingdom of Prussia, German *Reich*
SEPTEMBER 16TH, 1916(B)

T here are special trains, Elisa, and then again . . ." Horst began.
        "And then again there are *special* trains," Luz finished with a
sigh. "I doubt the two . . . eminent personages . . . we met with are being
shoved onto sidings like this."

Though it's an opportunity to gather intelligence, too, she thought.

She kept her hands in the sleeves of her orange coat; it was not only
stylish but warm, something the carriage most manifestly had not been
since the coal ran out—the new orderly had said he was going out to
get more, though he was taking a long time about it and the train might
leave at any moment. It suddenly occurred to her that she ought to
have a loop for her *navaja* sewn into the left sleeve of this coat if she was
going to be in cold-weather country. It wouldn't alter the drape much,
and a knife you couldn't reach quickly wasn't much use except to excite
suspicions if it was discovered.

I am a true professional, she thought whimsically. *It is starting to override
my fashion sense.*

And the fabric was bright, which her surroundings weren't either.
Now that they were into the gray chill autumn of the North European

plain it even smelled differently, more of the damp scent of waste steam and lubricants and a certain staleness. Coal smoke was the main contribution from the rail yards outside, though the drifting misty rain was laying some of that.

Nobody thought it odd she was wearing the coat; Europeans were used to buttoning up inside, being far from the land of central heating and even farther from California. Horst had his greatcoat on too, and Ciara her cloak, and Daubigny an overcoat with a raccoon-fur collar. The company was a bit different this time too; von Bülow was somewhere else—nobody had told her and she'd known better than to ask, but she suspected Berlin where he'd be cooking up some other devilment in his laboratory, or helping some less politically adept version of himself cook up other devilments. And she knew Horst was extremely annoyed by the fact that he had to share one of the two small sleeping compartments at the rear with the knight of the KKK, though to his credit he hadn't had the unimaginable brass to suggest putting Ciara in with a man.

Horst really is *a gentleman, in his way . . . but this isn't a century for knights. Not real ones, unlike that* puto *from the KKK. I suspect* he's *going to fit in perfectly.*

Their not-all-that-special train was sitting idle but with steam up on a siding in the industrial sector of Lehrte, a town that existed because about seventy years ago the then-king of the then-Kingdom of Hanover hadn't wanted any such ugly newfangled things as railway stations in his beautiful capital city.

That had made this former farming village a few miles away the center of the Royal Hanoverian Railways, and that reactionary attitude had played its part into turning the Kingdom of Hanover into the Prussian province of Hanover and the Royal Hanoverian Railways into part of the Royal Prussian and Grand Ducal Hessian State Railways about fifty years ago. Not that Prussian kings and nobles couldn't be ferociously reactionary in their way, but they rarely turned down something that would make their army more effective, from needle guns and steam locomotives to the monster killing engines of the twentieth century.

Lehrte had grown up as a typical grubby Victorian railroad-junction industrial town, as witness the sugar factory to one side of them and the cement plant to the other and acres of crowded workers' dwellings. And added to the scents of industry was the odor of a big cattle mart—*Baedeker's Guide* said it was the largest in the northern half of Germany—that didn't smell as bad as the Union Stock Yards in Chicago, but not for want of trying and possibly only because the weather was cold. The fact that it was drizzling and dark in late afternoon helped keep down the stench, but it didn't do anything at all for the view.

Living here would undoubtedly drive you to drink, socialism, suicide, or all three in succession, Luz thought. *Places like this make me love California in general and Santa Barbara in particular more and more. It makes you understand European painters like Munch, too, and why they're always doing things titled* The Scream *or* Ashes *or* Melancholy *or* Despair.

Luz had seen a Munch exhibition while she was at loose ends in New York in 1912, before the election, before the Black Chamber. She'd come away convinced that despite his difference from her preferred Academic painters like Leighton—that was one area in which she'd agreed with the Party's official aesthetics even before the Party—he was an extraordinary genius. And that it was even more extraordinary that he'd only gone mad and had to be locked up once, and even more that they'd let him out again. It was the sort of art that made you think:

What genius! How compelling! I think I'll slit my wrists now!

Of course, that had been much closer to the murder of her parents, and she'd been more or less insane then herself.

It was to the north that interesting things were happening, and she craned her head for a better view through the rain-streaked window beside her armchair. A main east-west line—quadruple tracked—from Berlin to the Rhine ran there. Trains were thundering by westward on three of the lines at a steady twenty miles an hour, a pace that spared strain on engines running on reduced maintenance and poor-quality coal but ate the miles well enough on this crowded continent. Germany was only about six hundred miles across, smaller than Texas, though you'd have to add in the distance from the dissolving Eastern Front to the Western in France. At this pace they could get men from one to the other in about five days, or allowing for a realistic degree of friction perhaps a bit more than a week.

Europe, where a hundred miles is a long way; America, where a hundred years is a long time, she thought.

Each troop train was fifty-four cars long, enough to hold a battalion and its equipment; she counted only a few that deviated from the norm. At precise intervals one would leave the main tracks for a siding, refuel and take on more water for the boiler, and rejoin the stream. Luz wasn't surprised at the mechanical perfection that kept the flow going at exactly the maximum the tracks and rolling stock could carry; the Germans and more specifically the Prussians had invented this sort of thing. In 1914 the head of the Great General Staff's railway section had been General Wilhelm Gröner, a man who spent his off-duty weekends with his wife enjoying their joint hobby: drawing up railway schedules.

Most of these *were* troop trains, men jam-packed into ordinary passenger cars or even slatted boxcars that probably had the proverbial *forty men or eight horses* stenciled on the side and where the amenities were straw and a bucket. One had something else as well: *Ein Lebewohl dem schönen Polen und seinen anhänglichen Läusen* chalked on the side, the letters still legible despite having smeared and run. Luz laughed aloud.

"What's funny, Elisa?" Ciara asked without looking up from her chessboard.

"What those soldiers had put on the side of their train. It means . . . *A fond farewell to lovely Poland and her* . . . anhänglichen . . . that would be *companionable or cuddly* . . . *lice* in English, wouldn't it, Horst?"

He looked up from his book, a copy of *Ardistan und Dschinnistan* with a luridly Oriental cover featuring curved daggers and robes, and spoke in an amused tone:

"Yes, but it's more sarcastic *auf Deutsch. Anhänglichen* . . . more like *sticks close to you* or *affectionately inseparable*. And their hopes will be disappointed; the lice in France are just as bad. Up at the front, at least—

there aren't as many in the rear areas among the *Etappenschwein* and the civilians, I grant."

About a third of the trains *were* carrying horses or their fodder, which took up more space per head. Lances and sabers might be obsolete, but armies still needed the big beasts as much as they did bullets or bread or artillery, not least because they hauled the bullets and bread and artillery from the railheads to the actual fighting line, or as close as they could get before men's arms and backs took over. Even the U.S. Army still used a lot of horse and mule power, and everyone else far more so. Others were mostly flatbeds holding chained-down artillery under tarpaulins, everything from the ubiquitous little 77mm field guns to monsters weighing scores of tons that had to be disassembled even to be shipped by rail.

An interesting variant was hundreds of captured *Russian* guns.

"Those aren't German artillery, Horst?" she asked; Elisa Carmody probably would know enough to realize that, if not the details.

"They're Russian, war booty. The light ones are Putilov 76mms . . . those are 107mms, a copy of a French design, a really fine piece . . . those are medium howitzers—from a Krupp model they bought before the war. All perfectly good guns, the Russians just weren't very good at using them. We captured thousands last year and this, and lots of their ammunition too; the Ivans were too demoralized or just too pig-stupid to destroy much before they surrendered, and I heard that we're going to be getting more shells as part of the peace terms. One thing this war's proven is that you can't have too many guns, so we're using some of it to fill out the artillery brigades of the newer *Ersatz* divisions and giving most to the Austrians and Turks and Bulgarians. Almighty Lord God knows *they* need every piece they can get, even if it shoots by shoving nails and black powder down the muzzle."

More trains passed, and more. And hospital trains and freight trains, and more, and more, and more . . .

It's an impressive display of efficiently handled power, Luz thought. *Fighting Germany isn't going to be a pushover even if we manage to stop the Breath of Loki. We're not making war on Mexicans anymore.*

"Every ten minutes on the dot," Ciara said.

She looked up again and glanced at the old-fashioned pocket watch she'd left open on the table beside the board as Daubigny frowned over his next move. She was winning handily for the third time in a row, to the Southron's badly concealed dismay. Luz had won exactly one game of chess with her so far, and that by dint of telling stories that made her laugh to distract her.

Ciara went on thoughtfully: "I'd read of that, in newspaper articles in 1914. That trains crossed the Rhine bridges every ten minutes for hour after hour, day after day, but sure I hadn't quite believed it; the scheduling problems would be monstrous. Yet this is the same. Though I also read that the trains were like holiday excursions, with the men singing and waving to the crowds."

She'd spoken in English, and Horst put his book down and replied in the same language, speaking softly and with his eyes fixed on distant memories, not really seeing her:

"No, this is not like 1914, Miss Whelan. Two years can be a very long time. And yes, we sang then, as we marched in our stiff new boots from the depots to the stations to board our trains for the front, past the cheering crowds. The sun was hot on our backs and the fields were golden with the harvest and the linden trees rustled overhead. We sang, yes . . ."

His voice was deep and well-controlled, and he could make the music seem rich even a cappella and done very quietly:

"Es braust ein Ruf wie Donnerhall,
wie Schwertgeklirr und Wogenprall:
Zum Rhein, zum Rhein, zum deutschen Rhein,
wer will des Stromes Hüter sein?"

Luz translated it mentally:

The cry resounds like thunder's peal,
Like crashing waves and clang of steel:

The Rhine, the Rhine, our German Rhine,
Who will defend our stream divine?

He was silent for a moment and went on: "The girls threw flowers and kissed their men good-bye, laughing . . . or hiding their tears behind smiles, for luck. We promised them we'd be home before the snow fell, and we chalked *Ausflug nach Paris* and *Auf Wiedersehen auf dem Boulevard* on the sides of the cars . . . *A weekend trip to Paris—See you later on the boulevards.* There were crowds at every stop westward giving us food baskets and fruit and wine . . . and more flowers and kisses, too. All our lives our fathers and uncles had drunk their beer on *Sedantag,* and boasted of *their* victories and *their* march to Paris, making us feel as if we were eternal children, a lesser breed. We felt like *men* that day, by Almighty Lord God, and it was good to be young and off to high adventures of our own. We'd be heroes with a tale to tell to our own sons one day!"

He fell silent again, rubbing absently at his side with one big long-fingered hand; Luz had seen the shrapnel scars there, rough against the smooth white skin and hard muscle. Very softly he finished:

"And then we crossed the Rhine . . . yes, a battalion's worth of us rattling over the bridges every ten minutes, Fräulein Whelan . . . and left the trains behind. Forced marches, twenty kilometers forward each day, week after week. Marching toward the sound of the guns. Two million pairs of *Marschstiefel* with their hobnails in the white dust of the roads."

His voice was almost dreamy now: "White roads, the white dust smoking in clouds, and the endless heat and the foundered horses in the ditches and the men staggering like drunkards with lack of sleep . . . and soon nobody was singing and there were no laughing girls or kisses or flowers or wine. The snow fell, but we didn't return . . . or reach Paris, either. Not yet."

Luz reached across and laid her hand on his; the gesture was genuine enough. He might be an enemy, but he was a man to respect, clever and brave and in his way honest, one who had suffered willingly for his loyalties and could laugh in the face of hardship and danger. He smiled and squeezed her hand for a moment, then released it. Ciara looked aside and swallowed at the byplay. Then Horst clapped a palm to the table to break the mood and went on cheerfully:

"Well, these are no boys off on a holiday; they're tried and tested fighting men, good tough front-swine. These are the victorious divisions from the Eastern Front, less the garrisons left behind—those will be mostly the older reservists and *Landsturm*, enough to kick the Russians' backsides and get the juice out of the Rumanians with a few prods of the bayonet. These men will beat the Tommies . . . the English . . . for you, Fräulein Whelan. And you and I and Elisa and Mr. Daubigny here, we will make sure the Yankees don't come to their aid!"

Ciara nodded solemnly; she wasn't up to being deceptive while she smiled, and wisely didn't try. Instead she looked down at the chessboard again.

"I queen this pawn," she said. "That gives me a queen and a rook and a bishop . . ."

"And me a checkmate in about ten moves," Daubigny said, toppling his king over.

"Twelve, I think . . . Another game, Mr. Daubigny?"

"I think I'll write a letter to my sister, if you don't mind, Miss Whelan," he said. "I'll probably arrive before it does."

"Where does your sister live, Mr. Daubigny?" Luz asked casually, then imperceptibly slowed the cadence of her speech. "Charleston . . . or . . . Savannah?"

The KKK man started a little; and significantly *after* she'd mentioned Charleston, during the naming of Savannah.

He's headed for Savannah, then, she thought. *They probably were smart enough not to send him to destroy his hometown.*

"No, Macon in Georgia, she's there with her husband and children," he said.

"You're not married yourself?" she said.

That was something a woman could ask if she saw no ring on a man's hand, and in fact by convention was almost supposed to once they were introduced and on friendly terms, whereas it would possibly be a rude and definitely an odd question for a man unless the acquaintance was much longer and closer.

"Not yet," he replied. An artificial smile. "Our Southron belles are commonly so beautiful that it's difficult to choose."

Thirty-five was about as old as a healthy upper-class male of more-or-less her own generation could be unmarried without being looked at as a *confirmed bachelor*. In her father's youth that would just have meant he *was* a confirmed bachelor, the type who spent most of his time in male company at his club or in the army or the faculty of a university, what they'd called then a man's man or woman-hater like Lord Kitchener. These days it came with a suspicion that the confirmed bachelor preferred his own sex for pleasure—that he was a sodomite or what people in advanced circles called by the new terms of *invert* or *homosexual*. Luz studied him closely behind a bland smile and decided she just couldn't tell.

He hadn't reacted at all to her or Ciara, not even the usual brief covert glances at hips or bosom or bottom, or to the few other women they'd seen, but that might just be extremely good self-control. Gentlemen weren't *supposed* to look at you that way, which generally meant they did it very quickly and covertly. He certainly wasn't effeminate, but that wasn't the same thing at all; in the terms she'd grown up with he wasn't a *maricón*, but could easily be a *bugarrón*. That ambiguity was a pity, since the knowledge would be potentially useful to blackmail or discredit an enemy agent. It was a matter of profound indifference to her personally, but that wasn't how the world in general looked at it, and you used the world as it was to accomplish your mission. Winning was all that mattered.

I'll ask Horst what he thinks, she thought suddenly. *It will plant a suspicion in his mind, which will* also *be useful; any sand you can put in the enemy's gears is a good thing. He's pretty conventional that way. Men with men revolts him; women and women he just disapproves of because the Church says he should.*

Instead of prolonging the conversation with Daubigny she brought out the violin case.

"Does anyone mind?" she said to the compartment at large.

"Really, Elisa, I didn't expect you to actually *steal* it," Ciara said disapprovingly; she seemed a bit annoyed in general today.

Unusual for her, Luz thought. *She's a very sweet girl most of the time. Not something you can say about me; I can be charming, and I'm good company . . . but not sweet. I never was, not even as a child, I think.*

"I'm not stealing it; I'm being *una buena gente* and taking it to the owners," she said reasonably. "I'll send it parcel post to them in Dresden from . . . wherever we end up on the seashore. If I'd left it at Schloss Rauenstein someone definitely *would* have stolen it and they'd never see it again. Meanwhile I keep it in trim by using it."

"I suppose," Ciara said dubiously.

Horst laughed. "Elisa has a true soldierly attitude toward property," he said, and dropped back into German: "*God provides the nuts but it's up to us to crack them*, as the old saying goes."

"That'll be possible?" Luz said to Horst. "Posting it back to them? Honestly, I wouldn't want to risk wrecking a violin this beautiful on a submarine."

"One way or another, Elisa," he said absently. "Either by mail, or someone I know will dispatch it later if I leave it with them."

Just then the orderly dashed past the windows of the special train and came in panting; he was older and plumper than the one they'd had on their trip from the border to Schloss Rauenstein. The *plumper* was notable in a low-ranking noncom in Germany these days. He had cloth and paper-wrapped bundles in both hands and his haversack bulged, and he was grinning until he put his burdens down and saluted Horst sharply. There was a faint smell like a bakery about them too, and something spicy and meaty.

"*Keine Kohle, Gefreiter?*" Horst said.

"*Nein*, Herr Hauptmann," the man said.

He was speaking good schoolroom-and-military *Hochdeutsch* but from his accent he came from the working class in this general area of the country, where the Low German dialects spoken day-to-day were virtually a different language and more like Dutch or Frisian than the tongue Martin Luther had cobbled together. Beaming, he continued:

"I can get coal from the tender that will do well enough with a little skill at laying the fire. What I have here is actual *bread*, not *drööch* sawdust held together with potato starch but fresh-baked *Bauernbrot* from real rye and wheat with caraway seeds. And real butter, some strings of good *Landjägers*, and a *Harzer Roller* cheese that may be older than the war—"

Luz looked at him with interest; *Landjägers* were a type of pressed, smoked, and dried beef-and-pork sausage made with red wine and spices. Hunters used them—hence the name—and other travelers, since they kept well and one link made the meat portion of a meal. They would go extremely well with the fresh dark rye bread, and the pungent yellow *Harz* cheese.

"—and greens, kale mostly and onions. *And...*"

He paused for effect:

"Some Leibniz butter cookies! This is what I have tracked down for my commander and his guests, sparing no effort in the hunt!"

"Corporal Jäger, you are a shameless thief, not a hunter," Horst said sternly.

But the sentence was a joke of sorts since *hunter* was exactly what the man's surname meant. Luz had noticed that Horst had a born aristocrat's easy mixture of authority and familiarity when dealing with subordinates whose position in the hierarchy was well established.

Retainers, in other words. His family's estate in Silesia is probably very well run, if they're much like him, but God help any peasant who tries to do the Freiherr *wrong.*

"And you are a very good scrounger," he went on. "What will you do with this... plunder?"

"I would never plunder my fellow Germans, Herr Hauptmann," the noncom said with a straight face. "It was my winning charm and explaining that even a stationmaster's wife had no prospect of hanging on to this stuff with a major movement passing through so she might as well sell to a handsome, charming, well-funded worthy like me before it's sniffed out by some ruthless swine who picked up bad management habits from the Poles—"

That was a joke itself too: *Polnische Wirtschaft*, Polish management, was a common German saying for dirt, chaos, and dishonesty.

"—and left his conscience behind in the East."

"Your quick fingers and my money, you scoundrel," Horst said, visibly suppressing a smile. "So?"

"I will make a lovely stew, Herr Oberst. Not a true *Grünkohl mit Pinkel*, since I have no *Pinkel* and smoked pork, but *Landjägers* will do. I will begin the simmering at once to make the kale tender and sweet. And there is a little lard for potatoes fried with some of the onions."

"You may go," Horst said. "And leave some of the butter cookies, and save a few for *our* dessert too while you're stuffing your own belly."

"*Jawohl, Herr Oberst! Zu Befehl, Herr Oberst!*" the man said.

He braced to almost comic rigidity for his salute, as if implying all the *Kadavergehorsam* in the world, then gathered up his swag and headed back to the miniature kitchen.

"And get that coal and get the heating stove going!" Horst barked after him good-naturedly.

He chuckled openly when the man had disappeared. "Every good infantry company has one like that," he said. "And you learn to appreciate them when a decent meal is a rare treat."

"Very true," Luz said sincerely.

She'd noticed exactly the same thing working with the American Army, whose official supplies were usually abundant and healthy . . . but paralyzingly boring after a while. There were rumors that the Quartermaster's Office of the General Staff taste-tested them to make sure they *weren't* very tasty, on the theory that the troops would increase the logistics strain by childishly gobbling more than they really needed if it was actually appetizing. There came a day when the prospect of another can of Libby's corned beef on crackers just made your stomach seize up, not to mention your bowels bind into immovable knots.

And *usually* abundant didn't mean *always* abundant, either. There were times when the units you were working with outran the supply trains and it was tortillas and beans and whatever someone like Corporal Jäger could work their sleight-of-hand on, coming up with a chicken or a piglet or some blessed tomatoes and eggplant in the most unlikely places.

"How about some Ysaÿe before dinner?" she asked, raising the bow of the violin again. "The Malinconia?"

L uz sat on the edge of the bed and smiled a small secret smile to herself as she composed the letter later that evening. There was an art to using book codes. They were unbreakable, yes, as long as the person who intercepted it didn't have the right book and edition; but they were also very obviously codes if you used the most straightforward method, with page and line and word rendered as numbers. The real trick was to compose an otherwise innocuous message in clear text that *contained* the reference numbers disguised as words. The only really safe coded message was one that nobody but the recipient would know was a coded message.

In this case she was using *The Mucker*, revealed by using Billy as the first word in the first paragraph, and then substituting alternating first and last letters in each line of her writing for the numbers. That type of code was easily breakable in itself, but not when used as a key to a book code—the numbers were meaningless without the book—and it made a convincing plain text cover much easier to write without convoluted syntax or odd word choices to activate someone's suspicions.

The grin died a little. It also made it impossible to convey complex mathematical data, which would have been perfect. She could . . .

"What are you doing?" Ciara said; she was sitting on the chair at the other end of the bed, combing out her hair for the night.

"I'm writing a message," Luz said. "In a code I can't tell you about, to someone I can't tell you about but who isn't who it's addressed to, who can get it out of Germany *if* they get it. And they may or may not get it in time, and international mails are slow and undependable these days . . . but it might get to the U.S. of A. in time to do some good."

"*Oh!*" Ciara said, relief flooding her face. "You mean they won't have to depend on us getting the information to them at the last moment—"

"No, unfortunately. *¡Maldito sea!* You see, it has to be a message that Horst and the German postal censors can read without realizing it's in code; he'd never let me send a sealed note. I have a plausible cover story for that—"

It had been her own suggestion, about two years ago, to develop that finishing school she'd attended—and Elisa had, though nobody had thought about that then—as a drop box for the Chamber's European operations. It had a natural reason to receive and send mail abroad, with its multinational clientele, and enough German women from socially prominent families had gone there to give it protection and respectability.

All that they'd needed to do was slip in an agent who could access the school's correspondence—Luz of course had no idea who that was or how they did it—and then keep the school going by an occasional infusion of funds from the secret accounts disguised as contributions by alumni. The woman in charge of the place was an impoverished German countess of impeccable lineage—a *Reichsgräfin* if you wanted to get technical—and from the reports hadn't noticed a thing, which Luz had anticipated.

Because poor old Countess von Weilbach wouldn't notice a badger if it bit her on the bum, she thought, mentally quoting a British fellow pupil. *I don't think anything since the Congress of Vienna was really real to her.*

And of course there were plenty of graduates in Switzerland and other nearby countries, where the odd letter could find its way to an American embassy and out in the diplomatic bag or sent telegraphically via standard diplomatic coded cables. It was an excellent conduit as long as it wasn't overused and you weren't in a hurry. She *was* in a hurry, but it was what she had.

"—but that means I can give only a general warning. And the actual precise day of the attack will be set by wireless message once the

U-boats are nearly in place, so I can't give an account of that. Even the exact locations wouldn't be enough without the precise time. And even this message is only possible because of the violin."

"The violin?" Ciara said.

"That's my excuse for being in a post office in the first place, or sending someone."

"That's . . . very clever, in a sneaky sort of way," Ciara said. "I thought you'd really stolen it!"

"I'm a spy, *querida*; it's my job to be clever in a sneaky sort of way. And to steal things when necessary; I have several perfectly good violins at home, though. There! Now the Navy will be expecting something, if we're lucky. They'll be on alert anyway with the war about to officially start, but knowing that U-boats are trying to sneak into our ports is better than nothing."

Ciara blew out her cheeks in relief. "Then it doesn't all depend on us?"

Luz hesitated and decided on honesty. "I'm afraid mostly it still does. Only getting—"

She patted her upper chest to show the location of the photographs.

"—this to the Navy will really do . . . and I don't dare let my only copy out of my hands and I can't make duplicates, not in the time we have. *And* we'll be reaching America about as fast as the mails, give or take a day."

"Oh," Ciara said, her face falling a little. "I would feel so much better if it were only us at risk!"

Luz nodded. *And she means every word of that*, she thought.

She'd used three iterations to compose the message; now she carefully ripped up the first two and ate the rice paper in small batches, washed down with water. A footfall outside brought her to her feet, and she cracked the door a little. Horst was reaching for the door of the men's compartment.

"Ah, sweetie," Luz said quietly. "Where's Herr Daubigny?"

"Still in the sitting room," he said. "Why?"

"Ummm . . . Horst, how shall I put this . . . do you sense anything rather odd about him? Not politically, I have no doubt at all he's what he says he is that way, but . . ."

"He is rather private and he is completely obsessed with Negroes," Horst said, mildly surprised. "And he plays chess badly."

"No, he's a *middling-not-bad* chess player, like me; Ciara's really good. What I meant was . . . this is a little embarrassing . . . it's because he's a man. Now, I may be vain, but I think I'm quite attractive . . ."

"Das ist wohl wahr, meine Süsse!"

"And I can tell when a man isn't paying any attention that way at all, however politely . . . and he wasn't. Or to Ciara, who's quite pretty too in a completely different way from me. So, just as a warning on a personal level . . ."

Horst's square handsome face changed for a moment, and then he clamped down iron control.

"Thank you," he said grimly. "There were swine of that sort at cadet school. They are unreliable, but for the present he is useful to the Fatherland, arse-bandit or not."

A grim smile: "While I'm more than willing to give up my life for Germany . . . or even my ability to sleep well . . . certain things I will not. I *will* see that he attends to his task and nothing more, and pass on your warning to those who will watch over him. Quietly, of course."

"I'm not *certain*, Horst," she said, frowning and managing to convey that she was, but was also trying to be fair. "You're a man; you should be able to tell more easily."

Except that I have now poisoned the well of perception, so you'll see what you expect to see . . . and you were predisposed to dislike him personally from the beginning, because he's a traitor to America. You'll use traitors, but you'll never like *them, or really trust them. Not that there's the slightest connection between one's tastes and one's patriotism, but* give a dog a bad name and hang him *is something that works everywhere.*

They both swayed as the train finally lurched into motion. "Ah, the scheduling difficulty has been resolved at last!" Horst said sardonically. "We will be in Wilhelmshaven tomorrow."

Luz chuckled, her face lighting, and got an identical fighting grin from Horst at her eagerness.

"The game is afoot!" she said. "After all this waiting . . . well, waiting is part of it. But I've never liked it."

"Yes, there is much of it in war," he agreed; then he looked both ways, leaned the short distance, and kissed her.

She returned it with interest, then spoke a little breathlessly as they drew back: "I really would like to send that violin to the von Herders. It may be my last opportunity to do a good deed; our survival isn't really a high probability at this point."

"Perhaps it would be better for me to do that, *Süsse*," he said. "Don't seal it—mail from a military post has to be inspected and then stamped *passed*. I will be sending some letters to my family at the same time."

"That's a very kind offer, Horst. Of course, I've got the address ready. I would appreciate it if you would mail it for me. Oh, and send this letter to an old teacher of mine at the school in Bavaria too, if that's possible."

She handed him the letter, unsealed but addressed. "You should look it over, of course, and tear it up if that *isn't* possible."

Preoccupied, he took it and tucked it into his tunic pocket with a cursory glance.

"Yes, I remember you mentioning the school. It should be possible—the *Gräfin* is irreproachable, if a bit eccentric. In fact, I think one of my cousins on my mother's side went there because the *Gräfin* is also Catholic. Yes, and Seraphika came back from München mumbling and mooing like a true Bavarian cow."

"*Grüß Gott, i bî da Sissi und kumm vo Minga*," Luz said, dropping from *Hochdeutsch* into a broad Bavarian patois.

"By Almighty Lord God, you sound like the missing link between Austrians and human beings!" he said with a laugh and a salute.

She was grinning again as she ducked back into the sleeping compartment. She pressed an ear against the door and laid a finger on her lips until she heard the click of the one opposite. Experience had shown that you had to shout for a voice in one compartment to be audible in the other; this train had been a rich man's toy before the war, and it was well made even by German standards of craftsmanship. The sleeping compartments were very compact, as they had to be to allow a passageway, but nicely laid out with their own electric lights, basins, and water taps.

"Do you really think Mr. Daubigny is that way?" Ciara said doubtfully.

"I'm not sure—about one chance in three, maybe? Though don't hold me to that."

"Isn't it a bit, well, cold to say so to Horst? I don't like him either; he wants them to use that horrible stuff on America—even his own part of it! But I mean—"

Since you are yourself, at least sometimes hung unspoken.

Luz shrugged. "Just business, *querida*. I really don't care a bit if he is or not. And there's absolutely no chance in this world or the next he'd try anything naughty with Horst! Not unless he's been reading too much Entente propaganda about the German officer corps, in which case God have mercy on him because Horst would not. And Horst is much more likely to post that letter for me now. Let that be a lesson: If you want someone to trust you without thinking about it, arrange for them to feel they're on the same team as you, or that you have a common enemy. Human beings are made that way. I've been convincing Horst of that since we met, in one way or another."

Ciara gave her an odd look; Luz could see she was wondering exactly how much of a puzzle-palace of deceptions her own interactions with the Black Chamber operative had been. Then she shook her head ruefully.

"Luz . . . do you *like* Captain von Dückler? I mean, do you think he is . . . handsome?"

"*Oh*, yes. He's pretty much the *definition* of handsome, as I personally think men go. And on that if nothing else the Department of Public Health and Eugenics would agree with me!"

They shared a chuckle that most Americans who followed public affairs would have understood.

At least the ones with a sense of humor, Luz thought. *Which Ciara definitely has and which I must admit is not generally the Party's strongest point.*

She'd always been a Progressive and had been glad when Uncle Teddy's legions took over the GOP in 1912 and made it the *Progressive* Republican Party—though part of that had been a simple lust for revenge on the *revolucionarios*, and the fact that Uncle Teddy was . . . Uncle Teddy. She'd been grateful for the Equal Rights Amendment and had approved of most of what the Party had done after that, too. The only thing that gave her pause occasionally was that so many of the Party stalwarts were po-faced, self-righteous sanctimonious scolds absolutely sure they knew better than other people what those benighted, ignorant just-plain-wrong other people needed to do for their own good, that and their conviction that everything could be reduced to science and time-and-motion studies.

The Department of Public Health and Eugenics was where the Progressive movement stashed the people the *rest of the Party* looked at that way, its more eccentric and crankish enthusiasts for Race Improvement, along with the ones who had useful phobias about germs and bodily fluids and social diseases, the type who walked around with a pocketful of sanitary wipes and pulled on a glove before they shook hands. The Race Improvement cranks tended in person to be—quite notoriously and to the joy of opposition cartoonists—very unlike the handsome, healthy, fecund exemplars on their propaganda posters and booklets with the *Yea, I have a Goodly Heritage* slogan or even the winners of the Fittest Family and Best Baby contests they staged at state fairs and other gatherings these days.

Most of the ideal types on the posters and in the books *did* look at least a little like Horst von Dückler or a female equivalent, or like idealized young farmers from Wisconsin dressed in ancient Greek robes and surrounded by abundant naked toddlers. Uncle Teddy had a lot of the same ideas in the abstract, but at least he really *was* an impressive man with a wife who was pretty much a match for him and he really *did* have six healthy, handsome, and intelligent children.

Though if there were a way to breed thousands of Alice *Roosevelts . . . por* Dios, *nobody would be safe! They'd keep the rest of us on leashes and make us sleep on rugs in front of the fire.*

"And Horst's charming too, in his way," she went on. "Not as clueless as most men, that is. A bit vain of his effect on women, but men are. And handsome, charming, intelligent, extremely virile men with a noble title and an officer's uniform like him are *very* vain of it."

"But do you *like* him?" Ciara said earnestly.

"Yes, I *do* like him in the way you mean, though of course he's on the other side and when he finds out I've taken him in he's going to be *extremely* annoyed. With himself, and with me because of that. It's a pity, though a minor one as war goes. I'm not smitten, but I think we might have been very good friends if we weren't enemies. Though as I've told him, quite truthfully, I wouldn't *marry* him for anything on Earth, even if there weren't the war and so forth."

"You wouldn't?" Ciara said. "But . . . you said you thought he was handsome and you like him, and . . ."

"It would be strictly church and *Kinder* and bossing the servants back at the *Schloss* for Freifrau von Dückler, with an occasional carriage ride among the fields of sugar beets for variety and having the *Gräfin* over for tea. Exactly the life my mother absconded to avoid, but with worse weather and white peasants. I'd end up assassinating him and he'd never know why."

"He seemed . . . quite sensitive, this afternoon. Almost like a poet," Ciara said. "I was surprised. He looks like such a soldier, so hard and ruthless and . . . I didn't think there was anything else there."

"Well, he's a secret agent now and then, too. And most human beings are complex at some level or another. I wouldn't have seduced him if I hadn't found him attractive, despite it being convenient from a professional point of view . . . it's called a honeypot trap in the trade . . . and I don't regret doing it. Nor am I very unhappy that it's over, though, either."

Luz noticed that Ciara's expression and the way she held herself changed at that.

I don't think she *noticed, though. Interesting.*

"I don't want to be doing that when the knife goes in. Even a spy has to have some standards, or at least I think so. Sorry if I'm shocking you, but I *did* promise what I told you would be true."

"I just . . . can't imagine doing that," Ciara blurted. "No offense intended!"

"None taken," Luz said, smiling. "Tell me something: If you imagine *kissing* Horst, what do you feel? Not think, feel?"

"Ummm—" She obviously considered it honestly. "I can't imagine wanting to, to be sure. Though he *is* handsome, I suppose. Like the hero on the cover of an adventure story in one of the magazines. It just seems it would be like . . . like kissing an arm, perhaps? The thought of it's not *bad*, like when Desmond Byrne kissed me—without warning!— at the parade and I felt like a dog had slobbered on my mouth and I gave him a belt about the chops."

Oh, my, Luz thought. *I don't suppose that's definitive, but it's very indicative.*

Aloud she went on: "Upper bunk or lower?"

Ciara hesitated, then said, looking down at her hands: "Luz, to be honest I'm more frightened the closer we get to this place where they're preparing the . . . the horror, and I'm very afraid I'm going to have that dream about those men's faces again. All twisted and bloody and . . . and if it wouldn't be too hard for you . . ."

"Not at all," Luz said with a fond smile. "But we should turn in, then."

The bed wasn't too small for two; in fact it was much more comfortable than most Pullman berths. Ciara turned out the light and inched backward. Luz gave her a chaste kiss on the top of the head and held her as she sang softly to the clicking beat of the rails:

"Aruru mi niño, arrurú mi amor
Aruru pedazo de mi corazón
Este niño lindo que nació de día
Quiere que lo lleven a la dulcería . . ."

Ciara's breathing slowed; after a moment it was calm and even. Luz smiled to herself and carefully slid her right arm under the pillow beneath her head—she usually slept on her side in that fashion anyway, so that solved the perennial third-arm problem with spooning neatly. Feeling safe and warm and contented . . .

Then her eyes opened wide in the utter darkness.

¡Ten cuidado, muchacha! *Watch out, girl! This snuggle isn't just fun; it's extremely soothing. Just lying here like this makes me feel happy. As if something is telling me* I could get used to this.

Her mind skipped backward.

And I enjoyed making her giggle until she lost track of the chess game just for its own sake and to see her laugh, and making music together is wonderful, and talking . . . I'm . . . getting in deeper waters than I thought. And I'm about to see her into hideous danger on a mission that's more important than either of our lives. ¡Ay, Luz! *You didn't have enough pain in your life? You couldn't help loving Mima and Papá . . . Your heart heals a bit, and then you offer it up as a gift for the dogs of fate to tear?*

Was that risk better than having it dead as a stone?

I don't know. I really don't.

FIFTEEN

O nce upon a time long ago—about seven hundred years ago— there had been an outlaw lord's castle and a pirate fleet based on the bay that now held Wilhelmshaven. A few generations later, the rising Hanseatic League of merchant cities had gotten around to burning the castle and sinking the fleet and hanging all the survivors they could catch, and the bay had lain empty save for fish and migrating birds. The current Kaiser's grandfather had bartered it from the Grand Duchy of Oldenberg to build a base for the growing Prussian Navy . . . and in a brilliant but eccentric stroke of humility had named it after himself. There were a *lot* of Wilhelms in the House of Hohenzollern family tree.

Not so much of a change, then, Luz thought, propping her chin on her hand and staring out the train window at a stretch of stained boards dripping with rain. *Fortified nest of pirates once again.*

From this railroad siding they would have had a good view of the harbor southward, with its dreadnoughts and battle cruisers and rows of cruisers and destroyers . . . if the wooden hoardings hadn't limited what they could see to a few of the rather archaic-looking pole masts with crossed yardarms the Germans favored on their otherwise exceedingly modern warships. The air had a smoke-and-metal reek that hinted at the shipbuilding yards, dry docks, forges, foundries, and machine shops that had sprung up to service the Kaiserliche Marine, and the sprawl of housing and buildings for the unfortunate civilian workers and those catering to sailors on leave.

It was yet *another* gray North European day—

I would go mad if I had to live here permanently, and strip myself naked and run screaming southward, looking for the sun!

—but the smell was of brackish seawater as well as coal smoke and oily mechanical scents. Other trains were unloading cargo onto wagons, mostly horse-drawn, a few motor trucks, and a surprising half-dozen steam traction engines pulling flatbeds loading thick curved metal shapes.

"Those are heavy turbine casings," Ciara said, peering past her. "See the spindle shapes, from the low- to the high-pressure blades? For geared marine turbines, I think. But we aren't going to see much, are we?"

Luz nodded. "Good basic tradecraft," she said. "What we don't see, we can't reveal—this is an operation where we might be captured. They *shouldn't* let us see anything we don't actually need to."

"A very good point," Daubigny said.

He was looking rather strained; Luz hoped that at least part of that was her doing. He was also in a German naval uniform, or the rather informal . . . in fact *extremely* informal . . . version thereof that U-boat crews wore when actually at sea: rough gray trousers, a gray jacket over a blue sweater, and a round brimless cap. They'd been given leather foul-weather jackets too, though they hadn't put them on yet, since Gefreiter Jäger had managed to scare up enough coal to keep the compartment warm, as well as a quite passable early dinner with pork and red cabbage and a quark cheesecake and some apples. If he wasn't an innkeeper in civilian life, he ought to be and would probably be very good at it.

An idle hope went through her mind: that the tubby cunning *Gefreiter* would survive these years of iron and death, and end up running a nice clean *Gasthaus* in some sleepily prosperous little German town where nothing much happened but seasonal festivals and a mild scandal now and then and the odd tourist passing through. With the appropriate shrewd, dumpy, bossy *Frau* running him, and some tow-haired *Kinder* and a comfortable potbelly, and a clutch of cronies who'd lie to one another with their highly colored war stories over beer and sausages and cards once a week.

She mentioned it, and Ciara gave her a rather odd look.

"Him, specifically?" she said.

And not Horst? was clear in her arched brow.

"I . . . or Horst . . . people like us . . . we chose to do certain things for our countries, and chose the risks, *por así decirlo*," Luz said. "So to speak."

The thought became clearer to her as she spoke. "I hope we live, but we don't have any real right to complain if we don't. It's . . . it's what we're *for*. We decided to play the role of hero or martyr, or possibly of villains depending on perspective and point of view, and we should take the consequences without wincing or whining. But little people like Jäger are just making the best of it as history breaks over them in an avalanche . . . and they're what *countries* are *for*, when you come right down to it. What countries *are*. The rest, kings and nobles and generals and presidents . . . and we secret agents . . . are waves on the surface."

"That's . . . kind," Ciara said, with a smile, and thoughts Luz couldn't quite follow behind her blue eyes.

She and Luz were in the same submariner's gear as the man, though it fit them rather worse, not having been designed for people with their proportions. Luz had tested and she had full freedom of movement; it just felt vaguely uncomfortable and looked lumpish, not like the field gear she'd had made to order. The girl from Boston looked down at herself and then stood and moved tentatively.

"This feels so *strange*," she said; she'd obviously never worn trousers before in her life and it bothered her nearly as deeply as a skirt and blouse and flowered hat would have done Horst. "It's as if . . . as if my legs belong to someone else. Or I'm all in bandages, or both. It doesn't feel *right*."

"I prefer skirts myself, *querida*, for everyday comfort," Luz said.

I've spent a lot of time in trousers, though, she thought. *When I was on hunting trips with Papá, and then in the field for the Chamber, which I can't really mention right now.*

"Especially I like modern skirts, not those hobble-skirt atrocities that were fashionable a few years ago."

"I saw them now and then, but I never wore one. They looked stylish if you were nice and slim, the way you are, but not very practical. What were they like?" Ciara asked.

"Terrible. They really did hobble you, *como un caballo cojeaba*. Once was enough and then I simply refused. Why should a bunch of men in Paris who mostly don't even *like* women get to tell us to wear things that hurt? But we're going to be climbing up and down ladders and squeezing through narrow corridors with thirty men, strangers, for a good little while now. About two weeks, I think. Pants are best."

"Oh. Well, I suppose so, then," Ciara said, thinking. "Yes, you're right, it's the only possible thing to do."

Daubigny had studiously avoided looking directly at their trouser-clad limbs, which might just mean he was a true gentleman. He started when Horst swung into the railcar, dressed very much as they were except that he had the leather jacket on, a scarf around his neck, a peaked officer's hat without any actual rank markings, and an automatic pistol holstered at his waist.

Wait, that's a .45, the 1911, not a Luger, Luz thought. Then: *Ah, yes, he expects the next landfall will be in America. That Colt will stand out a lot less there . . . and ammunition will be easier to get.*

A rather scruffy-looking man who seemed implausibly young—except for his eyes—in the same outfit but with a lieutenant's band and crown stood beside him stony-faced, the white-blond wisps of his beard seeming to bristle a little.

"Herr Daubigny, you will accompany Leutnant zur See Hansen to the U-144," he said, indicating the pale young junior lieutenant. "Fräulein Carmody, Fräulein Whelan, you will come with me."

Luz shook hands with the southerner. "Luck go with you!" she said, not specifying what kind; Ciara nodded silently from behind her.

"And good luck to you both, and good luck to the cause of freedom," Daubigny said gravely, and left.

Horst breathed out in relief as the two women put on their jackets.

"Come, then," he said, and to Luz: "I dropped off your items, Elisa."

"¡Ay! Now I can die with a clear social conscience! My last thoughts as I drown can be of joy in a noble house in Dresden as their cherished violin appears, and a lonely teacher happy that a pupil remembered her."

He grinned back at her; then it grew wider with the extra glee of a man who'd had his assumptions upset and now got to watch others go through the same uncomfortable experience. Germans didn't experience *Schadenfreude* more often than other people just because they had a word for it, but it wasn't entirely an accident that they *did* have a general noun form for the concept *to gloat over another's misfortune.*

"And I've just told the captain of the U-150 . . . Kapitänleutnant Karl Denke . . . just *who* the agents are that he has to take along on this voyage. He was . . . not happy."

The car that was drawn up waiting to take them to the submarine pens made Luz chortle slightly with laughter and point at it accusingly.

"Amsterdam!" she said.

Horst nodded as he handed them into the backseat; it was a little bull-nosed Renault taxi, just like the ones they'd taken from the airship hangar to the hotel where she'd had one of the best meals of her life . . . followed shortly thereafter by desperate hand-to-hand fights to the death.

Asi es la vida, she thought. *If* I *ever have grandchildren, what will I tell them about* What I Did in the Great War? *That I cut the throats of Frenchmen in a German's company and piled their bodies in a hotel bathtub to disguise the blood?*

"War booty," he said. "Very economical of fuel, too, though we will not be as short now with the Galician and Rumanian fields under secure control, and soon Baku. Perhaps in a few years we can convert our surface warships to oil fuel, as the English have done. Driver, back to the U-boat pens," he added with a snap as he took the front seat.

Luz set her suitcase on her knees. It held everything she and Ciara would absolutely need on a voyage where nobody would be doing much in the way of washing or changing their clothes, and her clandestine gear as well . . . all but the package of developed film. *That* was in her brassiere, a bit uncomfortably but unlikely to come to anyone else's attention. Ironically enough, Horst had sent Ciara's single trunk and her two to an address in Mexico; provided the freight got out of Germany to neutral Denmark in the next couple of weeks they'd probably get them back, since the address was a former *revolucionario* safe house in Veracruz that the Chamber had turned courtesy of the real Elisa Carmody and now used like an ant-lion trap.

Ciara craned her head openly to see as much as she could as they drove down the busy through-road behind the docks. It was a slow passage, since the traffic showed no sign of slackening for sunset and there were thousands on foot as well, in uniforms or worker's coveralls, shifts coming on duty or off. Instead a set of shielded streetlamps came on, and the work continued unabated by night or bad weather.

"That's interesting!" she said. "Look at the big ships—"

She pointed out the great gun-wagons they were passing, looming over them out of the gloom; a *Bayern*-class superdreadnought, and a *Derflinger*-class battle cruiser. They showed newly repaired combat damage, but what had caught Ciara's eye were sparks and flames on their upperworks where welders and riveters were at labor. Similar lights showed from more distant berths, and there was a smell of hot metal and ozone added to the harbor stinks.

"They're all getting the same modification to their superstructure. That big horizontal rectangular thing they're having fitted to their main masts over the bridge, just where the lower tripod section ends and the pole mast begins. Saints, I do wonder what that is; it's not like anything I've heard of. Look at the armored conduits for those cables; my goodness, that's massive. Something electrical, and with a high power demand! Far too big for a wireless transmitter, though. Oh, and how I wish I could take a closer look—"

"Fräulein Whelan," Horst said; there was amusement in his voice, but sternness too. "I suggest you contain your curiosity. That is a range-finding apparatus. And even so much is more than you need to know. Eyes front, please, and not another word about such matters."

"Sorry, sir," she said in a small voice . . . but she didn't stop looking, albeit now out of the corners of her eyes.

Horst chuckled. "If you were not needed on this mission, I would be strongly tempted to put you in a box and post you to the Siemens & Halske laboratories in Berlin, Fräulein Whelan."

The amusement died in his eyes as he looked back and forth between Luz and Ciara for a moment.

"Extraordinary," he murmured, then seemed to shrug and return his attention to the docks.

The big ships were coaling too, leaving a pall of black dust over everything, and net loads of unidentifiable cargo were being slung aboard. Smaller ships, tugs and tenders and barges and less identifiable craft, were chuffing about in busy throngs on the water as well.

Something big in preparation, for them to continue on into the night and with only a partial blackout, Luz thought. *Not just the Breath of Loki, though it's probably coordinated with that.*

The sense of raw power was palpable here, the hundreds of thousands of tons of Krupp steel and cannon and turbine horsepower and engineering skill coiling to strike. The German Kaiserliche Marine hadn't cut a very glorious figure so far in this war, except for the U-boats, and stealthy sinking of merchantmen wasn't what most of them had had in mind for *den Tag* in their long rivalry with the Royal Navy before the war. A few raids, a few skirmishes, one completely inconclusive fleet action that a cruel wit had described as the Kaiserliche Marine assaulting its British jailors and then returning to its prison cell. What they'd dreamed of and wanted was something like Trafalgar—or Tsushima, to be a bit more modern—with themselves as Nelson or Togo, and the British playing the hapless French or Russians smashed into burning splinters.

Evidently they thought they were due for a rematch, with the gun lines bellowing at each other in engagements lighting the horizon from one edge to the other, and probably someone like Privatdozent von Bülow had given them some sort of new toy to play with. It was turning out to be that sort of war, and every time springing a new toy on your enemies worked out, everyone—including the enemies—started working even harder on finding unpleasant surprises of their own. Sometimes she wondered where it would stop; in her more pessimistic moments she wondered if it ever would.

Sitting in harbor because you weren't strong enough to fight the people cruising around outside wasn't good for a fleet's morale, but her eye caught the indicators—quick steps, cheerful cursing, a snap when orders were given—of men eager for a rematch and expecting a better result.

Luz carefully filed the information; it wasn't as important as the Breath of Loki, nothing could be, but it *was* important. The First Sea Lord of the British Navy, a plump politician named Churchill, had defined his admiral commanding the Grand Fleet at Scapa Flow as the only man on either side who could lose the war in one afternoon. Taking command of the North Sea, even for only a few weeks or months, *would* give the *Reich* mastery of Europe—cutting the British armies off from their sources of supply, and Britain's people and factories from the seaborne food and fuel and raw materials they needed every single day.

I hope we have someone on that, Luz thought unhappily; she had no earthly idea, of course, and it would have been horrifyingly bad practice if she did. *I hope the* British *have someone on it. Or that someone does, Japan or . . . Bolivia or Siam, maybe, but someone.*

The submarine pens were in their own section of the harbor, with antiaircraft guns poking skyward not far away and the ground stations for barrage balloons winched down and deflated. The formerly French or possibly Belgian taxi halted for guards in naval sailor-suit uniforms—but with steel helmets and Mausers or machine pistols—to inspect Horst's documents. Those included those giving Luz and Ciara permission to exist here. He'd kept them on his own person, and without them neither of the women could have moved a hundred yards.

Meters, Luz thought. *Here, it would be a hundred meters before someone said:* Papiere, bitte. *Or didn't bother to say* please. *Apart from a few clerks and barmaids, this looks like a very masculine part of town.*

Many of the U-boats were docked three or four deep, with an occasional clank of steel on steel even here in the pond-calm harbor waters as men walked back and forth over bridging gangways on their errands.

Others had a dock to themselves. Several of those had conventional-looking hulls but were much bigger than the usual. Luz controlled the information-gathering itch she felt at the sight of them. These were probably the rumored cruiser submarines, built to operate at extreme range along the coasts of the Americas or in the southern oceans, and strongly suspected as the reason for the recent heavy losses in merchantmen across areas that grew wider every day. Rumor also said that cargo supply submarines brought them reloads of fuel and torpedoes and spare parts and food to make their cruises even more destructive.

Of course, rumor also says that they've got a secret base called Caprona in the South Pacific that has dinosaurs and cavemen on it, she thought. *Rumor has . . . what do the wireless technicians say . . . a lot of noise in the signal.*

And a dozen of the subs looked entirely different, each at its own dock and with additional guards manning yet another checkpoint. There were heavy rolls of camouflage netting nearby and knock-down frames, apparently just recently removed. All submarines to date were essentially like decked-over submersible torpedo boats or destroyers, and shared the spearlike hull form and narrow clipper bows of those classes. These were something else again. They were big, at least as big as destroyers in terms of displacement, but stubby and tubby and much less martial-looking, with a smooth overall shape and few protrusions.

The closest ready analogue she could think of for their shapes was the sort of French-inspired sourdough bread they used in San Francisco to make an oyster loaf—shaped like a fat bulging cylinder rounded at both ends. To add further strangeness, the conning towers were simple shark-fin shapes only about a third of the way along from stern to blunt bow, and there was no real deck on the forward part, just an elevated faring forward of the tower and then the bare curve of the hull, all painted in blue-gray. As the automobile halted a chugging, blatting sound came from within the nearest, and then a grating rumble and a burned-chemical smell along with a drift of black fumes from one of the tubes that stuck up from the conning tower.

"Starting the diesel engines," Ciara said. "Using electrics to turn it over. And they're not connected to the dockside power or water, see? They must be nearly ready to go."

"They are, Fräulein," Horst said.

Luz suspected that he'd come to view Ciara as a sort of holy fool, precociously brilliant at one aspect of life but rather mad otherwise. It wasn't *altogether* wrong, but it was an example of making snap judgments from inadequate information, too.

"This is very good timing," he went on. "Because we were delayed, of course, but it was a fortunate accident."

And we're being put on board at the very *last minute for security's sake,* Luz thought. *If we'd gotten here sooner we'd just have sat in the train car longer looking at those boards. The Germans are bad spies because they're bad at getting into the skins of people who aren't like them, but when it comes to keeping an eye on detail, they're very good indeed. Except that they tend to overconfidence in their security measures, of course, possibly because they're so meticulous. They really should change their codes more often, too, and their armed forces use the wireless too much.*

Horst dismissed the auto, hefted his own duffel, and strode to meet the officer waiting on the stained concrete of the deck with his arms crossed. The salute he received in return for his own—a ship's captain outranked Army officers of equivalent grade on his own vessel—was both a good deal more casual and a little reluctant. The German sub commander was stocky and powerful-looking, brown-haired and blue-eyed. He was Horst's age or a bit younger . . . which was very young for warship command, and he also wore a short-cropped beard that had an unflattering tinge of orange. Luz had heard that U-boat sailors often went bearded, or just stopped shaving when their craft left port and didn't start again until they got back.

U.S. Navy sailors called their submarines *pigboats* or sometimes *sewer pipes*, and had the same habit. Undersea warfare wasn't a specialty for the fastidious. Probably if you wanted spit and polish you stuck to battleships.

"The best I can do is give them one curtained bunk together," Kapitänleutnant Karl Denke said, ignoring the women after a brief irritated glance. "It's damned bad luck to have damned useless women on a submarine anyway, and it'll cause no end of trouble. The crew won't like it. Or will like it too much. Your Colonel Nicolai is making a—"

"First, Herr Kapitänleutnant, these ladies both speak German," Horst said. "Very well indeed for Fräulein Carmody if you don't mind a tinge of Bavarian, and passable fluency for Fräulein Whelan, respectively."

The naval officer gave Luz and Ciara a startled look and had the grace to flush a little. Luz glanced at him with cool hauteur, smiled and nodded, then shifted her view to the conning tower. Someone in a peaked naval cap was standing there, behind the chest-high bulwark on the top, and looking at them through a powerful pair of binoculars.

"Second, they are not essential to the accomplishment of our mission."

The naval officer looked surprised, then opened his mouth, and Horst cut him off.

"But they *are* absolutely essential to any of us *surviving* the mission.

The secret state police in America are very efficient and it will be hard for twenty-seven . . . twenty-eight including myself . . . Germans to evade them across thousands of miles until we reach sanctuary among the guerillas in Mexico and can be picked up, even if many of your men speak English of a sort."

Aha, Luz thought. *They made that one of the selection factors; not that it's all that rare for Germans to speak English, given how many have relatives in America. Still, that was clever.*

Horst went on like a trip hammer: "Or do you think if we are captured on their soil the Yankees will give us a kiss on both cheeks after we . . . have done what we plan to do? Or treat us as ordinary prisoners of war, even?"

"Well . . . no, Herr Hauptmann. They *should*, but I do not think they will."

Horst drove the point home like a bayonet: "If we were summarily shot . . . or as their so-charming habit is when the common people are angry at some outsider, lynched and burned alive . . . and no, that is not just propaganda . . . we would be more fortunate than I anticipate is likely. Have you heard of *die schwarze Kammer* and *das Bundesamt für Sicherheit*?"

From his blink and almost imperceptible wince, evidently he *had* heard of the Black Chamber and the Federal Bureau of Security.

"So, they come with us, Herr Kapitänleutnant. You will please instruct your personnel that they are to be treated with every courtesy, that their security clearance is of the highest, and that our lives depend upon them? I am willing to die for the Fatherland and the Emperor, but I would very much prefer to live on and serve them further."

"That is understood, Herr Hauptmann," the man said a little stiffly. "I knew that there would be Abteilung IIIb personnel aboard all the boats in this operation to arrange extraction for the crews, since your people are handling this rather than naval intelligence. I simply did not anticipate that such . . . charming ladies . . . would be among them."

He gave a heel click and bow as Horst introduced them, obviously wishing he could rewind the whole affair like a cinema film and start with a different script, and gave some emphatic low-voiced orders to a petty officer who hurried off. Luz was willing to go along with the rewind . . . but she squeezed a little when they shook hands, which made his eyes widen; men were always surprised when a woman had a strong grip.

Acrobatics and climbing did wonders for your hands, if not the sort of wonders her manicurists liked. She'd reduced a couple of those specialists to tears, though she did enjoy a full treatment and a pedicure.

"I do hope we can work together in an efficient manner, Herr Kapitänleutnant," she said in her most dulcet tones. "This is a mission of world historical importance, after all."

"Your boat is from a usual breed submarine very different, Captain Denke," Ciara said artlessly, after the formalities; the word she used for *breed* usually referred to different types of livestock, but it was understandable in context. "Isn't she by much and much larger?"

Brava, querida, Luz thought. *That's genuine interest, but you're learning to use it!* Then: *And you must be very used to men being astonished when you understand technical things. I've run into enough of that myself.*

"Yes, Fräulein, the original design was for a cargo submarine," Denke explained, blossoming as men often did when they had a chance to explain something they cared about to an interested young woman.

"Ah, is that why the hull to its length broader . . . is broader, shall it say . . . in proportion?"

"Exactly! Originally they were intended to carry cargo through the blockade, or to refurbish U-boats on distant patrols at sea. Though that form turns out to have other advantages."

"It is of a hydrodynamic shape more effect . . . efficient . . . when beneath the surface water is?"

"Yes! Why would you think that, though?"

"Because rapid fish . . . swift fish . . . some likeness in shape have?" Ciara said. "Such fish as sharks or—"

She turned to Luz and dropped into English for a moment: "What's *tunafish* in German?"

"*Thunfisch.*"

"Such fish as *Thunfisch*. Also most recent *Luftschiffe*, which have comparable problem of"—suddenly her German became more precise as she used a complex technical term—"traversing a resisting single-phase fluid with minimal drag in a certain range of speeds."

"That turns out to be very true. We had not placed any importance on it before because U-boats spend most of their time on the surface."

"How large?"

"Twenty-two hundred tons submerged displacement," he said proudly, pointing. "Much larger than the previous classes. Though that is only a little larger than the latest cruiser class of long-range war boats, the ones that we began to launch late last year, like my last command. Then it was determined that the planned cargo class be renamed *Loki* and the design be altered for this . . . special mission."

"Done with time enough to test much? Sufficiently? New designs always small problems of a many have, need to make better after . . . after testing in life as it is."

Denke was surprised into a bark of laughter. "You know which questions to ask! I very much hope so, Fräulein, and the shakedown cruise went . . . reasonably well."

Luz looked at the U-boat with interest as they spoke; she had long ago mastered the art of following a conversation inconspicuously and watching something else at the same time. There were no torpedo tubes in the rounded bow that she could see, and no deck gun, only a couple of light machine guns on the conning tower that could be easily taken down into the hull when the craft submerged. Rising from it behind the periscope was the reason it really needed no surface armament even to defend itself.

"And that the breathing tube must be?" Ciara said, in her fluent but clumsy German. "Oh, a streamlined faring of cross-section teardrop it has. Clever, clever!"

"Yes, gracious miss," Denke said. "That is the *Schnorchel*. With that, we can remain submerged and run on the diesels unless the weather is very bad indeed. The original two cargo holds were moved forward. Since this is a one-way mission, and the . . . cargo . . . is permanently installed, it's fairly easy to keep the hull in balance. Though to be absolutely frank, she maneuvers like a pig on the surface! The covers over the hold are thrown off by pneumatic bolts, and then the launching tubes are fired in sequence with an automatic counterflooding mechanism to keep her on an even keel."

"By connections of electro-mechanical?" Ciara said. "And the trajectories would be preset from the point of attack wanted . . . no I say desired . . . desired dispersal pattern to get, to each boat special?"

"Exactly!" Denke said, looking slightly sandbagged at Ciara's terrier pursuit of detail. "The gracious miss has been well briefed?"

"No, it logical solution only is," she said. "One right solution, in concern of one problem, as great thinker Taylor says."

She frowned. "Of displacement tonnage, cargo is much? Sorry for my handle of German; cargo is what . . . amount of whole?"

"*Anteil*," Denke said. "Proportion."

"*Ja, Anteil! Danke schön*. Proportion of entire."

"About seven hundred and fifty tons available for the . . . special loads, not counting structural supports," Denke said. "Since we didn't need enough diesel fuel for a return voyage, which more than compensates for room and weight taken by the extra batteries."

And it's some sort of low-velocity launch system, Luz thought, feeling something like a flush of heat followed by an icy chill over her skin. *Mortar or rocket or some combination of the two. So the payload will be high in proportion to the total weight. Between fifty and a hundred tons of* esa cosa horrible. *And five parts in a million will kill. One tiny little invisible drop. I've seen* that.

Horst cleared his throat; he found Ciara's artless charm amusing, but business was business.

Denke came to himself with a slight start, clicked his heels, and half bowed them toward the gangway, where two grinning junior petty officers waited. He'd probably also delayed a bit for the muttered instructions to be carried out.

"If you will accompany me . . ."

The conning tower had a hatchway in its front, where the companion-way from the dock ended. A breath of damp fetid air came out as it was opened, as if it were the door to a basement that gave on to a sewer. Denke called for a senior petty officer, then cleared his throat and said:

"Show the *gnädige Fräulein* to their . . . accommodation, Ober-steuermann."

U-150 moved away from the dock with a lurch, and began to pitch a little even in the calm waters of the harbor. Evidently Denke hadn't been lying about her characteristics on the surface.

"Let's get settled in and see what's what," Luz said to Ciara.

"Sure, and it's not much worse than the Norwegian freighter I came east on," she replied stoutly.

That's a lie, but a brave one, Luz thought.

The *Obersteuermann*—the word meant a senior noncommissioned rank—hustled them through the control room of the submarine. That was directly below the conning tower, and rather larger than most, though very crowded; the rudder helmsmen and those at the engine controls were busy as Denke gave his instructions through the intercom. Evidently the diesel and electric engines lay behind it, and the crew quarters forward.

Luz's immediate impression was that the U-150 was *insanely* crowded, and foul-smelling to boot, what with the swampy bilge and diesel reek and the faint acid tang of the batteries added to by fainter odors of vomit—what went into the bilgewater never entirely left, and the submarine had had a shakedown cruise already—and backed-up heads, as sailors referred to toilets. And while Luz was two inches shorter than the American average man, and Ciara a little shorter still, they both nearly cut their scalps on the profusion of pipes and obstacles as they were shown to their bunk.

The crew accommodation *was* forward of the control room, with a tiny cubicle for the captain opposite a nook for the radio operator, two two-bunk cubicles for the officers, and then the bunks for the noncoms and crew ahead of those and a tiny galley at the front. The bunks were stacked on either side of the passageway, three layers high with about two and a half feet between each and the lowest level a foot off the patterned metal plates of the deck; there were probably batteries in the compartment below.

"The U-150's hull is deeper than most, misses," the man said. "Here, you are to have a petty officer's bunk; on the lowest layer, larger, and with curtains of good thick canvas!"

Someone had done a good job of stringing those, made easier by the fact that the frames were metal tubing. She stood for a moment considering it; with two good-sized women it was going to be cozy, or very crowded, depending on how you looked at it. They could take turns using it some of the time, of course. Luz stowed the suitcase in the netting that was attached to the bottom of the bunk above.

"And no crates of provisions taking up space in the bunking area either," the man noted proudly. "Not on this boat. The galley is forward of this, and we have an actual electric freezing box to keep food from spoiling!"

First things first, she thought, and asked the man: "And the . . . head, I think you sailors call it, Obersteuermann?"

The man looked slightly embarrassed; he was older than his captain, and built like a stump with battered hands like spades, though no taller than Ciara.

"Gracious miss, you understand that . . . ah, we can rig a curtain as I have been instructed, as we did for your bunk, and perhaps a sign that you are using the . . . facility . . . but . . ."

"We all have to make sacrifices in the line of duty, and I am sure you will do your best," she said, and felt him reacting to the upper-class accent and manner.

He barked gruffly at other seamen, who did almost comical double-takes when they realized who was following him, but jumped aside—

which mostly involved pretzel-like contortions. The toilet was at least in a nook, and was fairly clean at the beginning of a cruise.

"Ah . . . not behind a door," he said. "And it is . . . tricky."

He used *vigeliensch* for that, which meant he probably came from Schleswig, but whether you said tricky or *vigeliensch* or *schwierig* the taps and valves around it showed that using it would require genuine technical skill. The petty officer began to stumble through an explanation—from what he mumbled she gathered you could literally sink the U-boat if you did it precisely wrong—but Ciara intervened.

"After use has been, close this, then this valve, this, this, and this—in that order—and trigger this, correct?"

The petty officer was startled out of his embarrassment. "*Ja*, miss!" he said. "You have been on a U-boat before?"

"No, just familiar with hydraulics am," she said. Then she smiled. "And pumps, engines, electric motors used to help my brother fix in workshop where he employment had."

"We are very sorry that security required our presence to be sprung on you as such a surprise, Obersteuermann . . ." Luz said.

"Obersteuermann Göttsch, miss. And now if you will pardon me—"

He took off at a fast scramble. The dim orange light of the bulbs used in the interior of the submarine gave everything a ghastly tinge as they made their way back to the control room, as if you were of the unburied, unquiet dead.

The passage outward from the harbor was a slightly unnerving experience in itself; only Captain Denke and his assistants up in the conning tower could see a damned thing. His voice came down via the boat's intercom system, and the submarine turned this way or that, but they could be about to pile into the side of a battleship for all either of them could tell.

Or be rammed, and the first we'd know of it would be the ship's bows coming through the wall. Pardon me, the hull.

The crew thought this was a luxury liner, for reasons starting with the U-boat's great size and adding in that she only had a basic sailing crew rather than a fighting one, and one intended for a single short voyage at that. The standard war sub needed men to reload torpedoes; man the deck guns; keep a four-man watch in the conning tower to detect vulnerable targets or dangerous warships, blimps, and aircraft, and others to relieve those people; and enough hands to maintain the complex machinery for months or repair it when long hard service wore it down. That meant squeezing them in like sardines and hot-bunking in relays, and sleeping on top of the torpedoes until they were fired off and left room for hammocks.

All the U-150 had to do was keep its engines going for one trip across the Atlantic, during which it was strictly instructed to travel submerged during the day and avoid all contact with anyone whatsoever if it could. And since it had only had one training voyage before this and a thorough overhaul afterward, apparently the submarine smelled like a meadow full of new-mown hay or fresh lavender-scented sheets in a good hotel compared to the rest of the U-boat fleet, which averaged several months-long cruises each.

Which makes me shudder at the thought of the usual sort of submarine, she thought. *Small spaces don't bother me, usually, but . . . You have to admit, these men are willing to suffer in the line of duty. Especially when you add in the continual risk of drowning in the dark. Germany would be a much less dangerous enemy if so many Germans weren't able and hardworking and brave and patriotic. A formidable people. Then again, every third American has German ancestry.*

Kapitänleutnant Denke's conversion from hostility to a rather condescending friendliness toward Ciara—he had more or less ignored Luz except for a few covert glances—extended to letting them into the control room below the conning tower, as long as they stayed strictly silent and jammed into one corner. His words to that effect came down when his executive officer, a thin dark dyspeptic-looking Rhinelander named Hans Roeckerath, called a query upward.

The walls were like nearly everything else inside the submarine; covered in pipes, electrical and pneumatic cables, and control wheels—large wheels, medium-sized ones, small ones, grouped apparently randomly as far as she could see and not labeled. Between them were even larger numbers of dials and gauges, levers and switches. The crew's hands and eyes went to the right places with practiced skill, their movements choreographed like a dance.

And this is much less complicated than the usual U-boat, Luz thought, pressing her back into the corner, where things dug in through her leather jacket and the wool beneath. *Of course, this isn't a warship armed with weapons. It is a weapon, meant to be expended like a bullet.*

Cold condensate dripped down on her occasionally, but that happened nearly everywhere on board. She was already damp and she'd stay that way until they crossed the Atlantic and came ashore; it was also the closest she'd get to a bath. The only real warmth was Ciara beside her, and the younger woman's eyes were virtually bulging with fascinated interest except for intervals when she couldn't ignore that this particular weapon was aimed at the city where she'd been born and raised and that contained most of the things she valued in the world.

And my period's started, Luz thought.

The cramps weren't bad and could be ignored, but she always felt slightly depressed and irritable at this stage; her preferred response was hot water bottles or friendly cats and solitude with a good book.

Oh, joyous voyage.

Her eyes strayed to the front part of the compartment, past the pedestal of the periscope and the compass binnacle and the little navigation table and just to the right of the watertight door. That large metal box was about six on a side and five feet high, covered in yet more dials and levers, and it was the control mechanism for the weapon that was the U-150's reason for existence. Two technicians did nothing but groom and care for it, and go over the electrical cables that ran in armored sheaths forward to the launching tubes.

Those men had the doom of a city beneath their hands, priests of a very modern, twentieth-century God of Death born amid retorts and catalysts . . . and because of a dozen laborers in German East Africa dying in uncomprehending terror after one dropped a wooden crate full of glass vials that some white man had yelled at him to carry carefully in a language he didn't know, or had only a few words of.

Luz had a sudden feeling that the box was like the altar on one of the old pyramids you still came across in Mexico, overgrown and ruined, where you could see the blood gutters that had poured the red salt flood like rainwater. There the Aztec priests had slashed chests open with knives of black obsidian and raised the beating hearts in their fists to feed their monster gods, then tumbled the bodies down the steps to the waiting crowds to be ceremoniously devoured.

I'd swear that thing has the same faint glow of evil about it. My imagination in both cases, but . . . Donde el diablo puso la mano, queda huella para rato. *The means change and become more terrible, but the wickedness men do . . . not so much.*

After two hours of dead-slow maneuvering and pitching and rolling Denke came sliding down the ladder that ran up into the conning tower, and the man behind him dogged the hatch that separated it from the pressure hull.

"We're clear of the harbor minefields," he said.

Which is deeply reassuring, Luz thought. *Except that this part of the world has broken out in minefields like an adolescent in spots. And speaking of breaking, sometimes the mines break free of their moorings and drift about killing people entirely at random. Just as dangerous in a surface ship, really, but this sense of being blind in a box makes it* feel *worse.*

There were types of danger she found exhilarating, almost pleasurable . . . and in fact by now as addictive as opium. But they all involved a degree of control—a sense that she was pitting herself against the peril and overcoming it by wit and skill. This purely passive waiting had none of that.

"Take her down, Karl. Periscope depth, and up with the *Schnorchel*," Denke said.

"Periscope depth. Aye, aye, skipper," the helmsman said, and he and his two assistants twirled some of the metal wheels.

I'd heard that submarines were more casual than most of the German Navy,

Luz thought. *Nice to get first-hand confirmation. It certainly doesn't seem to affect their efficiency. And of course they've got relatively small crews living in each other's pockets.*

The buoyancy tanks hissed and gurgled as air went out and seawater came in. The strong pitching action combined with a corkscrew back-and-forth roll damped down to a slower rise and fall. Luz had a strong stomach, but she was still glad of it, and from the smell *someone* on board had given back dinner . . . possibly assisted by a lingering hangover, given the way sailors usually acted in port. The U-150 was evidently one of those craft that could pitch and roll on wet grass when it was on the surface. The world beneath the waves was its true element.

"Up periscope," Denke said.

The instrument tucked up under the ceiling descended smoothly, and presumably the upper portion was doing the reverse, poking up through the surface. Denke reversed his cap so that the bill wouldn't interfere and put his hands to the twin levers and his eyes to the padded viewpiece.

"Almighty Lord God, what a wealth of targets!" he said, and his executive officer chuckled like a malicious skeleton while the men all grinned. "Too bad they're all Imperial German Navy. All ahead three-quarters. Report speed."

"*Schnorchel* on," the man at the engine control panel said. "Diesels feeding normally. Full fuel tanks, batteries at one hundred percent charge. All ahead three-quarters."

The rumble of the engines had continued without a break; now their sound became louder as he pushed on a set of throttles. Evidently the controls for the engines were managed directly from this control chamber, rather than being relayed to a separate engine room as on a conventional ship. Since they were electrical anyway, there was no reason *not* to do it that way except inertia from the days of steam, and it would reduce the lag between order and action. She made a mental note of it, since the U.S. Navy might want to try it out too.

"Eleven knots," another petty officer said.

"Come about to 315, I say again, 315," Denke said from the periscope.

"*Jawohl.* Changing course to 315," the helmsman replied, and the deck canted beneath their feet as the U-150 went into a curve and then straightened out again. "Course is 315."

"Steady as she goes," Denke said. "Hans, you have the deck. Maintain course and speed."

"Aye, aye, skipper. I have the deck; maintaining present course and speed."

Horst was standing near him; if Luz craned her head, she could make out the map that Denke turned to and the course he outlined.

"North of Scotland and the Orkneys," the U-boat skipper said. "A little longer but better than trying to run the Channel minefields and patrols. Then along this curve to the northeastern U.S."

"Haven't the English put up mine barriers?" Horst asked.

Thank you, Horst! Luz thought. *Elisa wouldn't have heard about that but I did and I'd been wishing I could ask.*

"They've started on one this summer. It's supposed to be eighteen lines of mines right across the North Sea from the Orkney Islands to Norwegian territorial waters when . . . if . . . it's ever finished. That would be four hundred kilometers long and twenty-five wide and need something like four hundred thousand mines . . . in water three hundred meters deep. Of course, they only have to mine the top sixty or seventy meters, which makes an area four hundred kilometers long by twenty-five wide and seventy meters deep."

From the quality of his laugh, Denke didn't think much of the idea. "Good luck to them making that many, and the reserves they'd need, and still keeping up their shell production."

"The Americans could do it," Horst said. "Fairly easily. And much else. Fortunately, we're taking preemptive action about *that.*"

Denke nodded. "Hence our course. Which is not so very different from a great-circle plot from Wilhelmshaven to the target, allowing for the British Isles being in the way. Mind you, they patrol vigorously there, and their Grand Fleet's base at Scapa Flow is not all that far away. Destroyer squadrons, armed whale catchers, flying boats, and those semi-rigid airships. But if we keep submerged in the daytime . . . which with the *Schnorchel* we can do and still travel at a reasonable speed . . . it should be fairly safe. Since we're not there to fight."

"Not to fight *there*," Horst said with a grim smile.

Denke nodded. "The Englanders have the devil's luck with maritime geography. They're perfectly positioned to keep Germany bottled up while they have the run of the world ocean. That's how they stole whole continents in the Americas and Asia and the South Pacific, shooting down Red Indians and walloping wogs and niggers who melted away before them, taking their land to settle. While we ended up fighting century after century over the same miserable scraps before the Wars of Unification, all over some stinking pig farm or what language we prayed in or which petty prince collected the taxes and then groveled to the Sun King or Napoleon."

Horst nodded agreement in turn. "But the geography is less important, now that we've beaten Russia, and now that railroads make it so much cheaper and faster to ship goods and troops by land," he said. "Still, that's what allowed them to settle the Americas, as you say. Even if the Englanders let the Yankees break away politically, they still speak the same language in more senses than one. We can beat the Tommies; beating whole continents full of Anglo-Saxons coming at us from all over the world is another matter."

Both men's eyes went to the control box for the Breath of Loki. "Well, we're going to do something about teaching them to keep on their own side of the ocean," Denke said cheerfully. "And then the Russians can be our Red Indians."

"And our wogs," Horst said, chuckling. "Once we get east of Rostov-on-Don . . . and one of our columns is due there soon. Really *before the snow falls* this time."

His eyes narrowed in amusement, and he made his voice diplomatically unctuous for a moment:

"Purely to assist the independence movement in the Ukraine, of course, and to secure order, protect property, and put down anarchists and Marxists and other revolutionary scum."

"Oh, of course, our altruism astonishes me. And aren't the *Turks* our wogs?" Captain Denke replied, chuckling with a mocking carnivorous grin.

"No, they're our honored and well-respected allies . . . until the war is over. *Then* they're our wogs, like the Bulgarians, since there won't be anything they can do about it," Horst said, with a matching expression. "Or our boss-boys over the *other* wogs."

His smile grew more wolfish still: "And in a generation . . . or two or three . . . when we're really ready . . . then our sons or grandsons will have a reckoning with the Yankees. By then we may have weapons that make this"—he jerked his chin forward—"look like a spray of French perfume."

O ver the next few days most of the sailors were as decent as possible about the privacy of averted eyes, and in things like the complicated business of passing one of the women in the narrow companionways; one who hadn't been when Luz went by had given a short smothered scream and completed his journey in a crouch that made him safe from bumping his head, to the amusement of his shipmates, and nobody had tried *that* again.

Particularly after the grilling he got from his captain, and then a briskly administered set of lumps from Göttsch and several other petty officers, who'd fully grasped how much all their lives depended on the two women acting as guides and contacts on the other side of the ocean. U-boats were far and away the most dangerous branch of the Kaiserliche Marine to start with, and the one with the worst living conditions, and then these men had volunteered for a very, very dangerous special mission, knowing only that it was even worse.

Every one of them was ready to die. That didn't mean that they *wanted* to die if they didn't have to. Luz understood the attitude perfectly; she'd alerted the U.S. Navy to the U-boat attack, and in a way she had to hope they'd use it to sink every one of Project Loki's vessels, including this one. That didn't stop her from really hoping things went the other way, the one that left her and Ciara alive and the heroes of the hour.

Four days later Luz and Ciara were on the forward hull of the U-150, in the early hours of the morning. Everyone in the fat metal cigar was cut off from the normal cycles of night and day, and there wasn't anything for the two women to do on the submarine but sleep and read and play chess most of the time. Though Ciara had made herself useful on minor repairs to the amusement of the crew, and Luz had taken to *helping* in the galley to their profound thankfulness.

Nobody thought it was strange that they had turned their sleep cycle around so that they were awake at night. That was when they'd be performing their part of the mission in Boston, after all. What they hadn't been able to do yet was talk frankly; too many of the crew could speak English, and they didn't know which ones.

They both wore a harness with safety lines running back to the door—

Hatch, since we're at sea, Luz thought.

—at the front of the conning tower. As Kapitänleutnant Denke had warned, the modified cargo submarine handled like a pig, and particularly swinishly on the surface, but by now their feet and stomachs had adapted. Fortunately the gray-blue surface of the North Atlantic was fairly calm, long smooth swells rather than white-crested chaos. Water purled away from the round bow of the submarine, and ripples flowed over the riveted steel plates about halfway back from the bow to the tower. Occasional stinging spray struck them when the bow dug a little deeper than usual.

Most U-boats had slatted decks built over their hulls, for men to work on when they were running surfaced. This one didn't, nor railings on either side, though there was a smoothly fared raised section forward of the tower. Members of the crew did get time to come out at night and breathe fresh air and stretch a bit and have a smoke, and so Denke had been persuaded to let the two women do likewise . . . though he had insisted on the line.

The cold air was intensely clean and full of the salt of the sea; there were wisps of cloud overhead but a sky full of stars as well, and a fingernail sliver of waning moon. Ciara looked up at it, and then down at the deck beneath their feet. The diesels' steady throb as they drove them along at fourteen knots and the chuckle and rush of water along the sides meant that nobody in the conning tower could hear a normal conversation.

"Luz, I'm frightened," Ciara said quietly. "This *thing* beneath our feet . . . there's a hundred and fifty rocket shells down there."

Luz nodded. They hadn't actually had to pry; the crew and the officers with whom they dined talked shop quite a bit, and the occasional casual question got them going on specifics. The U-boat would come into harbor submerged and dead slow. Then it would find its precise position by taking distance sightings through a coincidence range finder built into the periscope, aligning on various known points, mostly church steeples and the five-hundred-foot spire of the Custom House Tower that had been completed last year. They'd drop to the bottom then and place anchors that would keep the boat properly aligned.

If all the equipment functioned as designed, then they'd set the automatic controls and leave the submarine by an escape tube and rubber boats. If there was a problem, the two technicians would remain behind to do it manually. Ciara's Clann na nGael contacts would meet them at a warehouse that they'd rented with German funds, and there they'd find automobiles—good American Fords—and everything else they needed to make their getaway.

Meanwhile, a precise and rugged chronometer would be ticking away in that altar to chemical death in the control chamber. When it reached the preset point, a series of perforated metal cards would activate the U-boat's own systems in a precise order. Compressed air would blow the ballast tanks, and it would bob to the surface, held in position by the anchor cables. Pneumatic bolts would throw the deck covering that she and Ciara were walking on now off and to port. Below it was a set of sealed tubes with domed tops built into the hull.

Each held a stubby finned projectile, like the spigot mortar they'd seen at the grisly demonstration at Castle Rauenstein, but much larger. The base charge would produce enough high-pressure gas to blow the end of the tube out and loft the missile up a few dozen yards; then a rocket motor would push it in an arc a thousand feet or more into the air, higher than any building in Boston, spanning the sky to beyond the State House and the Common. Some would reach as far inland as Cambridge if they functioned perfectly—universities were a deadly weapon of war, in this new century of steel and fire and machine men as hard and cruel as either.

They would spin as they flew, and internal pressure would blow out hundreds of small precut holes in the outer casings. That pressure and heat and centrifugal force would disperse the Breath of Loki as a plume of tiny aerosol droplets along their whole path. Droplets just slightly heavier than the air in which they floated, a thousand pounds in the warhead of each rocket.

Drifting down across acres of Boston, down onto upraised faces and heads turned away, onto desperate hands trying to protect against the invisible death and arms holding children beneath bodies that were no protection. Sinking down ventilator shafts into office buildings and hospitals and schools, basements and subways, waiting on every surface for the unsuspecting hordes who'd rush out into the crowded streets when the screaming began.

Waiting for anyone who ventured in afterward, waiting in spots and hollows for day after day, month after month . . .

They'd told Ciara that the U-150's load was aimed at the Boston Navy Yard on the north side of the harbor. That was even the truth . . . partially. The right wing of the great fan of destruction would fall over those docks and dry docks and ships. The rest of it would come down on Boston proper, how far depending on the winds that day, and her sister U-148's load would cover the rest of the central city, the old tangle of colonial streets, the waterfront and South Boston's docks . . . and most of its tight-packed residential areas as well, the row houses and tenements of those whose strong backs and skilled hands made the city function.

Between them the two U-boats would turn the whole half circle that made up the central part of the harbor and the densely built areas to the north and south of it into a poisoned wasteland, where the untouchable bodies of a hundred thousand dead would lie rotting. Men would die, and women, and children . . . and the pigeons and sparrows and crows, the cats and dogs and dray horses and the mice. Even the rats that tried to eat the bodies would die with them.

The reign of the creatures of warm blood and thought and feeling would be done there, the rule of all the things that loved their young and their mates. It would be a kingdom of flies and cockroaches and maggots, and then an empire of silence and of bones.

Or more *than a hundred thousand, depending on the wind and weather,* Luz thought grimly. *And tens of thousands around the edges will be mad or writhing in fits or paralyzed or crippled for the rest of their lives. And everyone within fifty miles will run for their lives and never come back . . . or at least not for a long time. A whole great city of humankind, three centuries of history, of work and thought, joy and sorrow, life and death, wiped from the map in a few hours of horror as if it had never been at all. Who will recall that John Adams wrote there, or Sam Adams conspired with the Sons of Liberty and Revere made his ride, or that they fought for freedom on Bunker Hill?*

The only thing anyone would really remember of Boston was how it had died. And the other cities likewise.

"And it's my—" Ciara's anguished cry began.

"No!" Luz snapped.

She seized the shorter woman's shoulders in both hands and shook her a little. "Ciara! Look at me! *Look at me!*"

Luz waited until their eyes met, then slid her hands up until they cupped the other's chin. "Look at me. You didn't invent this. Isn't that true?"

A nod, though the bright eyes were full of tears. "Say it!"

"I didn't invent this."

"You didn't build it; you didn't bring it here; you're not going to launch it."

"But I went and—"

"Helped me! Spotted that electrical alarm and saved my life and the mission! If you hadn't been there, if it had been someone else, I couldn't have gotten the information out of Nicolai's office. This U-boat would still be *right here* and there would be *no chance* of stopping this!"

Shuddering, Ciara fought for control. After a while she nodded and they gripped each other in a fierce embrace for a moment. Ciara whispered:

"Luz . . . I think I could . . . sabotage the . . ."

"No, *querida*, no. We have to stop them all, and to do that we have to get off this submarine without them suspecting us until it's too late to stop us. If this were the only one, yes. Even if it killed us, yes. But it's one of many. Two for Boston. There are *six* of these nightmare things headed for New York. We have to string them along and then get loose and turn the package over to the Navy."

"I'm . . . I'm so frightened. I feel *sick* at what might happen and how it depends on *me*. How can I stand it for day after day? How can you?"

"It *is* sickening," Luz replied. "And knowing it depends on you is like carrying an anvil. We can hope the Navy gets them all . . . but submarines are just too hard to find to rely on that. They may not get any."

She drew back and looked down into the shadowed face. "But you can stand it because you must. I know you're brave. You showed me you were brave when you saved my life, and you showed Colonel Nicolai, too—even if he doesn't know *how* brave. Now show me again. You've braved danger; now brave the pain. Push it down. You can't make the fear and dread go away, but you can . . . not pay attention to it. Right now we've got too much to *do*, too much for fear or even anger. You pay for that *later* . . . we both will . . . but we can deal with that then."

Even now her omnivorous curiosity woke. "Pay for it?"

"Nightmares, mostly. When it's very bad, flashes of waking memory that leave you sweating or enraged or vomiting . . . that's how it hits me, at least. They . . . get a bit better over time. Being with friends helps too, and doing things that need all your attention. We are going to do this and we're going to win, and that's all that matters for now."

"Yes!" Her face firmed.

With a glare like a charioteer shaking her spear aloft and calling on the Morrigú, screaming her war cry as the scythed wheels beneath her rumbled toward the foe.

Her voice was firm: "We're soldiers, now, for our folk and our homes. Soldiers for America."

"We are!" Luz agreed. "And we'll be victorious soldiers, too."

SIXTEEN

Aboard U-150

Western Atlantic

SEPTEMBER 23RD, 1916(B)

S kipper," one of the crewmen who rated a stool in front of his working station said.

He looked up with a hand to one of the headphones on his ears, face underlit from the display lights of the dials.

"Ship detected. Ahead, and closing."

The U-150 was—in conventional terms—unarmed and intended for only one mission, but the Kaiserliche Marine hadn't stinted her of anything that might help that mission, even though self-destruct charges would turn it all into scrap once the missiles were launched.

Glad I'm here and hadn't turned in yet, Luz thought.

She slept as much as she could, but this wasn't likely to be something you wanted to wake up to. Luz doubted that all German submarines had hydrophones yet, but this one most certainly did, a Siemens set at least as good as anything the U.S. Navy could boast. Sound usually traveled well through water.

Maybe we shouldn't have publicized those experiments with long-range underwater sonic telegraphs, she thought dryly, trying to be invisible in the corner of the cramped control room, inhaling the smells of ozone and foul bilges that she scarcely noticed anymore.

Boasting about how advanced our hydrophone listening stations were, that they could not only hear the telegraph signals but ships miles away . . . that might have given the other *Institute ideas.*

The submarine sonic telegraph had been one of the National Advanced Research Projects Institute's first coups, back in 1913 when NARPI hadn't learned that the letters also stood for *keep everything secret, stupid!* Those easygoing days before the Great War—before even the Intervention had started to bite deep into the nation's life and the newly organized Party got a firm grip on things—seemed like another world now. Sometimes she wondered uneasily what the future would be like, if the empires kept butting heads for another generation.

The bit about hydrophones had stuck in some German scientist's mind, or in a naval officer who'd passed it on, and a U-boat with hydrophones could often detect prey far before they'd be visible on the surface.

"Off with diesels," Kapitänleutnant Denke said, head moving like a turret.

The throbbing of the powerful engines stopped. They drove generators that charged the big packs of batteries; it was quiet electric motors that actually turned the U-150's twin screws, and they went on regardless.

"Down *Schnorchel.* Engines ahead dead slow. Charge reading."

Luz hadn't really been conscious of the sound of the electric motors; they *were* quiet. It was the absence that she noticed, as they slowed to the point where the screws were barely keeping steerage-way.

"Three knots. Batteries at ninety-nine point eight charge," the helm replied.

One of the great advantages of the *Schnorchel* was that the U-150 could run fairly fast submerged and charge her batteries at the same time. She had many more batteries per ton than a regular boat, too; this was one of the first submarines designed to spend most of its—admittedly brief—lifetime underwater. The hydrophone man turned dials on his apparatus and concentrated, closing his eyes and putting a hand to one earphone again, his blunt-featured whiskery face blank as a corpse in the dim lights. The others were keeping half an eye on him, until a petty officer hissed at them and they returned full attention to their own jobs.

"High-speed screws, skipper, warship signatures," he said after a moment, his apparatus hearing much more clearly now that the submarine itself made less noise. "Multiple high-speed screws. Destroyers, and heading our way. Closing fast, I estimate at better than twenty-five knots."

"Yankee destroyer screen," Denke said. "They're doing a sweep."

The U-150's executive officer came through the watertight door at the rear of the compartment; he was tall enough that he had to be *very* careful of his head when he did that. The black stubble had turned to a dense beard on his thin face now—he was one of those men who had to shave twice a day.

His eyes turned upward. "Could be bad luck. Or an air patrol might have spotted the *Schnorchel* and sent our location in by wireless," he said. "It's not absolutely invisible if the observer's lucky and catches a patch of exhaust against a whitecap or something like that. And the American semi-rigid scout airships patrol this far out—their C-class have over twenty-four hours endurance and they're stable enough to use binoculars from their gondolas."

Denke shrugged. "The destroyers are here now at any rate. And they will conduct a *naval exercise*," he added, as if the word *Marineübung* combined obscenity, scatology, and bad taste.

Luz hid her smile for a moment. The U.S. Navy had been conducting anti-submarine exercises for some time now, as American neutrality wore thinner and thinner. Those exercises often coincided with the location of actual U-boats and involved dropping live charges, and complaints from Berlin were met with bland statements that putting submarines in the western Atlantic was *reckless endangerment.*

Which was exactly the same phrase the German foreign ministry had used about Americans taking passage on ships like the *Mauretania.*

She let the grin out, thinking how Uncle Teddy must have enjoyed reading the wording . . . if he hadn't been the one who'd come up with it. Across the control room Horst had a seat near the machinery that controlled the missile launch. He took her expression for a fighting grin in defiance of fate, which wasn't altogether wrong, and echoed it in kind; she knew he'd been feeling as useful as an udder on a bull.

"Silent running, pass the word, Hans," Denke said to his number two.

"Aye, aye, skipper."

The skinny dark-eyed Rhinelander slipped out. Ciara came in just after he left, and she saw Denke think of ordering her back to her bunk and then reconsider. The men had made her something of a mascot-cum-younger-sister, especially after she'd helped capably with several repair jobs. Luz greeted her with a smile and an arm around the waist, giving thanks to—

Nobody in particular, but feeling thankful.

—as she did that women weren't held to the same standard of stoic undemonstrativeness that men inflicted on themselves, but doing it sincerely. And it was good to have someone who was a real ally there. A spy operating undercover, particularly a double agent, was usually alone in a spiderweb of deceit where you had to tie a string around your finger to remind yourself of who you actually were now and then. They both looked up at the ceiling, then at each other with irony in their gaze.

Ciara made a side to side motion with her head, as if to say:

Who should we be cheering for?

Luz shrugged very slightly and raised a brow:

We've got a good patriotic reason to hope they miss! ¡Verdad!

"All ahead one-quarter," Denke said. "Come about to heading 220."

"All ahead one-quarter. Heading 220," the engine and helm replied.

"Take her down. Forty meters," Denke said, his face like something carved out of wood—if there had been a type of wood that sprouted a brown beard with orange tints; the lights brought them out.

"Aye, aye, skipper, forty meters," the depth helm replied.

More water gurgled into the ballast tanks. The U-150 banked downward and curved to the side as the hydroplanes at bow and stern bit the water and the rudder pushed. Creaks and groans came from the pressure hull itself as water pushed inward, trying to crumple it like an old tin can under a boot, but the Krupp steel held firm. Somewhere in the depths of the vessel there was a metallic pop and a wet hiss and muted cursing as the damage-control crew stopped a minor leak.

"Level at forty meters," the helm said. "Six knots."

"Skipper, the destroyers are maintaining course. Distance opening."

Then a new sound, through the sea and the steel of the hull itself:

Ping.

A metallic sound, vibrating through the hull of U-150 as if it were a bell and had been struck with a hammer.

Luz knew what it was; she'd never heard it, but she'd heard it described. It was an Echels, an echolocation system, mounted in the bows of a U.S. Navy destroyer.

Everyone else in the control room of the submarine seemed to know too. She had only a rough idea of how it worked—the details were deeply, deeply secret; she only knew anything at all because Uncle Teddy had mentioned it, one of his naval enthusiasms. You made a sharp sound, it bounced off underwater objects, and you measured their direction and distance by timing the return sounds through hydrophones. In theory it should make submarines instantly detectable; in practice there were so many unknown details on how sound propagated through real water with all its currents and temperature gradients, and so many technical difficulties in making the receiving apparatus work, that the first sets had only reached working prototype status this summer despite the desperate-haste priority.

Uncle Teddy took war in all its aspects seriously and thought about it deeply; he'd been a very good soldier himself, disgusted at the mass chaos of the war with Spain in which he'd won his spurs. He *really* thought about naval warfare. He'd written a history of the naval side of the War of 1812 that had become a standard in the U.S. Navy long, long before he became president, or even went into national politics, and he'd helped lay the foundations of the modern fleet as Assistant Secretary of the Navy and the real power there behind the pleasant old duffer who'd held the titular power.

Luz had heard that a scientist's offhand comment had resulted in the Institute being told, in no uncertain terms, to make the Echels system work, especially when it was discovered that the British had something similar under development.

I wish it worked much better, so that we didn't have to rely on what I've got tucked into my brassiere, she thought. *But I also have to hope it doesn't work well enough to destroy U-150, my personal desire not to be crushed and drowned completely aside, and the fact that Ciara's here, which has—¡maldición!—become very important to me too. Because the sets we have now aren't good enough to get them all and even if it gets* this *one most of the others will get through. So the great movements of history turn on little things!*

Ping. Ping. Ping-ping-*ping!ping!ping!*

"Ships closing again, flank speed, thirty knots or better. They're going to pass over us, skipper—at least some of them. They either know we're here, or suspect."

"For what we are about to receive . . ." someone said.

Now the thrashing screws of the destroyers were audible through the hull, a drumming roar less than two hundred feet away.

". . . may the Lord make us truly thankful." A voice completed the invocation.

The man at the hydrophones barked, managing not to make it too loud: "Splashes! Depth charges in the water!"

Luz and Ciara used their free hands to grab pipes and wedge themselves more tightly. Depth charges weren't a sophisticated weapon, and they'd been in use for about eighteen months: just metal barrels like the ones used to carry oil, packed full of cheap ammonal explosives with a simple pressure detonator that could be set for any depth. So far rolling them off the rear end of ships that had—or thought they had—a submarine beneath them was the only effective way of killing submerged U-boats anyone had found, though teams were working on better ones at full speed in all the Great Powers with significant navies.

Kapitänleutnant Denke had one hand above his head on the ring of brass tubing that surrounded the base of the periscope. His face was calm, but there were runnels of sweat on his forehead, and he blinked as they ran into his eyes and stung.

Everyone waited; Ciara's arm held Luz more tightly.

BAM!

The U-150 shuddered and jerked as if it were an automobile that had gone into a massive pothole at speed, throwing them backward painfully into the irregular metal surfaces, then nearly jerking them free onto the deck. The hull plates groaned again, far more alarmingly than they had before. The lights flickered, and one popped with a tinkle of broken glass. Thin, hard jets of water sprouted from the joints of pipes, and several gauges burst. Damage-control teams sprang into action with tools, closing valves with wrenches and stuffing pads into leaks.

BAM!

Another jarring jolt, and the U-150 lurched.

BAM! BAM! BAM! BAM!

"Course 210, all ahead full," Denke said.

"Aye, aye, skipper. 210, all ahead full."

The U-150 banked and leapt ahead with a surge of speed. The growl of the destroyers' screws faded.

BAM! BAM! BAM! BAM!

The next series of explosions was loud, but the U-boat shuddered rather than writhed. Denke grinned like a shark.

"The explosions deafen their hydrophones, and they can only use that damned sounding device in front of them," he said.

Ping. Ping. Ping...

"Moving away, skipper. They guessed wrong."

"Engines all ahead half," Denke said after a few minutes, as each successive volley of depth charges was a little fainter. "All they're doing now is killing fish."

"Aye, aye, skipper. Six knots."

"That will do. Come about to 300, I say again, 300."

"Aye, aye, Captain. 300. Course is 300, depth forty meters, six knots."

The executive officer came back. "Outguessed them, skipper!"

Denke shrugged. "Or they guessed port and I guessed starboard," he said. "Thank Almighty Lord God or the luck of the devil that that echo sounder of theirs is short-range and only works in a fan ahead of the bows. We'll keep this course and speed until we make our final approach to the target."

The Rhinelander's brows went up, and he stepped over to the map table. "On batteries all the way? That will bring us in at . . . no more than twenty percent charge, skipper. Maybe fifteen percent."

Denke turned a hand up. "Which matters exactly . . . why, Hans? We're *driving* away from the target in automobiles, not sailing."

His subordinate froze, blinked, and then smiled ruefully. "You're right, skipper. We're shooting off this boat like a torpedo, but it's still . . . unnatural to think about it that way."

Luz looked at the control console for the Breath of Loki. *¡Es absolutamente correcto!* Unnatural *is just the word!* she thought.

All ahead one-quarter," Denke said a day later.

"Aye, aye, skipper. Ahead one-quarter."

The tension in the control room was dense enough to slice; worse, she thought, because none of the men could smoke . . . and they'd been submerged for a long time now, longer than any other class of submarine on Earth could have managed.

The air was thick with the scent of male sweat too, and of a particular and familiar type that didn't depend on how hot it was, strong in these meat-fed men: throttled fear and tightly held aggression ready to burst into lethal violence, a peculiar rank musk. That was how an ambush party smelled as the enemy approached, or an assault group about to rush a strongpoint. It was the smell of the most dangerous thing in the world. She was used to it, though not in a sealed chamber with recirculated air, but she could sense it was adding to Ciara's nerves. She'd lived mostly among women or a few sedentary men until recently. And she was getting closer and closer to the home where she'd lived all her life, carrying mass death. That must be wearing at her too, but she was making an excellent stab at controlling it.

I admire this girl, I really do. I don't know if I could have done as well at her age or with her background.

Denke spoke, perhaps taking pity on his men: "I'm following a big harbor tug," he said. "She's got something like a corvette in tow— probably a minelayer with engine trouble. Take a look, Hans."

The executive officer briefly stepped in, stooping so as not to disturb his commander's setting of the instrument.

"Right you are, skipper," he said. "Moving slowly, too! I hope U-148 had as nice an escort through the minefields."

Denke resumed his position. "Now we just have to hope the *tug's* map of the minefields is properly updated," he said. "The Americans can be sloppy about details."

Ciara started as Luz joined in the hard snicker that went around among the sailors and Horst.

"It's times like these you need a laugh most," Luz whispered to her.

Ciara nodded. "I'm glad you're here," she said softly.

"*Y yo también, querida,*" Luz whispered back. "Good not to be alone."

Tense silence fell again, except for Denke's brief commands to the helm and their precise echoes. Luz glanced down; Ciara's eyes were closed, but she thought she knew what was playing out behind them. The approach to Boston by sea, the narrow entrance between the Navy Yard and South Boston, the golden gleam on the State House topping Beacon Hill, the Custom House, the church spires that were the tallest things, always coming into sight first to welcome the traveler . . .

Luz didn't dislike Boston; there were good bookstores and some lovely galleries and museums and a couple of really good trattorias in the North End, though she would never have lived there by choice.

And she had no single place where she'd spent nearly every day of twenty years; even the house in Santa Barbara had been a base to return to, despite her being born there. For Ciara the sensation must be much stronger, as if she were riding with the Four Horsemen to the doom of her world.

At last Denke sighed and relaxed. "We're in."

Nobody cheered, they were far too well disciplined for that, but backs were slapped and fists rose in exultation and a few bawdy jokes rang changes on Denke's phrasing. Luz felt something different, a hunter's keenness, as a wolf might after following a long difficult trail and seeing the prey at last in sight.

Now Denke did something with a lever on the side of the periscope. "Reference point number one in sight. Distance is . . . four point two-seven kilometers, bearing 177."

"Target distance is three point one-four kilometers, bearing 150," the exec said from the plotting table.

Silence except for the almost imperceptible whine of the electrics as the team went into their stylized dance of order and response. Luz felt her own sweat running down her spine, despite the dankness of the U-boat. She felt sticky with it, but she'd been places where staying clean was impossible before; it was probably harder on Ciara's morale. The dialogue between the two men went on until—

"Distance is—*down periscope!* Engines stop! Harbor patrol boat!"

Luz saw one of the petty officers biting his finger to keep from saying anything aloud; she sympathized deeply and swallowed acid at the back of her throat. Everyone waited in utter silence . . . either for enough time to pass, or for the bow of one of the ships in the busy harbor to slice into them as they waited blind and helpless.

"Up periscope," Denke said. He did a three-hundred-sixty-degree scan. "Distance to reference one is two point nine kilometers, bearing 160."

He began calling orders again in the same calm monotone. Twenty minutes later:

"Distance to reference three is three point eight kilometers, bearing 281."

"I confirm the plot," the second-in-command said.

The hitherto-silent *Bootswain*, who was also a navigator and had been running the calculations in duplicate spoke:

"I confirm the plot. We're where we're supposed to be, skipper."

"Down periscope. Vent trim tanks," Denke said, his eyes on the compass binnacle. "Take her down to the bottom."

Air gurgled out of the tanks and the U-150 settled. The sensation was familiar . . . until the submarine grounded on the mud of Boston's harbor. First by the bow, then with a long slithering sound and a *thunngggg* as the stern dug in. The deck canted to starboard and settled at about fifteen degrees off vertical. The sensation beneath their feet altered, too. Even the steady level swim of the submarine when far below the surface had a subliminal motion to it. This was stillness, the feel of solid ground.

"Our bearing is within the parameters set for the mission," Denke said formally. "Deploy anchors!"

More levers were pulled. There was a muted *clang* from behind them, and a whirring sound.

"Stern anchor deployed."

Another, the same sound but much fainter, from the distant bows, and then again.

"Bow anchors deployed."

Denke stood, grinning at his crew: "Men," he said ceremoniously. "We've done it!"

No, you haven't, Luz thought. *Not yet.*

SEVENTEEN

Luz tucked the little Browning pistol into the pocket of her leather coat. Then she put her hand into the one in her gray German naval trousers and touched the *navaja*, feeling the steel and brass and bone beneath her fingertips.

When she did that she could hear old Pedro's voice. Not speaking words of sympathy, but in cold command when he finally told her she had mastered all the technique he could teach her:

That *is an ass in the skin of a lion without* this, he had said.

He'd thumped his fist over his heart and reached out a finger to touch the air over hers.

As a navajera *you must fight with the cunning of the Moor, the passion of the flamenco, and the courage of a matador facing the bull. Should any of these be lacking, you will not be in control of the outcome. Then you should throw your* sevillana *away, or give it to someone who will use it properly. But if you have them, then you are like the wise in much, and like God in everything, and you will be the victor whether you live or die.*

"*Gracias*, Abuelo Cabo," she whispered to a memory, in the language they had shared, feeling her body washed clean, a fire like liquid steel flowing through its veins. "You were as one of my own blood to me, and I will not dishonor your teaching or your trust. I will give you pride in your granddaughter."

Ciara looked at her; there were dark circles under her eyes. She was inexperienced at this work, but far too intelligent not to know that they had a better-than-even chance of dying in the next few hours. The only way they could have a better-than-even chance of *survival* would be to go along with the German plan; that would find them a hundred miles away or better by the launch time.

And neither of us will do that, Luz thought. *Or even consider it.*

Ciara swallowed and leaned closer. "Luz . . . I—"

Luz smiled and laid a finger on her lips and spoke softly: "Ciara Whelan, I'm glad you're with me."

"I'm so glad I met you, Luz," Ciara said; even now, and with some distance between them and any of the U-150's crew she remembered not to use the full real name. "Even . . . well, even now. And I'm *very* glad it's you beside me."

They walked forward from the little galley. "And we never have to use that *maloliente* head again," Luz said thankfully, as they passed it.

That startled a giggle out of Ciara as they came back into the crew's bunking compartment. It was far more open now; all the bunks and their frames had been disassembled and stacked elsewhere, which made it merely rather crowded with half the crew in it; the rest were back down the corridor to the control room, or in it.

Horst looked up from the Thompson machine-carbine he was checking over and glanced between the two women, raising a brow at Ciara's little laugh. Luz gave him a thumbs-up sign, and he nodded, thinking that she was confident of keeping Ciara up to the mark for the task the Germans had set her. Right now she was angry enough—it was a cold rage—that she didn't regret deceiving him in the slightest. There wasn't much of morality or indignation in her anger; she'd killed for her country too, and sometimes in cold blood, though not on any-thing like the scale he was attempting. What she felt was the pure animal bloodlust of a she-wolf at having a rival pack step over the scent-marked boundary, toward the den and the cubs and the game that fed them, threatening the bond of blood between the generations.

No stranger on our tribe's land! Kill!

Horst nodded again and handed her the weapon and the webbing belt that went with it, with the carriers for another two of the fifty-round drums. Kapitänleutnant Denke looked at him in surprise as Luz reflectively checked the weapon over, made sure there was no cartridge in the chamber and that both safeties were engaged. The very first model of this thing had had an unfortunate tendency to fire if dropped—and sometimes to jump around like a piñata under the sticks firing all fifty rounds, if dropped.

"Herr Kapitänleutnant, how many men have you killed? Personally and on dry land, with bullet and grenade and knife?" Horst asked.

The sailor's brows went up. "At least hundreds at sea, none on land," he said promptly. "We all had that training course before this mission from those *Stoßtruppen* but I'm not in the infantry."

"Not until we get ashore; then you are. If there's fighting, you won't be doing it like a gentleman at several kilometers' distance."

Horst grinned, not an unfriendly expression but a savage one. "And with my own eyes I have seen Elisa kill about . . . six Frenchmen, wasn't it, Fräulein? All armed and fighting back."

Luz took the weapon in the crook of her left arm. It weighed about nine pounds loaded, and the feeling was very familiar indeed, along with the oily metallic-chemical smell. She didn't know if the Germans had acquired it through back channels or made this copy in their own shops—there were Springfield Armory marks and the serial number 9772 on the receiver, but those could be copied too.

"Six or seven, depending on whether they all died after I shot them or blew them up and they fell down," she said indifferently. "We were too busy to check, after those first few in the hotel, as I recall."

"That was not your first time dancing at the ball, either, eh? It didn't look that way to me!"

Luz smiled in a way that made the U-boat captain blink. The expression showed her white even teeth, at least.

"*¡No, por Dios!*" she said, which had the advantage of being quite true. "But I don't keep count. You do what you must. Only *bandolero* idiots waste time carving notches on perfectly good revolvers."

Denke laughed. "I take your point, Hauptmann von Dückler. If the women of Mexico are like the *Fräulein*, how did the Yankees ever conquer the men?"

And you probably think that is a compliment, Luz thought, and did not visibly roll her eyes. *Though to be fair, a lot of people would take it so. Elisa Carmody might.*

"They had superior numbers and better weapons," she said dryly. "And we were divided."

That too had the virtue of being true, if you threw in better organization as well. Mexicans in her experience were mostly extremely brave, often suicidally so, and sometimes very skilled, determined, clever, and tricky-dangerous fighters individually or in small groups. But organization wasn't their strong point. By the time the Intervention started there had been somewhere between three and seven distinct armed factions fighting it out down there over the ruins of old Don Porfirio's dictatorship, the number depending on how seriously you took their mutual alliances.

While they were fighting the flood of invading gringos they'd gone right on killing each other, too. As Díaz himself had said: *Poor Mexico, so far from God, so close to the United States.*

"Oh," she said, raising her voice slightly. "Would everyone please, *bitte schön*, pretty please, check the safety on their weapon again? An accidental discharge in here would get this whole day off to a bad start."

There were chuckles, but they checked, and one swore and corrected a potentially fatal mistake. Like any habit, that got more secure with practice. More weapons were handed out; the three Lewis light machine guns she'd noticed on the conning tower in Wilhelmshaven, another half-dozen Thompsons, the ugly angular shapes of Browning's self-loading rifles, and .45 automatics. There were also a scattering of brass knuckles and trench knives. They weren't going to put themselves wholly in the hands of their local allies—which showed solid good sense.

So did using American weapons. Someone who caught a glimpse would wonder what the auto rifles and Thompsons and brand-new .45 pistols were doing in the hands of civilians. If they were casual enough it might be written off as National Guardsmen or reservists on their way back from maneuvers—they kept their personal weapon at home with their uniform, their boots, and nowadays the steel helmet. But they wouldn't be waving something that shouted *Germany* to anyone with eyes to see. Too many interested men knew exactly what a Mauser rifle looked like, and Boy Scouts . . . and for that matter Girl Scouts . . . got badges for weapons recognition tests.

"I wish our men had something like this," Horst said, clicking a twenty-round box magazine into his Colt-Browning rifle. "We've got something as good designed and tested and in limited production, but the factories are too busy turning out Gewehr 98s to mass-produce new models."

"You are a true warrior, Horst," Luz said lightly. "Worrying about that and not whether we drown now."

Then he passed around something else: rolls of Indian Head ten-dollar gold pieces, along with bills and smaller change. There was laughter then, and mock-innocent questions about the cost of beer in America.

With all the interior gear out of the way, you could see that there was another hatch in the ceiling of the compartment, one of the massive ones that cut through the pressure hull. Various pieces of complex equipment surrounded it. Luz looked at them with mixed feelings. Ciara twitched beside her as she looked in the same direction. Luz knew enough about submarines to know that every time you put a hole in the thick steel that held out the sea you added another potentially fatal point failure source. Evidently Ciara knew more—or just felt it more directly, because technicalese was a language that spoke immediately to her soul.

"Nonsense, Fräulein," Denke said as he watched one of his crewmen put a foot in the cupped hands of another. "In the tests, this device worked over ninety percent of the time! Of course, those tests weren't after a real voyage and after being depth-charged."

"A pity we didn't have time to refine it until it *always* works," Horst agreed. "It would be a *great* pity to die a statistically insignificant death."

Some of the crew joined in the officers' laughter—since they were standing right there to share the common fate they had a right to joke. And would even be admired for it, among a crew of the sort who volunteered to go from dangerous duty to something even more so. Others were staring silently, and some were crossing themselves or otherwise praying. The man lifted his partner as he stood upright, and the second reached up and disengaged a locking pin that secured a long lever set into the roof of the compartment. This was the section of hull below the sloped metal faring ahead of the conning tower. That should have protected the mechanisms through the battering U-150 had taken from the American depth charges.

Operative word is should have, *I think*, ran through Luz's mind.

He put both hands on the grooved narrower end and looked down.

"Do it, Dieter," Denke said, his voice firm but flat.

The man who'd been holding Dieter up stepped back, and he brought the lever down as he dropped back to the deck. For a long moment nothing happened . . .

Bang!

The hull rang like a gong. Hissing, rumbling, clanking sounds followed. Then they dwindled, and after a few minutes there was silence again.

Denke spoke again: "Open it."

The tension built once more, but the crewman and his partner repeated their motion, until the one lifted—who was thin, but had big hands and thick wrists—was grasping the undogging wheel of the round hatch. He was whispering something; other voices took it up, and she recognized the Lutheran Bible's version of Psalm 20:

Now I know that the Lord saves His anointed;
He will answer him from His holy heaven
With the saving might of His right hand.
Some trust in chariots and some in horses,
Yet we trust in the name of the Lord our God.
They collapse and fall,
Yet we rise and stand upright.
O Lord, save our king!
So may He answer us when we call.

"Amen!" Dieter said, and twisted strongly at the wheel.

It resisted for a moment, then spun faster and faster. Then the hatchway slammed downward, and a massive slug of seawater struck him in the face. He shouted as he toppled backward under the impact, and hands caught him; there were more shouts, some that were really screams . . .

. . . dying off suddenly and sheepishly as no more water followed the first. Instead a metal-link ladder fell out of the dark hole above them, accompanied by the sort of dribble a small garden hose would produce.

"If you birds are through singing," Obersteuermann Göttsch said with heavy sarcasm, "then let's get going."

"I am first," Horst said; it was his duty, since he'd be in command ashore. "Then Fräulein Whelan, Fräulein Carmody—"

Who as far as he knew were his local liaisons and needed to be above for the plan to go forward.

"—and then the crew. Orderly but quick now, men!"

The two specialists stuck their heads through from the control room. "The Loki firing control mechanism is still working perfectly, skipper," one called. "We'll be the last through from here and dog the hatch."

Horst slung the rifle down his back; Luz did likewise with her Thompson.

Denke called: "Before we go, men, say good-bye to U-150. The lady got us here alive, and now she's ready for the Fatherland!"

The men murmured, many of them touching a hand to their lips and then reaching to press it to part of the U-boat. Horst did the same—he had very good manners, in his way—then grasped the metal ladder and swarmed upward with a parting:

"And douse the lights down here—we don't want to attract attention when I pop the lid at the top!"

Most of the lights died, leaving only a single orange bulb glowing, and a little scatter of light from the control chamber. Horst vanished, and Ciara put her hands on the rungs with Luz standing beside her.

"Don't worry, *querida*, I'm right behind you," Luz said quietly; the Boston girl was fit, but she hadn't trained as a runner or climber. "If you fall, I'll catch you. Don't try to hurry, just do it a rung at a time. Climb with your feet and legs, steady yourself with your arms."

"I won't fall, but sure, thanks for the offer!" Ciara said stoutly and began to climb.

Luz followed, and the escape tube closed about her, dark and cramped and smelling of seawater and rubber, the weapon on her back bumping against the other side with every rung. Most of it *was* thick rubber, a tube with a mesh of flexible steel wire in it, and a thicker steel ring every meter. It had lain tightly packed into collapsed form for the voyage. The lever had triggered mechanisms that shoved aside the fairing that had covered it and blown compressed air into it and much more into the three big inflatable rubber boats fastened to the top of the tube. Their ascent had dragged the tube upward . . .

It was one of those brilliant ideas that didn't necessarily take into account things like the rubber fabric working during the trip against the metal reinforcement that would keep it open against pressure when it was extended. And it was a rush job, without enough time to work out all the bugs. Little jets . . . and one or two not-very-little jets . . . of cold smelly harbor water struck her as she climbed the rungs made by loops of the steel rings protruding into the tunnel. And it was moving and flexing, rising and falling and swaying as the currents and tides in the water twisted it.

Ciara didn't climb nearly as fast as Luz would have, and the sound of her breath grew loud in the confined space. Once her booted foot slipped; Luz caught it on her shoulder and put a hand on it, guiding the sole back to the next rung.

"Sorry," Ciara said.

"Steady, steady does it," Luz replied.

The tube sagged and twisted still more as the rest of the U-150's crew climbed; someone was feeding them in at carefully controlled intervals, though, and subdued whispers kept them properly spaced except once or twice when someone's head bumped her feet. As she neared the top the contrast between the gusts of clean air from above and the fetid reek from the submarine almost made her gag even then.

And I smell no sweeter, she thought.

More light came from above as Horst cut loose the top cover. It was bright to her dark-adapted eyes, but really nothing but stars and the reflected glow from the city's late-night illumination. There was a cheerful "Here, Fräulein," and a squeak as Horst grabbed Ciara by the back of her jacket and effortlessly lifted her into the nearest of the boats.

If I had a couple of grenades . . . Luz thought.

Then she could just pull the pins in the darkness, drop them as she got out, cut Horst down with a burst from the Thompson, and row off to greet the harbor patrol. Horst *did* have some grenades and had kept them to himself, which might or might not be simply because he could throw them farther and more accurately.

She could shoot him, get them, drop them down the tunnel . . .

No. Too risky, she thought regretfully as she rolled into the boat alongside them.

"Up to the bow," she said to Ciara, her voice sounding odd in her own ears now that it wasn't confined by a metal tube. "This is going to be bumpy."

She absolutely could not risk a firefight here, not if there was the slightest chance of losing it or even of it going on for more than a moment. Her life didn't mean all that much—not in the greater scheme of things—but getting the data tucked into her brassiere to the Black Chamber and the Navy meant everything in the world.

Horst was crouched across from her like a great cat in the darkness, deadly and experienced and quick, and she could *feel* his senses combing through the night. She'd have only a few seconds alone with him anyway, and by then . . .

The skinny executive officer came up next, right on her heels, swinging neatly out of the top of the tube and into another of the rubber boats. His voice directed the others as they emerged, calling the crewmen's names and directions. Whatever you might say about the U-150's crew, they were sailors who knew their business on or under the water.

The lights of Boston glittered in the near distance west and north and south, even though it was well past midnight, enough to make about as much light as the gibbous moon would have if it were up. Modern cities of the electric age were *bright*; she'd seen that become more and more so over her own lifetime as that hard glow replaced the softer yellow flicker of gaslights, though traveling outside the United States or a few other countries was also like stepping back in time. The city silhouetted the ships at the docks; more lights there showed up those at anchor farther out waiting their turn in the busy port.

"What a set of targets, lit up like Christmas!" one of the U-boat men said. "And these *aren't* German."

"Don't worry, we'll take care of them all," someone else said.

"Quiet!" Obersteuermann Göttsch said. "Silence fore and aft."

It was chilly but not cold, around fifty degrees, though it felt colder in her damp greasy clothes. A light wind blew off the island-studded bay and the ocean behind them, and there was a slight swell that rocked the trio of boats. The South Boston harbor wasn't far off to their left. That was where the Clann na nGael would be waiting . . .

The two technicians who'd primed the launch controller came up next to last. "Everything good, sir," one of them said to Horst. "It's ticking away, purring like a kitten. Tonight, the day, the night, and then in the morning . . ."

I wonder if I can shoot them first? Luz thought idly.

She brought the Thompson around and clicked off the selector-safety, moving it from *S* through *SA* to *A*; the slotted cocking knob on the top still had to be twisted through ninety degrees and pulled back for the weapon to be ready to fire, but that could be done very quickly.

No, shooting them would be self-indulgent. They're not really fighting men. In fact, we want to take them alive if we can; they know more about the Breath of Loki than anyone else on the boat. Off to the local Room 101 with them, and a nice happy ending that will be. Though not for them.

Kapitänleutnant Denke was the last man up, having dogged the hatch in the roof of the crew chamber behind himself. He was even more sopping wet than the rest of them, and coughing as he emerged, too.

"Just in time," he said. "The leaks in the tube were getting worse fast—the water was pouring down on my head like a hose when I started, and by the time I'd closed the hatch it was climbing—I had to stick my head under to finish. *Dann sollten wir mal die Kuh vom Eis holen.* Let's get it done."

The three inflatable boats were simple boxes with a bluntly pointed bow at one end, more like rafts than anything else; they had paddles secured in loops on the floors, and the sailors used them to tow the escape tube backward, so that when they cut it free the water-filled sunken snake of rubber and steel would drape over the conning tower and stern of the U-150, not over the launchers.

"Fräulein Whelan?" Horst said. "Are you properly oriented?"

It was a serious question; if you weren't a sailor, getting turned around on the water was very easy. Ciara took a deep breath.

"Yes, Mr. McDuffy and I rowed out here half a dozen times at night. There's the light on top of the Custom House Tower. The warehouse is—"

Her hand moved in an arc, to point nearly southward. "They'll have been on watch for the last week, and they'll be watching now."

"Then you must do the honors, Fräulein," he said politely, and handed her a heavy flashlight.

Luz moved in the darkness, laying a gentle hand on her arm for a moment. Ciara took a deep breath and began to thumb the on-off switch. It was spring-loaded on this military model, which made it easier, and she adapted seamlessly.

That's my girl, Luz thought. *Well, no, she isn't, worse luck, but in the other meaning of the term, yes.*

The sequence was longs and shorts, like Morse but not any recognizable combination. Ciara repeated it twice and waited. The moment stretched, and Luz let her focus widen. Telling distances and directions in the dark was surprisingly hard, even on familiar terrain. Then a bright yellow light began to strobe at them from the spot Ciara had pointed at.

Blink . . . blink-blink . . . blink . . . blink-blink-blink.

"Sure and that's it!" Ciara gasped.

The light came from a little east of south; there were no ship's riding-lights there, nor cranes operating round-the-clock as there were in other parts. It looked quiet, away from the growl that never quite stopped in a great city.

Ciara repeated her initial signal, and it was answered again.

"Unhitch the line," Denke said. "This boat leads. Stay close."

The three boats each had about ten occupants, with four paddlers to a side.

"Stroke . . . stroke . . . stroke . . ." Obersteuermann Göttsch called softly.

The paddles bit into the brackish, stale-smelling water, full of mud stirred up by propellers and generations of bilgewater pumped out into the harbor and garbage dumped into it. A waft came from the land as well. Coal smoke was the universal scent of an urban area. So was stale horse-piss on the streets, though not as much of that as there would have been when she was a little girl, when a prosperous city had a horse for every fifteen or twenty people, or even a few years ago. A lingering tang of automobile exhaust; not as much as there would have been in Los Angeles, but more every year everywhere. And a *used* smell, one that she associated with big dense populations in a confined space. After the U-boat, it was all like the citrus orchards of California in blossom.

The light blinked again twice before they reached the dock. Once they lay quiet for ten minutes, faces down and paddles still as a steam trawler passed them a few hundred yards to the south, a strong smell of mackerel and cod coming from it. The new Fish Pier—it had opened in 1914—was there, and it never really closed; the stink from it was much stronger and more rank than the trawler's, two years' worth of guts and scales as the contents of holds were swung ashore in the nets. The warehouses there worked three shifts, and there were canneries not far away, and the throb of ice-making plants. The old T-Wharf on the northern shore mostly handled the smaller boats these days, while the big commercial fleets were based here.

They waited until the sleepy fishermen guided their craft in for one of the late-night landings that were part of their trade, along with the stink and hard labor and danger, and in winter the spray turning to ice in their beards, frozen winds hard as the teeth of hell.

Then more paddling; the crew of the U-150 knew how to handle small boats, and they'd trained on these models specifically as part of the run-up to the mission. Luz left it to the experts and kept her gaze focused ahead. At last the dock loomed over them, huge tarry timbers enclosing the landfill and supporting the decking, all fairly new and still smelling strongly of the chemicals used to treat the wood; this whole area had been reclaimed within living memory, from the sea and the old tidal mud flats. The water was conveniently most of the way up to the top, since the tide was still making and nearly at full.

Men were there, a half dozen of them dressed in workingman's dark rough clothing and cloth caps, and one carrying a shuttered lantern that he opened just long enough for the rubber boats to pull in. She noticed weapons there, too: sawn-off shotguns, and probably pistols and knives and blackjacks.

"A hundred thousand welcomes, but quick now," a man's voice said. "Is it that Miss Ciara Whelan is with you, gentlemen? Throw the rope!"

Irish-born and raised there most of his life at least, Luz thought. *Dat for* that *and* t'row *for* throw. *And listen to the way he treats his* r's *and turns* o *to* a, *he said* raawp *for* rope. *County Cork. And a hard man, and one used to giving orders, I'd judge; not too young, but still strong.*

"I am that, Mr. McDuffy," Ciara called back, a bit of a quaver in her voice.

Luz couldn't tell whether it was genuine, but she knew that her friend feared and hated him for deceiving her into the mission that had left her in Castle Rauenstein.

"And the German gentlemen, and a lady," she added.

"This way!"

Luz took the time to whisper: "It'll be soon," in Ciara's ear.

That would make her more tense, but it had to be chanced, and she'd just have to hope very hard that Ciara wouldn't freeze when it started.

Everything I've done . . . we've done . . . comes down to the next few minutes. Apostar por el todo o nada. *Do or die.*

Hard strong hands took hers and helped her to the dock. She hopped up and pulled on the sling of the Thompson, bringing it around so she could cradle it muzzle-up in her left arm.

"Thank you," she said, and added the same in Irish, a phrase she'd learned with a few others from her father: *"Go raibh maith agat."*

"Tá fáilte romhat," someone said.

That was an automatic *you're welcome* in the same language, and a safe bet among a group of Clann na nGael stalwarts whose reverence for Irish Gaelic knew no bounds, at least in boozy song and a few rote-learned phrases. Then he caught the outline of the weapon and started convulsively.

"Jayzus, lady!"

"I'm not here to take tea with Father Callaghan, boyo," she said.

She gave her voice a little more of the accent that her father had used when he was laying it on for effect or was a bit tiddly after a party, though not much. Elisa Carmody had first learned her English at the knee of an Irish-born grandfather, a self-made man born a peasant, though by report she'd smoothed it in later education.

"Now let's be about it. *¡Vámonos!*"

"An excellent idea," Horst said, dropping into his accented English and then adding, "*Schnell!*"

The wharf had cranes, silent now, and two sets of railway tracks set into its concrete surface tram-style, with a four-story warehouse on the other side, brick-faced over a steel frame with loading bays in its side. Some of the Clann na nGael men heaved the doors open; Luz noted that they were sheet metal and boards. Others helped the German sailors pull the inflated boats out of the water; knives slashed them open with a hiss of rubber-smelling air, and they were rolled up and tied into sausage-shaped bundles. The man at the door hissed himself and waved them in. Horst and McDuffy came behind, shepherding their followers to make sure nobody was left standing outside. Anyone who'd dealt with moving groups, especially in the dark, knew how appallingly easily that could happen. Luz could see McDuffy relax a little as they entered the building and the doors swung shut behind them.

"The others?" Horst asked with a snap. "From U-148?"

"Sent on their way last night," McDuffy said.

"Ah, excellent," Horst said.

Luz cursed inwardly; she hadn't expected anything else, but it was still bad news. Lights came on overhead, leaving the interior a crazy-

quilt of shadow and pools of brightness. The warehouse windows had
been covered on the inside with newspaper; anyone who saw it would
think that the owners were being conscientious and implementing the
blackout regulations ahead of time. She'd known what most of the
ground-floor storage was through her nose. Bales of tanned cow hides
and bales of raw wool loomed around them, both stacked up nearly to
the high ceiling of this ground floor in a massive checkerboard that left
just enough space for trucks or wagons to pass between.

That made it boringly ordinary, which was the best camouflage.
New England still had the greatest concentration of textile mills and
shoe factories in America, though plants farther south were starting to
give them hard competition on the lower end of the market, and Boston was the biggest port for the raw materials. All of those factories
were running on three shifts with the mobilization, sucking in the contents of places like this. Turning out uniforms and boots and belts and
knapsacks by the millions, to match the rifles and machine guns and
trench mortars and grenades pouring out of the region's machine shops
and foundries.

The way the goods were laid out had made it easier to use for the
Clann na nGael's purposes; they'd just taken advantage of a spot where
two of the stacks had been shipped out and not yet replaced, empty
space in the midst of pungent abundance. Five automobiles were parked
there, all products of the Ford assembly lines at Highland Park, all suit-
ably nondescript and battered-looking and in government military-drab
paint, a color used for uniforms and vehicles and equipment that somehow managed to combine dirt-brown and sagebrush-green. Four were
the long-body light truck version of the Model T with slatted board
sides and a canvas top, which could haul a ton or so of freight or a dozen
crammed-together men when they had bench seats like these. The military and the FBS had been buying them in bulk for years, and so had
everyone else from farmers to delivery companies.

The other vehicle parked beside the row of trucks was the passenger version of the omnipresent Model T, but the special type that had

only started mass production early last year; it had a shorter wheelbase, only two doors, broader tires, and a four-wheel-drive conversion. It was in the same dust-green-brown color but without branch or unit insignia. The Federal Bureau of Security used a lot dressed up that way; the Chamber did too sometimes, as double camouflage.

The Army had sprung on the first models of the nimble little vehicle with pantherish cries of joy when the inventor Livingood demonstrated them before General Wood and the divisional commanders down in the Protectorate.

Understandably, Luz thought. *Por Dios, how many times did I use one myself? They climb like goats and laugh at sand and rocks and mud. Everyone loved them except the diehards who think it's against God to ride anything* qué no comer heno y caga. *How I wish we'd had them from the beginning!*

The General Staff had immediately leaned hard on Ford Motors to get production going on the General Utility Vehicle—GUVe for short, universally pronounced *Guvvie*. Police forces had bought a good many of the others, and they were popular with ranchers and people who liked to imagine themselves country gentlemen. Uncle Teddy had three.

Ford Motors had been reluctant; Henry hated anything that distracted him from driving down the price of his standard you-can-have-it-in-any-color-as-long-as-it's-black model and was a bit of a pacifist anyway. But these days even a major business mogul knew better than to get the Party thinking he wasn't a patriotic New Nationalist.

Especially after the example we made of Hearst, Luz thought; she'd detested the newspaper magnate anyway and thought being allowed to sulk on his ranch was too good for him. *And Ford's making plenty of money out of it anyway.*

The light also showed faces. McDuffy was a man in his forties, lean but strong-looking, with a square chin and wiry black hair starting to recede into a widow's peak, and bright blue eyes; it was a nondescript face, except for batlike ears and a few scars. Most of his followers looked like dockers, or those who did similar strong-back labor, battered and thick-muscled and tough, but he was in a stiff-collared suit and tie with a bowler hat on his head, the sort of thing a clerk or shopkeeper would wear.

He looked at Ciara and nodded; then his eyes skipped over Luz, stopped, and visibly backtracked for a second puzzled look.

"We need to get you out of town quickly," he said to Horst. "They're expecting the declaration of war within the next week, I hear, and the Navy is jumping about like a frog on a griddle the last few days for some reason."

Horst nodded. "Your plan?"

"With these autos . . . and one of our men riding shotgun with those lovely Thompsons in each . . . it'll look like an FBS squad taking prisoners off to work on some road project or the like. Those bastards don't put their names on the side of their trucks, and the local police don't ask them questions. There've been some protests about the draft, you see—people with German names, mostly, and a few of us who don't fancy fighting to rescue the empire of the Sassenach. Section Fourteen arrests. That's a disguise as will get you as far as . . . Poughkeepsie, didn't you say?"

"Yes, your men can drop us off there," Horst said, giving no further details. "I know my route past that point."

"Good luck go with you."

Horst nodded approval of the scheme, though most of his compatriots were baffled by the details, even if they could follow the English. Section Fourteen of the Universal National Service Act of 1916 made it a federal offense to resist or encourage others to resist the draft for any but religious reasons—Quakers and Hutterites and the like could get away with it, as long as they couched it strictly in terms of absolute religious pacifism with no political overtones, but nobody else. The precise wording, which a Chamber operative of course had to know, was:

Such persons are subject to arrest and detention in the custody
of the Federal Bureau of Security; detention and trial shall be by

administrative procedure on suspicion of actions prejudicial to the
security of the state in time of war or apprehended war.

That in turn was a modification of the statute that had been passed several years ago when some of the usual suspects—including William Randolph Hearst—tried to organize a movement against the Intervention, the way some had in the political campaigns against the wars with Spain and the Philippine rebels, back at the beginning of the century in Uncle Teddy's salad days at the head of the Navy and then commanding the Rough Riders.

He took an extremely dim view of giving aid and comfort to the enemy in any way, shape, or form, and he'd gotten fiercer and fiercer about it as time went by. As far as he was concerned, the politics stopped when the first bullets were fired at American soldiers, and after that the only permissible debate was over how to win most efficiently. Anything else was treason, only marginally better than shooting at the American flag and uniform yourself.

The usual sentence after conviction by Bureau administrative tribunal—*guilty* was nearly but not quite inevitable—was five or ten years of corrective labor. It certainly *corrected* any tendency to publicly blame the United States for any war it was engaged in, since the earliest enrollees hadn't graduated from their course of educational labor yet. Seeing their scruffy, miserable forms in pictures or by the side of the road certainly *corrected* the speech and actions of most onlookers from the small minority who didn't share Uncle Teddy's opinions in the first place.

"That is a clever deception," Horst said. "What about clothing?"

He'd brought his own set of American street clothes with him, and was changing into them as they spoke. That wasn't practical for the rest, though.

"We have enough regular clothes, you can carry those in bundles for later after you, so to say, freshen up a wee bit . . . but it'll be the prisoner overalls at first; with those nobody will be surprised that you're not looking, ah, sweet as spring daisies, as it were."

That everyone's scruffy and stinking, Luz filled in, focusing on imper-sonal things to help beat down the gathering knot of tension within. *I can see a couple of them wrinkling their noses at the Germans, and I doubt Mr. McDuffy's friends are the most fastidious of men to begin with. From the one-bath-a-week set, the most of them.*

It would probably pass muster, too, since the U-boat men did look the part. A term of corrective labor under Section Fourteen wasn't sup-posed to *kill* you, but it wasn't supposed to be *pleasant*, either. There was enough food, just, but of the most bland and basic sort, and the work was hard—very hard indeed and dangerous too, for those not used to rough manual labor on construction sites in the blistering Colorado Valley, or digging irrigation canals around Bakersfield or logging in Alaska or the like. Among other things the whole process was intended to make a three-year hitch in the Army look attractive by contrast even to the imperfectly patriotic.

A few judges had tried to rule that sort of thing unconstitutional, years ago. They'd apparently forgotten—God alone knew why, since he hadn't been at all shy about it on the stump—that Uncle Teddy had put snap judicial recall elections into the Party's platform in 1912. Possibly they thought he'd been bluffing or only meant to use it for things like upholding the workman's compensation and child-labor laws that conservative judges were in the habit of striking down back then. A few demonstrations of just how quickly he and the Party could mobilize voters to yank offending judicial backsides off the bench had made the remainder . . . or their replacements . . . much, much more pliable.

"Your weapons will have to be concealed . . . unless you'd prefer to leave them with us . . ."

A single pale, coldly arrogant *Uradel* glare from Herr Hauptmann Freiherr von Dückler showed the Irishman how far he'd get with *that* idea. His lips went thin in annoyance, but he nodded silently.

And let that be a lesson in exactly how much liberty Ireland would have in a world where the Reich *has the victory,* Señor McDuffy-Venganza. *What you*

really want is to see the English brought down and their pride humbled in the dirt;
everything else is a distant second.

McDuffy's men handed out the overalls, loose canvas striped in black and dirty white, with a number preceded by the letters *FBS* stenciled on breast and back and brimmed caps of the same coarse material. While the Germans changed and stuffed their uniforms into sacks for disposal, quickly but with a fair bit of chaffing, the Clann na nGael men cranked the engines of the trucks and the Guvvie. They were well cared for and caught immediately, blatted, and began to roar. Oddly the sound didn't echo, sounding more muffled than it would have in open country: The tons of soft leather and wool all around seemed to soak up noise, and Luz doubted they could be heard outside at all.

Another strong point of this warehouse, Luz thought with professional respect for the Clan na nGael leader. *I'd bet you couldn't hear gunshots very far, either . . . Mr. McDuffy is a problem in need of solution . . . and death solves all problems.*

The warehouse was dim, but Luz saw things with increasing clarity—the wart below an eye, dirt ground into a laborer's knuckles by decades that could never be scrubbed free, a young man's gingery wispy mustache. Her body felt lighter, too, and her movements more precise. That was something in the back of her head warning her that she was about to go back to a certain place, a place she dreaded and—in her most honest moments—admitted she had come to crave as well.

The feeling was never wrong when it warned that the dance was about to begin; that buried part of her mind was better at quick deduction than the conscious portion, too.

There's never been as much riding on it as now, though. These negatives are the most important intelligence since that random soldier picked up Lee's Special Order 191 just before Antietam.

The Guvvie had no top, and a pintle mount stood up between the two front seats. One of Denke's seamen brought over his Lewis gun, and he and a man of McDuffy's who knew the weapon—he'd probably done a hitch in the U.S. Army, possibly precisely to acquire training for the Irish Republican Brotherhood's purposes—capably clamped it home in the pivoting mount on top of the steel column.

As the Germans piled into the trucks, McDuffy's followers gathered around behind the Guvvie. He pulled a map with the American National Railways crest—a stylized wheel superimposed on the outline of the U.S.—off the seat and began to open it, and his men crowded around to get their final instructions. The map was part of a series put out as an element in ANR's campaign to integrate road and rail transport more effectively, now that so many miles of paved road had been finished and even more were under construction. The Party never saw a road that it didn't immediately want to straighten, widen, and pave, at state and federal levels both. McDuffy's followers continued going over it after he came back for a last word with the German leader.

"I will ride in the small auto," Horst said as he joined them; his clothes were a bit wrinkled, but would do, and he'd rather heroically shaved with his drinking water before they arrived. "In which of the motor trucks will Fräulein Whelan ride? Two women in the car of the secret police would be excessively suspicious."

McDuffy looked up sharply. "Sure, and she'll stay here with me, of course. This is her town, and she has kin here, who I'll take her back to. She's no use to you now, and she's of our people, not yours."

Luz caught Horst's eye and gave a single short *no* motion of her head. The German officer's nod was equally curt; from his point of view Ciara Whelan simply knew far too much. And could not be allowed to talk privately with her compatriots before the Breath of Loki was launched, not under any circumstances. Her usefulness was over.

"That is not possible," Horst said flatly. "She will accompany us. Let us go. *Sofort!*" he added, then realized he'd used his own language.

"Immediately," he repeated, which meant the same thing but didn't have quite the imperative snap or sense of: *Do it! Now!*

Luz turned, and casually nudged Ciara in the ankle with her toe as she did. It was time to break the situation loose.

The younger woman nodded vigorously. "Oh, sure and that will be for the best, Mr. McDuffy!" she said brightly, wetting her lips and letting her voice catch with fear. "I'm sure that I can be of help to the gentlemen, and they our allies."

Good job, querida*!* Luz thought, as things took on a diamond clarity.

McDuffy was no fool; his eyes narrowed as he looked at Ciara, obviously determined to wring out everything she knew. When he spoke, his voice was flat:

"She'll come with us. It's bad enough we had to use her as the courier; she'll spend no more time among strangers, a good Irish girl."

"Captain von Dückler!" Ciara said, grabbing his arm with a terrified gesture.

Luz thought it just a trifle overdone, but then she knew Ciara better, and it was certainly an excellent improvisation and fit for the purpose. The Clann na nGael certainly didn't know what the Germans had really planned . . . and letting them know would drive an instant, handy wedge.

"Don't let them keep me here!" Ciara went on. "I don't want to be here when everyone dies!"

"*Silence!*" Horst barked, but the local men were all looking at her.

Some simply seemed puzzled themselves, but several were starting to look very curious, or alarmed. Sean McDuffy took a step forward; Horst's hand went to his .45, but the Irishman wasn't intimidated.

"Talk, girl!" he said, as she cowered backward . . . and away from the German. "Why should explosives launched at the Navy Yard kill everyone?"

"Bombs, they told you? It's poison gas over the whole city—" Ciara blurted, giving a very convincing imitation of someone panicking.

If I didn't know *she was brave as a lion, I'd think she was panicking too. I am* in love*!*

Horst's hand with the heavy automatic pistol in it made a hard smacking sound as it struck the side of her head. It wasn't lethal, as it might have been without the half step he had to take and her dodging, but she reeled against the Guvvie's side and slid down it, bleeding from a pressure-cut over the temple.

"Miss Carmody! Miss Carmody!" she called shrilly. "Don't let them leave me here to die! Everyone here's going to die of the gas, Miss Carmody!"

That was beautifully done, Luz thought, checking her impulse to shoot Horst with a little difficulty; first things first.

But it may have been a step too far. Don't complicate the story you're selling— though that does make it impossible for Horst to just brazen it out . . . And so does that attack on Paris back in May. The photographs in the papers were fairly dramatic.

Horst's pistol came around to cover McDuffy, whose eyes darted between him and Luz and Ciara and then went very wide. His mouth opened.

"*Carmody*—" he began.

Luz had grabbed the cocking knob on the top of her Thompson's receiver as soon as the men began their confrontation, twisted it to unlock it, and racked it back in the same movement. She was pivoting on one heel as McDuffy spoke, letting the forestock fall into her left hand and clamping the butt between her side and her right arm, and then her finger tightened on the trigger—

Braaaaaaap.

The rattling snarl was a precise controlled burst, eight or nine rounds, directly into the clump of Clann na nGael men behind the Guvvie. The Thompson's muzzle kicked up and to the right when it was fired on full automatic, but she'd started with it pointing at groin level and clamped down hard against the torque. The muzzle blast was a leaf-shaped blade of flame in the dimness of the warehouse, and she slitted her eyes to keep it from blinding her.

Braaaaaaap. Braaaaaaap. Braaaaaaap.

The men collapsed as the heavy .45 slugs punched into bodies and limbs from only ten feet away; a few sparked off the concrete floor and flew away with peening sounds. Luz's thumb clicked the selector switch back to *SA* as she stepped briskly over and brought the butt to her shoulder. One of them was struggling to lift a pistol he'd pulled from his pocket, shaking with the effort as blood ran down into his eyes. Others were moaning or thrashing or screaming, or still.

Crack. Crack.

Two rounds into the center of mass, and the man with the little .32 went limp. The Thompson was very accurate at close range, and the recoil of a single pistol round, even a powerful one, did very little against the weight of the weapon.

The German and the local man who'd been mounting the Lewis gun on the Guvvie were wrestling over it now, hammering clumsily at each other and making the vehicle rock on its springs. Luz stepped close and extended the Thompson until its muzzle was only a few inches from the local's stomach.

Crack. Crack.

The man pitched backward off the auto and landed in a boneless sprawl; the German leapt down and did what someone in his situation normally would, ran back to his comrades. She walked behind the vehicle and finished off the others quickly and methodically, starting with the least injured, double-tapping with precise shots into the upper chest or the equivalent on the back. That was the spot where you blasted into the bunch of arteries and veins above the heart, and the .45 round had been designed as a shock-action man-stopper that ripped things apart within. It worked just as well here as it had against Moro fanatics in the Sulu isles hopped up on religion and hashish.

Blood sprayed across her jacket and pooled about her shoes as she did so, and the coppery-salt smell of it was rank under the sweeter odors of leather and wool, and the chemical stink of auto exhaust.

¡Otra vez la misma historia! she thought, the words distant in her consciousness. *Back in business at the same old stand.*

Men were shouting in the trucks, and a few started to jump down. Less than half a minute had passed since her first shot, and they weren't used to this type of fighting. Horst's voice broke through the brabble in crisp German:

"Quiet! Two men in each truck, change into street clothes; one to play guard, one to drive. The rest—"

He paused a little; Luz thought he was probably remembering that the men were sailors, and more likely to shoot each other than McDuffy if they tried to hunt him through this maze.

"—the rest watch carefully for the American in the suit. Shoot him if you see him but do not shoot *me*."

"He got away?" Luz said sharply, turning back to him.

"Yes, *Herrgottdonnerwetter*!" the German noble said angrily. "You startled me. I wounded him but he's still mobile. My fault, I should have expected you to act quickly. Finish off the girl, I'll get Herr McDuffy and we'll salvage what we can from this *beschissen* mess. It shouldn't be too serious."

Horst turned away, keeping the rifle slung and his pistol ready, more suited to the close-in stalking among the maze of bales; he was going to have his work cut out hunting the IRB gunman down in this tangle, even with a blood-trail to follow. Luz crossed to where Ciara was slumped against the Guvvie and bent, forcing down concern with a massive effort of will. Her eyes were open, but her gaze looked vague. She'd been able to speak coherently after Horst hit her, so she couldn't be *too* badly concussed.

I hope!

"Lie still when I shove you!" Luz hissed. "But be ready to move. Understand?"

A weak nod. Luz looked around for an instant, then fired into a bale of leather nearby and pushed her to one side. Ciara toppled to the floor and did her best to go limp as death.

"Taken care of!" Luz called in German; none of the U-boat crew could see details and Horst was looking in the other direction.

Silence fell; one of the sailors started to talk and someone else whapped him on the side of the head. Then Luz heard a sound she hadn't expected: laughter.

"Ye dim thick gobshite!" McDuffy yelled; the accent was stronger in his voice now.

Then there was a guttural sound of pain, probably from the effort of the yell.

"Ah, Christ Jayzus!"

From the sound of it he was lying on top of one of the piles of leather or wool. From the sound of it he was also wounded and fairly badly; there weren't many places a flat-nosed .45 round *wouldn't* do that, if it hit you at all.

"Ye've kilt me, but you'll be dyin' too, and soon. Elisa? Elisa Carmody de Soto-Dominguez—isn't that the full name of her?" McDuffy called out to the German.

Mierda, he noticed what Ciara called me, Luz thought with icy concentration; things were going to move fast now.

The Irishman spoke quickly, to get the knife in while he could:

"We got the news of that one ten days ago, to the message we sent asking where she was! She was took, took in Mexico by the Black Chamber in March and they squeezed her dry in Lecumberri dungeon and swept up most of the PNR that was left on the strength of it! That whore with ye's a Black Chamber bitch, a fookin' viper of a spy ye've been nursing amidst all yer secrets, ye treacherous *amadán*!"

"*¡Recórcholis!*" Luz said mildly as Horst answered, which meant *Uh-oh* or *Oooops*, roughly.

Horst is more than smart enough to remember that Ciara didn't use Carmody's full name, so McDuffy would have to have known it on his own. And he's disciplined enough to remember it even when he's about to kill. And if he talks to McDuffy for more than a few seconds—

The German officer replied, and he wasn't shouting, and neither was McDuffy when he answered; she could just make out their voices, but not the words among the sound-absorbing piles.

"*Eso lo tronó*," Luz said; that had torn it. "Ciara! Up, quick!"

Ciara did her best; Luz bent and gripped her around the thighs as she rose and pitched her into the rear seat of the Guvvie, where she landed with a *thump* and a groan. Luz was already vaulting into the driver's seat and dropping the Thompson on the passenger side.

"Stay down!" she snapped.

Fortunately none of the U-150's sailors spoke English well enough to instantly grasp what was going on. Infantrymen would have known what to do by reflex when she pulled the cocking handle and turned the Lewis gun on them, but they hesitated fatally because their minds still saw her as someone on their side.

Bratatatatatatat—

Luz walked short bursts along the row of Model T trucks, aiming low—the fuel tanks were under the driver's seat. Tracer showed the path of the bullets, like bars of red light through the dimness at this close range, and then as she turned it back the first vehicle took fire with a *whump* that was not quite an explosion but close enough for government work. Men ran screaming as their clothes caught fire in the spray from the ruptured tank.

Crack.

That was a bullet, and far too close to her ear. She twisted and loosed off the last six rounds in the flat-pan magazine at Horst as he ran toward her with a face like something out of the deep oceans, firing the .45 as he came. Enough sanity remained for him to throw himself flat, but his body jerked as he rolled aside. She'd hit him, though there was no way to tell how seriously. But the surviving sailors would be recovering in instants, though the plume of flame and smoke from the first two trucks gave her cover.

She'd survived on surprise and ruthlessness and the equalizing effects of automatic weapons, but now they'd start shooting, and that much firepower would shred her and Ciara in a few seconds.

She dropped down into the driver's seat. The engine was running and warm. Luz slapped the spark timing control on the left side of the steering column down and the engine's purr rose to a roar; her left foot stamped to hold the gear in neutral as she let the handbrake off and held the car in position with her right foot on the brake pedal. Even with the brake on it started to move; she increased engine revs up to near full speed with the throttle lever, let the gear pedal off to engage top gear, slowing the engine with the throttle lever to get a smooth gear change . . . and lifted her foot from the brake.

Guvvies had bounce when you did that. She braced herself as it leapt forward toward the doors like a mule with ears laid back and teeth bare.

Crunch.

Things smashed; Luz gave an *ooof!* as the steering wheel punched her painfully in breasts and belly. Guvvies were also tough, and they had a sturdy bumper and mountings for a winch in front, rather than the naked radiator of the usual Model T. You could hope . . .

She threw the Guvvie into reverse, which made Horst roll aside just as he was about to reach the rifle he'd dropped; it also made the sailors stop shooting at her for fear of hitting him.

"Keep firing, you pigdogs!" he screamed. "Kill the—"

That involved calling her a name which accused her of a practice she actually found delightfully pleasant, with the right lady.

"*You should try it; you'd be less boring in bed!*" she shouted, and threw the Guvvie forward again. "*Germans are the world's worst spies—like taking candy from a baby!*"

As she went she shot across her own body with the little Browning automatic to keep his head down.

Always help an enemy make mistakes, she thought. *Poor Horst, this is . . . well, not more than you deserve, but really it must be quite distressing. A pity, but needs must when the devil drives. I need you as upset as possible and not thinking straight.*

Luz hadn't expected to hit him, but accidents did happen; he was three-quarters of the way to his feet again when his head snapped around and he screamed, clapping his hands to his face. Liquid fire had run across the path to the doorway. She ignored it and slapped the throttle lever down as far as it would go, braced again . . .

Crunch-bang!

Blood filled her mouth with copper and salt and iron; she spat to the side. The auto had had time to reach better than twenty miles an hour, two-thirds of the way to its maximum speed. The chain and bar that secured the doors burst; Luz ducked and yelped involuntarily as the chain whirred through the darkness and plucked the flat German naval cap from her head. An inch lower and it would have ripped off her face . . .

An ordinary Model T would have gone straight into Boston Harbor beside the wharf where the rubber boats had first pulled in, if nothing else because the brakes only affected the rear wheels. The Guvvie's front axle was a modified *back* axle from the standard model, and she managed to slow with a squeal of brakes and of wheels on the rough concrete, and wrestle the little auto into an insanely sharp turn to the right. Both wheels on that side came off the pavement, and for an instant she thought the auto would tumble into the water instead. Out of the corner of her eye she saw Ciara move, face death-white and blood-red, and clumsily throw herself forward on the seat so that she lay half-out of the auto on that side.

Whether or not that was the final hair's-worth of weight, the Guvvie crashed back down on all four wheels and sped up the silent southbound street between the streetlights' yellow pyramids. She shot out a hand to catch Ciara's jacket and make sure she went back onto the seat, and drew a breath to relax . . .

. . . and a flash of light showed in the rearview mirror; the last two trucks had made it out in her wake, though one of them was in flames. Both followed her, and Horst was ahead in the burning one, firing his Colt-Browning rifle at her with that distinctive *tunnnk-a tunnnk-a* sound it made. The sailors in the back had tossed the canvas cover free and were beating at the flames with their jackets, whipping them down for a moment before the rushing speed fanned them alive again. Another was standing in the bed, leveling a Lewis gun and loosing off bursts from the hip. So was someone in the second truck, whenever the frantic weaving of the first gave them a shot, and the green streaks of tracer rounds went by on either side and overhead.

Luz would have felt a flash of concern under other circumstances—the .30-06 bullets they were spraying with abandon could penetrate a brick wall and kill at half a mile, and they were approaching densely populated residential neighborhoods, with people and their children sleeping. The knowledge of what waited with cold mechanical patience beneath the harbor's water killed that impulse.

A policeman in his double-breasted blue jacket and peaked cap gaped at the cavalcade blasting by in a roar of flames and hail of bullets, raising his whistle toward his mouth and dropping his hand toward the pistol at his waist. Both were presumably by reflex; then he let the whistle bounce on its lanyard and ran for the nearest call box.

And more speed to him; the police arriving in force would be very good, right now.

Luz laughed wildly.

"It's an utterly secret undercover operation, and I'm driving fast through the streets of Boston at two in the morning, pursued by German submarine sailors shooting machine guns!" she shouted. "And—*¡Esto es lo más absolutamente delicioso de todo!*—the Germans are *on fire!*"

"Oh, shut up, you madwoman!" Ciara managed to choke out, before being noisily sick on the floor of the backseat.

Luz called up the map of the city in her mind, thankful for a good visual memory and the fact that she always studied the layout of a town before a visit.

"And . . . here!"

She stamped on the brake again and cut right, bouncing onto North Street, then accelerating again. The trucks slowed more, because they were carrying a lot more weight for the same engine, and because their drivers had to *find* her.

"Now, *don't* stop and shoot from a good position where you can aim properly," she urged. "Forget that a Guvvie can't outrun a stream of bullets from a Lewis but it can outrun a motor truck. Just come bouncing after me again shooting on the move! Put your trust in *la suerte de los pendejos y la intervención divina.*"

Instinct overcame the sailors' scanty infantry training ... and Horst was probably too caught up with pain and rage; that was why she'd taunted him, to flick his pride on the raw when he was most vulnerable. They did indeed count on the luck of fools and divine intervention.

The rearview mirror showed what she'd wanted to see ...

If they didn't just run away!

... both motor trucks screeched around the corner and swung wide, but pursued without stopping. The blinking of muzzle flashes continued, tracers arching out toward her and then going by with a *zip* ... or sparking off the roadway or arching out into the night, or in one case shooting out a streetlight with a spectacular strobing effect.

"I can feel my reservoir of luck draining," she muttered.

A bullet went *ptank!* into the Guvvie's structure somewhere, and then another one peened off something hard and substantial, probably a spring or part of the frame. Enough bullets, and ...

Then the water of Fort Point Channel loomed ahead, a darkness spotted with glitter from the lights. An intense relief from a fear she hadn't consciously felt ran through her, like a winding punch in the belly, when she saw that the swinging structure of the Northern Avenue Bridge was locked in place rather than opened to let watercraft go by.

The girders of the bridge flicked by overhead. She braked at the end of the long arch, suddenly aware that the firing from behind had ceased. A quick glance showed that the Germans had stopped at the beginning of the bridge. They were abandoning the burning motor truck; several of them were rolling on the ground, with their comrades smothering flames with their bundled clothes. Two carried Horst between them from the front seat, his arms over their shoulders and his feet dragging limp.

It occurred to them that driving shooting into downtown Boston wasn't a very good idea, and that they're dressed like Bureau labor-camp prisoners, and that the one man who knows their escape route is wounded and now unconscious, Luz thought. *Don't relax,* muchacha*! This isn't over yet until the film's in the right hands!*

Once she was sure the Germans were leaving—and leaving the second truck to burn, turning in moments to a pyre blocking the entrance to the bridge with a minor fireworks display as ammunition cooked off—she stopped for a moment. A few motions and she had unlocked the Lewis gun from the pintle mount; then she threw it to the roadway. It was likely to attract too much attention driving through central Boston, and if the police were put on alert and getting jumpy . . .

"Ciara," she said to the figure huddled on the rear seat. "Look up. Let me see that."

The younger woman obeyed sluggishly. Luz wiped her face with a handkerchief, then gently turned her head and looked at her pupils. Both were contracting and expanding as she turned them away from the streetlight, but the left noticeably less. The pressure cut had bled freely, scalp wounds always did, but a couple of stitches and some time would handle it.

"How do you feel?" Luz said, gently but firmly.

"Dizzy . . . where are we?"

"Boston."

"I know *that*!" Ciara put her hands to her head. "Mary, Mother of *God* but that hurts."

"Ciara, you've got a concussion. I don't think it's a bad one but they're no joke. Just hold this against the cut on your temple and lie quiet as you can. I've got to get us to the Chamber office."

"Where . . ."

"The Custom House Tower. I'd like to get you a doctor, but this has to come first. Lie still, now, *querida*. We're almost there."

Luz drove on, taking Ciara's cap and tucking her hair up under it. She would still look odd, but not automatically female; it was amazing how eyes slid over you if you didn't wear the uniform. With luck, she'd benefit from the same assumption McDuffy had been counting on: that this was an unmarked FBS car and should be left strictly alone. Two or three Boston police cars—ordinary Model T touring models painted dark blue with a shield on the doors—passed her as she drove on, heading fast for the bridge, and presumably the reports of fires and shootings. In the distance she could hear the clang of fire engine bells as well. The silent factories and showrooms of the leather district slid by . . .

Now she was into the part of Boston that was almost European-old, with streets laid out by the cows and sheep of English Puritan settlers three hundred years ago and straightened only slightly as the city grew up around them. Waves of fatigue crept in at the corners of her vision as the juices of mortal peril faded from her blood, leaving head aching and throat dry and stomach twisted with nausea that left a sour taste at the back of her mouth to match the heavy smell of blood and vomitus in the Guvvie.

She flogged herself back to full alertness by an act of will as she pulled up in front of the Custom House building. It stood as it had since the 1840s—this had been the waterfront then—of foursquare granite with huge Doric columns on two sides, in the heart of the financial district. Though there was a homely structure one space away that advertised *Carter's Tested Seeds*, and another had two wireless masts.

Originally it had been topped with a dome, but a decade ago the work had already outpaced the available space. The nearly five hundred feet of skyscraper that reared out of it now ignored Boston's height restrictions since this was federal property. Just before it was completed in January of last year the Chamber had quietly secured one of the top floors, below the clock-tower part and level with the four giant eagles at the corners, looking out over the city from between Ionic columns. The combination of steel-framed grandeur and Classical detail was very modern, and very much to the taste of the new organizations the Party had spawned.

The problem is, she thought, *the Chamber station in Boston is new and small and I don't really know the people here—I think I met the station chief last year, but nobody else. That can be awkward. And I think I'm not operating at my best right now. Also I stink, I'm in a German uniform of sorts, and I'm sopping with harbor water and blood.*

She brought the Guvvie to a halt before the main entrance. A doorman clattered down, limping; there was some business here every hour of the day, though this was probably a low ebb. Jobs like this were reserved for veterans who wanted them, often for lightly disabled ones. He slowed and stopped, his narrow eyes going wary and broad shoulders tensing under the gray uniform greatcoat; he was several inches over six feet. That reaction was probably to the smell, and from the scar on his cheek and the hitch to his stride he'd recognize the bloodstink; he had a hooked nose and graying raven hair and skin a darker olive than hers, obviously part Indian.

"Ma'am?" he said warily. "Can I call you help?"

He pronounced *can* and *help* as if they were spelled *kin* and *heyp*; that variety of twang said southwest, probably Texas or even more likely Oklahoma, with a trace of something else underneath that wasn't English at all. He might even have been a Rough Rider, since he was the right age and a lot of them had been Sooners.

"Yes," Luz said crisply.

She carefully held the Thompson gun up by the butt and set it down again; this wasn't a man you wanted to startle late at night.

"My friend and I need to get to the Universal Exports Inspection offices; they're on the seventeenth floor. Please call with the name *Verloc.*"

He recognized a code; and from the expression on his face when he glanced upward, he also knew that Universal Exports Inspection wasn't actually part of the customs service. Then his face went carefully blank.

"And help me with the young lady," she said, forcing steadiness to her voice. Screaming for haste wouldn't help at all.

Ciara was nearly unconscious, but she gave a small whimper as the doorman picked her up as easily as a child, carefully cradling her injured head against his shoulder rather than letting it roll free . . . which confirmed her original opinion of his experience with injuries.

"A doctor?" he asked as he walked carefully up the stairs and into the marble and faux-Roman splendors of the rotunda, frowning down at her.

"We'll handle that in the office," Luz said firmly, if reluctantly.

There were only three people on duty in the offices with their vast view of Boston, and the floor had the feel of a space mostly unoccupied, a matter of the way footsteps echoed and a smell of varnish and new paint. One of the three was a woman of about thirty, in a drab shirtwaist suit with her dark hair up in a bun, working on some accounts and probably doing it to while away the dull early-morning hours. She gave a shocked cluck and hurried forward to help move Ciara into the second office and onto a couch there.

The other two were men, both implausibly young—no older than Ciara, in natty modern three-piece suits but with their jackets off, showing their shoulder holsters as well as their waistcoats. One of them sprang up, short, slim, and dark, with black eyes and crisply curled black hair cut short. His companion had his tie loosened, but this one's was snug under his wide stiff white collar.

"Good God, what's this?" he said, speaking very rapidly but clearly. "Is that *blood*? What is going on? Who's that girl?"

"Don't worry, it's not my blood," Luz said, extending a hand. "Senior Field Operative Luz O'Malley, Mr. . . ."

"Hoover, Operative John Hoover. I'm Assistant Station Chief here," the young man said.

That was making much of his position in a place that probably had about fifteen or sixteen personnel, including the clerks and typists not in the chain of command. They only had anyone here now because regulations said a station had to be manned round-the-clock; she was surprised to see the other man.

"That's Miss Ciara Whelan. She's been assisting me."

His eyes widened a little, first as he realized he was talking to a woman and then as he recognized the name; he'd undoubtedly heard of her, but it would be difficult not to in the small world of the Chamber, even if he'd been recruited recently. What he'd have heard would depend on who he'd been talking to, since she had both allies and enemies.

The grip was a little hesitant, and his nose wrinkled as he leaned back slightly. Luz didn't altogether blame him—after ten days unwashed on a submarine, harbor filth, and then the sort of blood and matter that spattered around when you were close to multiple bullet impacts, she knew she was ripe and beyond it.

Still, he's going to have to get over that. The Black Chamber isn't a job for the fastidious.

His very neatly organized desk had a framed Bachelor of Law diploma from George Washington University dated from this year's spring class; and his voice sounded as if he was trying very hard and nearly successfully to disguise both a speech impediment and an Upper South accent as East Coast General American, only a little softening on the *r* sounds and final *g*.

"What can I . . . what's going on, Miss . . . Special Operative O'Malley? Ciara Whelan? We've got a Ciara Whelan on our arrest list as a Clann na nGael member suspected of treasonous correspondence!"

"I've been operating in Europe under deep cover. She's been *assisting* me, and I have information that needs to go straight to the top. Get me a Red Line to the Director immediately."

"I—" There was a flash of resentment as she snapped the order.

"I'm afraid the station chief is at home. He would have to authorize getting the Director out of bed. And Ciara Whelan is on the *list!*"

This one is a natural bureaucrat, Luz thought. *I suppose it's inevitable we'd get some eventually; we can't all be cowboys and adventurers and desperados.*

She closed her eyes for a second, gathering her forces, then spoke:

"Operative Hoover, I am authorized to use a Red Line whenever I damned well please at my own discretion. I'm not *asking* you to do it, I'm *telling* you, and while I know you've only been with the Chamber a little while, you must have noticed that we do have a rank structure— and I outrank you by both position and seniority. Now *do* it. That's an order."

His full-lipped mouth set. "I can't do that, miss. We should get Whelan into a cell, and you're obviously under strain; when the station chief comes in at nine you can—"

"*¡Ya basta!*" Luz snapped. "Enough!"

The *navaja* snapped into her hand and opened with that metallic crackling snap. Hoover didn't have time for anything but a convulsive jerk as the point dug in slightly under his jaw; his eyes glared at her levelly. The other man froze with his hand halfway to his armpit.

"Quiet, Frank!" Hoover said.

"Those are the first sensible words to come out of your mouth to-night, *muchacho*. You are in danger of being the Chamber's sacrificial goat right now; how close you get to being actually sacrificed is up to you. *Get me that telephone.* Before something slips. This thing is sharp. *¿Me hago entender?*"

Hoover was up on the balls of his feet and his neck stretched back-ward. A single bead of blood slowly ran down his neck, across the dense but closely shaved black stubble; he used a musk-scented shaving soap or cologne.

"Just get the telephone, Frank, and then stand back," Hoover said.

He's not in a panic, he's realizing he made a very bad mistake and hoping he can get out of it, Luz thought. *He's got* cojones, *at least, and he's not technically stupid.*

Frank approached; he was glaring at her with blue-eyed fury, but he put down the heavy black instrument at the end of its cord.

"You're insane, you bitch!" he said.

"*Sólo un poco, güey*, but if you're right then they'll know at head-quarters, *ey?* Now stand back."

"If you hurt Edgar, I'll—"

"Die a few seconds later. *Back!*"

He backed up, keeping his hand away from his gun, and stood glaring.

Luz pressed the red button with her left hand and brought the instrument to her ear; it was a very modern type, with combined speaker and hearing apparatus. Clicking and whirring sounds came to her ear, and distant voices; the red button signaled the Boston city headquarters of Bell that the call was to be routed to a particular Washington, D.C., number. Not having to talk to the local operator in an emergency was a particular privilege of the Chamber.

Intercity calls still weren't all that frequent, though New York had been connected to Chicago nearly twenty years ago and Luz had seen the first transcontinental call go through from New York to San Francisco at the Panama-Pacific Exposition last year. They'd even dug up Alexander Graham Bell and his original assistant to reenact their historic *Mr. Watson come here* for it, only this time over thirty-four hundred miles instead of a few yards.

Wonders of the modern age, Luz thought, and twitched her right hand very slightly as Hoover stirred. *I hope Ciara got to see it; she'd have been thrilled.*

"Hello, Service central," a voice said in a rather tinny tone.

"Hello, Miss Sanders," Luz said, recognizing the operator in the carefully unmarked office building on Pennsylvania Avenue. "Luz O'Malley here. No, I don't want the Director, though you'd better wake him. You've got a Red One Priority file there, with one-time codes. Take out the one with A-77-1B-422—"

Which was her service number, the one on her standing file and pay slips.

"And open it."

The sound of a seal being broken came over the line, and the crackle of stiff paper.

"I have opened the file, Senior Field Operative O'Malley," the operator said, with a hieratic intonation.

There were only five of those codes, and to Luz's best knowledge they'd only been used once before.

"The code is as follows: *Sagamore Bear Growl Pull Nose.* I repeat, *Sagamore Bear Growl Pull Nose.*"

It actually commemorated a memorable occasion when her parents had been visiting the Roosevelts at Sagamore Hill when the century was young and she'd given the then *vice* presidential nose a hard yank in the middle of a roughhousing game with the Roosevelt children and their father—only Alice had been absent, having loftily decided she was too old for such things at sixteen.

"I acknowledge the one-time code." A sound as it was stamped *used.* They'd have to come up with a new one. "Connecting."

Hoover's eyes had gone wide; no, he was no sort of fool, and he realized just who her call was being put through to at this ungodly hour in the morning. It was a wonder to her that her enemies in the Chamber accused her of being a teacher's pet, and then were astonished when it turned out she could *use* that patronage at need . . . not least because she never did without good-of-the-service reasons. She'd never used her direct access to the president before at all, but she was fairly confident he'd approve.

Luz smiled thinly and lowered the knife, wiping the point on Hoover's starched shirt-collar and closing it. The young man stepped backward, pulling out a handkerchief and pressing it against the tiny wound. He held a hand out.

"Frank, it's no worse than a shaving cut, and *just don't say anything,* all right? Nothing at all, not now."

There were more clicks and whirring. Then a sleepy voice:

"Luz? You're back? Bully!"

"Yes, Mr. President, and I have full details on the attack I warned about in my dropoff message . . . you did get that? *Bueno!* Yes, it's very big. Unfortunately I was improperly dressed in a German uniform and a bit bloody and smelly from the U-boat and the fight when I got into the Chamber station here in Boston and the assistant station chief is being uncooperative. If you could straighten him out, Mr. President? And then get someone fairly high-ranking over here from the Navy Yard; we've got a little time, but not much."

Luz's smile grew as she handed the phone to the young man, and became even more unpleasant. She'd been called a hysterical female before, but rarely had she been able to pay the man in question back so thoroughly and so soon. He put it to his ear.

And he's going to feel a lot of pain, she thought happily. *Of the sort that hurts longer than a kick in the crotch.*

She went on to the others as he stood wincing at the bellows coming out of the instrument:

"You, Frank . . . get your station chief out of bed and get him here, and all your people."

Hoover made frantic *do it* motions without daring to speak or take the telephone from his ear.

"That's a good fellow. And notify your liaison in the Bureau and with the local police. The Navy will be taking care of the information I've just brought—"

She extended a hand down the neck of her German tunic, wiggling a little as she brought the oiled-paper packet out of her brassiere.

"—but *we* have a manhunt to arrange, and that's just the beginning."

To the woman. "And you are . . ."

"Miss Sarah Perlman, Senior Field Operative O'Malley," she said in a carefully neutral voice, one that from the glance at Hoover out of the corner of her eye was very probably hiding an intense satisfaction. "Clerical Support section."

"Get a doctor for Miss Whelan, one of the ones we keep on call. Then . . . you take shorthand, Miss Perlman?"

"Gregg and Pitman, and we have a dictation machine, Field Operative."

"Good. I need to debrief. Urgently. And some of that coffee I smell would be very welcome because I'll fall asleep otherwise."

The need to debrief felt like desperately needing to pee, in a rar-efied informational way. Some knowledge was just too important to be limited to one, very mortal, skull. They went into the other office. Ci-ara was on a sofa and covered by a throw, her face still frowning slightly in sleep; Perlman had sponged away the blood and applied iodine tinc-ture and a bandage—any Chamber office had a well-equipped medical kit. Luz smiled down at her and then sat in the chair beside the couch.

Perlman already had a pad ready, and was inserting a cylinder in the dictation machine; she nodded with a finger on the switch, threw it, and took up a mechanical pencil and a steno pad.

Luz began: "Senior Field Operative Luz O'Malley A-77-1B-422: as per previous report of 1st September of 1916, on the afternoon of that date I boarded the ANA airship *San Juan Hill* in New York under the cover identity of—"

After a while the secretary's pencil stopped scritching on the pad. Luz opened her eyes—she'd just gotten past the point where she'd bur-gled Colonel Nicolai's office and felt a little chilled in retrospect—and looked over.

"Is there a problem?" she said.

Perlman's professional veneer had cracked a little; she was staring at Luz wide-eyed.

"This is all *true?*" she blurted.

"*Absolutamente*, Señora Perlman," Luz said cheerfully, then blinked as she realized she'd spoken in Spanish.

I'm more exhausted than I thought . . . And when you look back on it . . . there was some drama, yes. I won! ¡Viva la magnificencia suprema de mí!

"Then it's a pity you can't publish it, Senior Operative," Perlman replied, with a smile. "You'd be famous!"

Luz took up the narrative again. It *was* going to make a stir when it hit certain desks in Washington, the more so when the Navy found the U-boats exactly where her photographs of the German maps said they were.

I don't particularly want to be famous . . . not with the general public . . . but there are other rewards . . . and Uncle Teddy always pays his debts, for good or bad.

She looked at Ciara and smiled again. *And I'll see that you get what you deserve too,* querida.

The observation platform of the Custom House Tower gave an unexcelled view of Boston and its harbor, even on an overcast day. The weather was warm for October, about sixty degrees or a bit more, and Luz was comfortable in a light jacket. This high up the air was intensely fresh, and a peregrine falcon was standing on the head of one of the great sculpted eagles at the corners, casting her an occasional resentful golden glance as it scanned for pigeons.

And I'm developing a tendency to grin at random intervals, she thought. *Despite still being exhausted.*

"I've never dreamed of seeing Boston like this, and me born and raised here!" Ciara said cheerfully.

Luz had to admit that it gave the sort of view an aeroplane or airship did, only with solid decking under their feet. She still felt a glassy detachment—there had only been a nap as far as sleep went, really—but a bath and clean clothes and a hearty if stodgy lunch and some coffee made it possible to go on. Ciara was feeling passable herself, if still a bit wobbly from Horst's blow to her head, though she'd had a good deal more of the sleep and a dose of painkiller. There was a wheeled chair behind her, but the doctor said a little careful standing was permissible and that the blurred memories of the time around the injury were normal.

The Navy had helpfully brought them a tripod-mounted telescope, and Luz had it trained on the site where the U-150 rested on the bottom, its launch controller ticking away with blind mechanical malevolence. There was confusion down in the streets; the military were taking no chances, and they'd evacuated the areas nearest the U-boats with help from the police. And a hasty turnout of Boy and Girl Scouts, who were probably having the time of their lives living out Baden-Powell's dream and getting to—very courteously and politely—tell adults what to do.

Barges and ancillary ships were anchored over both of the U-boats now, and divers in hard-hat suits were peeling an entrance with cutting torches. The same was happening in the better-equipped of the other target ports; some of the rest were simply going to blow the submarines up, which was more risky but would probably work . . . though those locations were evacuating more people, and farther.

"There!" Luz said, and yielded the telescope.

"A green flag!" Ciara said, and clapped her hands without taking her eye from the viewing end. "They've disabled it!"

"As per your instructions, *querida*," Luz said.

She sank down into the chair, with Luz's hand under her arm. A nurse in white uniform and headdress was standing at a discreet distance, and so were several Bureau men in their unimaginative almost-uniform of conservative dark suits and snap-brim gray homburgs, with bulges under their left armpits and Thompson guns in their arms.

"What now, Luz?" Ciara said, her smile fading.

She's still . . . subdued, poor thing.

"I heard . . . didn't that awful little man say I was on an arrest list?"

"Not anymore, *querida*," Luz said. "That's been taken care of. In fact, you're very much the government's blue-eyed . . . well, green-eyed girl, right now."

"*Taken care of* meaning you put a word in?" Ciara asked.

"Well, yes, but that only worked because you actually have helped to save the country! And as for *what next*, you've heard of the Federal Express?"

"Ah, that's the train the senators and swells take when they go down to . . . *Washington?*" she said, her eyes going round.

Luz chuckled. "You look *so* charming when you make that expression, you know. Yes, Washington. The president has a . . . very important speech on Thursday with the special joint session, but he's made a little time for us. We'll have a nice dinner on the train, sleep ten hours in good Pullman berths, and then have some time to rest and get ready."

Ciara squeaked. Then she said: "Will we have time for the Smithsonian?"

"I think we might, but you're staying in this chair for it. I'll push."

Ciara's smile returned. "And Luz . . . it's over! It's over!"

"*Tienes razón*," Luz said in agreement, putting a hand on her shoulder.

And I don't have the heart to say: It's over . . . for this time.

EIGHTEEN

Wwhat the dickens happened in Savannah?" President Theodore
Roosevelt asked, seating himself behind the desk.

The mood in the Oval Office was serious, but with an undertow of
profound relief. Europe had experienced the full horror, but America
had escaped—and because of that, the world still might be saved.

He himself still felt primed for combat, after the speech he'd just
given to the Joint Session. All but one of the senators and representatives had voted for the declaration of war—and that one was a Quaker
lady from a district in Pennsylvania. And after his revelations on the
Horror Plot, as it was coming to be called, the response that followed
his demand for war hadn't simply been applause.

They had *roared*.

And there had been a baying for blood beneath it; he didn't think
Kaiser Wilhelm would have been happy if he'd heard it, or Ludendorff
or von Hindenburg. No president had ever had such unity behind him.

General Wood answered: "As far as the Navy can tell, that collision
with the munitions carrier last week left wreckage exactly where the
U-144 was due to put itself down. They just couldn't find the secondary
position it used in time to stop the launch. Casualties were about a

thousand, more than half of those military; that . . . thing is even more deadly than we imagined. That's a small fraction of what they'd been if we hadn't had warning and evacuated the civilians, of course, but the port is useless and will be for months."

He turned to Director Wilkie, officially of the Secret Service and more importantly of the Black Chamber.

"Your agent saved us. Saved the country, and I'm not exaggerating."

Everyone nodded, Wood and Wilkie and the two military aides, Omar and George. If the Director hadn't been a man of restraint Roosevelt knew he'd have purred . . . and he had a right to look just a little as if he were licking cream off his whiskers. There had been a lot of luck involved—the report he'd stayed up late to pore over read like a list of risks barely survived—but it had been Wilkie's organization who'd sniffed out the first hint of the hideous plot and his agent who'd exposed it.

"That's why I'm taking this time," Roosevelt said; the thought of what would have happened if the risks *hadn't* been survived chilled the blood. "Certain things need to be done. What can you give someone who saved America, and therefore the world? Little enough, but we will do what we can. God knows the rest of the day's going to be grim enough."

Wilkie nodded. "I'm expecting more detailed information soon, but my own people in London and Paris were . . . well, there's not much hope for them. The zeppelins got in, ten to a dozen for each of the three attacks, even if not many of them got home again after they came down to bombing level. Even the ones shot down shed their poison."

"It's the last hurrah for zeppelins as bombers, in my opinion," Wood said dispassionately. "Those were all they had, we think, but they're going out with a bang. They killed more people in a single day than we lost in the whole of the Civil War; three-quarters of a million at least, possibly more. Probably more, say at least a quarter million each in Paris and London and a hundred thousand in Bordeaux, potentially many times that. Eventually aeroplanes will carry similar loads, though, and it doesn't *take* all that much."

Wilkie's face showed disgusted agreement. "They released something like a hundred tons of that horrible stuff on each city, and from an altitude that gave a very thorough dispersal pattern. The whole central parts of both cities are gone as far as human life is concerned, and Bordeaux too."

Which was where the French government had relocated after the May attack on Paris. The ghastly news had been part of what drove Congress to such fury.

"And fires are raging out of control. The French and British governments are . . . just not there anymore, along with . . . well, civilian casualties were very heavy. The British Parliament and House of Lords were in session and they're . . . well, they're dead, all of them and the prime minister and the cabinet and the War Office. We think the British King-Emperor, Queen-Empress, and their immediate family were all lost as well, except for Princess Mary. She was definitely in Bristol and is alive. Viscount Milner was in Birmingham, and he's trying to cobble something together—some of the reports are calling him Lord Protector of the Empire."

Wood spoke: "The situation at the front is absolutely chaotic, but what information we have from our surviving liaison officers is . . . bad. They used the horror gas shells to interdict parts of the trenches and then large areas behind the front, particularly the artillery positions and rail junctions. After that they smashed through the areas they'd left clear while the French and British were cut into bite-sized pieces, using fire-waltz barrages and infiltration tactics. There's been panic and surrender among some of the British and quite a few of the French units, too, and I don't really blame them. Truck-borne *Stoßtruppen* units and armored war-autos are twenty miles behind what used to be the line, on the outskirts of Paris."

One of the aides who'd commanded armored war-autos in Mexico himself spoke: "Looks like they took a leaf out of our book there, sir."

Roosevelt nodded, and asked the general: "The Western Front is broken?"

"As it existed before this, yes, Mr. President. What's left of the French are in full retreat and what's left of the British are trying for the nearest ports. *If* we get enough divisions across immediately through Marseilles, we *may* be able to stabilize a new front on the Loire, or at least delay the Germans long enough for a large-scale French evacuation to North Africa. If Marseilles is still there by then. But it looks as if the Kaiser's High Seas Fleet is going to sortie with some sort of new devilment, and if that goes wrong . . . things will be very bad. If the attacks here had come off, we'd be totally wrecked, Mr. President, and the German Empire would have gobbled up the whole of Europe and most of Africa and western Asia while we recovered."

Roosevelt sighed and shook his head. "And the situation in the south?"

"Much better, again because we were forewarned. We've got the 32nd Infantry Division in Jackson, and the 11th in Montgomery and Atlanta, and the FBS has action battalions in Charleston and Memphis, and mechanized cavalry brigades are on alert and moving in."

Wilkie took over from Wood for a moment: "We know the 32nd and the 11th are fully reliable. The local units are locked down while we investigate; I'd suggest sending them to Europe in the first wave."

Theodore Roosevelt grinned, showing his teeth. Those two divisions *should* be reliable; they were both composed of Negro regiments like the buffalo soldiers he'd fought beside in Cuba. Right now, nobody was going to object, even in the capital of Mississippi. Or if they did, the FBS would be paying them a call with an invitation to a new lifetime calling in helping build up the nation's roads, bridges, and dams.

And damned few people anywhere were going to object to *that* given the news from Europe and what America had just barely escaped.

"General Wood, in the general order to the 32nd and 11th, mention that the president has the highest confidence in their soldierly qualities and their iron discipline," he said.

It'll make up for the Brownsville affair, he thought.

He'd been profoundly uneasy about that ever since the full facts came out, long after his impulsive action.

"And we're looking for this Daubigny and his . . . Klan," Wilkie said. "Membership will be prima facie evidence of treason under the Emergency Act, so formalities won't be any problem. Good God, Robert E. Lee . . . and even Nathan Bedford Forrest . . . must be spinning in their graves!"

"Standards have declined since their day," Roosevelt said, then looked at his watch and up at the Secret Service man near the door, an old Rough Rider who'd stayed with the protection detail because he wanted to watch over the colonel personally.

"Agent Whitlock, let the ladies know we're ready for them."

"Colonel."

O h, Mother of God, I can't meet the *president*!" Ciara half wailed as the clock in the anteroom ticked away toward three p.m.

She looked at the tall white door that led into the Oval Office, with the Great Seal over the door.

"What will I *say*?"

Luz grinned down at her in the wheeled chair, ignoring the tug of her own bruises, and set gentle fingers on the bandage at the side of her head, half concealed under the artfully arranged strawberry-blond curls Aunt Edith's own hands had set.

"You're not supposed to over-excite yourself, *querida*, so be quiet."

"I could walk in. The dizzy bits have gone away. I don't need the chair."

"You *really* don't need to fall flat on your face in front of the President of the United States, either," Luz pointed out, and Ciara subsided . . . about that, at least.

"What will I *say*?" she asked again.

"He'll do most of the talking, if I know him . . . and I do."

Then, softly but firmly: "He's my Uncle Teddy, and he's a gentleman . . . and a gentle man, with friends. And he admires what you did, admires it very much. Don't worry about a thing. This is where he gets to tell us *well done,* good *secret agents*! And pats us on the head and gives us a cookie. I want my cookie!"

Ciara touched the bandage herself. "And I must look a fright!"

"Now you're slandering Aunt Edith," Luz said dryly. "In fact, you look wonderful. We *both* look wonderful."

Edith Roosevelt and her dressmaker had indeed worked wonders in the limited time available. Luz thought that a little of Ciara's self-consciousness was that she'd never in her life worn anything like the afternoon dress of silk and flowered chiffon before, with its long-shouldered underbody and high neck and gathered sleeves, perfect for her full figure. The two-piece skirt had a slightly raised waistline and a soft fullness at the top, the upper part lengthened by a lower part with a tuck at the joining.

She went around to the front of the chair, leaned down, and said behind a pointing finger:

"And you saved the country, Ciara Whelan, and don't you forget it! Not to mention saving *me.* You *deserve* this!"

Ciara drew a deep breath. "Then so do you, Luz. And you saved me, too."

"I most certainly do deserve my pat on the head and my cookie!" Luz said sincerely. "And I intend to enjoy every minute of it and wring every ounce of advantage out of it I can."

Then she did a slow whirl. "And this . . . it's almost worthy of me!"

Luz wore a summer frock in organdy and lace voile, a bolero top with a graceful pointed outline, and the sleeves short and pointed to match the bolero. Beneath the surplice underbody was a French lining that permitted the open-style neck, and from a slightly raised waistline the skirt hung in gathers. Its two sections joined together in a deep Spanish flounce effect.

"You look lovely," Ciara said after a moment's wondering silence. "And—"

The Secret Service man who opened the door to the Office was a tall lanky westerner named Whitlock, a former Rough Rider with a kink in his nose, a graying yellow mustache, and gray-streaked dark-blond hair that curled over his collar in a style that had been common in the Dakota Territory in the 1880s and obviously hadn't been changed since, modern tight crops for men be damned. He made a half bow, a spontaneous gesture that went with his smile and the warmth in his pale eyes.

"*Executive* Field Operative O'Malley," he began.

Luz blinked; that was as high as you could get without being stuck behind a desk, a prospect she notoriously loathed.

"Well, I've been promoted!"

"And Operative Whelan. The president will see you now, ladies."

Ciara swallowed, then squeaked: "*Operative* Whelan?" she said.

Luz gripped the handles of the chair and leaned down to whisper: "Uncle Teddy will explain. Now buck up, heroine! *¡Animo!*"

She pushed the chair forward; the soft rubber wheels rutched and squealed a little on the hardwood floor. Ciara gave another small gasp as they entered the Oval Office itself. Luz had seen it when the décor was still the original style from the administration of Taft, who'd made the West Wing a permanent feature and built the office in the first place. There had been a rather ghastly dark-green wall covering that actually looked like burlap, for starters, and an even more hideous green rug from Patterson, New Jersey, or some similar *olvidado por Dios* place.

The current incarnation was mostly Aunt Edith's taste—Teddy's was incurably Victorian-masculine, tending to dark wood and bits of preserved dead animals glaring at you accusingly out of glass eyes, and he knew it and had always had sense enough to defer to her. The walls were papered in pale old gold now with moldings and ceilings of white carved plaster, and mostly bare apart from the swags of the cream-white curtains and a few portraits—Uncle Teddy always had a portrait and bust of Lincoln in his main working office. She'd had the floor covered in light marble tile, too, and the rugs were Tabriz.

Today the sofas were all against the walls, and the space before the president's desk—the famous one made from the timbers of a British warship—was bare. He stood there, in the same morning suit he'd used to address the Joint Session that had just not-quite-unanimously declared war on the Central Powers. General Wood was beside him, in his blue dress uniform, and Director Wilkie looking formal and grave—but also giving Luz a slight smile and nod.

I've always gotten on fairly well with the Director, once Uncle Teddy made him take me on, Luz thought. *But I'm his blue-eyed* Hibernio-Cubana-American-girl *now—there won't be any more mutters about the Chamber needing to be trimmed back for a long time, now that we've* literally *saved the nation. In fact, the Chamber may end up as the boss-cat and the Bureau at our beck and call. Which is* just *as it should be. And it means I have a long, long list of favors due me when I ask in the future.*

She didn't resent the element of bureaucratic calculation; the Director *had* to think that way, to get the Chamber the resources it needed. And it *was* literally true. There were three other men present, an aide to the Director being determinedly invisible and two of the president's military household. One was a Californian colonel she knew socially and professionally who still had a deep tan from leading a regiment of armored war-autos down south, known as Patton's Rough Drivers, and a very young major named Bradley. Both of them would probably be heading for Europe and higher commands soon, but right now they were carrying small polished rosewood boxes with golden wreaths set into their surfaces intaglio-style.

Luz blinked again when the military men all came to attention and saluted, and heard a muted squeak from Ciara as the President of the United States and the Director of the Secret Service—and hence of the Black Chamber, though really it was the other way around now—bowed. She was a bit shocked to see Wood here anyway; the Chief of the General Staff would have a *very* full plate the day the United States had declared war on the Central Powers.

Then Theodore Roosevelt grinned, the famous fighting grin that bared all his teeth, his eyes gleaming behind the pince-nez glasses. He looked older—Luz was a little worried at how *much* older since the last time she saw him in person eight months ago—but dogged and strong. And glad of this one bit of gladness, before a long stretch when all the days would be grim.

"Bully, Luz! Just *bully!*" he said. "I'm finally wholly glad I listened to you back in '12. I had my doubts, but they were wrong."

Luz cleared her throat, conscious of a frog in it, a rare thing for her. "I'm glad I didn't disappoint you when you trusted me, Mr. President," she said.

She was suddenly horribly aware that she'd nearly said *Uncle Teddy* instead.

Where's my steely self-possession? she thought. *He's just a man. A very great man and my president and the most powerful man on Earth, but I knew him when I was nine years old.*

From the twinkle in his eye, he was completely aware of her near-slip. She went on:

"This . . . I just did what had to be done, Mr. President. I'm only glad that it all *worked.* I don't think I'm more frightened of danger to myself than the next person, but I can tell you honestly that I was flatly terrified of *failing* whenever I let myself think of it. And I would have, if it weren't for Miss Whelan . . . Operative Whelan . . . volunteering her help."

Wood surprised her by chuckling, and Patton and Bradley nodded. "That's the way it works, Miss O'Malley," he said. "War wouldn't be possible without that fear of letting the side down."

Roosevelt switched his gaze to Ciara.

"Dee-lighted to meet you, Miss Whelan! And your nation is very grateful to you as well," he said, his voice as always surprisingly light, with that precise patroon-patrician New York accent that had just a hint of Britain in it.

Ciara straightened in the chair as they shook hands.

"It's I am grateful to my country," she said. "It was when I met its enemies that I . . . well, Mr. President, I told Luz . . . Executive Field Operative O'Malley . . . that in Boston I felt Irish, but in Germany I realized it was an American I was, heart and soul. I'm . . . I'm glad I could do something for my country, for I know now my country's been doing good for me all my life."

"*¡Brava, querida!*" Luz whispered.

The words were obviously sincere but couldn't have been better calculated to capture Theodore Roosevelt's heart. He turned to General Wood and nodded slightly. The tall ramrod-straight New Englander spoke, his soft accent dry and precise:

"Mr. President, Miss O'Malley, Miss Whelan; I would like to say for the record that if a report had passed through my hands detailing like actions by soldiers in the uniform of the United States I would without hesitation recommend both those involved for the Congressional Medal of Honor. Courage in the heat of battle is one thing, and you have demonstrated that. But the courage necessary to stay among deadly enemies for as long as you did and then strike instantly and skillfully in cold blood . . . that is distinctly unusual."

"Thank you, sir," Luz whispered, and Ciara swallowed and nodded silent agreement.

The president nodded and spoke with a formal cadence:

"But the agents of the Black Chamber, as they do their deeds in secret, so receive no public honors. Instead, we have established an equivalent that is granted as secretly as it is earned. Only three have been bestowed, and all before now posthumously."

Luz nodded somberly. She knew the details of those, and death had been far from the worst of what the recipients had endured.

"I am very glad that that is not the case with these," the president said, showing his teeth again.

The soldiers ceremoniously presented Director Wilkie with the rosewood boxes; he opened each and held it while the president removed the Black Chamber's highest award. The ribbons were black silk, and the medal itself was a gold circle wrought like a wreath of grasses, wheat stalks, and flowers, with a simple black feather across it in jet, modeled on a pinion of the bald eagle. The inspiration was the Roman Empire's highest decoration, the *corona obsidionalis*.

Horrified, Luz felt tears welling in her eyes as she bent her neck for the ribbon and the ritual words were spoken.

... beyond the call of duty ... best traditions of the service ... deserving well of the Republic ...

She managed to blink them back and stand upright, her hand on Ciara's shoulder. When it was over and the medals were resting on their chests the president smiled again and handed Ciara a folder after a handshake.

"Miss Whelan, your initial trip to Germany was ... irregular. This is your copy of your Black Chamber service papers, dating your enrollment from January of this year as a probationary field operative. That'll take care of any future legal complications. It's a formality ... if you want it to be. You're noted as on indefinite paid medical leave for injuries sustained in the line of duty."

"Th ... thank you, Mr. President!" she said.

"But if you want it to be more than that," Director Wilkie said, "that can be arranged too. We can use a young woman of your talents, Miss Whelan. The country can."

One of the aides-de-camp went to another door at a soft knock, spoke with someone outside, then murmured in General Wood's ear, and he nodded.

"Yes, that is urgent," he said. "Mr. President? The second set of reports on the German horror weapon attacks on Paris and London are ready, and I'm afraid it's not a pretty picture even compared to what we anticipated. The situation at the front is very grave too. I'm afraid it won't wait."

Luz could take a hint. "Thank you, Mr. President. And . . . I'm ready to serve again. You were right, when you asked for the declaration of war. That was a *deed that will live in infamy.*"

"I am too, sir," Ciara said. "Whenever you need me."

"First you will rest and heal from your honorable wounds," Theodore Roosevelt said firmly. "You too, little Luz," he added less formally. "And *that's* an order. Agent Whitlock has instructions to arrange things just as you please."

Several hours later Luz heard Ciara gasp as she leafed through the folder.

"Luz!" she called.

"Yes, *querida?*" she said, her eyes still closed as she leaned back in the padded chair.

So good to rest . . . So good to be clean . . . So good to be home . . . So good to be myself *again . . .*

The easiest way to avoid the baying mob of reporters around the White House who might wonder who the two of them were was simply to stay there overnight. Some of the reporters *thought* they had a bribe-oiled conduit into the building via members of the service staff. Those were actually working on retainer for the Chamber, and told the journalists just exactly what they needed to know in the president's opinion, or the Chamber's. Nobody had dared to *actually* leak anything private for quite some time, especially not when they got to keep the bribes anyway. Uncle Teddy had always known how to handle the press, one way or another.

"Luz, this says I have a bank account that's been paid into since the beginning of the year! There's a checkbook and slips and a billfold with an ungodly amount of cash and even a receipt from the IRS for paying a *hundred dollars* in income tax!"

Luz nodded. "It's automatic for Black Chamber operatives," she said. "Your weekly salary gets deposited straight into it, with the taxes deducted if you're over the triggering limit. Very *Progressive*, you know. Efficient . . . modern . . . clean . . . untouched by human hands."

"But . . . but . . . Luz, *thirty dollars a week?*"

"For your probationary year. Plus two weeks paid leave and reasonable sick time—very reasonable, for injuries taken on the job, and we have a special medical section with a good staff alienist I've used myself. And the pension that goes with the Black Eagle Medal we just got adds another fifteen dollars per week, by the way, for life, and *that's* tax-free."

"*Forty-five* dollars a week?"

She opened her eyes and looked over. They were in a parlor outside the two guest rooms Aunt Edith had found them, probably originally for the Roosevelts' now-grown children. Like most of the White House residential sections it was done in a pale neo-federal white-and-gold, with an electric overhead light in chandelier form. Ciara was at the oval mahogany table, examining the contents of the folder.

"But . . . Luz . . ."

Luz smiled; what Ciara was exclaiming over was a solid middle-middle-class salary even in these days of rising prices and taxes, about twice what a coal miner made, or a third again a high school teacher's pay. That made it just above the lower limit for paying income tax at all.

It was very much in excess of what most working *women* made, but the Chamber had had equal pay for equal work from its inception—something the rest of the civil service was just starting to establish, and which was only a dark cloud on the horizon for the private sector for the present. A year of it wouldn't quite buy passage across the Atlantic on an airship like the *San Juan Hill*.

Luz herself used her—considerably higher, given her rank and seniority—income from the Chamber as found money, to be squandered on impulses like the automobile she'd bought last year. For that matter, most of what she got from her inheritance went back into more shares in Du Pont and U.S. Steel and General Electric and Ford Motors and Treasury bills.

You could buy a Model T on what she's getting, though, Luz thought with satisfaction. *And get a nice flat too, or a mortgage on a house in L.A., and buy books and a few pretty things and tickets to plays. Or enroll at a university. That's a do-what-you-want income, a life pension if she didn't want to join the Chamber for real.*

"*Querida*," she said. "Please, control your Irish Catholic guilt. That is yours, and yours alone, by right and merit and your own accomplishments. You bled, and sweated, and went under the shadow of an ugly death, and you fought and won for America. *¡Tu lo mereces!* Or at least the President of the United States thinks so, and the Director of the Service."

"So do soldiers risk their lives and suffer, and they don't get anything like this!"

A private's base pay was a dollar and a half a day, fairly good wages for an unskilled laborer. Though it was steady and they didn't have to pay for their food or shelter or clothing, of course.

"They *should* get it, it's just the country couldn't afford it. And you ran risks soldiers don't, as well as the ones they do," Luz said.

Ciara opened her mouth, closed it, sighed, and relaxed. "To tell you the truth, I'd just started to think of such things as buying groceries and shoes and paying rent again. It was like an engine starting up after long disuse! And a bit of a relief, in a way, as if to say I could be a real person again, with ordinary things going on that couldn't be put in one of those magazines with the bright covers full of flashing swords and aeroplanes and such. Life can't be all adventures. Mother of God, I *hope* it can't be!"

Then, slowly: "So . . . what shall I do now?"

Luz met her eyes, turquoise-green as the flickers of sunlight in a deep summer forest, and quelled a quiver in her own stomach and a sudden impulse to bolt for the door.

"Well—oh, *por Dios*, this is harder than I thought it would be—well, *querida*, I was hoping . . . hoping very much . . . you might want to come and stay with me."

Ciara smiled and tapped the folder. "But you didn't say a word of that until I had money of my own, and could choose what I did freely. Am I right, now?"

A long moment while Luz nodded and then looked away. Ciara chuckled and went on:

"See, you're not such a hard woman as you think, Luz! And yes, I would like to stay with you, just the two of us. Where?"

Luz forced herself not to gasp in relief, or go limp, or giggle hysterically.

Or all three at once and grin like a demented chipmunk too, she thought. *And no pouncing, Luz, despite how utterly adorable she looks. Not yet. Be gentle, wait for exactly the right moment. She's understandably nervous about all this.*

"Mmmm . . . my home in Santa Barbara, for starters? It's . . ."

She waved at the White House around them. "A bit more private. I'd like to get away from the war and peering eyes for a bit."

"Oh, *yes!*"

Luz nodded: "The headlines and public life are going to be full of thunder and storm. We've earned a little respite from that too, I think."

Ciara smiled, a long slow expression that came with a flush. "That sounds very nice. A bit . . . scary, to be sure, but nice."

"Not *too* scary, I hope," Luz said.

A laugh. "Scary in a good way, I think. And an adventure of a better kind."

NINETEEN

Ciara looked up at the letters in the wrought-iron arch as Luz vaulted easily out of the auto to open the gate; the car had been waiting where the presidential train dropped them off.

"Casa de los Amantes . . . House of the Lovers?" she said as Luz returned to the wheel.

Luz nodded. "It was, too."

She pulled through and looked up as she came back from closing the gate; big coastal live oaks stood on either side of the laneway, their branches meeting overhead to make a tunnel of shade.

"Ah, they're early this year. I hoped so. See?"

Ciara followed her finger, and gave a little gasp. "So many!" she said. "God, Luz, they're gorgeous!"

Monarch butterflies were drifting between the branches of the trees, or resting with their wings gently moving like living jewels of orange and black. A swirl of them went by at head height, bound about their own business, and Ciara passed her hand through the swarm with a look of delight.

"They winter here—more so as we planted more trees. Clouds of them, sometimes, until they leave in the spring. Mima loved them and put in the things that draw them. She had a gift for gardens."

Green lawns surrounded the house, and banks of flowers—gladioli, dahlias, late roses trained up trellises on arches over graveled paths. There were trees, single towering palms or the great evergreen oaks that had been growing before the first Spanish missionaries came, clumps of tall branching sycamores just beginning to turn toward autumn and edging green with gold, thickets of bamboo and banana and deodars and umbrella-shaped stone pines and more. Rows of orange and lemon were setting golden fruit on the south side of the house nearer the beach, in a little orchard that included almonds and apricots and figs and trellised grapevines.

Toward the outer edges of the property the trees grew into open woods, amending nature less and half hiding a few outbuildings in the same style. The ground right beneath the house eaves was planted to Cashmere Bouquet, trained to chest height and starred with masses of red-purple flowers that filled the air with a warm, languorous scent that she remembered from a hundred nights of summer and fall. The deft hands of Taguchi Gardens kept them so while she was away.

The building itself had a single central block of two stories of pale yellow stucco and Roman-tiled roof, with wings extending backward on either side to surround its court and make a long asymmetric H-shape. The driveway curved up to a set of four semicircular steps that led to the arched doorway; there were windows to either side set with wrought-iron grills, and a row above with a balustraded balcony above the entrance. The studded oak doors were open, leaving only the inner ones of wrought-iron and brass fretwork in the shape of peacocks locked—she'd wired ahead instructions to have the house aired out for today, and the kitchen stocked from Diehl's Grocery on State Street.

Through the hall and the arched inner doors you could see the fountain playing in the central court, bright with *cubano* tile. Sheets of purple and crimson bougainvillea climbed the trellises between the arches of the loggia around it.

"Luz!" Ciara said, looking around as they carried their bags in;

what they'd sent ahead would be unpacked and ready, but they had the building to themselves. "You didn't tell me it was a *palace*!"

"Oh, this isn't a palace; that's Arcady or Piranhurst up in the hills. Those are *palaces*, and it must be like living in a hotel. This is just a big house, sixteen rooms counting kitchen and storage. But it's . . . home."

Luz stopped and looked around the entrance hall; the floor was warm brown Saltillo, and the walls pale for better contrast with the paintings and the exposed redwood beams above. More bright-colored *cubano* tile in Moorish geometric patterns marked the risers of the twin staircases curling up on either side of the arched passageway to the courtyard, up to the landing and the second story.

"It's like being inside a jewel box," Ciara said wonderingly.

Luz took her hand and spoke slowly.

"My father . . . was a poet, in his way; a poet of made things, of the things that are seen in the mind and then made by the work of our hands, as he made my rocking horse and dolls and swing. This house was his gift to my mother, the vision in his heart made physical—a new home in place of the one she gave up for him. The central bit here was finished just in time for me to be born in it, and the rest over the next ten years as time and money allowed. He never left it to contractors; it was all done under his eye and some of all of this with his own fingers."

Ciara's hand tightened on hers. "This is his love letter to her, isn't it?" she said wonderingly, looking around to catch each detail.

"Yes, exactly; to her and me. They wanted a big family, but . . . well, that didn't happen. And the gardens around it and the life within it, that was her answer to him—if ever he had to go where we couldn't, for his work, she'd have something new growing for him to see when he came back. I enjoyed our traveling life, but I always felt . . . safe, here. It's my private place, close to my heart."

Ciara hesitated, her face white, and then blurted: "I love you, Luz."

Luz sighed and smiled and touched the forefinger of her free hand to Ciara's cheek. "And I love you, my darling one. You woke my heart that I thought had turned to dead stone. That's why I brought you here. It's a house made for love. And for happiness, and I want to make you happy."

There was a moment's singing tension, but without awkwardness.

"Ummm..." Ciara said, turning away a little, obviously shuddering with relief that her words had been matched. "I'm glad I consulted Aunt Colleen about this. About *us*, you and me."

Luz blinked in surprise. They hadn't had time, surely, and Ciara had been hurt in Boston and still recovering in Washington...

"I remember you speaking of her many times, but when did you have the chance to speak *to* her?"

"I consulted her in my head," Ciara said with a shy smile. "I mean... I didn't know what I was feeling except that it was important and very strong, and I so wished I could talk to her about it, she was always the one I took my troubles to, there being no mother and she the best and wisest person I knew... and then I realized that she and Auntie Treinel, they lived together all the time I knew them and I'd never made anything of it and just at that moment things sort of clicked in my head and I suddenly *knew*... which was as good as talking to her, you see?"

Luz laughed aloud. "Well, here's to her and Auntie Treinel for their good advice by example!"

They kissed, and it grew hungrier. Ciara spoke into the collar of Luz's blouse.

"Luz, you *do* want to take me to bed, don't you?"

"Oh, yes, *querida*. For a long time now. Like a flower wants to follow the sun, or a ripe grape wants to burst on your tongue. Your eyes and hair are like the sky around the setting sun, and your skin is like white alabaster and you fill me with longing and passion and desire. Yes, my love, yes, yes."

When Ciara drew back she grasped the front of Luz's jacket and shook her a little fiercely, spots of color high on her cheeks.

"Then why didn't you *say* anything! I keep feeling like I'm going to faint or my skin will crawl off into a corner by itself and cry! I don't know what I want, not exactly, but I keep *wanting* it more and more! And—"

Luz laughed outright and stopped the words with a kiss.

"I didn't because I wasn't sure how I felt; then because I wasn't sure how *you* felt; then because I wasn't sure how well you *knew* what you felt. Because we were alone among enemies and our lives were in danger. Because you'd taken a knock on the noggin and needed rest. Because I wanted you to be very sure it was as much your idea as mine ... and ... well ... this will be your very first time with anyone, won't it?"

"Yes. A kiss or two but ... yes."

"*Querida*, you want to share that with me and that's . . . a wonderful honor. So once I was sure, I wanted to make it very special and beautiful for you, and this is the most special and beautiful place I know. And we have it all to ourselves and we aren't hurried or exhausted or in danger."

"Oh," Ciara said breathlessly. Then: "I'm a bit ... I'm afraid I'll disappoint you because I have *no idea what to do.* I mean I know a little about men and women but nothing about ... and I so want to make you happy, and ..."

"*Querida.*" Luz met her eyes. "You are not going to disappoint me! I *am* happy, right now. It's your time to be a little shy and feel a little awkward and strange. And my time to be tender and patient and gentle. And I am going to make you feel *absolutely marvelous.*"

Ciara swallowed and nodded. Luz stood back a little, holding her hands.

"Let's get settled in, and then perhaps a swim, and we'll change into robes and I'll make you dinner and we can watch the sun go down together."

"You *cook,* too, don't you, Luz?" Ciara said, her voice trembling for a moment, then firming. "I remember you telling me about it."

"Quite well, *querida*, even if I say it myself. You've never tasted what *fresh* means until it's something right out of a Californian kitchen garden. A salad, and then I'll make us *pollo de coco* and *plátanos maduros fritos.*"

Photo by Anton Brkic

S. M. Stirling is the author of many science fiction and fantasy novels. A former lawyer and an amateur historian, he lives with his wife, Jan.